JIGSAW ON THE KHYBER
THE SOLDIER'S SON
BOOK IV

MALCOLM ARCHIBALD

Copyright © 2024 by Malcolm Archibald

Layout design and Copyright © 2024 by Next Chapter

Published 2024 by Next Chapter

Cover art by Lordan June Pinote

This book is a work of fiction. Names, characters, places, and incidents are the product of the author's imagination or are used fictitiously. Any resemblance to actual events, locales, or persons, living or dead, is purely coincidental.

All rights reserved. No part of this book may be reproduced or transmitted in any form or by any means, electronic or mechanical, including photocopying, recording, or by any information storage and retrieval system, without the author's permission.

For Cathy

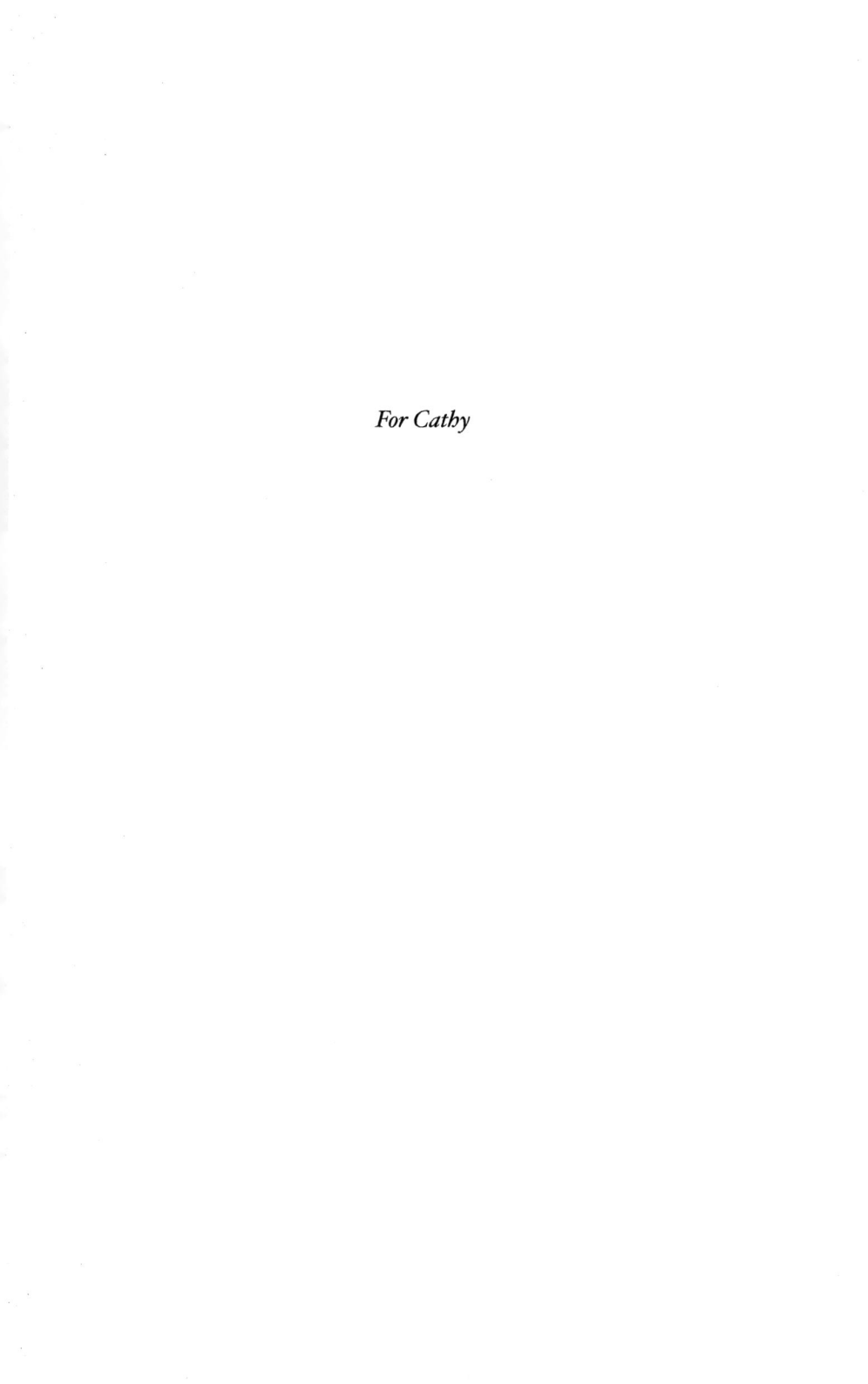

Can anything be more ridiculous than that a man should have the right to kill me because he lives on the other side of the water and because his ruler has a quarrel with mine?
Blaise Pascal (1623–1662)

GLOSSARY

Aga: Fire
Al-Shaytan: The Devil
Ayah: Children's nurse
Babu: Native clerk
Badmash: Bandit, outlaw
Bajke bajao khabadar: Look out
Cantonment: Where the British lived in an Indian town
Caraja: Charge
Caravanserai: Roadside inn with central courtyard
Caterans: Highland warriors and cattle thieves
Charpoy: Bed of string or webbing
Chokra: Small boy
Dak: Mail or post
Dhotie: A form of loose trousers
Djinn: Supernatural beings – the genie of the lamp
Feringhee: Foreigner, particularly white man
Ghazi: Muslim warrior, often a religious fanatic
Havildar: Infantry sergeant
Houri: Beautiful woman, or companion of the faithful in Paradise
Istishadi: Martyrdom
Ika lā'īna banā'ō: Form a line
Jai Mahakali, Ayo Gorkhali: Victory to Goddess Mahakali, the Gurkhas are coming
Jhampan: Old fashioned, clumsy vehicle
Jezail: Old fashioned long-barrelled firearm
Jirga: Tribal gathering or discussion
Jihad: Holy war
Jungle wallahs: Men who lived apart from society in remote stations
Jo Bole So Nihaal, Sat Sri Akaal: Shout Aloud in Ecstasy, True is the Great Timeless One
Khalsa: The Sikh army
Lashkar: Tribal army
Lecht: A steep hill pass in Scotland's Cairngorm mountains
Madrasa: Islamic religious school
Malik: Village headman
Mufti: Plain clothes
Mullah: Religious leader
Munshi: Teacher

GLOSSARY

Naan: A form of bread
Naik: Corporal
Narodnaya Volya: Russian secret society dedicated to bringing down the Tsar
Northwest Frontier: Northwest border between British India and Afghanistan
Okhrana: Tsar's secret service
Pashto: Pashtun's language
Pice: Small coin of little value
Poshteen: Afghan sheepskin coat
Pulwar: Single-handed curved sword common in Afghanistan and on the Frontier
Punkah: Fan suspended from ceiling and pulled by a punkah-wallah
Sepoy: Native soldier in the Indian Army
Shabash: Congratulations; well done
So Nihaal, Sat Sri Akaal: The Almighty is the eternal truth
Tonga: Two-wheeled carriage pulled by horses
Udēśa: Aim
Uhanāṁ nū mārō: Kill them
Uhanāṁ sāri'āṁ nū māra di'ō: Kill them all
Vālī aga: Volley fire

PRELUDE

HEREFORDSHIRE, ENGLAND, JULY 1894

The faces loomed over him, wide-eyed, screaming and shouting, promising him death. Some belonged to John Company sepoys, others to local natives, but hate filled them all. Jack writhed and struggled to avoid the hungry bayonets and lunging tulwars, hearing the terrible threats. He knew he must escape, or these men would murder him, then rip Mary away, rape and kill her.

"No!" Jack shouted, fighting to escape the bonds that held him. He tried to free himself, lifted an arm, and punched out, flailing at empty air. The faces were everywhere, leering, screaming their anger. The moonlight reflected on the naked blades, and the smell of woodsmoke mingled with jasmine, cinnamon, and raw blood.

"You can't have her!" Jack punched again, wrestled a leg free and kicked out, swearing. He lifted his revolver, aimed between a pair of staring eyes, and squeezed the trigger. Nothing happened. The revolver misfired. The eyes widened further; they were brown, with long lashes, Jack noted, and the tulwar, the deadly sword of the Indian sub-continent, swung down, hissing through the air in terrifyingly slow motion.

He felt somebody touch his shoulder and twisted around, grabbing for his assailant's throat. "Leave her alone!"

"Jack!" The voice was calm through the dark. "It's all right! It's me! It's Mary!"

"Mary?" Jack sat up, blinking the sleep from his eyes. He looked around the familiar room with the furniture he had known for decades and the thin morning light seeping through the window at his Netherhills home.

"Was it that same dream?" Mary held him gently.

Jack nodded, feeling the sweat drying on his body. "I was back in the Mutiny," he said.

"You haven't had that for years," Mary said.

"No." Jack took a deep breath. "I haven't." He swung his legs from the bed and stood up, stepping to open the window and allow fresh air to clear his head. "Something's going to happen."

"What?" Mary followed him to the window, looking out over the peaceful Herefordshire countryside to the soft slopes of the Malvern Hills.

"I don't know," Jack said. "Something bad." He felt her arms closing around him.

"Whatever it is," Mary said, "we'll cope. We always do."

CHAPTER 1

BERWICKSHIRE, SCOTLAND, JULY 1894

"I rather like Rudyard Kipling, you know," Mariana said, placing a finger in her book to mark her place.

Andrew looked up from scrutinising his newspaper. "Even better than Tennyson?"

"He's different to Tennyson," Mariana said. "More contemporary, yet he has written about Arthurian themes. Have you read *Sir Galahad?* It's one of his earlier pieces."

"I've never read it," Andrew admitted.

"How Kipling writes about India and the Northwest Frontier is so romantic," Mariana said. "It reminds me of Walter Scott and the Border Ballads, with the Border Reivers and Bold Buccleuch, except it's *Barrack Room Ballads* and the Guides."

"Ah, I see," Andrew nodded. He returned to the paper, scrutinising an article about cattle disease in the farming column.

"Kipling even writes about Mandalay," Mariana said. "You were at Mandalay when I was in Rangoon."

"I remember it well," Andrew admitted. "I had to leave in a hurry when King Thibaw's soldiers murdered half the prisoners and rioted through the streets."

"Do you miss it?"

"Do I miss Mandalay?" Realising he would not get peace to read his newspaper, Andrew folded it carefully and placed it on the table. "No, I can't say I do miss Mandalay."

"Not so much Mandalay as the adventure," Mariana asked. "Do you miss the excitement of it all?" She put her book face-down on the table and held Andrew's gaze.

"I am quite happy in our house, with our wee bit land, thank you," Andrew said. He did not mention his growing desire to ride long distances again or the pull of the hills.

"I miss it," Mariana told him. "I miss travelling and seeing new places, the spicy smells, and different people."

Andrew stood, stepped to the window and stared out. He could see the ancient Corbiestane Tower fifty feet away, the blue surge of the Tweed and the couple of hundred acres he called home. "We've built this place up over the last eight years," he said.

Mariana joined him at the window. "We've done it well, haven't we? It seems just like yesterday when we stood at the altar. I can't believe that was eight years ago, Andrew. The time has flown past. I think we deserve a change, a bit of adventure, and seeing something different." She linked her arm to his. "You feel the same."

"Do I?" Andrew asked.

Mariana led him to the second of their three glass-fronted bookcases. "Read the subjects of your books," she said.

"Why?" Andrew asked again and read out the nearest titles in the bookcase. "Joshua Slocum's *Sailing Alone Around the World*, Robert Louis Stevenson's *An Inland Voyage* and *Travels with a Donkey in the Cevennes*, William Curtis' *The Capitals of Spanish America*, and *The Land of the Nihilist: Russia: It's People, It's Palaces, It's Politics. A Narrative of Travel in the Czar's Dominions.*"

"That's enough," Mariana held up her hand. "They are all travel and adventure, Andrew," Mariana told him. "Your feet are getting as itchy as mine."

"Perhaps," Andrew said. He had been married long enough to understand his wife's reasoning. "How long were you thinking of being away?"

Mariana shrugged. "I don't know," she admitted with a smile. "Quite some time, I thought. We've no children, and I doubt any will come along after all this time."

Andrew nodded. He would have liked to have a son or daughter to follow him, but their once-enthusiastic efforts had not produced any heirs. The Windrush-Baird-Maxwell line seemed destined to end with them. He tried to hide his disappointment. "I think you are right."

Mariana looked downcast, for she desperately wanted children. "We're in a bit of a slough just now, Andrew, doing the same thing, meeting the same people. Maybe a change will make things happen." She patted her belly. "Are you listening in there?"

Mariana is still hopeful of having children. "Maybe," Andrew agreed cautiously.

"It's worth trying, surely," Mariana said.

"Maybe," Andrew said again. He opened the glass door of his bookcase and ran a finger across the spines of his favourite books. Mariana was correct; they were all about travel and adventure. *That woman knows me well, but does she want to travel because she is bored or to get herself with child?*

"You have this all worked out, don't you?" Andrew said.

"I've been thinking about it for a while," Mariana admitted. "And I've been watching you take longer rides each week."

Andrew nodded. He had taken to riding over the Cheviot Hills and across country, wandering the lonely paths of the Borders and riding to hounds, although he disliked hunting for fun. "That's true," he said. "I didn't think you noticed."

Mariana smiled at him. "I notice everything about you." At thirty-two, she had matured without losing the vitality of youth, while Andrew, three years older, was as athletic and vigorous as his active lifestyle could make him. "What do you think, Andrew?"

"Our factor will keep the farm running," Andrew decided. "Maybe you are right. Maybe a few months away from the same old routine will be good." He grinned. "It will be like the old days, except without people shooting at us."

"That's always a good thing," Mariana agreed solemnly. "No Zulu Impis, no Boer commandos and no dacoits to chill your blood."

Andrew smiled as the idea began to appeal to him. "Find a map of India, and we'll work out where you want to go."

Mariana laughed. "How strange," she said. "I happen to have one here." Opening a drawer, she produced the most recent Bartholomew map of India, folded to reveal the northern section and with half a dozen places already circled.

"You are remarkably well prepared for a woman who just had an idea," Andrew remarked.

"Call it a woman's intuition," Mariana said as she cleared Andrew's newspaper from the table and spread open the map.

"Call it anything you like," Andrew said, peering over her shoulder. "So we're going to Peshawar, are we? The city of a thousand and one sins. My father knew that town well."

"I've already written to him," Mariana replied.

"Was that a woman's intuition, too?"

"Not at all," Mariana shook her head. "That was Mariana's foresight."

Andrew shook his head. "Have you booked tickets on the boat as well?"

"Good Lord, no," Mariana said. "That would be terribly presumptuous of me."

"Oh, terribly," Andrew said, grinning. "I presume you'd like me to do the hard work?"

"Of course," Mariana said. "Isn't that what I employ a husband for?"

"I can't think of any other reason," Andrew agreed solemnly. "I'll arrange the passage; you arrange the packing." He knew

Mariana would only take the essentials, with everything expertly stored to occupy the minimum of room.

Mariana smiled. "I've trained you well," she said.

After some consideration, Andrew booked them first-class tickets for India at £55 each, rather than the £42 second-class, and endured Mariana's curtain lecture about wasting money on luxuries.

"We can afford it," Andrew told her, "and two weeks is a long time to exist in a cramped cabin with no outside portholes."

Mariana nodded reluctantly. "If you say so," she said. "I don't want to return from India a pauper."

"Nor do I," Andrew said. "But I do want you to enjoy the trip."

Mariana looked at him. "I know you do," she said softly. "I promise that I will."

They took the train to London and boarded the P and O steamer for Bombay. The voyage lasted slightly less than a fortnight, with the ship leaving London on Saturday and arriving in Bombay on a Friday morning.

"Here we are then," Andrew said as they stood at the rail, watching India unfold before them.

❄

Bombay was busy, bustling and hot. The ship was three hours late, and by the time they arrived, Mariana was tired, hot and irritable.

"Welcome to India," Andrew said as they hurried to the train station to catch their up-country train.

The station master greeted them anxiously. "I've held the train for the P and O ship," he said. "Please hurry up!"

"We're hurrying," Andrew assured him.

He saw a window open in one of the first-class carriages, and a whiskered face leaned out to glare at them. "Why are we delayed? Get the damned train moving!"

"That's Colonel Neville," the station master said. "He doesn't like to be kept waiting."

Mariana stopped on the crowded platform. "Look, Andrew. Are these what I think they are?"

Andrew looked through the open door of the guard's carriage of their train. "Coffins," he said. "I believe most trains in India carry a coffin or two in case a passenger dies on board."

"That's reassuring," Mariana said. "I didn't read that in *Murray's Handbook,*" she held up her well-thumbed copy of the recommended guide to India and its railways.

"Murray must have left that part out," Andrew said. He shooed away the gaggle of beggars who clamoured for attention, money or anything else the travellers could provide. "This place is even busier than London King's Cross."

Mariana glanced at the people in saris and dhotis, in ragged loincloths and scarlet uniforms, in yellow robes and dirty turbans, and stiffly formal European suits. She nodded. "India is how I imagined it," she said contentedly. "Except for the coffins."

Andrew nodded. "Not quite what one would expect on the North British Railway." He gestured to the station master. "Excuse me, sir! Where is our carriage? The name's Baird."

"You are Captain and Mrs Baird?" the station master asked.

"We are," Andrew confirmed.

"You are very late," the station master said.

"The ship was late," Andrew reminded the man, "and we couldn't find a porter." He saw the testy face of the impatient colonel watching through their first-class windows.

"Who the devil are we waiting for?" the colonel asked. "Who are you?"

"Captain Andrew Baird, sir," Andrew told him. "Late of the Natal Dragoons."

"The what? You're a junior officer from a damned colonial unit! I've never heard the like!"

"Come on, Mariana," Andrew encouraged.

The station master ushered them into their carriage, and the train emitted a gush of steam, a loud chuffing, and the creaking of woodwork. Andrew waited for Mariana to sit before he joined her.

"I rather liked Port Said," Mariana straightened her skirt and sat opposite Andrew on the dusty train. "I had forgotten how noisy it was out East."

"After the quiet life we've led these past few years, it was a bit of a shock," Andrew replied. He looked out of the window. "At least we're moving again."

"Slowly," Mariana said. "I think Africa begins in Alexandria, and the East begins at Port Said or Suez. Those bumboat men were very entertaining."

Andrew nodded. "They throw up the basket on a rope, we put in the money, they retrieve the basket and pile in bananas or oranges," he reminded her.

"And the gully-gully men with their magic tricks," Mariana said. "Why didn't we go ashore there?"

"It's not a place for ladies," Andrew told her. "You'll notice that even the men went ashore in groups."

"I'm not a blushing virgin," Mariana said. "After the Zululand Frontier and Burma, I'm hardly likely to be shocked."

Andrew smiled. "No, but Port Said is notorious for casinos, dirty pictures and brothels. I would not like you taken for one of the ladies of the night." He ducked away as Mariana threw a cushion at him.

"Oh, you pig, Andrew Baird!"

Andrew laughed. "It is better that you retain an appearance of respectability, Mariana. I know the truth, but to the outside world, you are a quiet, well-brought-up British wife."

"I am a quiet, well-brought-up British wife!" Mariana retorted, realised Andrew was still teasing, and launched another cushion, which landed smack on his face.

"Is that how well-brought-up British wives act?" Andrew asked solemnly.

"It is when their husbands start being cheeky," Mariana retorted. "Give me my cushion back so I can throw it again."

The train jolted on, day after day, with the flat, dun scenery rolling past. Mariana stared out the window, pointing out the occasional village, the bullock carts and groups of palm trees. "India is vast," she said. "The sky is as huge as Africa, and the land stretches forever. Only the trees and the people give it scale. I'd love to paint here to give some idea of the immensity of the country."

"You don't paint," Andrew said.

"I said I'd like to paint," Mariana replied. "I didn't say I could paint! Oh, Lord, we're stopping again!"

They pulled into a siding at a small railway station. Mariana looked at the platform, crowded with people, beggars, station vendors and hawkers with their high-pitched calls of "*Hindi pani*," "*Mussulman pani*" and "*tahsa char, garumi garum*," "water for Hindus", "water for Muslims", "hot fresh tea."

"I forgot how crowded the East is," Mariana said. "There are people everywhere." She swung her hand at the flying insects that invaded their carriage. "And flies."

"You'll always get flies," Andrew agreed. He took a deep breath, lay back and closed his eyes. "You may as well try to sleep, Mariana. We could be here for some time."

"It's too interesting to sleep," Mariana said. "I wonder why we've stopped."

"To allow you to enjoy the sights, sounds and smells," Andrew told her. "Particularly the smells."

"No, there's another train coming up the line," Mariana said. "It's slowing down."

"Maybe some bigwig," Andrew said. "Sir Pomphrey Piddlewick or the Lord High Commissioner of somewhere-or-other come to inspect the drains."

"It's going to stop," Mariana peered out the window. "The train's stopping beside us, Andrew."

"So I see," Andrew glanced at the arriving train with little interest. Clouds of steam emerged from the engine as the second train hissed to a stop, and a moment later, a smartly dressed young officer leapt from the first of three carriages and hurried across the tracks.

"That lieutenant's coming here," Mariana said. "He's boarding our train."

Andrew grunted, leaned back and closed his eyes. "I hope he doesn't waste too much of our time," he said. "Colonel Neville will have a fit with his leg in the air."

Mariana gave Andrew a running commentary as the lieutenant moved from carriage to carriage, peering in windows and returning to the platform at frequent intervals. After a few moments, the lieutenant tapped on their door.

Andrew sighed and pushed the throw-over catch that ensured nobody could enter the carriage from the outside.

"Terribly sorry to bother you, old chap," the lieutenant was around twenty, Andrew estimated, with a sunburned face and sweat patches around his armpits. "I am Lieutenant Cotton, and I'm looking for Captain and Mrs Andrew Baird."

"That's us!" Mariana replied before Andrew could respond. "What do you want, Lieutenant?"

"The general requests your presence on his train, sir," Cotton slammed to attention and saluted.

"Which general?" Andrew asked angrily. "And why does he want to see me?"

"The general ordered me to bring you both, sir," the lieutenant replied. "He is waiting."

Andrew glanced at Mariana, who was smiling.

"Come on, Andrew! We're in the middle of a mystery. Who is this mysterious general, and how does he know we were here?"

"No mystery about that," Andrew replied. "We reserved a carriage, so our names are on the passenger list."

"What the devil's happening now?" Colonel Neville descended from his carriage and stormed to the lieutenant.

"Look here, you! We've been delayed already by that colonial pipsqueak, and now you're making matters worse!"

"Yes, sir," Cotton said. "My apologies, sir. I am sure you'll be on your way again in a few moments."

"Who ordered this damned stop!" Neville asked. "If it was you, Captain Baird, I'll have your commission."

"I did," a tall man in the uniform of a full general limped up. "Do you have any objections, Colonel Neville?"

Neville stepped back. "No, sir. I beg your pardon, sir."

"I suggest you return to your carriage, Colonel, and stop interfering in matters that don't concern you."

Colonel Neville grew red in the face, apologised, and withdrew while a hundred people in the second- and third-class carriages watched this free entertainment. The first-class passengers were more reserved, hiding their amusement until later. It was a minor incident on the railways, but it reduced the tedium and would be recounted in officers' messes and barracks over the coming months.

"I thought you might prefer to travel in some comfort rather than in that rattletrap of a train." General Jack Windrush extended his hand. "Welcome aboard, Andrew, and you, Mariana."

Andrew shook his head. "I should have known you would be involved, Father," while Mariana watched Colonel Neville's retreat with open glee.

Mary was smiling, watching her son and his wife through fond, intelligent eyes.

"Rank has its privileges," Jack said as Andrew and Mariana stepped onto the private train, after Mariana ensured the porters transported all their luggage.

"What are you doing in India, Father?" Andrew asked as they settled into his carriage. "I thought you were based in southwest England."

"There's some trouble on the Frontier," Jack replied and smiled. "There is always some trouble on the Frontier."

"Surely there are plenty of locally based men without calling you over from Herefordshire," Andrew said as Mary winked at Mariana.

Jack nodded. "I welcomed the opportunity to do more than train the men," he said. "I was growing bored with inactivity, as were you two," he nodded to Mariana. "Farming has its attractions, but the Windrushes are a fighting race."

"You're not going fighting," Mary scolded her husband. "You are here in a purely advisory role."

"Advising on what?" Andrew persisted.

"Russian involvement," Jack said quietly. "Our political agents have reported Cossacks infiltrating in the north."

"I thought all that nonsense had finished years ago," Andrew said.

"It was only sleeping," Jack said quietly. "You know about the Northwest Frontier, the jumble of hills, mountains, valleys and passes that mark the boundary of British India with Afghanistan. The Afghans can be troublesome, and the Pashtun tribes are nominally on either our side or the Afghan side of the Frontier. In reality, they despise any authority except their own, or Allah, when it suits them. To the north of Afghanistan, Russia has taken over all the Central Asian khanates and is peering over the Hindu Kush at India. They're building a railway across Siberia, and in Turkestan, I hear, and may attempt to annex Tibet."

"Yes, Father," Andrew said, knowing he was set for a long lecture on Indian affairs. His mother's expression told him he should have known better than to ask.

Jack continued as the train rattled across India. "In 1893, Sir Mortimer Durand, an Indian-born British civil servant, demarcated the Frontier between India and Afghanistan, and we are trying to keep Abdurrahman Khan, the Amir of Afghanistan, sweet with bribes and guns. We're also putting pressure on the Pashtun tribes by building new roads, strengthening boundary posts and creating forts in the territories of the Afridis, the

Waziris and the rest." Jack shook his head, "telling the Pashtun that we control their land is a bit like poking a wasps' nest with a stick to see what happens."

Mary touched Jack's arm. "Enough politics now, Jack. These two are tired. Talk about something else."

"In a minute, Mary," Jack said, smiling. "I won't bore you much longer."

"If you say so," Mary winked at Andrew and glanced significantly at Mariana.

"I saw that!" Jack growled. "Russia is biding its time, awaiting its opportunity." He reached inside his tunic, extracted two cheroots, lit them both and handed one to Mary. "Here, Mary. Smoke that and look out the window until I'm finished. Show Mariana the points of interest." He grinned at Andrew. "Russia is like a hunting cat; she waits with infinite patience until the time is right and she strikes."

Andrew sighed. "You don't trust the Russians, do you?"

"I know them too well to trust them," Jack said. "I can never work out if they were the most eastern of the Europeans or the most western of the Asiatics." He drew on his cheroot. "Every so often, they try to Westernise and modernise their country, but it's still a vast, mysterious place with a mindset all of its own and an autocratic Tsar."

"Politics can keep till later," Mary told him severely. "Let's talk about something more cheerful than Russia." She smiled at Mariana. "Tell me all about life in Berwick, Mariana. How are you both?"

Andrew saw Mariana's face as she settled down to talk and knew she was in her element. Travelling to new places and talking to other people were two of Mariana's fondest experiences. Andrew sighed and settled down, happy to allow his wife to be the centrepiece as he absorbed all that India had to offer.

CHAPTER 2

PESHAWAR, BRITISH INDIA 1895

The Pashtun tribesman stood at the side of the track, balancing a Martini-Henry rifle on his shoulder and with a Khyber knife at his waist. He was tall, with a finely chiselled face framed by long bobbed hair beneath a carelessly tied turban, with a sheepskin coat hanging loosely over baggy trousers. A bandolier stretched across his chest, and his gaze never strayed from the train.

"Is that man from the Khyber Pass?" Mariana asked.

Jack glanced at him. "He's a Waziri from the upper Peshawar valley," he said. "Good fighting men and loyal friends as long as it suits them."

"He looks like a warrior," Mariana said.

"He is a warrior," Jack replied. "He's as unlike the down-country Indian as it's possible to get. This entire area is part of the Indian subcontinent, but I always feel we leave India behind at Peshawar and enter Central Asia."

Andrew studied the warrior until he was out of sight. The Waziri seemed as immobile as the distant mountains. He seemed to belong to this landscape, while the train was an alien, British intrusion.

"What's Peshawar like?" Mariana asked.

Jack considered for a moment before he replied. "It's a frontier town," he said. "On a frontier between India and the wild lands. It's like nowhere else on Earth, where cultures collide and mingle, yet never seem to merge." He glanced at Mariana. "You take care in Peshawar, Mariana. Don't wander on your own."

"Berwick-upon-Tweed was a frontier town too," Mariana reminded him. "And I grew up on the border between Natal and Zululand."

"I know," Jack said. "And Berwick still retains some of the tense atmosphere of the old Border. Don't believe all that poetical nonsense, Mariana. There is nothing romantic about the sweep of a Khyber knife or a raid by Waziris or Orakzais. You stay near the British cantonment and always have an escort if you enter Peshawar proper."

There was something about Jack's voice that made Mariana shiver. "I will," she said, looking at Andrew.

Jack grinned. "Peshawar is not the end of the earth," he said, "you'll be fine if you are careful. Mary will look after you."

Andrew will be with me, Mariana thought.

"Of course, I will look after you," Mary said, smiling at Mariana. "I've been looking forward to spending time with my daughter-in-law."

Jack looked out of the window. "Andrew and I also have things to discuss," he said.

❅

Peshawar was hot, dusty and crowded. Andrew had visited a few frontier towns in his career, from Newcastle in Natal to Bhamo in northern Burma, but as his father had said, Peshawar was different to any other.

Peshawar was older than any city in Britain, with a history

stretching for hundreds of years before Christianity. It had been the capital of the Kushan Empire, and the Kanishka Stupa one of the tallest buildings in the ancient world, with remnants standing for Andrew and Mariana to admire.

"We met Buddhists in Burma," Mariana said. "It's strange to come across the remains of one of their temples thousands of miles away on the other flank of India."

Andrew agreed. "When the Kushans left, the White Huns ruled Peshawar, then the Hindus, followed by various Muslim empires."

Mariana admired the city. "And then us," she said.

"Not quite," Andrew said. "The Mughal Empire controlled it, then the Durranis from Afghanistan, the Marathas and then the Sikhs took it in 1823."

"All these empires in poor India," Mariana said.

"The world has always been about empires," Andrew said. "We're just one of a long succession. In 1849, after the Second Sikh War, John Company gained control of the area, including Peshawar. When the rule of John Company ended, the Crown took control, the Raj as people call it."

Mariana smiled as they returned to the city. "It's a lovely name, Peshawar." She ran the word around her mouth. "Peshawar. I wonder what it means?"

"Some think it means frontier town in Persian," Andrew said. "It's the first city that travellers arrive at when they survive the Khyber Pass." He grunted. "If they survive the Khyber Pass."

Peshawar's streets were busy, with merchants from India, Afghanistan, and Central Asia, mostly Pashtuns but including a mix of races leading proud camels. Andrew watched the men, tall and rangy, with a long-striding walk and most carrying a firearm. Some had modern weapons, such as the British Martini-Henry, while others had *jezails* with long barrels and a curved stock.

"They're a wild-looking bunch," Andrew said.

Mariana nodded. "These are the sort of men your father fought in Afghanistan," she said.

"More than once," Andrew agreed.

A British regiment marched into the cantonment. Andrew knew they had newly arrived from Britain by their stiff khaki uniforms and peeling red faces. He watched the crowd of itinerant prostitutes, sand rats to the soldiers, offering themselves or being offered by their smooth-faced pimps.

"Jiggy-jig, sahib!" the pimps shouted as Andrew quickly ushered Mariana away.

"It's all right, Andrew," Mariana laughed at the expression on his face. "I've been married to you for years. I know what's happening."

Andrew relaxed. "Of course you do. We shut ourselves up in our enclosed little world for too long, Mariana. We needed to get out and about."

"I knew that too," Mariana told him quietly. "We were too young to shut ourselves up on a farm."

"Maybe so," Andrew said. "You have pioneer blood in you, and I am a Windrush. Maybe this is where we belong, at the fringe of civilisation where progress shakes hands with the wild people of the Frontier."

"And when there is no more Frontier ?" Mariana asked in sudden introspection. "What will we do when we've tamed the last wild land?"

"We'll explore ourselves," Andrew said quietly. "Or implode."

"That's very sombre," Mariana said. "Let's enjoy the colour and vitality while it's still here."

Andrew laughed. "I think it will outlast our lifetime," he said, checking his watch. "Father wants to see me at six, so we have a few hours yet. Where do you want to go?"

※

When Jack grinned at Andrew, the years rolled away, and he looked much younger. Only the grey hairs on his black whiskers and slight balding at his temples gave his age away.

"It's good to have you with me, Andrew," Jack said.

"It's a queer coincidence that brought us both here," Andrew replied.

They sat in Jack's spacious office with the slow *punkah* rotating the air and the sound of the cantonment floating through the open window. Andrew listened to the NCO's staccato barks with something like nostalgia. He had never thought he would miss the army.

"It was only a coincidence," Jack said. "Mariana told your mother why you are here. India seems a strange place for a holiday."

"India is a strange place for a holiday," Andrew agreed. "But Mariana has not had a conventional life, so it's unsurprising she chooses India rather than Brighton, Paris or Rothesay." He smiled, shaking his head. "I could not imagine Mariana walking along the pier in Margate or joining the crowds to go down the water on a Clyde steamer."

Jack nodded, scrutinising Andrew's face. "I don't think you would be reluctant to agree with her," he said. "Farming in the Borders might be fascinating, but you were always a man of action." He stepped from his desk to fetch a whisky decanter and two cut crystal glasses. "Time for a sundowner," Jack said. "It's a tradition, and you know what people say about traditions."

Andrew watched Jack pour two stiff glasses of whisky. "One must never make a tradition or break a tradition," he said.

Jack nodded. "That's the ticket. Now you are here, you may as well make yourself useful."

Andrew smiled. "Are you talking as my father or as a military officer?"

"Both," Jack said soberly. "Now listen."

"I'm listening," Andrew settled back in his chair.

"I've received an urgent *dak* bag informing me there is

trouble brewing at Chitral," Jack said. "The Chitralis are unsettled and are threatening to besiege the fort, with the neighbouring Hunza Pashtuns helping."

Andrew nodded. "Why are the Chitralis unsettled? I don't know much about the history of that area. I am not even sure where it is."

"Chitral is right on the northern frontier of India," Jack explained. "It's isolated by high mountains, with Afghanistan and Russia close by, making it vulnerable to both."

Andrew nodded again. "A long way from help, then."

"A long way for any relief column to march," Jack agreed. "Three years ago, the *mehtar*, the ruler, died, which led to the usual bouts of bloodletting, murder and mayhem. I won't bore you with the details, but the eldest son, Nizam-ul-Mulk, struggled to the top, and we recognised him as the *de facto* ruler." Jack lifted his glass. "Here's health."

"Thank you," Andrew said. He sipped carefully at the whisky.

"Then, a couple of months back, Amir-ul-Mulk, Nizam's half-brother, murdered him. Our agent in Chitral refused to recognise Amir as the legitimate *mehtar*, so Amir-ul-Mulk asked his neighbour, Umra Khan, for help. Umra Khan is a Pashtun, and in my experience, the Pashtuns are always ready for mischief, particularly if it means twisting the British lion's tail."

Andrew tasted more whisky. "So I believe."

"Rather than have Amir-ul-Mulk in charge, backed by Umra Khan, we sent Surgeon-Major George Robertson and a few hundred men to Chitral with orders to depose the usurper and put his younger brother, Shuja-ul-Mulk, in charge. Robertson and his men have occupied Chitral fort." Jack swirled the whisky in his glass, allowing the evening light from the window to reflect on the cut crystal. "It's a bit like the situation in Afghanistan back in 1839, except on a much smaller scale. If we show weakness here, the Russians may befriend Amir-ul-Mulk, and Umra Khan undoubtedly will extend his influence. I'd think that half the tribes on the Frontier are watching, wondering if we have the strength to act."

"Do you think there could be a tribal uprising?" Andrew asked.

"That's always a possibility on the Frontier," Jack replied. "We're on constant alert, having to nip minor troubles in the bud before some fanatic escalates the situation. In Chitral, a troublemaker named Sher Afzul, the original mehtar's brother, has stirred the pot. He's demanding that Robertson leaves Chitral and returns with his men to Mastuj. Umra Khan has raised his *lashkar*, his tribal army, and moved into Chitral, ostensibly to support Sher Afzul and ultimately Amir-ul-Mulk."

"Ostensibly?" Andrew asked.

"I suspect Umra Khan will wait his chance, oust Sher Afzul and try to add Chitral to his domain," Jack said. "And that will lead to more bloodletting."

"Is the fort sufficiently strong to hold out?" Andrew asked.

Jack shook his head. "I wish I knew the answer," he replied. "I've never visited, and few Britons have, so my information is sketchy. From what I can gather, it's a typical frontier fort, maybe eighty yards square with fifty-foot-high towers at the corners and twenty-five-foot-high walls built of stone, dried mud and stout wooden beams."

"It sounds like something out of the Middle Ages," Andrew thought of the scientifically constructed walls around Berwick-upon-Tweed.

"It's probably stood there since Alexander the Great rampaged through the passes," Jack said. "I believe there is a covered way from the fort to the Kunar River for water, but mountains overlook the fort."

Andrew nodded. "Not an ideal position, then. How big is the garrison?"

Jack lifted a sheet of paper from the table. "We have Surgeon-Major Robertson in command, with Captain Charles

Townshend of the Central India Horse, Lieutenant Gurdon and a handful of other officers."

"How good are the officers?" Andrew asked. The years of peace since his last military campaign seemed a dream as he slipped into military thinking.

"Robertson is solid, as is Gurdon," Jack knew the value of good men in charge. "Townshend, I have mixed feelings about. I've never met the man, but I've heard he's a bit of a misfit who spends more time with actors and actresses than soldiers and takes part in amateur theatricals."

Andrew grunted. "Sounds a perfect man to defend a fort in the middle of nowhere. He can entertain the Chitralis with songs and dances. How many men are there?" Andrew asked.

"About four hundred, some unreliable, but including maybe a hundred Sikhs, thank God. Do you have any experience of the Sikhs as soldiers?"

Andrew nodded. "I met them a couple of times in Burma," he said. "They were good men, stolid fighters and loyal. I'd rather have them with me than against me."

"In my opinion, the Sikhs are equal to the best British soldiers," Jack said. "When I was in a tight spot, I was always thankful to have the Sikhs under my command."

"I can understand why," Andrew said.

"We are organising two expeditions to relieve Chitral," Jack said. "Colonel James Kelly will command one, and Major-General Sir Robert Low another." He faced Andrew across the whisky decanter, his eyes troubled. "Low will have the larger expedition with fifteen thousand men and British regiments, while Kelly has a much smaller unit with less experience."

Andrew waited, anticipating what was coming next with a mixture of hope and trepidation.

Jack held Andrew's gaze. "I'd like some experienced officers with Kelly, and you are at a bit of a loose end. I can't order you to go, and God knows I don't want to put you in danger."

"I'll go," Andrew volunteered at once. "If Mariana doesn't mind."

"I thought you would," Jack said. "Your mother will take care of Mariana." He swallowed more of his whisky. "I don't want Mary or Mariana in Peshawar if the tribes rise, so they'll travel to Simla."

"Mariana wants to see Simla," Andrew said.

"She'll either love it or hate it," Jack replied. "It's not a place I've ever taken to, but Mary likes the socialising, and Mariana may be the same. We'd better get you ready." He smiled. "You're going into virtually unexplored territory at the roof of the world, above the snowline and not far from the Russian border."

"Yes, Father," Andrew said. He waited, knowing there was more to come.

"Speaking of Russia," Jack said so casually that Andrew knew he was about to impart some important information. "Our agent in Chitral has seen some Cossacks in the area."

"Have they, Father?"

"When you're up there, keep an eye open for any Russian infiltration, will you?" Jack asked. "I want somebody I can trust in Chitral, and your arrival is a godsend. I want you to be my eyes and ears up there, but for God's sake, keep out of trouble."

"I'll do my best," Andrew promised.

Jack sipped at his whisky, his gaze never straying from Andrew's face. "There is one more thing," he said.

"There usually is," Andrew said.

"I want you to take a man with you." Jack lowered his glass. "He knows what he's doing, but it's better to have somebody watch your back out there."

"What sort of man?" Andrew asked.

"The sort of man who will find out what's happening with the local tribes, the Russians, the Afghans and anything else on the Frontier," Jack said.

"A spy?"

"An agent of the Indian government," Jack amended with a

wry smile. "You don't have to do much. Ensure he arrives safely and leave him there when you return." He smiled. "A nice little jaunt for you. It shouldn't take long. A few weeks at most."

"Yes, indeed," Andrew swallowed more of his whisky, barely noticing the bite. "I am to accompany a spy on a small expedition into barely explored territory where the tribes are hostile, and there could be hordes of angry Cossacks waiting for us."

"That's the ticket," Jack said with a smile. "It takes me back to my early days. God, how I envy you!"

Andrew felt a once-familiar surge of excitement. "It could be interesting," he agreed. "It's certainly different from raising cattle and wheat beside the Tweed."

"We'll get you to Gilgit," Jack scribbled quick notes. "I'll tell Colonel Kelly you are on your way, and you have vast experience of irregular warfare against Zulus, Boers and Burmese."

"And the Galekas," Andrew reminded him.

"I'll add that as well," Jack said. "It's a bit of a journey, but you'll get to know India on the way."

"Mariana won't be pleased," Andrew said.

Jack grinned. "You leave Mariana to your mother," he said. "She'll have plans to keep her busy while you're away."

"I'm sure she will," Andrew said.

CHAPTER 3

KABUL, AFGHANISTAN 1895

Asad heard the droning voice from within the crumbling building. He huddled close, hoping to understand the words. When people passed, he held out his hands for charity, sometimes being rewarded with a few *pice* or a handful of rice or raisins, but more often ignored and occasionally kicked or cursed.

After a few days, people grew accustomed to the *chokra* crouched outside the *madrasa*, and some even smiled at him.

"What are you doing here?" one kindly man asked.

"I want to go inside," Asad replied. "All the other boys go inside to learn the words."

"Can you afford to pay the *munshi*—the teacher?" the kindly man asked.

"No. I have no money," Asad said, holding out a hopeful hand.

"You'll have to earn some," the kindly man said. "Remember, the Quran teaches that wealth is only a worldly pleasure. When you have money, it is merely of this life and does not follow you into the afterlife." Duty done and wisdom imparted, the kindly man walked away, leaving Asad more desperate than ever to enter the *madrasa* and increase his knowledge.

Asad had no means of counting the passage of time, as one day was much like the last or the next. He did not know how old he was or what city he was in. He only remembered hunger, cold, heat and begging to survive each weary day. Asad remained outside the *madrasa* until he saw the merchant riding his camel. He watched the man, not envious, for he had no concept of such a feeling but knowing that even a fragment of the merchant's possessions would help his quest. When Asad held out his hands for charity, the merchant rode on, ignoring his plight.

Asad did not understand the emotion that surged over him. He only knew the merchant would not miss the few coins that would pay for entry into the *madrasa*, and they would change his life forever. Rising from his habitual station on the street, Asad followed the merchant's camel at a distance, instinctively keeping out of the man's sight.

After a long time, the merchant rode into a *caravanserai*, where other travellers greeted him like an old friend. Asad slid inside the building beside a gaggle of servants and slaves. They ignored him, intent on their own misery, ate their meagre food and turned away. One man, the poorest there, gave Asad a handful of rice.

Asad waited with infinite patience until the merchant was asleep and slid quietly beside him. He moved slowly, keeping to the shadows as he rummaged through the merchant's possessions until he found his purse. The merchant mumbled in his sleep as the contents of the purse chinked.

Asad pulled at the soft leather, saw it was chained to the merchant's wrist and tried to unfasten the chain.

The merchant stirred in his sleep, turning over, and Asad merged into the dark, waiting, barely breathing until his quarry settled back down. Asad tried the purse again without success. When he heard movement nearby, he eased away to see a latecomer into the *caravanserai*, the kindly old man who had educated him about money.

The old man settled into his place and quickly fell asleep. Asad crawled towards him and searched his possessions, lifting a handful of rupees to pay for his entrance to the *madrasa*.

"You will be dead soon, old man," Asad said softly, "and wealth is only a worldly pleasure."

Satisfied he had done the kindly old man a favour, Asad pressed a rupee into the fist of the slave who had fed him, left the *caravanserai* and returned to Kabul.

❄

"Mariana can come with us to Simla when you're away adventuring, Andrew." Mary glanced around. "It's a different world from Peshawar, Mariana, with safe streets, balls and parties and a much better climate."

"What do you say, Mariana?" Andrew asked.

Mariana nodded. "I don't want you to return to the army," she said, sighing. "But I suppose we did come here to see new things and have an adventure," she said. "You'll be soldiering again, and I'll see the Indian elite."

Andrew was surprised Mariana had so readily accepted his decision and suspected Mary had spoken to her. His mother could charm the birds from the trees when she had a mind. "How far away is Simla?"

"About four hundred miles," Mary replied, laughing at Mariana's expression. "India is a huge country, but you'll soon get used to the distances." She glanced at Andrew. "Don't worry, Andrew, we'll take care of your wife."

"I am sure you will," Andrew agreed.

"You'll pick up the languages too," Mary said and snapped at him in *Urdu*.

Andrew instinctively replied in the same language. "When did I learn *Urdu*?" he asked.

"You grew up here, remember," Mary said. "India is your home. From now on, I'll only speak to you in *Urdu* and *Pashto*, as we did when you were small."

"That would help," Andrew said. "I'll have to leave soon, though." When Mariana looked at him, he saw the tears glistening in her eyes.

❄

ANDREW FOUND THAT TRAVELLING TO GILGIT WAS AN adventure in itself, with the train terminating at Rawalpindi and over two hundred miles of road still to come. He was fortunate the weather was dry and cold, for often blizzards and deep snow blocked the two high passes. Andrew could not take his hired pony over the highest pass at 13,500 feet and felt relief and a sense of achievement when he finally arrived at Gilgit. High in Kashmir and surrounded by spectacular mountains, he breathed in the sharp air and felt as invigorated as he had in years.

"You'll be Captain Baird," an enthusiastic young subaltern greeted him with a quick salute.

"I am," Andrew said.

"Second-lieutenant Harry Symington, sir. Welcome to Gilgit, the roof of the world, home of the forgotten and base for the hills."

"Thank you," Andrew said. "I am meant to meet a civilian here. Has he arrived yet?"

"There are no civilians here, sir," Symington told him. "Except the local Gilgit people."

Andrew nodded. "He must still be on his way. What's the position here?"

The subaltern grinned. "It's all good fun, sir, and we're waiting for the word to go forward to Chitral, a couple of hundred miles to the west. Surgeon Major Robertson is in Mastuj Fort, about 170 miles up the road to Chitral. He'll keep an eye on developments and let us know what's happening, unless deep snow blocks him in or the local tribesmen decide to cut his throat."

Andrew nodded. "I see." He was not surprised by how easily the subaltern accepted the dangers of his situation, having worked with eager young British officers in the past.

"We also have Lieutenant Edwardes in Gupis Fort, about sixty-seven miles along the road. He will watch the path to Mastuj." Symington sounded very assured for a man of his years and rank.

"How did you know my name?" Andrew asked.

"I've been waiting for you, sir. This way, if you please," Symington said. He was medium height, slim, with a wind-battered face and expressive brown eyes that seemed to dance with excitement. He ushered Andrew to a small, stone-built house with snow piled against the outside walls and a bright fire sparking inside.

"We've had bad news from Mastuj." Symington poured a generous amount of gin into a mug of hot tea. "The fort there isn't up to much, sir. It's the usual small Frontier structure, but with saltpetre swamps surrounding it. A dismal place in any weather and grim with the Chitralis calling for our blood."

"Bad news?" Andrew repeated. He sipped at the tea. "That's very welcome, Symington. Thank you."

"Yes, sir. Two officers, Lieutenants Fowler and Edwardes, left Mastuj with sixty men, stores, and ammunition for the fort at Chitral. They didn't know it was besieged, so it was just a routine march."

"They didn't take any special precautions, then," Andrew said.

"Exactly so, sir," Symington agreed.

"What happened?"

"The Chitralis ambushed them," Symington said. "They rolled boulders on the column from the hills above. Edwardes withdrew his men into a deserted village called Reshun and is making a stand, holding out against the Chitralis without food or water."

"They rolled boulders?" Andrew repeated. "That suggests they don't have many guns."

"Perhaps, sir," Symington said. "It also shows they can use the country against us."

Andrew recognised Symington's intelligence. "That's a good point."

Both men looked up when somebody banged open the door.

The newcomer fixed Andrew with a cold stare. "Are you Captain Baird?"

"I am," Andrew admitted, standing to greet the newcomer. Bundled in a sheepskin coat and with a turban swathed over his head, Andrew could not distinguish the man's rank.

"Captain Ross," the newcomer introduced himself. "Welcome to Gilgit. Have you heard about Lieutenant Edwardes?"

"Symington just told me," Andrew said. "He's trapped in Reshun."

"I'm organising a relief expedition," Ross told him sharply. "Are you coming?"

"Yes," Andrew said immediately.

How about my agent? He's evidently not arrived here yet, and I'm not going to kick my heels waiting for him.

"I know you've just arrived, Baird, and you'll be tired." Ross looked Andrew up and down, assessing his potential. "It will be a stiff march and probably end up in a scrap."

Andrew smiled. "I would not have it any other way."

"Get something to eat, grab yourself some travelling rations and extra ammunition," Ross ordered. "We have about twenty-five miles to cover along a rough track." His grin failed to conceal his anxiety. "Welcome aboard, Captain Baird."

They left later that day: Captain Ross, Lieutenant Jones, Andrew, and sixty Sikh infantrymen. Andrew was glad to be back with the Sikhs, sturdy, competent soldiers who faced the march with equanimity.

"Are you sure you're up to the march, Baird?" Ross asked.

Andrew nodded. "Lead on, Ross," he replied. "I didn't come all this way to admire the scenery."

"Good man!"

Ross led them along the winding track, with the surrounding snow-streaked mountains seeming to mock the toiling strangers. Andrew touched the revolver at his belt, held his sheepskin *poshteen* coat tighter, and strode on. He had not expected to be involved in another campaign, and here he was, right at the northern fringe of British India, in an area not even his father had visited.

Stay safe, Mariana. I'll be back as soon as I can.

"We're being watched." Andrew found that some of his old skills had returned. He could sense the enemy's presence as he automatically watched the surrounding hills, noticing and analysing every movement.

"Where?" Ross asked, reaching for his revolver.

"Don't stare," Andrew advised. "Walk normally and look casually." A pair of predatory birds circled above, tiny specks in the white sky.

Those birds sense trouble, Andrew thought. *They know that men marching here invariably bring them fresh meat.*

The column marched doggedly through rough terrain, with the hills closing in around them and a turbulent river roaring and bubbling at their side.

"Have you any scouts out, Ross?" Andrew asked.

"We don't have the numbers," Ross said and grinned. "We're our own scouts."

"I could go ahead," Andrew volunteered.

"This isn't Africa, and these people aren't Zulus," Ross replied. "A lone man here is likely to be captured or killed. Once we pass Buni village and the Koragh Defile ahead, we're only a short march from Reshun."

Andrew wished he knew the area better. He had studied a map, but names on a map were only a guide to the soaring hills with snowdrifts, scattered trees, broken rocks, and harsh, tumbling rivers. He looked around, searching for the hidden watchers.

Buni was a small village of stone-built houses huddled beneath the grim hills. The inhabitants greeted them civilly, although some watched the Sikhs with suspicion. Ross's column rested and ate there, with the officers consulting a map of the area and calculating how far they had to travel.

Buni's *malik* – the headman – elderly, grave, and serious-eyed, approached Ross and spoke urgently. Andrew saw Ross shake his head.

"What's the to-do?" Andrew asked. The two birds continued to circle above, calling harshly to each other.

"The *malik* thinks there could be trouble ahead," Ross said.

"Do you?" Andrew asked.

Ross shook his head. "There hasn't been any sign."

"Somebody is watching us," Andrew reminded him.

"I can't see anybody," Ross replied.

"Nor can I," Andrew told him, "But they can see us."

Ross smiled and tapped the butt of his revolver. "We'll deal with them if they appear." When Ross led his tiny army out of Buni the following morning, most of the population gathered to watch them. Andrew was unsure if they were wishing them well or watching the condemned march to their death. He felt the once-familiar tingling at the base of his spine and knew again that somebody was watching him. He paused, pretended to examine a rock at the side of the road, and looked around. The hills looked empty: bare rock and a few scrubby trees, bare of greenery, with snow piled on the weather side and dark shadows on the other. Andrew looked for movement or footprints in the snow.

He saw neither.

The last of the Sikhs watched Andrew. Tall, bearded and dignified, he murmured something Andrew did not understand but knew to be a warning.

"You feel it too, don't you, my friend?" Andrew said.

The Sikh held Andrew's gaze for a moment, nodded, and hurried after the column. Andrew joined him, still studying the slopes above.

"What's your name, soldier?" Andrew asked in Urdu.

"Kuljit Singh, sahib," the man replied with a grin.

Just before twelve, the column arrived at the small village of Koragh near the entrance to the sinister Koragh Defile.

"It's empty," Ross said.

"Why have the people deserted their homes?" Andrew asked.

"They must have run away when they saw us coming." Jones was young and excitable. He pulled on his luxuriant moustache. "Do we go on, sir?"

"We go on," Ross said. He looked behind him when the Buni *malik* hurried to catch up. "Danger ahead, sahib!"

"There's no danger!" Ross laughed off the warning. "Everybody's left before we arrived. The road to Reshun is clear."

People don't leave their homes without a reason, Andrew thought. *The Buni malik is correct; we're walking into trouble.*

"Sangars," Jones said.

Andrew saw the stone-built defensive sites on either side of the Koragh Defile. A sangar was a simple structure to erect, with a circle or semi-circle of loose stones piled on each other. Andrew had seen the like during the Boer War and wondered how the Boers would deal with Ross's column. He lifted his field glasses and scanned the sangars. "They're empty," he said.

Ross laughed. "I knew that old man was talking nonsense."

Andrew saw a flicker of movement on the hill above. "We're still being watched," he said.

Ross looked up. "They probably want to see who we are."

"It might be an idea to have the men open up," Andrew said. "Have them march in extended order."

"Do you have much experience in the Frontier?" Ross asked.

"Not on this Frontier," Andrew said. "But the Cape Colony Border, Zululand, Transvaal, and Burma."

"I know these people," Ross told him. "They won't attack us." He motioned for the column to advance.

They marched on, entering the Koragh Defile. The hills closed in like cliffs around the small column, grim rocks rimmed with snow and frost. The hills magnified the sound of the river, so it seemed to roar, a nearly sinister sound that plagued Andrew's mind. When he closed off the noise of the river, he heard the hollow echoes of the men's boots on the ground and the wind whispering around the rocks.

Andrew could see a sliver of daylight ahead where the cliffs opened at the end of the defile. He felt a surge of relief, glad that Ross had been correct. As the river surged closer, the path eased up the side of the cliff, narrow and steep. Andrew unbuttoned the flap of his holster as the prickle returned to the nape of his neck.

"What are you doing, Baird?" Jones asked.

"The *malik* knows something," Andrew replied.

As Andrew spoke, he saw men moving on the cliff above and heard voices echoing from rock to rock. "Spread out!" he shouted to the toiling Sikhs. "Extended order!"

The single gunshot reverberated from the steep walls, and Andrew saw the jet of smoke, although he did not see the fall of the shot.

"Don't take any notice," Ross shouted. "We don't react to snipers on the Frontier. Keep moving!" He repeated the order in Punjabi as the Sikhs swung up their rifles, searching for the marksman as they struggled upwards.

The echoes died away, leaving only the crunch of feet on the narrow path and the eldritch whistle of the wind.

"Nothing to worry about," Ross said. "Probably only a youth proving his manhood by firing at the silly foreigners." He laughed and moved on, long-striding despite the yawning drop at his side.

A moment later, half a dozen shots cracked out from above, and Andrew saw men bobbing about among the rocks. Ignoring

Ross's advice, he drew his revolver and fired at the closest puff of gun smoke, heard Ross and Jones shouting to the Sikhs, and fired again.

Andrew heard a rumble above them and saw darting men throwing stones and rolling rocks at them. Some boulders thundered down the path, and others crashed from the cliffs to bounce on the roadway, raising clouds of dirt and frozen snow.

"Fire back!" Andrew said, emptying his revolver and hastily reloading. He shoved the brass cartridges into the chamber, closed the weapon, and peered up the steep slope, searching for targets.

Some of the Sikhs replied, firing their rifles and shouting in defiance. Andrew saw a head-sized rock bounce from a boulder a yard from him, sending splinters in a wide arc before it rolled onto the path and over the lip to raise a mighty splash in the river far below.

The gun battle continued, with the Sikhs firing at their largely unseen attackers and Andrew firing and reloading. The enemy was also throwing rocks, barely seen as they briefly emerged from cover to attack and dodged back down.

"Who are they?" Jones asked. "Who's attacking us?"

"They'll be the men from Reshun," Ross replied. "They don't have modern rifles. They're firing jezails!"

Andrew had heard of jezails, the long-barrelled muskets of the Frontier, often hand-made and fired by a flintlock or even a slow match. "Jezails can kill," he said. He looked upward as the old fighting thrill returned. "We can storm up and defeat them." He readied himself to charge upwards, sheltering behind a rock as he reloaded. *That's twelve shots I've fired already. I'd better be careful with my ammunition.*

"No!" Ross said. "We don't know how many there are. Withdraw down the path."

Andrew shook his head, but Ross was in charge, so he obeyed as the Sikhs returned to the defile, with their attackers shouting, firing, and throwing rocks after them. Andrew took the rearguard, five tall Sikhs who fired upwards, replied to the shouts, and moved from cover to cover like the natural soldiers they were.

Kuljit Singh was the last of the rearguard, reloading his Snider as he slid behind a rock.

"Jones!" Ross ordered when they reached the defile, "Take ten men back and secure the entrance to the defile. Hold it until we get here."

"Yes, sir!" Jones replied, choosing his men.

Three of the Sikhs were wounded, and one man had died on the path. The remainder waited stoically with loaded rifles.

"Make a firing line in case the Chitralis follow us," Ross ordered. "We'll withdraw back to Buni."

Quiet descended on the defile, with only the gurgle and swish of the river and the constant whine of the wind breaking the silence. Andrew surveyed the cliffs, seeing nobody.

"They've all gone," Ross said.

"They'll be there," Andrew replied. He could taste the tension. One of the Sikhs coughed; a pebble fell from above, and the Sikhs were instantly alert. The silence returned, sinister in its intensity.

A gunshot cracked out from the entrance to the defile, followed by a distinct volley.

"Damn! Jones has met trouble!" Ross said.

The firing increased, with the cracks of the Sikhs' Sniders distinct against the deeper boom of jezails and the rattle of weapons Andrew did not recognise. "I'll take a section down and see what's happening," he volunteered.

Most of the Sikhs looked up hopefully, and Andrew randomly selected half a dozen men. "Do any of you speak English?"

A naik lifted his hand. "I do, sahib."

"You're with me, then," Andrew said. "What's your name?"

"Manbir Singh," the naik replied.

Andrew set off down the path, weaving from side to side to upset the aim of any potential sniper. The Sikhs followed, with their boots crunching on the ground. The firing ahead continued.

"Jones!" Andrew shouted as he found the Sikhs lying behind rocks, firing forward.

"Sir!" Jones crouched in the lee of a boulder, reloading his revolver. "The Chitralis have occupied the sangars in force."

Andrew saw three Sikhs lying on the ground, still in death. Others were bloodstained and wounded, with the survivors loading and firing. The men in the sangars commanded the entrance to the defile so that any advance would be through intense crossfire, with terrible casualties.

"We don't have sufficient men to take the position," Andrew said.

"What should we do, sir?" Jones asked.

"Return to Captain Ross," Andrew said. "He'll have to make the decision."

CHAPTER 4

SIMLA, 1895

Jack had never taken to Simla, the summer capital of India, although he recognised the necessity of the establishment. When the Plains and the low country were too hot for the administration, it made sense to move everything—bags, baggage, and clerks—to the cooler climate of the hills.

"How far is Simla?" Mariana asked.

"A fair bit yet," Mary told her as Jack ushered them into the Punjabi village of Kalka and hired three *tongas*.

"Three?" The *tonga* hirer was fat, shrewd and smiling as he held up three fingers.

"Three," Jack confirmed. "One for me, a second for Mary and Mariana, and a third for our luggage." He laughed at the hirer's initial figure, beat him down to half the price, and watched the women supervise two porters loading the luggage. When they sat down, Jack took his place in the leading *tonga*.

"That's an interesting vehicle," Mariana said.

The *tonga* was a two-wheeled cart with a single driver and horse. A passenger sat beside the driver, with another seat facing the rear for a second passenger. A fabric canopy provided shade from the sun and minimal protection from the rain.

"All ready?" Jack asked. "Off we go, then."

He warned the drivers to take care of the women and the luggage. "Take us to Simla," he ordered.

The road climbed slowly and steadily upwards, leaving behind the heat of the Punjab plain. Jack heard Mary and Mariana talking about the scenery, the statuesque pine trees and the occasional troop of monkeys.

Mary gets on well with Mariana, Jack thought. *That's good.*

They passed the brewery town of Solan, with the driver blasting his horn to clear a string of mules from the road, then swerving to avoid a pair of carts laden with farm produce.

The road grew steeper, turning around sharp corners with the air becoming clearer and sharper until Jack ordered his driver to halt.

"There's Simla, Mariana," Jack said as they followed a slow-moving buffalo cart.

Simla was unlike any other town Jack knew. As the summer capital of India, Simla was one of the most important towns in the world for half the year, yet Jack thought it resembled a hill-foot holiday resort. The town descended in terraces on the southern side of a wooded ridge, with imposingly ugly bungalows of government officials, heads of departments, and the odd military man.

"It looks nothing like I imagined," Mariana said. "What's that tower there?"

"Christ Church," Jack said. "You'll hear the bell on Sunday, Mariana. Listen to it carefully, for it's made from a mortar we captured during the Second Sikh War. My father was involved in that campaign."

"The Windrushes seem to have been involved in Indian affairs for years," Mariana said.

"Since 1753," Jack said. "One of my ancestors was an ensign with the 39th Foot, the first royal regiment to serve in India."

Mary smiled. "The Windrushes are newcomers, you see," she said. "The Bairds were here with John Company a century before that."

Mariana laughed. "You're more Indian than the Indians," she said.

"Actually, I am," Mary said. "My mother's line, Andrew's grandmother's line, is pure Rajput. Anyway, no native calls themselves Indian. They are Rajput, Sikh, Maratha or whatever. Only the Indian-born British call themselves Indian."

"I didn't know that," Mariana said.

"It might change with this new idea of Indian nationalism," Mary said quietly. "Only time will tell." She smiled again. "My grandchildren or maybe great-grandchildren will know the answer." Mary glanced meaningfully at Mariana.

As the *tonga* wound its way up from the bottom of Simla to the upper level, they passed from the ramshackle shanty town around the Indian bazaar to the lower level of British-owned bungalows before the *tongas* reached the elite upper levels.

"We can't take the *tongas* through the town centre," Jack called over his shoulder. "Only the viceroy, the Commander-in-Chief of the Army, and the Lieutenant-Governor of the Punjab are permitted to drive their carriages there."

"How do we reach our hotel, then?" Mariana asked, as the incessant travelling had made her tired and irritable.

"Hotel?" Mary looked amused. "Your father-in-law doesn't use hotels unless it's absolutely necessary. We've hired a bungalow."

"Oh," Mariana was impressed.

Mary laughed. "Your father-in-law is a general, remember. He's been in the army since God was a schoolboy and knows everybody worth knowing."

The Windrushes' bungalow was in the Annandale district, the same area as Peterhoff, the Viceroy's official residence. Peterhoff looked out of place, a Tudor-style mansion with shingled eaves and wooden frames.

"I thought carriages were not allowed here," Mariana said as their *tonga* convoy rolled through the centre of Simla.

"They're not," Mary glanced at Jack, produced a cheroot from inside her jacket and lit up, blowing smoke. She nodded to her husband. "Would you like to tell him that?"

Mariana glanced at Jack, who sat upright in his seat, glaring ahead. "No," she said, smiling.

"Nor would anybody else," Mary said. "I pity the policeman or petty official who tries to stop General Jack Windrush."

The bungalow sat within extensive gardens with a team of gardeners who watched the tongas roll to the front door. The style was a mixture of Mughal and British, with a deep veranda to provide shade and extensive views of the Himalayas.

"What do you think? Do you like it?" Jack spoke to Mary first and then turned his attention to Mariana.

"It's lovely," Mariana replied, determined to be impressed by everything she saw.

"Let's see what it's like inside," Mary was more cautious. "One can't judge a book by its cover."

Jack stepped aside to allow Mary and Mariana to enter the house while he supervised the drivers in unloading the baggage. He had arranged for a quota of servants, who arrived to help, and only then did Jack enter the house that would be his home for an unknown length of time.

"How is it?" Jack asked.

"It's marvellous," Mariana enthused. She looked around. "It's very spiritual as well. I am sure I can feel the presence of the people who lived here last."

Mary shook her head. "That's only the dust they left behind, but I'll soon have things put to rights. The cleanliness leaves a lot to be desired, and some of the servants require gingering up." She frowned. "Give me three days, and I'll have this house running as it should be."

Jack grinned, knowing Mary meant every word. "I'll leave the house in your capable hands," he said. "I have to see the viceroy."

Mary nodded, used to her husband's official movements. "How long will you be?"

"That depends on the viceroy," Jack told her.

"I see. I'll have some cold food ready for you," Mary replied. "And the dishes better be clean, or I'll know the reason why."

Jack knew he had left the house in good hands. "I'll be back sometime," he said.

※

Eight of Jones's men were dead or wounded as the patrol returned to Ross. "We can't get through, sir. The Chitralis hold the sangars at both sides of the defile."

"Damn!" Ross said as he heard the news. "We'll shelter here until night and break out then."

"As you wish, sir," Jones said. He looked tired, with his face drawn and white under his tan.

Ross led them into a series of caves at the foot of the cliffs, where Andrew ordered the Sikhs to build a wall at the cave entrance. He helped gather rocks from the plentiful supply on the path, including those the Chitralis had rolled down on them.

"The Chitralis can fire into the cliff from the other side of the gorge," he said. "A wall will give us some protection."

As Andrew spoke, a Chitrali on the cliff opposite sniped at them, with the bullet pinging and whining off the rocks.

Naik Manbir Singh glanced at Andrew and grinned. "You were right, Sahib."

Andrew glanced at Ross. "I'd suggest we detail a couple of our best shots to return fire," he said. "We might not hit anybody, but we might discourage them."

"Do that," Ross agreed.

For the remainder of that day, two Sikh marksmen exchanged fire with Chitrali snipers as the remainder of Ross's command sheltered in the cave. Andrew remained near the entrance, encouraging the marksmen and occasionally borrowing a Snider to fire at the enemy.

"Have you hit any?" Jones asked.

"I doubt it," Andrew replied. "Firing uphill at a near-invisible enemy who has plenty of cover is not the easiest of tasks." He shrugged. "But they haven't hit any more of us, either."

When daylight faded, Ross glanced up at the slit of sky above the cliffs. "Right, men," he said in English and Punjabi. "We'll try the path again. The Chitralis might not want to fight at night."

They filed out of the cave in the dark, keeping noise to a minimum by speaking in whispers and carefully avoiding any loose stones on the path. Ross led from the front, with Jones taking the rearguard and Andrew in the middle of the column. Two men helped each of the wounded.

"We never leave wounded men behind on the Frontier," Ross explained. "Take it slow and steady."

The first couple of hundred yards were easy, with the men feeling their confidence grow as they ascended the steepening path. When they reached the spot where the Chitralis had ambushed them, Andrew felt some of the tension pass, and they moved on faster.

Andrew saw the muzzle flash ahead and heard the shot and then a score of rifles fired at the column; men were shouting in the night, rocks were crashing down, and all was confusion.

"They've built a sangar across the path!" Ross shouted.

"Charge forward!" Andrew roared. "Go for the throat!"

"No!" Ross countered Andrew's order. "Fall back! Retire!"

Andrew swore. His instinct was always to attack when ambushed, to take the enemy unawares rather than what they expected.

The Sikhs obeyed their officers. They withdrew, scrambling back down the dark path with shots whistling after them and rocks bounding in their wake. Ross was last to reach the cave, where Andrew stood at the entrance, counting in the men.

"Any casualties?" Ross asked.

"Three men with slight wounds, but nobody's dead," Andrew replied.

"We'll have to rethink the situation," Ross said. He set sentries at the entrance to the cave and ordered the others to rest. Andrew tried to sleep, dozed fitfully, and awoke before dawn.

"Good morning, sahib," Naik Manbir Singh crouched behind the barrier, watching the cliff opposite. Andrew thought it must have rained further upstream, for the river was higher, surging between the road and the cliff face.

"Good morning, Naik," Andrew replied, rasping a hand over his unshaven chin. "Anything to report?"

"No, sahib," Manbir Singh replied.

"Any movement across the river?"

"Two men are on a ledge halfway up," the naik replied. "They've been there half the night." He tapped the lock of his Snider. "Shall I shoot them?"

"Only if they fire first," Andrew said. "Save your ammunition in case we need it later."

Manbir Singh looked disappointed. "Yes, sahib."

They breakfasted on the rations they had brought, augmented by three fish Andrew caught by throwing a line into the river.

"You're a fisherman, sahib," Manbir Singh approved.

"Where I live," Andrew said, "nearly everybody is a fisherman, either legally or illegally."

Manbir Singh grinned. "Where I live," he said, "we are all farmers or warriors."

"We have farmers too," Andrew said, "and the area has seen many battles between Scots and English."

The naik nodded. "It sounds like the border where the Punjab meets the Afghan lands."

"Very similar," Andrew agreed. *People of the land are much the same the world over, with similar experiences and histories.*

Half an hour after breakfast, the first bullet of the day

slammed into the barricade, and Manbir Singh replied immediately. Andrew saw one of the Chitralis pitch forward from the cliff ledge, somersaulting on his way down and landing in the river with a mighty splash. The naik chuckled and reloaded.

"Good shot," Andrew said.

The sniping continued, with Kuljit Singh taking the naik's position later in the day and replying whenever the Chitralis fired. Except for the sentries, Ross pulled the Sikhs further back into the cave, where they learned to ignore the occasional crack and ricochet of bullets. Twice, Ross left the cave on private reconnaissance patrols, and the second time, he returned looking thoughtful.

"We'll try again tonight," Ross decided. "We can't stay in this cave forever."

"If the Chitralis have blocked the path in both directions," Andrew said, "maybe we should advance as close as possible in the dark and then charge. It's not subtle, but it might work."

"No," Ross said. "We'll try to climb the cliff. The Chitralis won't expect that, so we'll take them by surprise."

Andrew looked around at the Sikhs. They were stalwart men, solid and professional. If Captain Ross ordered them to climb the cliff, they would do their best, but Andrew did not think they looked like mountaineers.

The day passed slowly, with the Sikhs finishing the last of their rations and the intermittent sniping and replies breaking the monotony. Ross ordered the men to sleep if they could, ensuring they were fresh for the night.

Andrew learned a few words of Punjabi, took a spell at the mouth of the cave, and returned the Chitralis' fire. He grunted with satisfaction when he saw one of his adversaries jerk backwards when his bullet hit.

"That's one less," Andrew said as Manbir Singh grinned at him.

"There are plenty more," Ross said. "We're leaving an hour after nightfall."

Andrew nodded, suddenly feeling tired. He closed his eyes, and in what seemed like two seconds, Jones was shaking him awake.

"Sir! Sorry, sir, we're moving in five minutes."

The darkness seemed to magnify the sound of the river, which roared between rocky banks. Ross led his men from the cave, moving quietly and with Jones as rearguard. Andrew took the left flank, with Naik Manbir Singh on the left and the Sikhs marching in between, obedient to Ross's command.

"Here!" Ross halted the men. "I noticed this fissure in the rocks when I was on a reconnaissance. It should get us most of the way to the top. The last fifty feet or so might be a bit of a scramble, but we'll manage. Follow me!"

Ross lifted himself onto the fissure and began to climb, with the Sikhs following. Andrew allowed fifteen men to pass him and then joined in, pulling himself up the damply cold rocks. He heard the slither of feet and gasps of straining men above and below, searched for foot and handholds in the dark, and hoped the climb did not take long.

If any Chitrali marksman across the river hears us, he needs only point and fire to hit. We are very vulnerable against this cliff.

Andrew heard the skiff of boots on rock above. He glanced up, heard a man shout, and hugged the rock as somebody plunged down in a flurry of arms and legs. The man landed with an audible thump.

"Halt!" Ross hissed. "There's no way up. Get back to the cave."

Climbing down was more difficult than scrambling up. Andrew slipped and slithered to the path. The Sikhs gathered in a confused group, unsure of what to do.

"Head back to the cave," Andrew repeated Ross's order, searched for the naik as a translator and repeated his words.

The man who fell was dead, with his neck broken. "Bring this poor fellow with us," Andrew said. "We won't leave him for the Chitralis."

The Sikhs huddled in the cave, despondent after their three failures. "Jones!" Ross called. "We have things to discuss. You come too, Baird."

The three officers gathered at the back of the cave, peering through the gloom. Nobody lit a match in case the light attracted a sniper.

"We can't remain here indefinitely," Ross said. "We've tried to push on and tried to outflank the Chitralis by climbing the cliff. I am afraid there's no choice but to return to Buni and gather reinforcements."

"Yes, sir," Jones agreed.

Andrew nodded. "I think that's the wisest decision."

"The Chitralis will hold the sangars, but they might not stand against a determined rush," Ross gave a rare smile. "I hope not, anyway."

"I'd say we advance quietly as far as possible," Andrew repeated his earlier advice, "and charge them with the bayonet when they see us."

Ross nodded. "Sound advice," he agreed. "We'll leave in ten minutes, before the men lose heart entirely."

Andrew nodded, taking a deep breath. *Into the valley of death, as Tennyson said.*

CHAPTER 5

KORAGH DEFILE, NORTHWEST FRONTIER, 1895

Most of the Sikhs seemed pleased to leave the cave, with the naik and Kuljit Singh even smiling at the prospect of fighting their way clear. However, the three reverses had left their mark, and one group of sepoys refused to leave the cave. Andrew watched as Naik Manbir Singh, Jones, and Ross harangued them.

"What's the problem?" Andrew asked.

"These men are not coming, sahib," the naik said. "They are disgracing themselves and the regiment."

Despite the officers' attempts, the six sepoys sat tight, refusing to leave the cave.

"Come on, men," Ross led the remainder of his Sikhs out of the cave. "We don't have time to waste."

With a final glance at the men who remained, Andrew followed. He hoped the river's roar would blanket any noise Ross's men made as they marched to the entrance of the defile.

I'm meant to be escorting an agent to Chitral, not playing around with caves.

Stars glittered around the scimitar of a moon as Ross

increased the pace, with the Sikhs moving as silently as possible on the rough track. Andrew could feel their tension and frustration as they advanced and heard the harsh gasps as they stumbled and slithered in the half-dark. The river was loud on their left, roaring over ragged rocks and crashing against the uneven banks.

"Fix bayonets!" Ross ordered, and the sinister click sounded as the Sikhs attached the eighteen-inch bayonets to their Sniders.

"Chitralis!" Naik Manbir Singh was the first to give the alert as they neared the entrance. Andrew saw the dim figures of men around the sangar and heard a warning call.

"*Caraja!*" Ross ordered. "Charge!"

"*Jo Bole So Nihaal, Sat Sri Akaal!*" The Sikhs shouted their war cry as they surged forward with their bayonets extended. The Chitralis must have been waiting, for they fired at once. The flare of a dozen rifles temporarily blinded Andrew, with the noise echoing from the cliff walls. He ran forward with the rest, holding his revolver in his right hand.

"Forward, lads!" Andrew shouted, knowing very few would understand his words. He saw a Sikh fall in front of him, heard another scream as a heavy bullet ripped his arm from its socket, and then they were at the sangar. The Chitralis rose to meet them, fighting with swords, shields, and muskets against the attackers. In the desperate insanity of hand-to-hand combat, Andrew temporarily lost his humanity.

He fired point-blank at a lunging Chitrali face, avoided the sideways slash of a sword, fired into the swordsman's stomach and kicked out, feeling savage satisfaction as his boot made solid contact. He was no longer a caring man, no longer Mariana's husband, but a fighting soldier, desperate to kill to survive.

"*Uhanāṁ nū mārō!*" the naik roared. "Kill them! *Uhanāṁ sāri'āṁ nū māra di'ō*; kill them all!"

The fight at the sangar lasted short minutes, with Sikhs and Chitralis slashing, thrusting, and firing at one another, gasping in fear, anger and the knowledge that defeat meant death. Andrew did not see Ross fall, but when the last of the Chitralis fled, and the Sikhs stood, panting, bloody and triumphant after their victory, Ross lay on his back, shot through the head.

Another good man gone, another sacrifice on the altar of imperial glory. Is the human cost worth painting the world pink?

"What now?" Jones crouched, bleeding from a gash across his arm.

"Now we fire into the sangars to help any stragglers come through," Andrew said. "The lads in the cave might decide to join us."

Jones grinned through his pain. "I've already got the men ready for that," he said, straightening up.

The Sikhs fired volleys into the sangars and up the hillside as the Chitralis sniped and rolled rocks at them.

"Here they come again!" Jones shouted as the Chitralis mounted a desperate charge with swords and shields. The Sikhs met them with bayonets and rifle butts, with Jones and Andrew firing their revolvers. Thin moonlight allowed brief glimpses of the skirmish, wide eyes, mouths open in fear and anger, the glitter of blades and the horror of torn bodies and spurting blood. After a few desperate moments, the Chitralis withdrew a second time.

Andrew glanced at the panting Sikhs. "Reload," he said, pushing cartridges into his revolver. "They'll be back."

"They're only regrouping," Jones agreed. He glanced at Andrew, trying to staunch the flow of blood from his arm. "I think we should stay a little longer, sir, in case some of our men come through."

Andrew nodded. "Another five minutes won't do much harm." He looked along the ravine. "Although I can't see any of our men."

Kuljit Singh shouted a warning, and the Chitralis came again, yelling their war cries as they charged with swords.

"Here they come again!" Jones panted.

The Sikhs fired a quick volley and met them with bayonets. After another hectic few moments of screaming faces and slashing blades, the Chitralis retreated, carrying their wounded with them.

Andrew hardly remembered firing his revolver as his instincts took over. He reloaded, hurriedly thumbing cartridges into their chambers. He heard himself breathing deeply and forced himself to relax.

A British officer should never be seen to hurry. Whoever created that statement had never been in a skirmish on the Frontier.

While the Sikhs were repelling the attack, other Chitralis filtered in their rear, cutting off their retreat to Buni.

"They're getting behind us," Andrew warned.

"I think we'd better retire to Buni," Jones said.

Andrew counted the casualties. Of the original sixty men, only seventeen Sikhs remained with them, many wounded.

"How about the dead?" Jones asked.

"We can't take them with us," Andrew decided. "Let the dead care for the dead; we must look after the living."

A succession of shouts from the defile told Andrew more of the enemy were approaching. "Come on, Jones. Half of Chitral will be after us in a minute."

Jones nodded. "I don't like to leave my men behind."

"Nor do I," Andrew said. "But unless we get out, we'll all join them. They're your men; you must make the final decision."

"Move out!" Jones ordered in English and Punjabi. Andrew noticed the blood was seeping through his shirt sleeve and tunic. "Move out, lads!"

The Sikhs obeyed, marching towards Buni, leaving their dead and supporting the wounded. Within five minutes, the Chitralis were following, yelling in triumph and firing as soon as the Sikhs cleared the defile.

When Jones glanced behind him, Andrew saw the determination on his face.

"Form a line," Jones said quietly. "*Ika lā'ina banā'ō!*"

The Sikhs obeyed, with Manbir Singh taking the right of the line. They waited, checked their Sniders were loaded, and stared into the moonlit gloom.

The Chitralis closed, shouting encouragement to one another as they saw the steady line of Sikhs.

"Aim! *Udēśa!*" Jones ordered.

The Sikhs levelled their Sniders, seventeen trained riflemen aiming at their pursuers.

"Volley fire! *Vālī aga!*"

Andrew lifted his revolver, aiming at the enemy mass descending the path. The countryside was more open here, with the Sikh line extending on either side of the track. The noise from the Chitralis drowned the sound of the river.

"Fire!" Jones ordered grimly. "*Aga!*"

The volley hammered out. Half a dozen of the attackers fell, some knocked back by the force of the bullet, others crumpling to the ground. One man screamed as a bullet smashed into his stomach.

"Reload!" Jones again spoke in English and Punjabi. The Sikhs reloaded, thumbing shining brass cartridges into the breeches of their Sniders.

"Present! Aim!"

The Chitralis pushed on, still yelling.

"Fire!"

Seventeen Sniders crashed out, and seventeen .577 bullets hammered into the advancing Chitralis. More men fell, one bullet taking off the top of a man's skull and spattering those behind him with blood, bone, and brains.

Andrew fired with the rest, aiming for what he hoped were the Chitrali leaders.

"Reload!"

The aimed volleys stopped the Chitralis. They halted, with some men turning back and those at the rear urging them on.

"Present! Aim!"

The Sikhs aimed again, but the Chitralis did not stand for

another punishing volley. They broke and fled, leaving a scattering of dead and wounded on the ground.

"Fire!" Jones ordered, rubbing salt into the Chitralis' wounds and getting some small revenge for the reverse and loss of so many men.

The final Sikh volley cut down three more men.

"Reload!" Jones ordered.

Andrew pushed cartridges into his revolver. He glanced at Jones; the subaltern had matured in the last few days. He was a man now.

"Back to Buni, lads," Jones ordered as Andrew ordered the men to lift the dead men's rifles.

Don't leave any weapons for the enemy to use.

"If I know anything about tribal people," Andrew said, "they'll follow us, waiting for any opening to attack. Shall I take the rearguard?"

"Do that, sir, if you please," Jones replied.

The Chitralis followed at a distance, sniping whenever they found an opportunity, so Andrew and his two-man rearguard were hard-pressed to hold them back. By the time they reached Buni, the Chitralis had shot three more Sikhs, and only two of the remainder were unwounded. The forty Sikhs of the 14th Sikhs greeted them like long-lost brothers, asking about their adventures.

"Look ahead!" Jones said. "The Chitralis are all around us."

In the cold light of morning, Andrew saw the tribesmen clustering around the village.

CHAPTER 6

KABUL, AFGHANISTAN 1895

The *madrasa* was small, dark and stifling hot. Asad sat in the back, struggling over the texts as he tried to absorb the concepts of Islam while simultaneously learning the Arabic language in which it was written.

"Pay attention! This morning, we have a visiting *mullah* who will teach you important things!"

Asad looked up. The resident *munshi* was a young man with a quick hand and a nervous tic. Asad did not like him. None of the students liked him, but they endured his teaching style because they needed to learn the Quran. The visiting *mullah* was much older, with a red beard and the kindest eyes that Asad had ever seen. He took his place at the head of the class and smiled benevolently at the class.

"I will not strike anybody," the *mullah* announced, much to the relief of the pupils. "Today, I will teach you about the blessings of martyrdom and the passage to Paradise."

The *mullah*'s smile seemed to wrap around Asad as he sat in the back of the class. He felt the *mullah*'s eyes staring into his and tried to smile, which was a strange concept under the usual *munshi*. This red-bearded *mullah* smiled back.

"Martyrs are the most blessed of individuals," the *mullah* told them. "And martyrdom can come in many forms, with the most favoured by Allah being violent self-sacrifice in the course of a *jihad*, a holy war against the infidel."

Asad had heard of infidels, although he had never seen one. He pictured them as the epitome of evil, Iblis himself, cast from heaven for refusing to bow to Adam. Asad vowed to destroy any infidels he saw for the love of Allah.

The red-bearded *mullah* continued. "Martyrdom, *istishadi*, will ensure a Muslim, however much he has sinned in life, will never go to hell and will immediately go to Paradise."

Asad had heard of Paradise, where all pleasures were available, a place of tinkling fountains, shade and peace.

"Martyrs smile at death because they have sight of the joys of Paradise," the *mullah* continued, smiling at the pupils. "*Istishadi* is the ultimate aim for life on earth, and a martyr will receive seventy-two virgins when he passes through the gates of Paradise."

Asad listened intently. He suddenly wanted desperately to enter Paradise, wherever it was. It might be behind the tall walls of the palaces where the wealthy merchants lived. When he saw some of the older boys glance at each other in anticipation, Asad also wanted seventy-two virgins, whatever they were.

The *mullah* saw the expression on Asad's face and knew the boy was a willing convert to martyrdom. "Our chance is soon coming!" he spread his hands to encompass every young student in the class but kept his mesmerising gaze fixed on Asad. "We are spreading the news of a *jihad* to push the infidels out of our lands!" He raised his voice. "Who here wants to be a martyr and enter Paradise?"

Asad was the first to stand, although he knew he risked the wrath of the incumbent *munshi*, who shook his head warningly.

The red-bearded *mullah* smiled on Asad fondly.

❋

Victor Alexander Bruce, GCSI, GCIE, the 9th Earl of Elgin and Viceroy of India, looked younger than his fifty-six years. Of an ancient Scottish family that had included King Robert the First, Elgin had been born in Montreal and educated at Eton and Oxford. He had been Viceroy of India since 1894 and did not enjoy the position. With a straight nose, firm mouth and full beard, he looked Jack full in the eye across the width of his desk.

"Welcome to Simla, General Windrush."

"Thank you, Your Excellency," Jack replied.

"You know this country well, I believe," Elgin said.

"Yes, sir. I was born here and have served here in the past."

Elgin sighed. "You fought in the Second Burmese War, through the Mutiny, on the Buner Campaign of the '60s, and with Roberts on his march from Kabul to Kandahar," he said, proving his knowledge of Jack's military experience.

"That's correct, sir."

"The Mutiny seems a long time ago now," Elgin said. "Yet India remains the pivot of our Empire. If we lose any other part of its dominion, we can survive, but if we lose India, the sun of our Empire will have set."

"I agree, sir," Jack said. "Many of our possessions are only there to maintain the trade routes to India or are coaling stations for our steamships."

Elgin sighed. "I didn't want this position, Windrush, and all we have is trouble, with famine, political agitation and now the Russians poking their noses into our north-west territories again."

"I have read the reports, Your Excellency," Jack said.

"Do you think the Russians will create trouble?" Elgin asked.

"I think it's possible," Jack replied. "Their ambitions are boundless."

Elgin sighed. "Simla is the most inaccessible of places," he said. "We're seven thousand feet above sea level, you know, and eighty miles from the nearest railway station."

"Yes, Your Excellency," Jack did not remind the Viceroy he had arrived from the railhead at Kalka that day.

"I have to send the government mails to Kalka by two-pony *tongas*, Windrush, or use elephants when the rivers are flooded." Elgin shook his head. "I am responsible for the lives of over three hundred million people, from Rangoon to Aden, and I depend on elephants to carry the mail."

"Yes, Your Excellency," Jack agreed. "I doubt I am here to discuss elephants."

Elgin smiled. "No, General Windrush, you are not. Do you know what we have here in Simla? We have scores of British civil officials, the men who run India; we have the local people, the hillmen of the north; we have an occasional Tibetan, cheerful men and women from that most mysterious land beyond the mountains, and we have the foreign diplomats." Elgin pressed his hands together. "These foreign diplomats are the ones we must watch, General."

"Must we, Your Excellency?"

Elgin nodded. "Officially, they're here to look after their nation's interests in India. Half probably hope British rule collapses, and the other half are working towards that end."

"I'll bear that in mind, sir," Jack said.

"You'll meet them soon enough when I host a ball for the international diplomats, General. I hope you have brought your lady wife with you?" Elgin looked benign for a moment.

"I have, Your Excellency," Jack confirmed.

"Good," Elgin said. "Ladies always temper any tension on these occasions, while diplomats can be wary of men on their own, particularly military men."

"I agree, Your Excellency," Jack said.

"Your wife is half-Indian, isn't she?"

"Yes, Your Excellency. Her mother was a Rajput. I am also Eurasian."

Elgin surveyed Jack for a long moment. "As is Lord Roberts, I believe."

"Indeed, Your Excellency," Jack said.

"Friday evening, General," Elgin said. "Seven o'clock. Be careful not to say too much to Victor Demidov, the Russian diplomat. I hesitate to call him an ambassador, General, but that's what he is, the Tsar's *de facto* ambassador to the Queen Empress in India."

"I'll be careful, Your Excellency," Jack said.

"He's a minor Russian nobleman," Elgin continued. "And very conscious of his status."

Jack nodded.

"Please warn Mrs Windrush not to say too much," Elgin said and hesitated. "I would not give her too many details of your duties here, General."

"My wife knows what not to say, sir," Jack assured him.

Elgin sighed again. "I didn't want this position, Windrush, but now I am here I'll do it to the best of my ability. Viceroys are like senior civil servants on a five-year contract." He gave a lopsided grin. "When my tenure of office ends, Windrush, the Indian Marine will take me as far as Suez, the limit of my rule. I must disembark there, and after that, I make my way home with the Vicereine, Lady Elgin, at my own expense. That is what the government thinks of me."

"I see, Your Excellency," Jack said.

Elgin eyed Jack levelly. "I'll meet you both on Friday, General." He returned to the papers on his desk, an unhappy man with too much responsibility.

※

"What do you reckon, sir?" Jones asked.

"We have fifty-four men and two officers in Buni and an unknown number of Chitralis who may or may not attack," Andrew replied. "We can hold out in Buni or return to Mastuj

Fort. I have no official position here, Lieutenant, so the decision is yours."

"Yes, sir," Jones said. "What would you advise, sir, judging by your experience?"

Andrew considered for a moment. "Return to Mastuj," he said. "We can collect reinforcements there and have a proper attempt at Reshun, maybe with artillery as well."

Jones nodded, white-faced from strain and loss of blood. "That's what we'll do then, sir."

"Here come the Chitralis!" Naik Manbir Singh shouted.

Like most villages on the Frontier, Buni's houses were enclosed by a mud and stone wall, with a small tower at one corner. The Sikhs ran to the walls, ready to fight despite the rigours of their march.

The Chitralis mustered a thousand yards away, watching the village without attacking. They beat drums as more men gathered to their standards and then moved in a great arc to surround the village, careful to keep at extreme rifle range.

"Here they come!" Jones said. He ran a finger across his neat moustache and grinned at Andrew. "Isn't this exciting, sir?"

"It is," Andrew agreed. "And to think I could be farming back home."

Jones laughed, ignoring the blood that seeped through his sleeve. "I wouldn't miss this for the world. What a story to tell my grandchildren."

Andrew thought of Mariana's desperation to have children. "I can imagine their smiling faces," he replied. "Where's Buni, they will ask. And why were you fighting there?"

"Ours not to reason why, old man," Jones said. "Ours but to bleed and cry."

Andrew nodded to Jones's arm. "You're doing the bleeding."

"But not the crying, eh?" Jones said. He laughed, high-pitched and slightly hysterical.

The drumming increased as the Chitralis gathered their courage. When the drumming stopped, there was a few seconds' silence, and the Chitralis gave a single shout and ran forward, waving their swords and rifles.

"Volley fire!" Jones said in English and Punjabi. "On my orders!"

The Sikhs waited, aiming at the oncoming horde. Nobody spoke.

"Fire!"

The Sikhs fired, reloaded, and fired again. After three volleys, the heat departed from the Chitralis' attack, and they withdrew, leaving a trail of bodies and wounded, gasping men.

"First round to us," Jones said cheerfully. He touched his moustache. "Do you think they'll come again, sir?"

"I don't know the Chitralis," Andrew replied. "They might. The Pashtuns certainly will. You'd best get your men fed, Jones, and send some to grab some sleep. We could be here for some time."

Baird nodded and organised his men into three, with a third on watch and the remainder resting, waiting for the enemy to attack.

"You and I should take watch and watch," Andrew said, "so there is always an officer on duty."

"I can keep awake, sir," Jones said.

"Not forever," Andrew replied. "I'll need Naik Manbir Singh with me as he speaks English."

"I'll arrange that, sir."

The day passed without any further incident, followed by a night broken only by a lone sniper who chipped the wall without hitting anybody. Andrew was on duty shortly after dawn the following morning when he heard a warning hiss.

"Somebody's coming, sahib!" Naik Manbir Singh reported.

"Where?" Andrew asked.

"On the road to Mastuj, sahib," Manbir Singh replied.

Andrew lifted his binoculars to peer through the pre-dawn dark. "I can't see anybody," he said. "I can hear them, though."

"Can you smell them, sahib?" Manbir Singh asked. "Tobacco

and Kashmiris." He grinned, with his teeth white in the gloom. "It's Moberley Sahib with a detachment of Kashmiris."

"You're a marvel, Manbir Singh," Andrew told him.

Lieutenant Moberley arrived fifteen minutes later. He greeted Andrew with a nod, ordered his medical orderly to attend to Jones's wound, and asked what had happened. He listened to the explanation and made his decision, as Andrew wished he had an official position in the column.

"I agree with Captain Baird," Moberley said. "With the Chitralis up all along the route, further progress is impossible with our small number of men. We'll return to Mastuj and regroup there." He looked to Andrew for approval.

"What about my men in the cave?" Jones asked. "Can we not try to bring them back?"

"They're deserters," Moberley decided. "They've made their decision. If we happen to come across them, we'll rescue them." Again, he glanced at Andrew, who nodded in agreement.[1]

"Get whatever food you can find in Buni, and we'll get on our way," Moberley said. "The longer we stay, the more time we give the Chitralis to organise themselves."

They left within an hour, with Andrew taking charge of the rearguard and Moberley leading as Jones's wound weakened him. Andrew carried one of the dead men's Sniders, a rifle he had rarely used. Only ten minutes after they left Buni, the Chitralis appeared in the rear and on the flanks.

"Don't fire unless they do," Andrew ordered. "Keep moving."

Andrew taught the rearguard to turn every few steps so that somebody was always watching the rear. The Sikhs learned quickly, followed Andrew's example, and kept the Chitralis under observation.

The column pushed on, with Moberley setting a fast pace.

---

1. The Sikhs in the cave held out for ten days before surrendering to the Chitralis. Although the Chitralis promised them quarter, the following day, they murdered all the Sikhs except one.

When the Chitralis began to snipe, Andrew fired back. He did not see the result of his shot.

"If they fire at us," Andrew said, "fire back to discourage them."

As the column marched towards Mastuj, the Chitrali attacks grew bolder, with men standing in the open to fire at the Sikhs. Andrew's rearguard responded, firing and moving, covering each other.

"Keep them back," Moberley said. He ordered another ten men to act as flank guards. "Fire on sight."

The Chitrali pressure increased, firing almost continually, with the Sikhs returning fire and gun smoke lying in a thick grey-white pall along the path.

Andrew knelt behind a waist-high rock, aiming at a patch of brush from where a Chitrali fired. He put first pressure on the trigger and waited until he saw a slight movement, then fired. The Snider kicked, and he reloaded and jinked away, expecting the Chitralis to target him.

"Did you get him, sahib?" Manbir Singh asked.

"I think so," Andrew replied.

By the time they reached Mastuj Fort, the Sikhs were tired, with two more men injured. The fort reared up like a sanctuary, with the square corner towers contrasting with the wild mountains behind. Andrew studied it for a moment. The builder had chosen his site well, on a plateau at the confluence of the Mastuj River and the Yarkhun River.

The situation is similar to Roxburgh Castle in Scotland, Andrew thought. *Mariana was correct; these people are a mirror image of the old Border clans.*

The column entered Mastuj Fort with a sense of relief. Moberley ensured the men were fed while Andrew called all the officers to a meeting to inform them what had happened.

"The Chitralis will besiege us, like as not," Moberley said calmly. "We're a bit isolated here."

Andrew looked around the area. "We can hold out for weeks," he said. "Or break through and make our way to Gilgit."

"We're better behind stone walls," Moberley said.

"The Chitralis and Umra Khan could besiege us for weeks, even months," Andrew said. He remembered the long sieges during the Boer War. "Who knows we are here?"

"They know about us in Gilgit," Moberley said. "But they don't know we're in trouble."

"That's a hundred and sixty miles away," Andrew said. "A long way to send help even if they knew." He leaned back, looking around the room. Illuminated by flickering candles and a smoky fire, the officers sat around a central table, some with papers in front of them and two with loaded revolvers.

"I have no official position here," Andrew said. "You will not miss me if I leave to get help."

"From where?"

"Gilgit," Andrew said and waited for the incredulous looks from the gathered officers.

"You wouldn't have to go all the way to Gilgit," Moberley said. "The nearest British post is Ghizr. Lieutenant Gough is there with a detachment of the 2nd Gurkhas. He's a good man." He paused for a moment. "Once you reach Ghizr, you'll be safe, but you'll have to negotiate the Shandur Pass first."

Andrew nodded. He remembered the high Shandur Pass. It had been snow-free when he crossed, but the season had progressed since then. "That will be an obstacle," he said.

"It depends on how much snow has fallen," Moberley said. "You outrank me, Captain, but I know the area better, and I'd not advise anybody to travel alone over the Shandur, especially with the tribes up. I could ask for volunteers from my men to accompany you."

Andrew shook his head. "Thank you, but no. I'll travel faster alone. Anyway, the Sikhs are people of the plains and are not popular with the hill folk."

"As you wish, sir." Moberley did not argue. Andrew suspected he would be glad to have a senior officer out of the way. "When you reach Gilgit, tell them we could sit pretty here for weeks," he said. "Mastuj is a fairly strong fort, and we have Sikhs. I'd pit my Sikhs against any number of Chitralis or anybody else."

Some of the other officers nodded. One man lifted his revolver, spun the chamber, and replaced it on the table. He grinned. "Let them come."

Andrew knew these men would fight. "Is there a pony anywhere in the fort?"

"Yes," Moberley said. "We have a couple. Are you thinking of riding over the pass?"

"I am," Andrew said.

Moberley shook his head. "The horses here are hardly thoroughbreds."

"What are they?" Andrew asked, hardly daring to hope.

"Kabul ponies," Moberley said.

Andrew grinned. "Could not be better," Andrew said. "A Kabul pony will continue when all other horses fail." He thought for a moment. "I'll need to look the part, so I want a *poshteen* and a turban, a rifle, bandolier and sufficient food to get me through to Gilgit." He considered for a moment. "I also want a jezail. No British soldier would carry a jezail."

"We have a few in the armoury," Moberley said. "I don't know if they can fire."

"I won't be firing it," Andrew said. "It's part of the deception. A jezail across my back and a Martini at my saddle, if you have a spare."

Moberley shook his head. "You can't speak the language," he said.

"I speak Urdu and Pashto, but not Khowar, the Chitralis' language. I'd like a local guide," Andrew said.

"None are available," Moberley said. "Or none that I'd trust."

"In that case, I will go alone." Andrew was suddenly desperate to be on the road, away from the confines of the fort.

He already felt claustrophobic at the thought of being trapped in Mastuj for an unknown period.

"You won't last a day," one of the other officers told him cheerfully.

"I'll save you a man's rations," Andrew replied. "I want you to arrange a diversion ten minutes after I leave at the opposite side of the fort. Draw the Chitralis away from me."

"I can do that," Jones replied. He had his injured arm in a sling and looked as relaxed as Andrew had ever seen him. "Take care, sir."

Andrew nodded and rose. "Where are the horses?"

CHAPTER 7

MASTUJ, NORTHWEST FRONTIER, 1895

Andrew ensured the fort's normally squeaky gates were well greased that evening and opened them quietly an hour after dark. He had muffled the ponies' hooves with rags to deaden the sound and led them onto the road outside, alert for any movement from the surrounding hills. Thick clouds concealed the moon and stars, with the patches of snow reflecting only the faintest light.

Andrew had studied the surroundings carefully through his binoculars without seeing any Chitralis but was still cautious as he walked along the road, leading the ponies.

"All right, boys," Andrew whispered. "I'll name you Teviot and Tweed as a memory of less dangerous times."

After a quarter of a mile, Andrew climbed onto Teviot, whispered in his ear and pushed on.

The darkness was a friend; it wrapped around him like a shield, keeping his mission a secret as he rode away. He could sense the presence of the Chitralis, and an occasional slant of wind brought a whiff of their scent. Andrew put his head down and plodded on, knowing that every hundred yards away from the fort increased his chance of success. A lone horseman in this part of the world was a novelty, but with the Frontier disturbed, he could pass for a wandering warrior.

Andrew heard a voice, faint against the whine of the wind, lifted a hand in acknowledgement, and rode on. The man had spoken in Khowar yet had not sounded threatening. No doubt, he did not expect a lone British soldier to saunter from the fort.

Andrew kept the pace slow, knowing that running would attract suspicion. The voice sounded again. Andrew ignored it, bowed his head, and hoped his apparent lack of concern fooled the challenger.

The shot seemed to come from far away, a single sharp crack from a Snider followed by a score more. *That had better be Jones's diversion,* Andrew thought. He increased his pace slightly, feeling a prickle of apprehension at the base of his spine. Teviot was steady beneath him, with Tweed walking happily on a long rein at the rear.

Twice, Andrew looked back, certain somebody was following him, but the road was empty. The wind increased, blowing snow from the hills and sending fingers of mist across the path. Grey against the black of the night. Andrew pushed on, not hurrying in case he drew attention to himself. Used to travelling alone among the Cheviot Hills, he did not mind the solitary ride. The hills seemed watchful, leaning towards him with their towering peaks, abrupt cliffs, and patches of scrubby vegetation. He passed an occasional village, where men watched him without comment and raised a hand to acknowledge his silent greeting.

The night eased to a dull day of intermittent snow flurries and harsh sunlight. Andrew rested for two hours at a patch of rough grazing for the ponies, checked his surroundings through the binoculars and moved on. When the light faded, Andrew found a quiet place to sleep, knee-tethering the ponies and moved off long before dawn. He stopped whenever he found grazing and walked on.

When Andrew reached the village of Laspur, the inhabitants

stared as he rode past. One shouted something that Andrew ignored. He plodded on, keeping his head up and his hand on the butt of his revolver.

The Shandur Pass loomed ahead, and even from the foot, Andrew could see the snow was deeper than he expected, with ominous clouds clustering high up. Shifting mist shrouded the twelve-thousand-foot summit.

Andrew took a deep breath. "This will be difficult," he told his ponies. "If we stick together, we'll make it."

The ponies nuzzled him, and he began climbing the narrow path. Frozen mud soon changed to frozen snow, with the ponies' hooves crunching through the hard surface to the softer snow beneath.

The pass rose before him, sharply white and with the flanking mountain peaks lost in slithering mist. Andrew thought of the gentle green slopes of the Cheviot Hills. *This place is savage in comparison.* He half shut his eyes against the snow glare and plodded on, with his ponies walking slowly, their feet secure even on the treacherous ground. At this altitude, the enemy was not the fierce Chitrali warriors but the weather, the low temperatures, and the deep snowdrifts.

One step at a time. Andrew realised his breath was laboured as he sucked in bitingly cold air. He moved more slowly, forcing each step.

The path thrust upwards, then eased into a small plateau, allowing some relief from the climb. The ponies stood in thigh-deep snow, resting as if they knew there was worse to come. Andrew allowed them a precious half hour to recover before he plodded on again, moving more slowly with every few hundred feet.

As he climbed, Andrew found breathing more difficult. He felt as if somebody had tied a belt around his chest, a belt that tightened the higher he reached. With the snow becoming deeper, he whispered to his ponies, encouraging them with English, Urdu and Pashto words as he slogged on, gasping.

"Keep going, boys," Andrew urged. He helped pull Teviot from a drift and stopped for another rest. Mist closed around him, cold, clammy and uncomfortable. Andrew looked uphill, trying to follow the pass. He moved on, concentrating on putting one foot in front of the other, feeling himself stagger and leaning on the ponies.

"Come on, boys," Andrew gasped. He squinted his eyes against the snow glare, feeling his tears freeze on his cheeks. He moved on, each step smaller than the last, each step taking more effort as the band around his chest tightened and his breathing became increasingly painful.

Andrew did not feel himself fall. He looked around, confused, with his chest constricted and his breath laboured. His heart pounded, hammering to pump his blood while his mind was confused. The snow was hard beneath him, with the wind howling above his head. Keeping his eyes open was agony, yet despite the cold, his tears felt red hot.

I'll lie here for a minute, Andrew told himself. *I'll catch my breath and then continue.* He felt a pleasant numbness in his feet and hands and closed his eyes, allowing darkness to ease over him.

Somebody was shouting, the words and voice harsh. Andrew tried to shake him away. Rough hands grabbed his coat, slapped his face, and hauled him upright.

"Go away!" Andrew said. "Leave me alone!"

Two men held him. They spoke in a guttural language he did not understand, half pushing, half dragging him up the track with the snow cold around his legs. Andrew took another breath, gasped and choked when one of the men thrust something into his mouth.

Andrew looked around with his eyes burning from snow blindness. "Who are you?" He retained sufficient sense to speak in Pashto, then choked as fiery liquid trickled into his mouth and throat.

"What's that?" Andrew did not recognise the taste. The liquid burned his throat, making him cough. He tried to push the pewter flask away, but the man persisted, holding it in place. Andrew swallowed, tasting alcohol, swallowed again and nodded.

"Thank you. Who are you?"

Nobody replied, but Andrew saw light blue eyes staring into his. He thanked the man again, and the man withdrew the flask.

Fighting the pain, feeling as if something was compressing his chest, Andrew forced himself to walk. His companions were silent now, supporting him until he regained some strength.

Andrew knew he was at the summit when the ground levelled beneath him. The band tightened around his chest, and he drew a rasping breath. One of the men pushed him onwards, and he blundered downhill. The men released their hold but remained at Andrew's side as he pushed through thigh-high snow.

The ponies trudged beside him, sliding in the snow without failing. Andrew felt the pain in his chest easing as he plodded on, and when he turned to see his companions, he realised he was alone. He looked behind him, seeing nobody. Teviot and Tweed stopped when he stopped, waiting patiently.

Did I imagine them? Was I hallucinating? Andrew tasted the alcohol in his mouth and remembered the pale blue eyes. *No, I wasn't imagining them; they were as real as I am.*

Leading the ponies, Andrew staggered on, ploughing through the snow, weak as a kitten but aware that the worst of the journey was behind him.

Squinting through red-rimmed eyes, Andrew saw the group of men through a haze. He lifted a hand in salutation, hoping they did not ask any questions. They were small, neat men who spoke to him in another language Andrew did not know. Half blinded by the snow, it was only when one came close, pointing his rifle, that Andrew recognised what he was.

"Are you a Gurkha?" Andrew said, repeating the question in Urdu.

The man nodded.

Andrew allowed himself to smile. "I am Captain Andrew

Baird, late of the Natal Dragoons. Could you direct me to Ghizr, please?"

※

Mary looked around the ballroom in Peterhoff, the viceroy's palatial house. "His Excellency holds a magnificent party," she said, holding a champagne flute and observing everything around her.

Jack nodded. "It's more like an international bun fight than a social gathering. I suspect most of these men and their wives are jockeying for position rather than attending for pleasure."

Mary smiled. "To that type of person, Jack, jockeying for position *is* pleasure."

Jack grunted. "You're probably right," he said.

They stood on the upper landing, looking down on the swirling dancers below. Jack was not a lover of social events and hoped Mary would cut the evening short.

"Come on, Jack," Mary said, smiling as she smashed Jack's hopes. "I'm looking forward to this evening. It's years since we last attended a ball."

"Yes, my dear," Jack said, steeling himself for the coming ordeal.

Resplendent among the evening suits and ball dresses, the senior officers' scarlet uniforms and medal ribbons attracted interested women. A few women were single, most were married, bored, and seeking attention, and a very few wanted more. Jack stood in the corner of the room, listening to the small orchestra and avoiding the efficient waiters with their trays of champagne and spirits. He watched Mary dancing with a nervous, heavily tanned man from the Forest Service and thanked the Lord she had found a better dancing partner than he was.

"General Windrush?" The woman was about fifty, Jack estimated, with brown hair, fine eyes and high cheekbones. She stepped to his side, holding a long-stemmed champagne glass in her left hand.

"At your service, ma'am," Jack bowed formally, wondering who she was and what favour she wanted.

"I am Kira Demidov," the woman introduced herself with a smile and a curtsey. "My husband is Victor Demidov."

"The Russian representative in Simla," Jack said.

"The Russian ambassador to India," Kira corrected with a smile.

"He is an important man," Jack said diplomatically.

Kira tapped Jack's chest. "As are you, General Windrush." She half turned away, showing her profile. "Come and meet my husband, General Windrush."

Demidov greeted Jack with a formal bow and a steady gaze. "Your name is known in Russia," he said, glancing at the medal ribbons on Jack's chest. "You are a soldier of distinction."

"Thank you, sir," Jack replied. He noticed Kira watching him closely, sipping at her champagne.

"What brings you to India, General?" Demidov asked. "I thought you commanded the troops in southwest England."

Russian intelligence is first-rate, Jack thought. *Tell something of the truth; he already knows as much as I do.* "We have trouble in the north," Jack said smoothly. "The viceroy thought my experience might help."

"Ah," Demidov smiled. "Were the men on the spot incapable of solving such a small local issue as a disputed regime in Chitral?"

"I am sure they are, sir," Jack replied. *He knows I am here for Chitral.* "But there may be outside influences at work."

Demidov nodded. "I see, and you can provide advice." He bowed. "Each of our empires has its problems, General Windrush, internal and external. I hope we can work together to have peaceful cooperation."

"That would be best for everybody," Jack agreed. *Internal and external?*

"Our countries have had their differences in the past, General," Demidov said, pointing to the yellow-edged blue medal ribbon that denoted Jack's service during the Crimean War. "I hope these unhappy days are all behind us now."

Spoken like a true diplomat, Demidov, while your agents are trying their best to stir up trouble in Chitral. "I hope so too, sir," Jack agreed. He looked up when the orchestra began to play.

"Shall we dance in this spirit of friendship?" Demidov asked. "I shall dance with the lovely Mary and you with Kira."

Mary came towards them as they spoke, curtseyed to Demidov, and nodded to Jack to signify her approval.

The dance was a simple waltz, but Jack was unused to having any partner except Mary. He started as Kira's hand strayed slightly onto his right buttock, saw the mischief in her eyes, and smiled back.

"In the spirit of friendship," Jack said.

Kira's smile widened. "I have had enough of war and disputes," she said.

"As have I," Jack agreed. He led her in a circle that allowed him to watch Mary and Demidov. He saw Mary moving Demidov's hand from her hip to the small of her back, and then the music quickened, and a press of dancers swept between them.

Kira moved her hand again, exploring further. "You have the body of a soldier," she said. "Hard and muscular."

"And I also have a soldier's wife," Jack reminded her.

Kira laughed shortly and shifted her hand to his back.

When the music ended, they found seats around a circular table, with Mary ensuring she was between Jack and Kira.

Demidov raised his eyebrows to Kira, who shook her head in a hidden message.

"What did that mean?" Mary could be very blunt for a diplomatic general's wife.

Kira patted Jack's arm. "We tested you, Mrs Windrush. I tested the general, and Victor tested you. You would have failed if you had accepted where our hands strayed."

Mary nodded. "I see." She did not smile.

"A married man who allows himself to be seduced is not to be trusted, and nor is a married woman," Demidov said.

"What would have happened if we had allowed you to continue?" Jack asked.

Kira laughed. "We would have had a happy night, you and I," she said.

"And a very unhappy tomorrow for you both," Mary told her with a sweet smile that fooled nobody.

Demidov laughed. "I like your wife, Windrush," he said.

Jack nodded. "Thank you, Mr Demidov, so do I."

When the evening ended, Jack shook hands with Demidov.

"What did you think of them?" he asked Mary as they made their way home.

"I rather liked them," Mary said.

"So did I," Jack said. "They were nothing like I expected." He grinned. "That's the first time I've met a Russian socially. Demidov would fit in well in most of the officers' messes I've been in."

"Kira liked you as well," Mary said. "Oh, I know she was testing you, but she was genuine." She smiled. "You know I understand such things."

Jack grunted. "I'm not sure I want to be liked by a Russian ambassador's wife."

"It's all right, Jack," Mary rubbed his arm. "I'll make sure she doesn't carry you away to her evil lair."

Jack grunted again. "I don't understand them, Mary, and I don't like not understanding people. There are undercurrents here that disturb me."

Mary looked at her husband. She knew that Jack would gnaw and worry at the problems until he found a solution. Whatever game the Russians were playing, they had chosen a dangerous opponent in Jack Windrush.

CHAPTER 8

GILGIT, NORTHWEST FRONTIER 1895

As he approached Gilgit, Andrew saw the garrison lining the walls. A group of horsemen emerged from the gate, riding in extended order with rifles in their hands.

"Stand!" the lieutenant in charge ordered, pointing a pistol at Andrew. "Tell me who you are and what your business is here!"

Andrew lifted a hand. "I am Captain Andrew Baird, late of the Natal Dragoons," he said. "Come from Mastuj with news. I hope you have hot water for a bath, and a stiff whisky would be welcome!"

"Good God!" The lieutenant lowered his pistol. "Glad to see you back, sir. We've heard disturbing news from Mastuj."

"Is Colonel Kelly here yet?"

"Yes, sir," the lieutenant replied.

"Take me to him," Andrew ordered.

Colonel James Graves Kelly welcomed Andrew with a warm handshake. A veteran of the Northwest Frontier, he had served on the Hazara and Miranzai expeditions. However, Kelly was in the area as a road-building engineer rather than a fighting soldier. White-bearded and grave, he brought Andrew into his office for a private meeting and listened to his account of events around Mastuj.

"You've had an interesting time, Baird," Kelly said. "You must feel like Doctor Brydon, the last survivor of the Kabul massacre."

Andrew felt waves of weariness sweeping over him. "Not quite, sir. The garrison at Mastuj was holding out when I left, and hopefully, so was the fort at Chitral."

"Are you fit to join my expedition to relieve them?" Kelly asked.

"Yes, sir," Andrew replied. "Allow me a few hours' sleep and something to eat, and I'll be ready."

"Good man," Kelly said. "Is there anything else?"

"Two things, sir," Andrew said. "Do we have telegraph communications with Simla?"

"I can arrange that," Kelly said.

"Thank you, sir. I'd like to send a telegram to General Windrush there. And another to my wife."

Kelly nodded, unsmiling. "She'll be worried about you," he said. "Women have the hardest part in war."

"And, sir," Andrew added.

"And the second thing, Baird?"

"I believe there is a civilian waiting for me here."

Kelly shook his head. "No, Baird. The only man waiting for you is Lieutenant Symington, a special service officer."

"Special service officer? He didn't tell me that," Andrew said. "Where is he, sir?"

"In his quarters," Kelly said. "Inside the tower. Is he very important to you, Baird?" His eyes were shrewd.

"I hardly know the man, sir," Andrew admitted.

Kelly nodded. "Don't keep secrets from me, Baird. Who is he?"

"General Windrush wants Lieutenant Symington in Chitral, sir."

Kelly held Andrew's gaze. "I see. We'd better ensure Lieutenant Symington arrives safely then. Is that why you're in my column?"

"Partly, sir. That and because you're light on experienced officers."

Kelly did not blink. "It appears I have two extra officers," he said dryly. "When you've rested, give me a verbal report on the road between here and Mastuj."

"I will, sir," Andrew said.

❋

SYMINGTON WAS STUDYING A MAP OF THE NORTHWEST Frontier when Andrew entered his quarters.

"You didn't tell me who you were," Andrew accused.

Symington gave a lazy smile. "You didn't give me much time, old boy," he replied.

"If I had known, I would not have joined Ross's little adventure," Andrew did not hide his anger. "Stand up! And say, sir, when speaking to a superior officer."

Symington stood up slowly. "I was always a bit hazy about the rules in this military game," he said. "Sir. I don't need a nursemaid to get to Chitral, with hundreds of soldiers to look after me."

"That's probably what the Prince Imperial of France thought," Andrew replied, "and look what happened to him!"

"Ah, yes, sir," Symington nodded sagely. "The Zulus did for him, didn't they? I hope you do a better job than old Captain Carey, sir."[1]

"That depends on your conduct, Mr Symington," Andrew

---

1. Captain Carey had been detailed to look after the Prince Imperial of France during the Zulu War of 1879. However, when they separated, the Zulus killed the Prince Imperial.

snarled. "I expect you to obey my orders unless a more senior officer countermands them."

Symington smiled. "Yes, sir," he said. "We're going to rescue Alphonse, aren't we?"

"Who?" Andrew asked.

"Old Alphonse, sir, Charlie Townshend," Symington said. "He was the lead in a dramatic production with which I was involved."

"I believe Captain Townshend is with the Chitral garrison," Andrew confirmed.

"Thank you, sir," Symington said.

"Remember what I said, Symington." Andrew treated Symington to a parting glower and withdrew.

❄

"Give me a report of the road between here and Mastuj," Kelly ordered, pulling a pen and pad of paper towards him.

"I managed to get through," Andrew said, "but one man with two horses is different from a mixed force of infantry and artillery."

"How were the passes?"

Andrew considered for a moment. "Not too bad," he said. "The Shandur Pass was the worst. I got over them with difficulty." He did not mention the men who helped. "Moving the guns will be tricky, and the mules might find it hard."

"How about the enemy?"

"They're buoyant, unfortunately," Andrew said. "When I left Mastuj, the Chitralis were starting a siege, but Jones and Moberley are good men. I can't see them capitulating."

Kelly wrote neat notes on his pad.

"I believe Umra Khan, the Khan of Bajour, is throwing in his hand with the Chitralis," Kelly said. "At present, that is speculation, shave and rumour, but I would not be surprised. These people tend to join whoever they think is strongest." He sighed. "Self-preservation, probably."

"I'd imagine so, sir," Andrew agreed. "And a touch of religion, perhaps."

"Perhaps," Kelly agreed. "Religion is important to the Pathans." He unfolded a map and stabbed a finger onto Chitral. "We are around 220 miles from Chitral, Baird. Our men have created a mule road to the fort at Gupis; you'll know that road."

"Yes, sir, although I was in no fit state to appreciate it," Andrew remembered passing Gupis in a blizzard. He had been tempted to call on the garrison but decided to push on rather than burden them with an exhausted traveller.

"Probably not," Kelly agreed. "Gupis sits at about 8,000 feet and will be under snow by now. We have a rough track beyond that, running some fifty miles uphill to Ghizer, at about 10,000 feet above sea level. You'll remember that."

Andrew nodded. "The road is rough, sir, but passable."

Kelly added to his notes. "Ghizer is a summer pasture for the herdsmen escaping the heat of the valleys. A bit like the Highland shielings."

"Yes, sir," Andrew agreed.

"Twenty-five miles on, and we reach the Shandur Pass over a spur of the Hindu Kush."

"I remember it well," Andrew said quietly. "I'd say that will be the hardest part of the journey, sir, except for any Chitrali resistance."

Kelly nodded. "Once over the Shandur, it's down the valley to Mastuj with its fort, and we're only seventy miles from Chitral, past gorge after gorge with the Chitral river on our right," Kelly spoke without emotion. "I expect the terrain to be as challenging as the enemy."

"Yes, sir," Andrew said.

"If the warriors of Tangir and Darel, on the south side of the Shandur Pass, join in, or even the tribesmen around Gilgit, the situation could become interesting," Kelly said. "They are an independent-minded bunch of *badmashes*,[2] always ready for mischief, and only the prestige of the Sirkar[3] keeps them quiet. If we ever lose that prestige, God knows what will happen."

"India will likely return to the chaos it was in before we took over," Andrew said.

"Let's hope not," Kelly smiled for the first time. "You did well to get here, Baird, and you won't be alone on the return journey. I presume that Symington has a separate agenda from us?"

"I believe so, sir," Andrew replied.

"I'll keep him out of harm's way as much as possible," Kelly said. "You're not with us officially, Baird, so I can't give you a command. You handed in your papers years ago, I believe."

Andrew nodded. "That's correct, sir."

"Very well, you may accompany us as long as you don't get in the way."

"I'll try not to, sir," Andrew said.

❄

ON MARCH THE 23RD, 1895 AT NINE IN THE MORNING, THE first detachment of the Chitral Relief Expedition left Gilgit. Lieutenant Borradaile commanded two hundred men of the 32nd Sikh Pioneers, with Andrew and Symington at his side.

"The *Gazetteer* states that it never rains in Gilgit," Lieutenant Borradaile said, looking up at the bruised clouds. "What do you reckon, Baird?"

"The heavens are going to open," Andrew said. "You can depend on it."

"Are you sure you're up to marching?" Borradaile asked. "You look pretty done up."

Andrew patted Teviot. "I'm right as rain. The sooner we

---

2. Badmash: bandit, robber
3. The Sirkar – the government or state, in this case, the British ascendancy in the Indian sub-continent.

relieve Mastuj, the better." He glanced over his shoulder, where Symington rode Tweed with an expression of bemused wonder on his unshaven face.

Twenty minutes later, the rain began, slicing down on the marching men. Andrew had little experience with Pioneers and wondered how they would cope with the actual fighting, but they did not complain about the weather.

They're Sikhs, of course. They'll be tough and enduring, whatever the world throws at them.

After eight hours slogging through the rain, Borradaile halted the Pioneers at a small village. Officers and men found shelter in local barns, while Colonel Kelly and the rest of the column arrived shortly after.

"We'll spend the night here, Symington." Andrew led him into a small barn near the centre of the village.

Symington grinned. "Yes, sir." He looked around. "It's better than most lodgings I stayed in."

Andrew was surprised Symington accepted the hardships of campaigning so readily. "Lodgings?"

"Yes, sir," Symington scratched his chin, where his five-day growth was beginning to itch. "When we were touring with the company, we stayed in some of the worst lodgings you can imagine."

"Which company was that, Symington?"

"It was a theatre company, sir," Symington said, smiling. "Didn't you know? I was an actor before I took on this job."

"Good God!" Andrew said. "No, I didn't know. Do you know what you're letting yourself in for?"

Symington laughed. "It can't be worse than playing the music halls on a Saturday night when the boys have had a drink."

"Good God," Andrew said again. "Were you trained before you came out here?"

"Fully, sir," Symington said.

Andrew nodded. "I'll leave you here, then."

Andrew found the Pioneer's officers a cheery bunch of young

men. They were high-spirited and eager to enjoy the expedition's adventures without worrying about any possible danger. Rather than having half a dozen different messes, all the officers in the expedition messed together.

"Join us, Baird," Borradaile invited. "You know the route better than anybody." He grinned. "It'll be home territory for you." Borradaile glanced around. "Where's that other chap? Where's Symington?"

"He'll be here in a minute," Andrew said, immediately liking these enthusiastic young warriors. He answered their questions about the route and the Chitralis.

"Will Chitral fall?"

"I haven't been there," Andrew said. "And when I left Mastuj, the garrison was holding firm."

"Jones and Moberley won't let the flag down," Borradaile said.

Colonel Kelly was the only officer to sleep in a tent, and a bugle woke everybody up before six the following morning. After a welcome breakfast of bacon and eggs, Andrew glanced over his fellow officers before they left.

Although the officers wore uniforms, they also had poshteen coats against the cold, as did the men. Some wore the regulation helmets, others adopted turbans, and many, like Andrew, wore the local *chuplies* instead of boots. Andrew liked the practicality of the *chuplies*, which were like sandals but worn with leather socks.

It's hard to believe that these men are the same kind of British officers that march so rigidly at Horse Guards, the stiff marionettes in bright scarlet uniforms.

Symington was laughing with the officers, wearing a similar mixture of formal and informal dress and appearing quite at home.

"Did you wear snow goggles in the passes, sir?" Borradaile asked.

"No," Andrew remembered the pain of the snow glare on his

eyes as he forced his ponies through. "I wrapped a scarf around my eyes."

"Use these," Borradaile handed him a pair of snow goggles. "They might save you a lot of trouble."

"Thank you." Andrew held the goggles with their tinted green glass. His eyes still hurt from the journey, so the goggles were very welcome.

They left the village at seven, with the infantry in front, the baggage mules plodding patiently behind, and the rearguard last. Andrew rode Tweed, glad to have company as he retraced the route he had so recently struggled along.

The initial few days passed easily, with the column soon settling into a routine. They left at seven in the morning and camped in the middle of the afternoon, with time to post pickets and feed the men and animals before dark set in. They ate better than Andrew was accustomed to on campaign, with a plentiful supply of mutton, chapattis, and tea, while some kind soul passed around the whisky. Andrew was surprised at the hardihood of his fellow officers, who slept in the open without complaint and spoke of their hunting exploits in the Himalayas. Symington listened more than he spoke, and Andrew wondered about his cultured accent, which was so different from what he expected from an actor who toured the music halls.

When the rain was too heavy to sleep outside, they found one of the ubiquitous huts or barns. When armies of fleas descended on this new prey, Andrew and the other officers defended themselves with smoky fires and much slapping and cursing. Only Symington seemed immune, sleeping without complaint in the most uncomfortable surroundings.

Every evening, Andrew checked their progress on his now sadly battered map, marked where they were, and calculated how long the expedition would take.

On the hour and the half hour, Andrew found a prominent site, took out a pair of binoculars, and scanned his surroundings.

He did not see any Cossacks, and when he asked the villagers, they denied any knowledge of strangers in the area.

Any Cossacks will be in disguise, Andrew told himself. *They won't wear a sign proclaiming who they are.*

"Any Chitralis?" Borradaile asked him when Andrew returned from scanning the surroundings.

"Are you hopeful of a fight?" Andrew retaliated.

"It might enliven the journey," Borradaile replied.

"I've only seen peaceful shepherds," Andrew said.

At the settlement of Suigal, a smiling man greeted them with an invitation to stay the night in his village. Andrew remembered hurrying past with his face averted only a few days before and wondered what his reception would have been if hundreds of armed sepoys had not accompanied him.

"Suigal must be a lucky place," Symington said. "The rain's stopped for the first time since we left Gilgit."

Andrew nodded. The weak sun seemed to cheer everybody, and the column made good time that day, passing their intended destination of Gurkuch and stopping at Hoopar Pari.

"This is a desolate spot," Symington said.

Andrew agreed. He located his old camping ground, checked again for Cossacks, and wondered if he was wasting his time searching for invisible Russian soldiers.

It's my duty, Andrew reminded himself. *I promised to keep an eye open, and that's what I shall do.*

"You're very cautious, Baird," Kelly said. "Do you expect trouble so soon? There are British bases near here."

Andrew lowered his binoculars. "On the Zulu frontier or in the Transvaal, we never knew when the enemy would attack, sir," he said.

"In Burma, too?" Kelly revealed he had checked on Andrew's war record.

"We were mostly on the Irrawaddy River there," Andrew said. "The dacoits could ambush us from the forest."

Kelly nodded, watching Andrew thoughtfully. "Tell me the rest when you are ready, Baird," he said and walked away.

Andrew watched the men camping, laughing and joking happily. *Something's wrong,* he told himself. *I've missed something. Where? What?* He returned to his old campsite, retracing his steps. He saw the cigarette stub on the ground beside the black ashes of his fire and stooped to pick it up.

I don't smoke cigarettes, and neither do any officers with the column. They're pipe smokers.

He examined the stub. *It's foreign,* he realised. *I've never seen that brand before. The writing is Cyrillic. Russian.*

The realisation jolted Andrew. *That's my first proof that a Russian has recently been here. How can I get this cigarette end to Father?*

CHAPTER 9

GUPIS FORT, NORTHWEST FRONTIER, MARCH 1895

Kelly's column reached the fort of Gupis next, with its small British garrison happy to greet them. The fort was well built but poorly sited, with hills overlooking it.

"Here's Stewart!" Borradaile said, "Now all we need is the guns."

Lieutenant Stewart was the artillery officer, an enthusiastic Irishman who lived, breathed, and spoke of nothing except his beloved mountain guns. Although the guns were small, Andrew remembered how effective they had been on previous expeditions and welcomed their addition to the force when they arrived the following day.

Lieutenant Peterson led the detachment that brought the artillery, and Stewart ran to greet them, examining them in detail.

"How are they?" Stewart asked as Andrew and Symington watched in amusement. "You'd better not have damaged them, Peterson!"

"I cared for them as if they were gentle ladies," Peterson replied solemnly.

"You'd better have," Stewart told him. "I could try them out here, maybe fire a few shots at that village on the other side of the river."

"The inhabitants might object," Andrew said.

"It would give my men practice in ranging," Stewart said.

"No," Colonel Kelly said curtly. "Check your guns, Stewart."

Stewart commanded Number One Kashmir Battery, with four mountain guns, or screw guns, as the soldiers called them, because they came in pieces that screwed together.

"We're short of transport mules," Stewart said. "Which means we can't carry spare rations, reserve ammunition or kit for the men."

"What do the men think about that?" Kelly asked.

"Oh, they're happy as Larry on holiday," Stewart replied. "We have two sections, sir, left section and right section, with the right section, the Dogra section, mustard keen. If we're short of transport, I'll take the Dogras. They're as good as any home-grown artillerymen and half the trouble."

Andrew had learned that Dogras were high-class Hindus who were fussy about what they ate and who considered themselves of a higher caste than the Mazhabi Sikhs of the Pioneers. The Dogras with Kelly were Mian Dogras, who believed themselves the highest of all Dogras. To the Mian Dogras, soldiering was the most honourable profession, with farming a poor second, as having to grow food was considered a mark of poverty.

Symington was deep in conversation with the Dogra artillery-men, talking happily to them and exchanging jokes. When he saw Andrew, he lifted a hand in acknowledgement, returned the Dogras' salutes and walked across.

"Nice fellows," Symington said, saluting Kelly. "Hazara Singh commands the battery, with the havildars, Dhrm Singh, which means Lion of the Faith, and Buwan Singh, the Lion of Strength."

This man mixes with all kinds of people.

Kelly faced Andrew. "What do you think, Baird? You've been in action. Would you take the full battery or half?"

"I'd take the full battery, sir," Andrew replied immediately. "The men always like to have artillery with them, and four guns are more likely to give the enemy pause than two guns."

"Even with limited transport and ammunition?" Stewart asked.

"Even then," Andrew said. "The enemy doesn't know our weaknesses, and a show of force might be sufficient to dissuade them from attacking."

"Maybe the men could carry the gun," Kelly suggested.

"The gun weighs two hundred pounds," Stewart knew his equipment. "And so does the carriage."

Kelly pursed his lips. "You know much of the route, Baird. Could the men carry that weight on the road?"

Andrew considered for a moment. "With the Shandur Pass at nearly thirteen thousand feet and some bad roads, I don't think men could carry that weight over that distance and be in condition to fight at the end."

"How were the passes?" Stewart asked Andrew.

"Tough," Andrew replied, "but passable."

"Would the baggage mules get through, sir?"

"I got through with my ponies," Andrew looked ahead. "It wasn't easy, Lieutenant, and it's been snowing since then."

"We'll leave the mules here," Kelly decided.

In place of the mules, Kelly hired local men to carry the baggage. "Coolie transport," as Symington called them.

Andrew remembered the road improving at Gupis on his way to Gilgit, but on the return journey, the situation reversed, and the road deteriorated.

"It's hill tracks from now on," Andrew warned.

Kelly nodded. "The men will cope, Captain." He stood beside the track, surveying the snow glinting on the Shandur Pass ahead.

"Symington," Andrew rode beside the agent. "I found a Russian cigarette back there."

"That's a bit worrying," Symington said.

"I thought I'd better warn you."

"Thanks, old boy. I'll keep my eyes and ears open."

The column struggled on, with the road narrowing and becoming progressively more difficult, rising and falling. The officers had to train the labourers in their portering duties, keeping them in line and stopping the most reluctant, who tried to dump their loads and return home.

The names on the map were familiar: Dahimar, where a ragged forest provided firewood; Ghizr, where the river ran closest to the track; and Pingal, where the climb became steeper.

"The road opens up now," Andrew said as they approached Ghizr. "The snow line is not far ahead, and it's the last British-held post this side of the Shandur Pass."

The temperature dropped, the snow became deeper, and officers and men scrabbled for their green snow goggles. Remembering how painful snow blindness had been, Andrew immediately put on his goggles, surprised by their effectiveness.

"These things are a Godsend," he said.

"The Army should make them standard issue," Symington suggested.

Underfoot, the path softened, with ankle-deep slush and mud slowing the men.

"This is a lonely place," Symington observed as they arrived at Ghizr. A thorn zareba and basic entrenchments surrounded a group of simple houses. The garrison of Kashmiri troops and Gurkhas stared at the column, while a platoon of Kashmir sappers and miners stood at attention with their Snider rifles. Andrew recognised two Gurkha soldiers and returned their smiling salute.

"People think a soldier's life in India is all romance and glamour," Borradaile said. "They should try living in an isolated post up here, with temperatures below freezing for months at a time and always at risk of snipers or an attack by a *ghazi*."

Lieutenant Gough of the 2nd Gurkhas met them with a broad grin. "Good to see you again, sir, and you, gentlemen," he said. "Are you heading for Mastuj?"

"We are," Andrew replied.

"You'll remember the Shandur Pass, Captain Baird," Gough said. "It's been snowing up topsides since you came over."

"I remember it well," Andrew said sourly. "Do you have a message service to Simla?"

Gough nodded, "I can get a telegram to Simla. Write your message down, and I'll have a runner take it to Gilgit. They have a telegraph service there."

"I want a small packet sent down, not a telegram. Could you arrange that?"

"How small is small?" Gough asked. "Could one man carry it?"

"Easily," Andrew replied.

"I'll arrange it," Gough said.

❄

Asad quickly learned the basics of reading and writing. He was eager to learn, and the *munshi* recognised him as an enthusiastic pupil and reinforced his lessons with a supple stick.

"You must learn," the *munshi* explained.

Asad did not complain. The *munshi* was helping him achieve his destiny. He was one of the chosen, bound for Paradise.

The other members of the class watched Asad with some envy, yet soon learned not to bully him. Asad was slightly built yet fought with feet and fists and was not shy about using his teeth and head when required. Asad gained the respect of the boys in the class and proved a natural leader.

The *munshi* moved Asad to the head of the class and pushed him hard.

※

THE COLUMN PICKED UP AN ENGINEER NAMED LIEUTENANT Oldham and a competent body of Kashmir Sappers and Miners who had arrived in Ghizr the previous day.

"You men will be useful," Kelly told them. "We are heading into dangerous territory, and there will be fighting."

The Sappers looked pleased.

"It will be a change from improving roads in the Plains," Oldham said.

Andrew watched as Symington spoke to the Sappers, adopting their language and patois within minutes.

That man's a chameleon, Andrew thought.

As the fort at Ghizr was too small to hold the column, they camped in the village outside, with Andrew watching impatiently as another hundred men joined them, the Hunza and Nagar Levies. Andrew watched these men arrive, wondering at their loyalty. The Levies were lithe hillmen who carried Snider carbines and had walked a hundred and forty miles from the upper Hunza valley in an impressive four days. Wazir Humayun, a middle-aged man with a fine beard, led the Hunza Levies. He greeted the British with a grin, saluted Colonel Kelly with a flourish, and laughed to see the Nagars hurry behind his men.

Symington sat outside the fort, watching the Levies arrive. He studied the way they moved and listened to their speech patterns with his eyes narrowed.

"These are interesting people," Symington said. "I rather like them."

"I'm not sure that like is the correct word," Andrew replied.

Once again, Andrew considered the Frontier's similarity to the old Scottish-English border, for the Nagars and Hunzas were near neighbours and bitter enemies. Both were stoutly Islamic, but the Hunza warriors considered themselves of a higher class.

"Wazir Humayun," Andrew asked in Pashto. "You'll know the area well."

Humayun agreed, happy to talk.

"Have you seen any strangers in the area?" Andrew asked.

Wazir Humayun smiled and spread his arms to encompass Kelly's column. "Apart from these people?"

"Other strangers," Andrew asked, immediately liking the Wazir. "From outside the area?"

Wazir Humayun considered the question for a few moments. "There was one man," he said thoughtfully. "He was writing in a book," he made gestures to show a man writing.

"Did you see what he was writing?"

"He was looking at the fort when he wrote," Wazir Humayun replied.

"Could you describe him?" Andrew asked. "What did he look like?"

The stranger was tall and tried to disguise himself as a merchant, Andrew learned.

"Thank you, Humayun," Andrew said.

Kelly listened to the conversation and sent Humayun and his Hunzas to the village of Teru, close to the Shandur Pass, from where they could watch for the Chitralis.

I cannot remember passing Teru. I was in a worse state than I knew. These travellers on the Shandur saved my life. Good Samaritans still exist.

When Andrew asked the same questions in the village of Ghizr, a few others had seen the stranger drawing the British base.

This fellow has been very open about his spying. He is either very foolish or very confident.

Andrew wrote another note to his father and had Gough send it.

Gough glanced at the address. "Do you know General Windrush?" he asked.

"I do," Andrew replied.

"It's none of my business," Gough said, "but are these telegrams related to the questions you've been asking?"

"Yes," Andrew said.

"I'll keep my eyes open for strangers, sir," Gough promised. "Shall I give the information to you or direct to Fighting Jack?"

"I'm going up country," Andrew said. "Send it directly to the General, please."

"Yes, sir," Gough replied. "I'll say that I am acting on your instructions."

Andrew nodded. "Thank you, Lieutenant." He walked away, relatively pleased he was making some progress in his hunt for Russian agents.

CHAPTER 10

NORTHWEST FRONTIER, APRIL 1895

After a couple of days gathering the force and adding porters and ponies, Kelly's column set off again, with ten days' rations for the journey. Andrew counted the men. After much discussion, Kelly had decided on two mountain guns to augment his four hundred Pioneers, forty Kashmir Sappers and the newly arrived hundred Levies.

"Where are the porters?" Andrew asked. "We've less than half the number we had yesterday." He frowned. "Most of the ponies have gone, too."

Symington nodded. "The coolies fled in the night, and the pack ponies scarpered as well. They took one glance at that horror of a pass and decided their future was elsewhere."

"Get them back," Kelly ordered curtly. "We need them to carry food and reserve ammunition."

"And carry my guns!" Stewart said.

"I'll come with you, Stewart," Andrew decided. "You remain here, Symington."

"Yes, sir!" Symington threw an impressive salute.

"They must have left early last night," Stewart said in his rich Irish brogue.

A few gunners and a dozen Hunza Levies joined them as they rode back down the track, collecting the reluctant porters like collies rounding up sheep. The Hunzas herded them back to the column, laughing and prodding, until they returned fifty glowering porters to the fold.

"We'll have to watch these men constantly," Stewart said.

Andrew agreed. "We'll have to put a guard on them."

Travelling with a military convoy along the narrow road was tedious and much slower than Andrew expected. What had been a slight irritation for a lone rider proved major obstacles for hundreds of men, and Andrew felt his frustration rise. A rockfall he had skirted without noticing delayed the column for hours, and some of the ponies proved much less capable than Andrew's two mounts.

"Well done, lads," Andrew patted Tweed and Teviot as they passed the scattered village of Teru, the highest inhabited place before the Shandur Pass. The people watched them without expression.

More snow had fallen since Andrew had crossed the pass, making progress painfully slow. The men struggled on, helping the pack ponies and encouraging the porters with a mixture of threats, promises and humour.

When they reached a level stretch, the snow lay deeply, and the ponies and gun mules sank up to their girths. The wind whipped loose snow from the surface, forcing men and animals to duck their heads.

"Push on!" Andrew shouted above the scream of the wind.

"It won't do!" Borradaile yelled. "The beasts can't get any footing!"

Borrowing a long pole from one of the Levies, Andrew tested the depth of the snow. The pole was nine feet long, and when he probed, he found no bottom in many places. He heard the officers swear as the men looked on helplessly.

"What do we do?" Lieutenant Borradaile asked, scratching his ice-rimmed moustache. "We'll have to return when the snow melts."

Andrew thought of the two beleaguered garrisons that depended on them. "No," he said. "We push on."

Colonel Kelly appeared, looking as calm as ever. "Retire for the day," he said. "The night's closing in."

"We can't abandon the men in Chitral and Mastuj," Andrew had to speak loudly above the rising wind and blasting snow.

"I have no intention of abandoning our garrisons, Captain Baird," Kelly assured him.

"I could press on with some of the fittest men," Andrew volunteered.

Kelly shook his head. "We'll do better than that, Captain," he said. "We'll all go through and relieve the garrisons."

Unable to push the animals through the snow, the column retired. The officers were cursing, the men confused, and the animals tired after a day slogging through deep snow.

With daylight already fading at four in the afternoon, Kelly withdrew the column to Teru and called the officers to him. They stood in a disconsolate group as the wind sliced into them, carrying spatters of snow that threatened worse for the oncoming night. Andrew thought the wind's moan was like the souls damned to hell.

That's the sort of thing Mariana would say after reading one of her books. I hope she is all right in Simla.

Kelly called the officers together. "Borradaile, and you Oldham and your Sappers," Kelly said, then pointed to Andrew. "You too, Baird, as you know the area. Stay in Teru overnight with the Hunza Levies and the coolies, the porters. Hack your way over the pass tomorrow and halt at Laspur, the first village on the other side of the pass."

Andrew nodded, remembering the difficulties of his previous journey.

"When you get to Laspur, entrench yourselves in case the

Chitralis attack, send back the porters and try to contact the garrison in Mastuj."

Andrew felt a surge of satisfaction that they had not abandoned the beleaguered garrisons. "How about Symington, sir? I'd prefer him to accompany me."

Kelly considered for a moment. "Yes, take him with you."

Teru was in confusion for the next three hours as Kelly posted sentries to ensure the porters did not desert and divided the ammunition and supplies. Eventually, Kelly led the bulk of the column through the slush and snowy dark to the larger village of Ghizr, leaving the forward party at Teru.

Stewart was the last to withdraw. He looked fondly at his guns, then forward where the snow on the Shandur Pass gleamed through the night.

"You may have won this round, Shandur, but my guns are going over that pass even if I have to carry them myself." He glared at Andrew as if blaming him for the topography and climate. "You may bet your boots on it, sir. I'll set my gunners to cut a road unless it freezes sufficiently at night to bear the weight of the mules."

"I am sure we'll get them across," Andrew assured him. "The men in the garrisons will expect you."

The reply mollified Stewart. "And they'll get me, by God!"

"Look after my ponies," Andrew ordered. "I'll leave them in your care."

Stewart nodded and stalked away, remaining close to his guns as the mules carried them back to Ghizr. Andrew watched him for a moment and returned to the hut where he would spend the night. He looked up at the pass, wondered who had saved him on his previous ascent and stepped into the warmth of the house.

"Sahib," one of the villagers approached Andrew, speaking in Pashtu.

"Yes, my friend?" Andrew replied.

"We can help you cross Shandur, sahib," the villager said. "We have a *mullah*, a holy man, in Teru who can stop the snow."

"Have you, now?" Andrew asked.

"Yes, sahib," the villager replied. "He will stop any more snow for two rupees."

"If he can stop the snow falling," Andrew replied solemnly, "he will be a great man indeed." He handed over two rupees. "I'll double that if the *mullah* succeeds."

The villager salaamed solemnly and withdrew with Andrew's money.

The Russians will have a lengthy report to send to St Petersburg if they are watching, Andrew thought.

"I thought these people were all devoutly Islamic," Symington observed.

"They are," Andrew told him. "With a healthy admixture of superstition. Djinns and whatnots are as popular here as in Aladdin's day."

Symington scratched his incipient beard. "I'll remember that, sir," he said.

They set out early the next morning, trudging through flurries of snow with the pass white and sinister ahead.

"You wasted your two rupees, sir," Symington said. "The *mullah* didn't stop the snow. I'd ask for your money back if I were you."

Andrew grunted. "Save your breath for the climb, Symington. You'll need it."

After another thousand feet, Andrew began to gasp for air, with the familiar and unwelcome tight band squeezing at his chest. The combination of wind, sun and cold peeled Andrew's skin, which flaked off, leaving him with an annoying itch.

Even without the pack animals and artillery, the climb was tough, but Borradaile and Andrew urged the men on. Andrew found the snow goggles a magnificent asset, helping him see where he was going rather than blundering forward and hoping for the best.

"Are you still with us, Symington?" Andrew asked.

"Still here, sir," Symington said.

The final section of the pass was a steep climb of a mile, followed by a gradual ascent to a level plain with two frozen lakes. Andrew could not remember passing the lakes.

"This reminds me of one tour we did of the Lancashire music halls," Symington said. "Cold, dark and damp lodgings."

Andrew fought the band that seemed to tighten across his chest. "At least you've kept your sense of humour," he replied.

"Yes, sir. I did some comedy sketches between the character parts."

Once they crossed the highest part of the pass, the column found walking easier as the track descended, with the snow gradually decreasing in depth.

"That's the most difficult part of the journey behind us now," Andrew said.

"Now all we have to worry about are the Chitralis," Borradaile said. "And maybe a few thousand Pathans."

"That's right," Andrew agreed. *And maybe some Cossacks.*

When the path steepened ahead, entering a dark defile, the officers stopped.

"That's a good place for an ambush," Andrew remembered the Koragh Defile and scanned the surrounding slopes through his binoculars.

"Can you see anybody?" Borradaile asked.

"No," Andrew said. "But better safe than sniped."

Borradaile nodded and sent the Levies to hold the slopes on either side of the ravine while the Pioneers marched down, heads up and boots crunching through the frozen slush.

"Push on," Andrew said. "Watch your backs. I remember the villagers of Laspur being less than friendly."

"We won't give them a chance to be unfriendly," Borradaile replied, pushing the column through the defile. They arrived at Laspur suddenly, debouching on the village with Sniders in their hands. The villagers greeted them with forced smiles and offers of help, which Borradaile accepted.

"You stay close to me, Symington," Andrew ordered.

"Find quarters in the houses," Borradaile told his men. The night was already falling, and Andrew insisted on double sentries around their quarters, with a strong guard on the porters.

"It's when it seems quiet that you have to watch the horizon," Andrew warned. "Keep indoors, Symington."

"You don't have to wrap me in cotton wool," Symington said, smiling.

"My job is to get you safe to Chitral," Andrew reminded. "After that, you can unwrap yourself."

The following day, as Andrew supervised the men in building defences around Laspur, Borradaile sent the porters with a strong escort back to Langar to fetch more supplies. By evening, Kelly had pushed the remainder of his small army over the pass, with the gunners and porters carrying the mountain guns and ammunition. They arrived at Laspur tired but satisfied.

Andrew watched them march in, each man wearing a sheepskin *poshteen* over their coats and carrying a rifle and eighty rounds of ammunition. Even the officers had helped carry the guns, with Gough and Stewart arriving with sore eyes, having loaned their snow goggles to sepoys.

As the men marched in, Andrew toured Laspur, enquiring about strangers. Only two of the Laspur men proved helpful.

One spoke of a lone stranger leading two ponies who had passed a few days previously.

That was me, Andrew thought.

"Two men followed the stranger with the ponies," the villager said.

"Who were they?"

The villager did not know. "They were strangers," he said.

The second man knew nothing about strangers but expressed surprise that a British force had crossed the pass. "We thought the snow had blocked you," he said. "We thought you were stuck in Ghizr, with the officers blinded by the snow and the men suffering from frostbite."

"Our arrival will be a nice surprise for Sher Afzul's warriors besieging Mastuj and Chitral," Andrew told him.

Ten minutes later, he saw a man running down the valley and knew the Laspur men had warned the Chitralis that the British were coming.

A pity, but it was inevitable. You can't hide a thousand men in a narrow valley.

Although the Chitralis had not resisted Kelly's column, the weather had taken a toll. Some men were frostbitten, and the officers dosed their peeling faces with Vinolia Powder to ease the pain of peeling skin.

"I've never heard of this stuff," Andrew said suspiciously.

"Don't you have any children?" Colonel Kelly asked. "I thought you were a married man."

"I am married, but no children," Andrew replied.

Kelly grunted. "Mothers use this stuff for nappy rash and the like," he said. "Don't ask me why I am carrying it."

"I won't ask," Andrew said. "As long as it helps."

The powder gave nearly immediate relief to his peeling face and cracked, bleeding lips. Andrew gave himself his regular dose of quinine to stave off malaria and found a space to sleep for the night.

❄

"SIR! CAPTAIN BAIRD!" ANDREW OPENED HIS EYES TO SEE Borradaile grinning at him.

"Yes?" Andrew shook the sleep from his head. He sat up, listening for gunfire. "Are we under attack?"

"Not even a little bit, sir," Borradaile replied. "I'm taking a patrol down the valley. Are you coming?"

"Am I!" Andrew got up. "When are we leaving?"

"Now," Borradaile replied. "I sent out a reconnaissance patrol yesterday, and they reported that the enemy was mustering a few miles away. I want to have a look." He grinned. "I'm taking the guns with me, or Stewart would drive me mad with his demands."

"Stewart is desperate to see his guns in action," Andrew agreed.

Ordering Symington to remain in Laspur, Andrew grabbed a handful of chapattis for sustenance, checked his revolver, borrowed a Martini, and joined Borradaile's patrol. They left Oldham and Symington in the village with the men suffering from frostbite or snow blindness and pushed on down the valley. Twenty grumbling Laspuri villagers carried Stewart's guns.

After three miles, Andrew saw circles of melted snow and blackened ground that told of previous campfires. He stopped to investigate, searching unsuccessfully for any sign of Russian activity.

"Come on, sir!" Borradaile urged as the column trudged on, with each step taking them downhill. Half an hour and two miles later, they reached the village of Rahman beneath the snowline, which cheered everybody up, so they quickened the pace.

"According to the map, we'll see a village called Gasht soon," Borradaile said.

"That's halfway from Laspur to Mastuj," Andrew replied quietly. "It's only eleven miles away." He pointed to a ridge in the centre of the valley. "I'll go up there and see what I can see."

"We'll all go," Borradaile said.

The ridge was only a hundred feet high, and Borradaile led the Levies up. They moved quickly from cover to cover, natural warriors who needed no schooling in familiar terrain. Andrew ordered some into defensive positions in case the Chitralis attacked, climbed to the highest point and peered through his field glasses.

The valley was empty for three miles, and then there was a flurry of activity, with hundreds of men digging entrenchments and building stone sangars on either side of the road.

"The Laspur men warned them we're coming," Andrew said. "They're looking for a battle."

Borradaile nodded. "I am very tempted to oblige them." He called the officers together. "What do you think, gentlemen?"

The officers seemed keen to fight, with Stewart already marking out targets and ranges.

"If I may," Andrew said. "I know I have no official capacity here, but I do hold the rank of Captain and I have seen some considerable service. We have a hundred and fifty men with us, including fifty Levies, who may not be reliable, and two small mountain guns. I'd estimate they have five hundred warriors behind stone sangars. We might well scatter them, but then we'd have to return to camp with hundreds of angry Chitralis buzzing around us."

"What do you suggest, sir?" Borradaile asked.

"We return to camp, return with more men and do the job properly," Andrew said.

Borradaile nodded. "That makes sense," he said. "Sorry, all you firebrands, but Captain Baird is correct. Fighting our way back in the dark against three times our number of local warriors is unwise."

The patrol withdrew, with the officers reluctant and Stewart claiming he could land his shells in every sangar one after another.

"You'll get your chance, Lieutenant," Andrew promised. "Maybe after your snow blindness clears up."

Stewart blinked, rubbed his eyes and followed Andrew back to Laspur.

CHAPTER 11

SIMLA AND LASPUR, NORTHWEST FRONTIER
APRIL 1895

Jack held the cigarette end in the palm of his hand.

"What are you going to do with that?" Mary asked. They sat on long cane chairs in the bungalow's living quarters.

Jack grinned. "I'm going to ask our friend Victor Denidov if he knows the brand."

Mary put down the month-old newspaper she had been reading. "Is that not like telling him how much we know?"

"We don't know anything," Jack said. "I might learn something from Victor's reaction."

Mary smiled. "I didn't realise you were on first-name terms with the Russian ambassador."

"Oh, we're old companions," Jack replied.

"And Kira?" Mary raised her eyebrows.

Jack laughed. "I doubt she'll be there."

Mary's smile lacked any humour. "Let me know if she is."

JIGSAW ON THE KHYBER

The officers crowded into one house in Laspur, enduring the thick smoke that clung under the thatched roof, although a sliver escaped through the central hole. Waist-high wooden walls divided the single room, with the officers' weapons hanging on hooks on the wall. They were fully dressed, with candles pooling flickering light around their gaunt, peeling, tired faces. Yet as Andrew studied each man, he saw something burning inside them, a bright determination that he knew would drive them forward to Chitral.

"Be careful not to let any hot ashes fall from your pipes, gentlemen," Colonel Kelly said. "You'll notice that *bhoosa* covers the floor of our sleeping quarters; that is chopped straw, feed for the villagers' cattle. One spark and the whole place will be ablaze and us with it."

"We'll be careful, sir," Andrew replied.

"We'll advance to Gasht on the 8th April, the day after tomorrow," Kelly said. "Tomorrow, we'll make the arrangements and ensure the local villages don't turn against us." He glanced at Borradaile. "You were right not to attack today, Lieutenant. We'll be better prepared on the eighth."

Borradaile nodded. "It was on Captain Baird's advice, sir."

"You had the final decision, Lieutenant, and it was correct."

The following day, Kelly sent his officers around the surrounding villages, ordering them to submit to British authority or have their houses burned around their ears.

"That's how we wage war on the Frontier," Borradaile explained. "It's an ugly, sordid business with no glamour. The enemy fights with kidnapping, extortion, vile torture, and murder, and we use threats, starvation through burned crops and punitive expeditions that fine whole valleys for the crimes of a few."

Andrew nodded. "I've never found war anything other than ugly."

"Yes, but we can't demonstrate the benefits of civilisation by starving civilians, sir," Borradaile said.

Andrew nodded. "I can't argue with you there, Borradaile."

When they left Laspur, Kelly's column was slightly over two hundred strong, with an advance guard, a main body and a rearguard. Andrew eyed the men, aware there were no regular infantrymen among them, yet they were in the middle of an operation that would try the skills of even the best regiment in the army. As well as the Levies, there were Pioneers, Sappers, Artillerymen, and a handful of British officers. Andrew grinned; one of the officers was an actor in uniform, and another was a colonial dragoon who had been out of uniform for the past eight years.

Andrew tried to gauge the mood of the men, for he knew soldiers' morale influenced their conduct in battle. Many of the Levies had relatives among the Chitralis, and Andrew wondered if battle would strain their loyalty. He walked past them, nodding to any man who saluted him. They seemed keen to fight.

Borradaile agreed with Andrew's assessment. "They are natural warriors," he said. "They'd be ashamed to remain behind if others fought. They tell me they could not face their wives if they missed a battle."

Andrew smiled. "Women can have that effect on men. Was there not a Norse mother who sent her son to invade Scotland, saying if she wanted him to live forever, she'd have kept him in her wool basket?"

"I don't know that story," Borradaile said.

"Am I allowed to leave the village?" Symington asked mildly. "Or do you intend me to remain in your wool basket, sir?"

Andrew had already considered that question. "You're probably safer with me, Symington."

"Yes, sir," Symington said.

Andrew marched with the advance guard, stopping to scour the surroundings for Chitrali ambushes and evidence of Russian activity.

"Can you see anything?" Symington asked.

"Not a damned thing," Andrew replied. "The houses are ominously empty."

"Ominously?" Symington asked.

"The Chitralis know we're coming," Andrew said. "If they're not here, they must be somewhere else. I suspect they are either gathering ahead or assaulting Mastuj before we relieve the place."

"Will they fight us?" Symington asked.

"Quite possibly," Andrew replied.

"I've never seen a battle," Symington sounded more interested than afraid.

Andrew lowered his binoculars. "Do you hold the Queen's Commission, Symington?"

"Yes, sir," Symington said. "I was at Sandhurst and commissioned into the Buffs."

"Then you became an actor?" Andrew asked.

"No, sir," Symington agreed. "I toured the country for two years before I attended Sandhurst."

They marched on, reaching the village of Rahman in the middle of a level, stony plain, where the local *malik* greeted them with civility. Andrew asked the usual questions and got the expected answers.

"Yes, we are friendly to the British."

"No, we don't intend to attack you."

"Yes, some warriors are besieging the British in Mastuj, but I don't know who they are, and none are from Rahman."

"No, I have not seen any strangers except two travellers who passed this way a few days ago."

When Andrew questioned the *malik* further about the two travellers, he got little information. They were tall and did not stop to talk. The *malik* thought they might be Pashtuns, except they did not walk like Pashtuns. They looked more like men used to riding horses than hillmen.

Andrew salted the information away, thanked the *malik* and rejoined the column.

Cossacks are famous horse riders.

After Rahman, Colonel Kelly was more cautious.

"The Chitralis know we are here," he reminded the officers. "Increase the advance guard, send the Levies to scout in front, and watch for ambushes. Remember what happened to Ross's men."

Andrew kept Symington at his side as he marched with the advance guard through now-familiar country. He remembered how narrow the valley was, with the bleak, rocky hills patched with snow. Mist slithered across the peaks, one minute hiding and the next revealing their snowy summits. Beneath them, the river raged and surged between cliff-like banks and over ragged rocks. Dark *nullahs* – dried river beds or ravines – gashed the hillsides, sometimes thick with vegetation, more often bare, barren and bleak or white with gushing snow-melt from the heights.

"This is some country," Symington said.

"It's not quite a pastoral idyll," Andrew agreed. "The village of Gasht is ahead."

"I like the wildness," Symington said. "Byron and Wordsworth would love it."

"They didn't have to fight the inhabitants," Andrew replied quietly.

Kelly sent the Levies to investigate Gasht, where the British officers had seen the enemy the previous day. "You go with them, Baird. Report what you see and leave Symington with us."

The Levies were a cheerful bunch, men as wild as the country from which they came, laughing as they ran ahead. Andrew called them back, put them in loose order, and cautiously entered Gasht. Nobody shot at them, and the residents only stared at them. Andrew reconnoitred a small hill at the bottom end of the village, positioned the Levies on the slopes and climbed to the top to survey the land ahead.

Andrew had hoped to see Mastuj, but the valley's configuration, coupled with an area of high ground, blocked his view. He saw a sizeable sangar about three miles up the valley on the left bank of the river.

"What can you see, Baird?" Symington joined him.

"I thought you were with the main body," Andrew snapped.

"I had to come. What's ahead?"

"A sangar packed with men," Andrew replied. "I'm not sure if they are Chitralis or Pashtun." He sighed as Borradaile climbed to his side.

These men treat this expedition like a Sunday School picnic.

"If there are sangars to delay our advance," Andrew said, "Mastuj fort must be holding out."

Borradaile nodded. "That's true, sir," he said. "I'd say that sangar is on the Chitralis' right flank."

"I'd agree," Andrew said. He scanned the area through his binoculars, focussing on a dozen men climbing up the steep slope on the right bank of the river. "See these lads? I'd wager they intend to start an avalanche as we pass underneath. That's what they did to Ross's party."

"We can't allow that," Borradaile said.

They studied the terrain, determining the enemy's dispositions. Andrew and Borradaile took notes and reported their findings to Colonel Kelly, who shared them with the other officers.

"I'll take a patrol of Levies forward and find out more, sir," Lieutenant Beynon volunteered.

"Off you go, Beynon," Kelly agreed. "Baird, you go too. You know the layout of the fort better than anyone." He glanced at Symington. "Not you, Symington."

Beynon ordered the Levies into extended order, and they climbed up the rocky slope, careful not to dislodge loose stones as they moved above the enemy's position. The hill rose in a series of ridges, some with scrubby vegetation clinging to the few patches of soil, others weather-scoured and stark, with snow in the hollows. The river roared angrily below.

The patrol settled on a ridge, with the men invisible from below as Andrew studied the Chitralis' position and Beynon drew a plan. The Chitralis were settled into their sangars, contentedly cooking an evening meal as they overlooked the garrison in Mastuj fort. Andrew saw men carrying water from the river to the sangars.

"The fort's still holding out," Andrew remarked.

"Why does the garrison not fire at the Chitralis?" Beynon asked.

"They'll be conserving their ammunition," Andrew replied. "They don't know how long the siege will last."

Beynon nodded, showed Andrew his sketch and glanced at the sky. "It's nearly dark," he said. "Time we were on our way."

Kelly studied Beynon's sketch and listened to Andrew's report. "We have more Levies arriving soon," he said. "Gentlemen, we will attack the Chitralis' positions tomorrow and relieve Mastuj in the evening."

※

Victor Demidov looked at the cigarette end Jack placed on his desk. "Are you thinking of smoking Russian cigarettes, Colonel Windrush?"

They stood inside Demidov's office with his sturdy manservant standing beside the door and a glass-fronted bookcase occupying one wall.

"No, sir," Jack replied. "A British soldier found that cigarette near Chitral."

Demidov laughed. "Do your soldiers always pick up cigarettes and send them to you, General Windrush?"

"Only Russian cigarettes, your Excellency," Jack replied evenly. "Do you have any of your men operating in the area?"

Demidov spread his hands. "Do I have any men, General Windrush?"

"Agents, spies or stray Cossacks," Jack replied. "You are a diplomat, sir; I am only a blunt soldier."

"I know nothing of such matters," Demidov replied innocently. He gestured to his manservant. "I only have Chornyi here and a handful of servants."

"I am glad to hear it, sir." Jack lifted the cigarette end and placed it in a small bag, which he pocketed. "I would not like to think of a gentleman like yourself being concerned with espionage. It is a dirty business and often has fatal consequences."

Demidov nodded. "I agree, General. I assure you I have no knowledge of anything of the sort in Chitral." He lowered his voice. "You have my word on that, as a Russian gentleman."

"Thank you, sir," Jack replied.

"Let us drink to international friendship and mutual trust," Demidov said and snapped an order to Chornyi, who produced a bottle of vodka and two glasses. When Chornyi poured the vodka, Jack noticed a Templar cross tattooed on his right forearm.

"International friendship!" Demidov lifted his glass.

"And mutual trust!" Andrew said and drank the vodka. They smiled at each other in complete understanding and mutual distrust.

CHAPTER 12

SIMLA AND THE NORTHWEST FRONTIER, APRIL 1897

"Demidov deliberately showed me the Templar Cross on Chornyi's forearm," Jack said. "The Cossacks have used the Templar Cross as a symbol for centuries. Demidov was warning me as much as I was warning him."

"Was it a threat?" Mary asked. "Check."

They sat in the front room of their bungalow, crouched over a chessboard, with moths fluttering around the lanterns and a whisky decanter with two glasses beside them.

Jack pondered for a moment and moved a rook to block Mary's attack. "I don't think so," he said. "We were exchanging information. I told him we knew the Russians were operating in Chitral, and he informed me his man was more than a servant."

"Why?" Mary lit a cheroot and moved her queen, renewing her attack. "Check."

"We're sparring, testing each other out," Jack replied, shifting his king out of danger.

"As long as their men in Chitral don't hurt our boy," Mary

contemplated her next move as she blew smoke across the board.

"Spies and agents gather information," Jack said. "They don't attack young British officers."

"When will you hear from Andrew next?" Mary moved a knight.

"Soon, hopefully," Jack threatened Mary's knight with a pawn. "Things are busy up there."

"What's happening?"

Jack leaned back. "While Kelly is pushing his little force over the rugged hills, we have Major-General Sir Robert Low gathering a much larger force to relieve Chitral by way of Swat."

"Swat?" Mary smiled at the name.

"It's largely an unmapped area, so Low will be killing two birds with one stone," Jack said. "He's got 15,000 men and 28,000 beasts of burden from the First Army Corps. He's already left Nowshera and headed into Swat, where we think the local tribesmen are friendly."

"Will that take Sher Afzul and Umra Khan's attention away from Kelly's expedition?" Mary lost interest in the chess game.

"I hope so," Jack said. He glanced at the clock. "It's getting late. We can finish this tomorrow."

❄

KELLY'S PLAN OF ATTACK WAS SIMPLE. HE ORDERED BEYNON with the Hunza Levies to leave before dawn, work their way behind the enemy and attack their right rear. As soon as Beynon was away, Kelly would send the newly arrived Punyal Levies to climb above the Chitralis on the right bank of the river. The rest would launch a frontal attack at nine in the morning, with only a small guard remaining in the camp.

"Baird, you are in a unique position as a military man with nobody to command," Kelly said. "Accompany Beynon."

"Yes, sir," Andrew said. "I'll take Symington with me."

"As you wish," Kelly said curtly.

Andrew rose before dawn, grabbed a quick breakfast of chapattis, added more to his haversack, woke Symington, checked his rifle and revolver and joined Beynon and the Hunza Levies.

"Ready, Baird?" Beynon asked.

"Ready," Andrew replied. He noticed that Beynon wore puttees and rope-soled canvas shoes for scrambling over the rocks.

Symington joined them, still chewing his chapattis.

They left the camp at six, with the sun not yet risen behind the mountains and the fifty Hunza Levies eager to march. Using the information gathered the previous evening, they climbed up a *nullah* in the hills and pushed upward as the sun rose in a glorious dawn. The Levies were tireless, moving easily across the rugged hillside as they climbed above the highest of the Chitralis' sangars.

Beynon sent a section further uphill to scout and kept moving. When full daylight arrived, Andrew knew Kelly's main body would be preparing for their attack.

"Stay with me, Symington," Andrew ordered, moving quickly to get in position but stopped when he saw a body of the enemy far below.

"Keep below the skyline," Andrew ordered, surprised at how well Symington kept up.

They negotiated a scree slope, careful not to dislodge any stones. Knowing his men, Beynon sent them across the scree one at a time as Andrew guarded the rear, watching for any stray Chitralis. The Levies ran across the scree and arrived, grinning, at the far side.

"Go!" Andrew urged Symington across and waited until he was safe before moving.

Andrew was last to cross the scree, looking around at the vicious slope down to the line of sangars. They crept along a spur above the enemy's positions, with the ground between white with frozen snow and divided into sharp-edged ridges.

Andrew heard the crack of a shot and saw a puff of grey-white smoke on his left.

"Chitralis," Beynon said calmly. "They have sangars up here as well."

Andrew saw men emerge from what looked like a clump of boulders, some waving coats at the Chitralis below and others pointing rifles at the Hunza Levies.

The Chitralis fired, with the sound echoing from the hillside.

"They're terrible shots," Beynon said. "I didn't hear any of the bullets passing us."

Andrew studied the Chitralis through his binoculars. "They're armed with carbines," he said. "They don't have the range."

Beynon smiled. "Let's see if we have," he said. "Gammer Singh, you have a Martini. See what you can do. They're about eight hundred yards away." Gammer Singh was a tall Hunza with an infectious smile. He set his sights at eight hundred yards, knelt, aimed his Martini and fired.

"Just to his right," Andrew said as Gammer Singh's bullet raised a spurt of dust a foot from the leading Chitrali's leg. The Chitrali dived behind a rock.

"We're out of range of their carbines," Beynon said with satisfaction. "And they're out of range of ours. Only our Martinis have the range."

"They know we're here," Andrew reminded. "We've lost any surprise, so the quicker we hit them, the less time they'll have to organise against us."

"There's a goat track," Beynon pointed lower down the slope. "We'll follow that."

As soon as the Levies moved onto the track, the Chitralis fired at them, with none of the shots coming close.

"Push on," Beynon said. "They can't have many rifles."

"Are you all right, Symington?" Andrew asked.

Symington nodded. "I've never been under fire before." Andrew noticed he had not flinched.

"Keep moving," Andrew advised. "That makes you a harder target to hit."

The Levies scrambled down the path, more surefooted than most British regiments. When they were five hundred yards from the first sangar, the Chitrali bullets pinged and screamed around them.

"We're in range of their carbines now." Andrew pushed Symington behind a rock. "Keep your blasted head down, man!"

They took cover between two sharp-edged ridges, with the Levies disappearing so easily that Andrew could only wonder at their skill.

"We'll advance ridge by ridge," Beynon decided. He divided his force into two equal units of twenty-five men. "We'll send one group forward while the other gives covering fire."

Andrew nodded. "I'll go with the first unit; you look after the second."

"Right, sir," Beynon said.

"You're with me, Symington," Andrew ordered sharply. "Move when I move and keep under cover."

"Yes, sir."

"Now!"

They edged forward over frozen snow, with the Chitralis shooting at them and the Levies shifting from cover to cover, making slow progress. Andrew urged them forward, hugging the ground, aware he was an easy dark target against the brilliant white snow. A bullet smacked at his side, lifting a fountain of ice as it burrowed towards the frozen ground. He eyed the next ridge, shouted, "Forward!" and scurried over the snow, sliding sideways as his shoes gave no grip. Symington stayed level, gasping slightly.

The Levies followed his example more than his words, nearly running to the ridge and throwing themselves down, rifles at the ready.

"Fire!" Andrew had no need to point at the sangars on the slope beneath, as the Levies were natural warriors. They fired with a will, covering Beynon's section, who moved to join them, experiencing the same difficulty over the slippery ground.

When Beynon's section arrived at the ridge, they covered Andrew's Levies to the next piece of cover. This area was worse than the first, with even more dangerous ground where the men had to move in single file on a narrow ledge between a terrifying drop to the valley floor far below. Andrew led, feeling as though every marksman in Chitral was aiming at him. He heard the crackle of musketry, but only one bullet came close, whistling above his head.

Andrew reached the relative safety of the next ridge, sank into cover and signalled for Symington to join him. He watched anxiously as Symington crossed and gestured to the next man. The Levies advanced willingly, nearly running along the narrow, ice-rimmed ledge, and within ten minutes, they were in position, covering Beynon's section with eager carbine fire.

"Each advance is taking us closer to the Chitralis," Beynon remarked.

Andrew nodded. "One more ridge, and their fire will increase." He raised his voice and warned the men what to expect.

Symington was panting hard but had followed orders unhesitatingly.

"Ready, men?" Andrew shouted. "Now!" He ran forward.

The Levies had learned that his single word, "Now!" prefaced an advance, and they followed eagerly, running through heavy musketry to the last ridge with loud shouts. They lined the ridge, holding their carbines ready and overlooking the uppermost Chitrali sangars.

The Chitralis were firing hard, with the Levies retaliating, although Andrew was sure most fired without aiming, so the bullets flew high.

Beynon's men joined them, doubling their volume of fire.

"Aim low!" Andrew roared, knowing only some of the Levies would understand his words. "You're firing downhill! Aim low!"

He pushed down the nearest man's carbine barrel to demonstrate what he meant when the Levies began to yell.

"The Chitralis are running!" Beynon said.

Rather than counterattack, the Chitralis left their sangars and fled downhill. The Levies fired after them without causing a single casualty. Andrew glanced over the Levies; for all the firing, nobody was missing, and nobody was wounded. Beynon had cleared the heights without loss.

Andrew was tempted to order the Levies to follow up their victory and chase the Chitralis, but Beynon was in command and made the decision.

"Colonel Kelly ordered us to clear the heights," Beynon said. "We'll hold here while the colonel takes them with a frontal advance."

Andrew fought the impatience that had earned him the sobriquet "Up and at 'em" during the Zulu War. Instead, he watched events unfold below.

"You three," Beynon pointed to the nearest Levies. "Try to find a path leading downhill."

"What should I do?" Symington asked.

"Keep your head down and observe," Andrew told him. "Stay alive."

Kelly's advance guard was first on the plain, half a company of the 32nd Pioneers marching in open order in the morning light. From above, they appeared like tiny figures, toys on a child's table, but Andrew knew they were living, breathing, struggling men, hoping they would survive the day. He watched as Kelly's main body marched a few hundred yards in the rear, another half company of Pioneers, and the Kashmir Sappers and Miners. The gunners of the 1st Kashmir Mountain Battery set out their seven-pounders, and Andrew imagined Stewart praying to Saint Barbara, the patron saint of artillerymen. As a reserve, Kelly had another Pioneer company.

Kelly sent forward his firing line in extended order. Andrew saw the Chitralis in the sangars open fire, with the jets of grey-white smoke visible a second before the sound of the shots carried to them. He saw Stewart's artillery fire with smoke and flame, then heard the crash of the guns.

"Stewart will be in seventh heaven," Beynon remarked, "having a chance to fire his pets at a genuine enemy."

Andrew nodded, fascinated by seeing the battle unfold below him.

Kelly's front line was firing in volleys, the 32nd Pioneers and Kashmir Sappers and Miners as steady as any British infantry. Andrew watched in admiration, slightly tinged with envy that he was not involved.

"This is fascinating," Symington said. "It's like a stage set seen from the Gods."

Stewart's first artillery shell burst in orange flame and smoke above one of the sangars, scattering shrapnel on the men beneath.

Kelly's frontal attack continued until it reached the river where the Chitralis had damaged the bridge. When the Sappers and Miners rapidly repaired the crossing, the Pioneers ran over and advanced on the sangars on the right of the Chitralis' defences.

The Chitralis had a line of sangars across the valley, blocking the road. A snow glacier protected their extreme right as it thrust to the riverbed, with another series of well-sited sangars beyond.

The firing line pushed forward, firing volleys against the Chitrali sangars. When another shell landed above the first sangar, the Chitralis scrambled away, joining the men who Beynon's attack had displaced. The British guns altered their target to the second sangar, firing shrapnel until the occupants also fled.

"It's very methodical," Symington commented.

"Kelly knows what he's doing," Andrew replied.

As more Chitralis began to retreat, Kelly's advance continued with the artillery firing half a dozen shrapnel shells into the mass. Kelly's reserve Pioneer company provided covering fire, ensuring the Chitralis did not double back to menace the flanks. As Kelly's men made ground, the porters carried the seven-pounders across the river, the gunners set them up, opened fire, and the Chitralis retreated from more of the sangars until the entire line was empty.

"Baird!" Beynon shouted. "We've found a path!"

Andrew realised he and Symington were alone on the hill, watching the battle unfold while Beynon ushered the Hunza Levies to the valley floor.

"Come on, Symington!" Andrew pushed the agent in front.

Andrew was last to descend the slope, where the Chitralis were in full retreat.

"Fine day for a battle," Kelly said.

Kelly's men continued to advance along the valley towards Mastuj. After another mile, Kelly halted the pursuit, ordered an advance guard to move a quarter of a mile in front, and checked for casualties.

"We had one man severely wounded and three slightly hurt," Kelly said. "No deaths, which is a mercy." He listened to reports from his officers before continuing. "We estimate the enemy were four or five hundred strong, with maybe fifty casualties."

Privately, Andrew thought the colonel's guess at Chitrali casualties was too high but said nothing. When Stewart arrived, he was rubbing his hands at having given his mountain guns a proper outing.

"That's the way, eh, Baird? We showed what my lads could do. Little beauties, my pets, aren't they?"

"Your guns were invaluable," Andrew agreed.

Kelly split his force, sending the Sappers to build a bridge over the river, while the Hunza Levies and the main force followed the left bank, and the Punyal Levies advanced on the right.

"On we go, Symington," Andrew said. "No rest for the wicked."

As the advance guard approached the hill spur that blocked their view of Mastuj, they saw a body of men standing on top and quickly reported to Kelly.

"The Chitralis might fight harder this time," Kelly said. "Take a dozen Levies and investigate, Baird."

Andrew moved forward fifteen minutes later, ordered the patrol into extended order and stopped at a copse of weather-battered trees to examine the enemy. He raised his binoculars and grinned.

"Stand easy, men," Andrew said. "They're not Chitralis. That's our men." Rising, he strode forward.

"Halloa there, Moberley!"

Lieutenant Moberley greeted Andrew with an enthusiastic handshake. "You got through then, sir."

"I did," Andrew agreed. "Colonel Kelly is behind me with a force of Pioneers, Sappers and a couple of seven-pounders. How is Mastuj?"

"Holding out well," Moberley said. "We heard gunfire, and all the Chitralis ran away."

"We had a little brush with them," Andrew agreed.

That's the first stage of the advance completed.

CHAPTER 13

NORTHWEST FRONTIER, APRIL 1895

With the Chitralis in full retreat, Kelly marched his little army into Mastuj. They bivouacked in a garden, built a dry-stone wall in case of attack and settled down for the night.

Andrew sought the officers, introduced Symington and the others and settled down to hot tea.

"Did the Chitralis press hard?" Andrew asked.

Moberley shook his head. "They didn't press at all," he said. "They built their sangars and blockaded us, and we sat inside and glared back at them." He smiled. "Apart from some sniping, they did little else."

"Did you see anybody else here? Any strangers from outside the area?" Andrew asked.

Moberley considered for a moment. "Yes," he said. "There were a couple."

Andrew's interest surged. "What were they like?"

"One was a Pashtun *mullah* with a dyed red beard," Moberley said. "He toured the sangars and spoke to the leaders. I always think that *mullahs* are bad news. They stir up trouble and make local disputes into religious wars."

Andrew dismissed the *mullah*. "And the other man?"

Moberley shrugged and thumbed tobacco into his pipe. "A tall fellow. I don't know who he was, and I don't think the Chitralis did either."

"What was he like?" Andrew asked.

"Once I knew he was not a threat, I didn't pay much attention," Moberley admitted. "Why do you ask?"

"A stranger helped me over the pass," Andrew replied. "I wondered if it might be the same man."

"He was tall," Moberley repeated. "And he didn't quite fit in. He was neither a Chitrali nor a Pathan. That's about all I can say."

"Thank you, Moberley," Andrew said. His investigations into possible Russian involvement in Chitral were not going well. He had found a single cigarette end and a few vague sightings that could be anybody.

I must be the most ineffective spy in the world, Andrew thought as he prepared a meagre report to send to Simla.

Andrew retired to his previous room when he heard a volley from outside. He grabbed his pistol and ran for the door to hear that a picket of the 14th Sikhs from the original garrison had heard somebody moving outside their area and fired.

Andrew returned to sleep.

"Don't you want to investigate?" Symington asked.

Andrew shook his head. "They're Sikhs," he said. "They don't need me." He closed his eyes.

That's Mastuj relieved. Now we can march to Chitral, and I can leave Symington to his own devices.

❄

"ANY NEWS FROM OUR ANDREW?" MARY ASKED. THEY LAY IN

bed, with Jack poring over official reports and Mary reading *A Lady of Quality* by Frances Hodgson Burnett.

"He's alive and well and in Mastuj," Jack replied. "Kelly's making progress."

Mary put her book down with a sigh. "How about the other expedition?"

"Sir Robert Low's pushing into Swat over the Malakand Pass, three and a half thousand feet high," Jack said. "Do you want the details?"

"Not really," Mary said. "As long as he's taking the pressure off Andrew."

"He is," Jack reread the report. When Low saw thousands of tribesmen ready to dispute the pass, he sent the Guides and 4th Sikhs up a scree slope, with the 2nd Battalion, King's Own Scottish Borderers, and 1st Gordons in a flanking attack. As Low's artillery hammered at the tribesmen's sangars, the infantry took the position one sangar at a time at a cost of seventy casualties, with an estimated 1200 enemy dead and wounded.

"Low's doing well," Jack confirmed. "How's Mariana?"

"Living the life of Riley's fortunate sister," Mary assured him. "She's attending dances nearly every day and listening to all the gossip."

❄

Before dawn the morning after he relieved Mastuj, Kelly ordered his officers to check all the supplies and transport in the fort. He sent the porters and a powerful escort back over the Shandur Pass to bring more food and scoured the area for ponies, grain and porters.

"When do we set off again?" Symington asked.

"When we're ready for the next stage," Andrew replied. "We can only carry a limited amount of food and ammunition, so must resupply every so often." He grunted. "We also need gun wheels and saddles for the artillery."

"Transport is a bit of a problem up here," Symington said.

"It is a problem in every campaign in untamed country," Andrew replied. He was about to elaborate when somebody shouted his name.

"Are these yours, sahib?" A grinning Levy led Teviot and Tweed to Andrew. "The snow on the Shandur Pass is melting now."

Happy to have his ponies back, Andrew wrote a report detailing his meagre findings and sent it off to Simla with a short note to Mariana. After feeding the ponies, he rested and prepared for the next stage of the trip to Chitral.

Colonel Kelly called a council of war of all the officers to decide the best route to advance to Chitral. With summer approaching and the high passes behind them, the officers left their cold-weather clothing at Mastuj, which freed some baggage animals for more essential supplies. By cutting supplies to the minimum, the column could carry sufficient food, fodder and ammunition for seven days if all the porters contributed and few deserted.

"All set for Chitral, Symington?" Andrew asked.

"All set, sir," Symington replied. His beard was respectable now, and he was fortunate that the wind and sun had tanned his face and hands. Where some other officers continued to suffer and turn red, Symington was walnut brown.

A few hundred reinforcements marched over the passes, adding to the number of rifles in Kelly's column, but also requiring food and ammunition. Andrew and Symington joined in with the officers as they struggled with weights and distance, the reliability of porters, and the availability of pack animals.

"Fighting a campaign is as much about logistics as about defeating the enemy," Andrew said.

Borradaile nodded. "If we get the logistics correct, the actual fighting is easier. Get there fastest with the mostest, as somebody said. Then, the fighting men have it easier, with the right men at the right spot at the right time. If the commanding officer can do that, he's done his part to win the battle."

As the officers worked and organised, Kelly sent the Levies to forage and scout the route towards a steep valley named Nisa Gol, where patrols had reported the enemy gathering.

The Levies' leaders, Raja Akbar Khan and Wazir Humayun, returned later that day to report to Kelly. Akbar Khan was an elderly man with a jovial smile and mobile eyes.

"What did you see?" Kelly asked them.

"The Chitralis and Pashtuns are building sangars," Humayun reported.

"How many of the enemy did you see?" Kelly asked.

Humayun looked confused. "Many," he replied. "Including cavalry."

Kelly did not hide his surprise. "Cavalry. I didn't expect cavalry." He looked over the camp. "My men will cope," he said. "Thank you, gentlemen."

Andrew waited until Humayun and Akbar Khan were alone, then asked them about any strangers.

Akbar Khan gave a broad smile. "Yes," he said immediately. "I had a stranger in my lands."

"What did he want?" Andrew asked.

Akbar Khan laughed. "He wanted to cause trouble. He was talking of a rising of the tribes."

Andrew felt his heartbeat quicken. "Did he mean a rising against our position in Chitral?"

Akbar Khan spread his hands. "I didn't hear, sahib. I ran him out of my lands."

"You did well," Andrew said. "What was he like?"

"I didn't see him," Akbar Khan confessed. "Some of my people told me about him."

Andrew cursed silently. "Did they say anything else? What did they tell you?"

"They said a foreigner was asking questions," Akbar Khan

said. "The foreigner told them there would be a rising soon, and he expected them to participate."

"Do you know where he went?"

"No," Akbar Khan said. "Once he was off my land, it was not my concern."

"Did you see this stranger, Humayun?" Andrew asked.

"I didn't see any foreigner," Humayun said. "And nobody mentioned one to me."

Andrew nodded. "Thank you." *That's something more to report to Father. I hope he knows what to do with this disparate information.*

"Beynon," Kelly said. "You've been to Chitral and you heard Humayun and Akbar Khan's reports."

"Yes, sir," Beynon agreed.

"Sketch the enemy's positions," Kelly ordered. "Then tomorrow, go and see for yourself."

The more we see the other side of the hill, the easier the battle will be; Andrew thought of one of his father's favourite maxims.

"Captain Baird!" Kelly snapped. "You are experienced in scouting in Zululand and the Transvaal. Accompany Beynon tomorrow and examine the enemy positions. Scout tomorrow, and we'll attack the next day, the 13th of April."

"Yes, sir," Andrew replied.

Dawn of the 12th showed the surrounding mountains as majestic, snow-capped and as beautiful as any range Andrew had ever seen. Beynon had called on Akbar Khan, Humayun and fifty Levies from Punyal and Hunza as escorts. He rode a transport pony while Andrew chose Teviot for the expedition.

"We're all very cheerful today," Beynon said.

"It must be the weather," Andrew replied. "Good weather always cheers people up, and we're all glad to be away from the snow."

The patrol moved up the valley, with Levies on the left flank and the gurgling Mastuj River on the right. Andrew watched the hills for snipers, thankful they were fighting Chitralis rather than

Boer marksmen who could have shot them from eight hundred yards.

They moved along the riverbed, watching the heights, carbines ready with the tension rising as they neared the supposed enemy position. Andrew held his Martini, waiting for the heavy thump of a jezail, or the loud crack of a rifle, and the whizz-thud of a passing bullet.

Beynon noticed Andrew's caution. "Don't you trust the Levies to guard the flanks?" he asked.

"I don't know them sufficiently well to trust them," Andrew replied.

"That's a bit cynical," Beynon said.

"Call it experience."

They left the riverbed and ascended a ledge that climbed at an angle above the river. Even Teviot could not scramble along the hand-wide ledge, so Andrew left the pony behind and moved on, sliding across a slope littered with loose rocks. The Levies had halted on a projecting spur a few hundred yards in front, keeping their heads below the skyline as they waited for Beynon and Andrew.

"What's happening?" Andrew asked.

"The Chitralis are on the next spur," Humayun said.

Andrew focussed his binoculars along the valley. A series of tongues jutted from the hills into the valley, with the next over half a mile distant. He saw movement on top as men, Pashtun and Chitralis, waited on the crest, careless of being seen.

"They're very confident," Andrew said.

"We can get closer," Beynon suggested. "What do you think, sir?"

"The closer, the better," Andrew said.

They moved on, with Andrew sliding from cover to cover as he had learned to do while fighting the Boers. The hill slope was steep and littered with shattered rocks, which provided protection against enemy fire, but the Chitralis either ignored the approaching patrol or kept a poor watch, for nobody fired.

After a quarter of a mile, they settled into a sheltered corner with an excellent view of the enemy's situation. Andrew ordered the Levies to picket the surroundings, and they took their positions, leaving the officers space to examine the Chitralis.

"We can see them, and they can see us," Beynon said.

"Ignore them and keep drawing," Andrew ordered.

The Chitralis and Pashtuns returned the British scrutiny. Andrew scanned them through his binoculars, seeing the usual well-sited sangars, with men waiting behind with modern rifles and more numerous matchlock jezails. A dozen tribesmen emerged from the sangars to view the Levies.

"Keep coming, lads," Beynon said quietly. "Let me count you." He sketched the Chitralis' positions, calculating the number of defenders and their possible fields of fire. Andrew studied each man, searching for a possible Russian while realising it was a nearly impossible task. He looked for a tall man with European features without success.

"Movement," Andrew said as a couple of Chitrali horsemen trotted on the far side of the river.

"That will be the cavalry our scouts reported," Beynon said, smiling. "Two lads on local ponies."

Andrew studied the horsemen, seeing their young, eager faces and the Snider rifles slung across their shoulders. The riders dismounted and came within a thousand yards when one aimed his rifle and tried a shot. Andrew did not see the fall of the bullet. After another few hopeful attempts, Humayun returned fire, which encouraged more Chitralis to try their luck, with several men firing at the British and Levies.

"Don't fire back," Andrew shouted. "Your carbines don't have the range, and you'll only encourage them."

After fifteen minutes, the Chitralis stopped firing. A second group of horsemen appeared, riding along the row of sangars. One rider was dressed all in white and accompanied by a man on foot carrying a flag.

Andrew studied these newcomers, but their features were

undoubtedly local. He sighed, wondering if the Russian had moved on to other pastures and if he was wasting his time in Chitral.

Ignoring the occasional Chitrali shot, Andrew stood up to examine the enemy positions. The sangars covered the track up the valley and extended into the deep *nullah* of the Nisa Gol, which extended far into the opposite mountain.

"We might need some scaling ladders," Beynon said. "I'll have the sappers throw some up. These lads could make a house out of a puff of smoke and a wisp of grass."

"Time we were back," Andrew said. "The Chitralis are getting too curious."

Beynon nodded. "All done here, sir." He raised his voice. "We'll be back tomorrow, boys!"

CHAPTER 14

SIMLA AND NORTHWEST FRONTIER APRIL–MAY 1895

"How's Andrew?" Mary looked up from trimming the lamps. "Is there any news?"

"The last I heard, he was fit and well," Jack said.

"How about General Low? Is he taking the pressure off Kelly's column?"

Jack nodded. "I get regular reports from General Low. He's still pushing across Swat."

Mary crossed the room and returned with a map. "Where is he now?"

"The last I heard, Low's engineers threw up a bridge of logs and telegraph wires across the Panjkora River. A flash flood took away the bridge and stranded the Guides on the wrong side of the river."

"The Guides!" Mary looked over as Mariana entered the room.

"Andrew's fine," Jack reassured Mariana.

"Colonel Battye took five companies of the Guides and cleared the Pashtun from the hillsides, then withdrew by companies. They held off five thousand Pashtun warriors with accurate musketry and a flanking attack."

"*Shabash* the Guides," Mary said quietly.

"The Devons did well to support them," Jack said. "We lost Battye, though." He glanced at Mariana. "More important for us, Low's column pushed on, using Maxim guns and star shells. He's making such good progress that Umra Khan has abandoned the siege of Chitral and is taking his men to stop the imminent invasion of his territory."

Mary smiled at Mariana. "That means Andrew and Kelly's column has fewer men to oppose them."

"That's good," Mariana said. "When will Andrew be back?"

"Not too long now, I hope," Jack said. "Get the cards out, Mariana. You could do with a quiet night after all your balls."

❈

"THE ENEMY IS WAITING IN A ROW OF SANGARS AT NISA GOL," Kelly had read all the scouts' reports, studied Beynon's sketch and created a detailed plan of attack. "Muhammad Isa commands them, one of their more able commanders. We will defeat him, thrust through and continue our march to relieve the garrison at Chitral."

The officers nodded as Kelly gave detailed instructions. They listened to their role in the forthcoming battle and readied their men.

"You stay with me, Symington," Andrew ordered. "Do exactly what I tell you, and you should survive."

At seven in the morning, Kelly briefly inspected his little army and marched them out.

With Symington at his side, Andrew watched the column pass him. The backbone was the four hundred Pioneers, with one hundred newly arrived Kashmir Infantry. Augmenting them were forty Kashmir Sappers and a hundred Levies from Hunza and Punyal. Lastly came Stewart with his pair of seven-pounder mountain guns, looking as proud as if he commanded a siege train of howitzers.

"How far do we have to Chitral?" Symington asked.

"Only seventy miles now," Andrew said.

"I hear Low's force from Peshawar is making good time, sir," Symington said. "They might arrive before us. They're going by Malakand."

"That's right, but we'll get to Chitral first," Andrew said. "A small, mobile force will always move faster than a large, cumbersome army."

Symington laughed. "I hope you are right, sir. It would ruin my mission if I arrived in Chitral to find no Chitralis or Pashtun warriors there."

"What is your mission, Symington?" Andrew asked.

Symington lost all expression on his face. "I am gathering intelligence, sir," he said.

"About what?" Andrew asked.

"You know I can't tell you," Symington suddenly seemed like a mature man rather than an eager young subaltern.

At seven in the morning, Kelly's column marched into the bright sunshine. Oldham's sappers had erected a bridge over the river, but it was narrow, so crossing was slower than Kelly hoped. Stewart took his guns to a ford a few hundred yards away and splashed them across, encouraging his men with imprecations in Irish and Punjabi.

Kelly sent Peterson and the Levies ahead as scouts and advance guards as the column reformed after crossing the river. After a short march, with no interference by the Chitralis, the road dipped and then rose to a maidan, a fairly level though undulating plain. In the centre of the plain was the line of Chitrali sangars, which ran from the hill spur to the deep *nullah* of the Nisa Gol Andrew had noted the previous day.

Andrew saw flags flying above the sangars and heard the sinister throb of drums. "The Chitralis mean to fight," he said, glancing at Kelly. The colonel looked unconcerned, as if he was on a parade ground rather than organising a battle to relieve a beleaguered fort in the heart of a hostile country.

"Peterson!" Kelly ordered. "Extend your Levies and form a firing line!"

Peterson acknowledged and moved forward with his volatile men as Kelly formed the main force into open lines and advanced, rifles ready. To Andrew, this felt vaguely surreal, as if these men could not be marching into battle on this high plateau surrounded by white-capped mountains.

"Do you realise we are fighting a native *lashkar*—tribal army —with a native force and not a single British unit?" Symington asked.

"I do," Andrew replied. "We trust these men entirely."

The sangars were ahead, with the defenders' bobbing heads visible through binoculars and the flags flapping bright under the sun. Most were green, with lines from the Quran written to encourage the Chitralis.

Andrew watched the Levies advance, with the men on the right out of position and edging Peterson's men to the left, where they would be exposed to a crossfire from two Chitrali sangars. Kelly sent Beynon to rectify the Levies' line, and the advance continued.

"Here we go!" Symington said as the Chitralis on the spur opened fire, with the bullets kicking up dirt around the advancing Pioneers. Kelly sent another company forward. "Baird! Go with them!"

"Stay in the rear, Symington," Andrew ordered and ran forward. He saw a few spurts of dust nearby where Chitrali bullets pecked into the ground and joined the men in the firing line. The Pioneers glanced at him and continued to move forward. The Chitralis on the spur were firing, with some in the sangars in front joining in.

"Keep moving!" Andrew spoke in Urdu and Pashto, hoping somebody would understand his words. He heard the bark of the mountain guns and saw the explosion of a shell above the closest sangar.

Thank you, Lieutenant Stewart. God bless Saint Barbara.

When they were about three hundred yards from the sangars, the Pioneer company descended into a hollow, protecting them from the Chitralis' fire. Andrew glanced along the line, where Peterson's Levies were in the same position.

"Give them a volley," Andrew shouted.

Peterson lifted a hand in acknowledgement, grinning as if fighting a battle was hugely entertaining.

Andrew watched as Peterson shouted, "Fira Volee!" and the Levies fired on the last word. When one man fired early, Peterson gave him a resounding smack on the backside and winked at Andrew.

"Fire!" Andrew shouted and watched as his Pioneers fired with a volley that the Brigade of Guards would have envied.

The Levies and Andrew's Pioneers exchanged fire with the Chitralis in the sangars for a few moments while Stewart's gunners fired shrapnel in support. The combination of volleys in front and shrapnel above discouraged the Chitralis, who drifted away from the nearest sangars.

"That's the way, Pioneers!" Andrew yelled. He saw Beynon take a couple of Levies towards the *nullah* to find a road across.

"I'll look after your men," Andrew shouted and walked across both companies, giving orders to aim and fire. The men responded well, firing, loading and firing again like veterans.

When Stewart altered his target, the Chitralis eased back into the sangars and opened fire again. "Return fire!" Andrew said, ducking as a bullet whined above him. The Chitralis on the spur were also firing, catching the Levies and Andrew's company in the flank.

"Three and Four Sections," Andrew shouted, "Left face, extended order, and return fire to the spur!" When he saw the Levies' confused expressions, Andrew repeated his order in

Urdu, wished he could speak Punjabi, and thanked Peterson when he translated.

Two Pioneer sections faced the spur, and the contest continued without many casualties among Kelly's men. Stewart's guns covered the entire battlefield from the spur to the *nullah*.

"We're holding them!" Peterson shouted.

"They're holding us, too," Andrew replied. He glanced to the *nullah* on his right, where Beynon was ducking under Chitrali fire. "We'll have to take them in the flank."

Peterson nodded, fired his revolver at the closest sangar and reloaded. "The *nullah* is too deep to cross."

Borradaile approached Andrew. "Colonel Kelly wants to know if the advance has stalled, sir."

"Can you look after my men?" Andrew asked. "Keep them firing at the enemy and advance when Colonel Kelly gives the order."

"I can do that," Borradaile said.

"Cease your men's fire until I get to the *nullah*," Andrew shouted to Peterson. "I don't want an over-enthusiastic Levy to shoot me."

"The Chitralis are still firing," Peterson pointed out.

"That's a risk I'll have to take," Andrew told him.

Andrew slid to the right, keeping his head under the lip of the depression as bullets whined overhead. Taking a deep breath, he rose and ran across to the *nullah*, jinking from left to right to spoil the Chitralis' aim.

One bullet snagged Andrew's sleeve, another raised a fountain of dust at his feet, and a third whistled past his head before he reached the *nullah*, where Beynon and his two Levies were sheltering behind a rock.

"Morning, Baird," Beynon said casually. "Grand day for a shooting party, don't you think?"

"Couldn't be better," Andrew replied. "We need to outflank the Chitralis."

"Let's find a path," Beynon said, "or at least a passable route."

They followed the lip of the *nullah*, ducking the occasional shot from the Chitralis. When the seven-pounders hammered the closest sangar, the enemy shooting faltered, giving Andrew and his men across a bare patch to another handy rock from where they could survey the opposite side.

"There's a small track on the other side," Beynon said, pointing to a goat path that straggled upwards from the bottom. "If we could only get there."

Andrew examined their side of the *nullah*. "There's a ledge down there," he pointed out. "That will take us close to the track opposite."

"Except for that cliff edge," Beynon indicated a significant obstacle. "It's sheer for seventy feet. Only an Alpine mountaineer could scale that."

Andrew nodded. "You had the sappers making ladders and ropes, didn't you?"

Beynon smiled as his face cleared. "For just this sort of thing. I'll get word to Oldham to bring his men and the ladders."

They waited as an active young Levy ran back to Oldham with a hastily scribbled note.

"Now we wait and hope the Chitralis don't see us," Andrew said. When they had arrived, the closest sangar had been empty, with the Chitralis facing Kelly's frontal attack, but now warriors filtered back. They began to take an active interest in Andrew and Beynon, sniping at them across the *nullah*.

"It's fortunate the Chitralis are poor shots," Beynon said and ducked as a bullet splintered the rock an inch from his head. "Except for that one!"

Andrew agreed. "It looks like they've saved their best marksmen for us."

"I wish they hadn't," Beynon said.

Sheltering behind a couple of rocks, they returned fire, with the double crack of their Martinis echoing across the *nullah*. They were firing when Oldham's Sappers arrived, escorted by Moberley and a company of Pioneers.

"Make us a route down the cliff!" Beynon ordered the Sappers.

"Typical infantryman," Oldham said with a smile. "When in trouble, call for the Sappers." He spoke to his men, who immediately began to work with picks and shovels as the Pioneers lined the lip of the *nullah*.

"Chase these troublesome fellows away, would you, Moberley?" Andrew indicated the Chitralis in the sangar.

"That will be a pleasure," Moberley replied. He snapped an order, and the Pioneers opened a hot fire on the sangar.

Andrew watched as a half company of Levies passed, trotting higher up the *nullah* to search for a better path as Kelly's frontal attack continued to occupy the Chitralis' attention. He joined the Pioneers in firing at the sangar, with the Sappers making good progress on the road.

The firing from the sangars slackened as the occupants realised they were outgunned. One by one, the Chitralis slipped away with the Pioneers firing at the retreating men, exclaiming in satisfaction whenever they hit their target.

"Those poor fellows don't stand a chance," Beynon said.

Andrew nodded. The ground behind the sangars was open, a bleak, bare slope, and the Pioneers and Levies were only four hundred yards distant. Whenever one of the Chitralis ran, the Pioneers and Levies fired a volley, which would invariably bring the man down.

"It's all good sport for our men," Beynon said.

The Chitralis fled singly or in small groups, with the sepoys shooting most, so the scree slope was scattered with what looked like piles of rags.

How easy it is to kill a man. A little pressure on a rifle's trigger and one ends a life, with all the hopes, loves and dreams coming to nought.

As the Pioneers practised their marksmanship, the Sappers were labouring away, ignoring the excitement all around.

"Up there!" Andrew pointed across the *nullah* and higher up, where a group of men appeared beside a jumble of rocks. "Tribesmen!"

"It's all right," Beynon said, grinning. "They're ours! The Levies must have crossed further up. Mountain goats, these boys!"

The men on the opposite side of the *nullah* stopped and fired at the Pioneers.

"Damn the fellows! They're not our men at all!" Beynon said, "And they have us at a disadvantage!"

CHAPTER 15

SIMLA AND CHITRAL, SPRING 1895

Jack sat at his desk as his agent stood before him. "Give me your verbal report," Jack ordered.

"I've been watching the Russian Ambassador, sir, as ordered."

"With what result?" Jack asked.

"He's been busy with social engagements, sir. Three dances or balls in three days."

"Alone?"

"No, sir. His wife and his servant are always with him."

"Chornyi? The stocky man with the Cossack tattoo?"

The agent screwed up his face. "That's him. He's a capable-looking fellow, sir."

"Watch him," Jack ordered.

"I will, sir."

Jack nodded. "Anything else to report?"

"Nothing out of the ordinary, sir. Only the usual comings and goings in Simla."

"I'll read your report later. Carry on."

"Thank you, sir." The agent half-saluted, remembered he was

out of uniform, and slouched away. Jack watched him for a moment, sighed, and opened the handwritten report.

※

"The Chitralis have us at a disadvantage!" Beynon shouted.

"Pioneers! Fire!" Andrew ordered. "Target those men across the gully!"

Andrew did not know if the Pioneers understood his orders, but they fired a quick volley that felled one man. A second, better-aimed volley staggered the Chitralis, and they fled, leaving their dead and wounded on the ground.

"That saw them off," Andrew said. "Well done, the Pioneers!"

"We're down!" Oldham shouted from a long way below. "How about a well-done for the Sappers?"

Oldham's Sappers had completed a path to the bottom of the *nullah* opposite the track leading to the far lip. It was narrow, with wooden ladders connecting hacked-out ledges and stretches where men would have to climb down ropes, but Oldham was at the foot, looking pleased with himself.

"Come on, Beynon!" Andrew said, and began the descent to the narrow ledge. The Sappers had done an excellent job, with the ladders more secure than they appeared and stout pegs holding the ropes in place. Balancing with one hand on the cliff face and the other holding his rifle, Andrew followed the ledge to a slithering shale slope that ended at the cold stream at the foot. Beynon and his orderly, Gammer Singh, were only seconds behind, where Oldham and the Sappers were waiting for them.

"With me, men," Oldham said, panting up the goat track on the opposite side.

Andrew followed, scrambling up with loose stones sliding under his feet and the stream loud in the confined space.

"The men aren't coming down the cliff!" Oldham shouted.

Andrew glanced over his shoulder to see the Pioneers lining

the lip of the *nullah*. He motioned for them to come down, wishing he spoke Punjabi.

Oldham was first up the other side of the *nullah*, with Andrew close behind and Beynon and Gammer Singh next. They stood at the lip in the bright sunshine, looking around as a dozen Sappers joined them. The Sappers carried short-range Snider carbines; Oldham, Moberley, and Beynon only had revolvers, while Andrew and Gammer Singh had longer-range Martini-Henrys. They saw the Chitralis mustering half a mile away, gathering to advance.

"Where are the Pioneers?" Beynon asked.

"Not here," Andrew gave the obvious reply. "Take a defensive position until they join us."

The ground was bare but lined with ridges. Oldham positioned his Sappers behind the tallest ridge in case of a Chitrali counterattack, as Beynon tried to bring the Pioneers and Levies across the *nullah*.

Seeing how few men had crossed the *nullah*, the Chitralis recovered their courage. A few opened fire, with the sound of their rifles strangely muted and unwarlike, and the Sappers retaliated. Andrew levelled his Martini, aimed at a tall Chitrali who seemed to be giving orders, took first pressure on the trigger, and fired. The man staggered backwards under the force of the bullet, and one of the Sappers cheered.

"The Pioneers are coming across!" Beynon reported.

Somebody was firing from the right flank, with the bullets kicking up chips of rock. Andrew could not see from where the fire came, fired at what he hoped was a puff of smoke, worked the underlever of the Martini, and thumbed in a cartridge. He wished he had brought more ammunition.

"Keep them back," Andrew ordered and glanced over his shoulder.

The Pioneers crossed the *nullah* one at a time, but each man was a welcome addition to their force.

"We can advance now," Beynon said when a dozen Pioneers

had joined them. With another Pioneer arriving every few moments and a score of Levies crossing the *nullah* further up, Beynon and Andrew pushed along the lip of the *nullah*.

"This way, lads," Andrew said, and saw the Pioneers following.

As Kelly's main force pushed ever closer to the sangars and Beynon and Andrew developed their flank attack, the Chitralis began to drift away. They left in ones and twos, and when the flank attack advanced to two hundred yards, a score of men burst free from the sangars.

"Fire!" Beynon ordered. "Volley fire!"

The Sappers fired the most ragged volley Andrew had ever seen, with few Chitrali casualties.

"Nobody's trained them in volley fire," Oldham excused his men. "They're Sappers, not infantry!"

"Independent firing," Andrew said. "Let the men fire at their own pace." He saw more Pioneers take their place in the firing line.

"Go on, lads," Beynon shouted.

The Sappers and Pioneers kept up a continual, if largely inaccurate, fire as they pushed back the Chitralis.

"They're running!" Beynon shouted.

The Chitralis abandoned their sangars as the flank attack pushed on. After three sangars fell, the Chitrali defence stiffened.

"What the devil's that?" Beynon started as a definite volley of bullets zipped past from the opposite side of the *nullah*.

"That's our Pioneers firing at the sangars," Andrew said. "If we continue on this route, we'll walk into their line of fire."

They altered the angle of advance half-right, heading for the open ground behind the sangars to cut off the Chitralis' line of retreat.

"Let's hope the Pioneers know we're on their side," Beynon shouted above the crackle of musketry.

"Head for those rocks!" Andrew indicated a jumble of rocks ahead. "We can stand there and cut them down as they run."

"Why not let them go?" Oldham asked.

"If we do," Andrew explained, "we'll have to fight them again tomorrow. Beynon's correct. A dead enemy can't shoot you in the back."

They ran across to the rocks and settled down, aiming at the increasing flow of retreating Chitralis.

"There goes the ferocious cavalry," Beynon said, smiling as half a dozen mounted men fled across the open ground.

Andrew grunted, fired, saw his man fall, and reloaded. With most of the Pioneers and Sappers firing carbines at the extreme range of five hundred yards, they were scoring few hits.

"Cease fire!" Andrew ordered.

When the rush of Chitralis subsided as the sangars emptied, the British officers checked the men and assessed the situation.

"We've pushed them back and constricted their defence line," Andrew said.

Beynon glanced behind him. "The Levies were not much use today."

Once they crossed the *nullah*, the Levies collected the Chitralis who chose to surrender, then busied themselves looting the sangars.

"They're not trained soldiers," Andrew reminded him. "They're only tribesmen joining the fight." He nodded at the remaining sangars. "Maybe they did enough. We've broken the enemy."

The last of the Chitralis had abandoned their defence line and fled, running across the *maidan* behind them. Colonel Kelly led his men forward, firing volleys at the retreating enemy.

"We've won this battle," Kelly said as he reached the flank attackers and halted his men. "With luck, we should have a clear run to Chitral now."

Andrew ensured Symington was unhurt and listened as Oldham admired the Chitralis' skill in building the sangars.

"See how they've sunk the lower reaches into the ground and used huge boulders with timber head cover. That's good building practice."

"Do you think they've had European help?" Andrew asked.

"You mean the Russians?" Oldham had heard of Andrew's quest. "I shouldn't think so, sir," he said. "These Chitrali lads are intelligent. They don't need anybody to teach them how to survive in this harsh environment."

Despite the volume of fire from the Chitralis, Kelly's overall casualties were relatively light, with six dead and sixteen wounded, two mortally. Andrew did not ask about the enemy casualties, although he guessed them at around a hundred, with a dozen prisoners.

If our shooting had been better, we'd have killed two or three times that number. Andrew stopped himself. *Do I want to kill people? I've been a farmer for eight years, and now, after a couple of skirmishes, I am thinking like a soldier again.*

Kelly reformed the column and moved on to the village of Sanoghar, where some of the local men met them. Andrew accompanied Kelly and Beynon as they spoke to the Sanoghar *malik*.

"The fellow says he lost some of his men in this morning's fight," Beynon told Andrew. "He claims they didn't want to fight. The others forced him, and he is glad that we won."

"I bet he is," Andrew had heard similar sentiments across the Cape Frontier, Burma, and Zululand, and had learned never to believe a word. Local people were always friendly when soldiers were present in numbers.

"I'd be the same," Symington read Andrew's thoughts.

Andrew nodded. "I see their point. Living in a society where blood feuds are a way of life, I'd use any artifice to remain alive."

Kelly listened to the *malik*, nodded solemnly, and said he appreciated Sanoghar's loyalty. He added they could prove their friendship by allowing their fit young men to act as porters and bring *charpoys* for the wounded and food for men and horses.

When the *malik* looked dismayed, Kelly promised he'd pay for the labour and supplies, which cheered the villagers immensely.

Kelly used the twelve prisoners as porters, adding any further Chitrali captives to the labour pool, with the higher-ranked prisoners ending with the heaviest loads.

When Kelly dismissed the *malik*, Andrew called him over and asked his usual questions. The *malik* had not seen any strangers apart from Kelly's column and did not know of any, except the three men who had passed towards Mastuj recently.

"Did any foreigners order you to fight the British?" Andrew asked.

"Only a passing *mullah*," the *malik* replied.

"What was he like?" Andrew asked.

The *malik* screwed up his face. "A big man with a red-dyed beard," he said.

"Thank you."

Frustrated at his lack of progress, Andrew headed back to the sangars to search for anything that could hint at Russian involvement. He had hardly travelled a quarter of a mile when he saw three Levies laughing and firing a pistol at a rock. Andrew stepped closer, surprised that any Levy should own such a weapon.

"Where did you get the revolver?" Andrew asked.

"In one of the Chitrali sangars," the Levy replied, showing his prize.

Andrew hid his sudden interest. Most Chitralis carried obsolete matchlock *jezails*, homemade Sniders, or weapons stolen from British or sepoy forces. He had never seen a Chitrali warrior with a pistol. "May I see it?"

The soldier handed his weapon over, smiling proudly.

Andrew examined the weapon. *This revolver is a Nagant M1895 and very advanced, with a gas-sealing system that pushes the cylinder forward when I cock the gun.* He looked closer. *That will increase the muzzle velocity as well.*

When Andrew held the pistol, he felt something raised on

the grip and looked closer. The insignia was small, about the size of his thumbnail, but he saw it was a double-headed eagle bearing a shield under an imperial crown.

What symbol is that? I don't know it.

"I'd like to buy this revolver from you," Andrew said. "How many rupees will you take?"

The Levy spoke rapidly.

"I want to keep it," the Levy said. "I don't want to sell it."

I wonder what such a weapon would cost in Peshawar.

"Perhaps an exchange then?" Andrew suggested, showing his Webley revolver.

The Levy smiled. "I want to keep the pistol." He tapped Andrew's Martini-Henry and smiled. "However, he would consider allowing you to buy it if you gave him your rifle."

Andrew considered for a moment. Keeping modern weapons from the tribes of the Northwest Frontier was a cornerstone of British policy, but the Hunza Levies were not a particularly aggressive tribe, unlike the Afridis or Waziris. On the other hand, the revolver could be very important in proving Russian interference in the area.

Andrew forced a laugh. "I'll swap him my revolver for his," he repeated.

"No," the Levy said.

"My revolver and ten rupees," Andrew said.

"Your revolver and the Martini," the Levy smiled, enjoying the game.

"The Martini for your pistol," Andrew countered.

Eventually, Andrew swapped his Martini and five rupees for the revolver, and both sides thought they had the best of the bargain.

That night, Andrew wrote a note for his father and handed it to Colonel Kelly to be delivered with the next messenger for Gilgit.

Kelly sat up at his folding desk beside the flap of his tent and looked at the sealed note. "You are searching for Russians, Baird, and sending messages to General Windrush, who has much experience in Russian affairs. I presume there is a connection."

"Yes, sir," Andrew agreed.

Kelly sighed. "Does your mission, whatever it is, endanger my men?"

"No, sir," Andrew said.

"I presume Lieutenant Symington is involved with this Russian affair?"

Andrew smiled. "I honestly don't know Symington's mission, sir. General Windrush asked me to keep an eye on him."

"All right," Kelly said, unsmiling. "I don't want to know any more. I'll see your note is sent."

"Thank you, sir," Andrew said.

※

ANDREW LAY IN THE OPEN, HALF ASLEEP, AS THE PAST FEW days' events raced through his mind. He saw the snow on the Shandur Pass, the wounded and dead of the skirmishes, Symington's laughing face, and the rivers rushing along the deep valleys. He closed his eyes, hoping they would reach Chitral soon so he could return to Mariana in Simla.

Andrew heard the scuffling through a haze of sleep. Without opening his eyes, he listened, gauging the direction of the sound, and lay still. The scuffling continued, and he sensed movement nearby.

Andrew half-opened his left eye. Stars glittered high above, reflecting on the snow of the high hills, while the ever-present rush of the river masked most sounds. He lay still, now fully awake and aware of a new smell.

What is that? Oil?

Somebody slid closer to him, breathing softly, and Andrew saw a naked man crawling at his side. He bunched his fists, prepared to kick off the covers and fight, but was interested to see the intruder's intentions. When the man began to search through his possessions, Andrew abruptly sat up in bed.

"What are you up to, fellow?"

The intruder started with his hand on Andrew's holster.

Andrew lunged forward, grabbed at the intruder's shoulder and swore when the man slithered away. "Come here!" Andrew roared, knowing his words were futile. The man grabbed at Andrew's holster and pistol belt and fled, with Andrew cursing as the bedclothes tangled around his legs. He threw himself forward, snatched at the man, felt his hands slide off his oiled body, and grabbed the trailing belt.

For a moment, Andrew and the intruder wrestled for the belt, and then Andrew threw a single punch. The intruder shuddered under the blow, dropped the belt, and ran.

"Sentries!" Andrew roared. "Stop that fellow!"

The noise had awakened half the camp. The closest two sentries, Pioneers, arrived quickly, took in the situation, and gave chase, with others joining in. One man fired a shot, another followed, and then everybody seemed to be clamouring for information.

"What's all the fuss?"

"What's happening?"

"Is it the Chitralis?"

"Are we under attack?"

By the time Andrew explained, a couple of hefty Sappers had flattened the intruder, and the NCOs were abusing the sentries for allowing the incident to happen.

"It's common on the Frontier," Beynon said. "He was after your revolver. Firearms are the most prized possession these people have. They'd sell their mother for a Martini."

Andrew nodded. "I grabbed him twice, and he slipped free each time."

"They grease their bodies," Beynon said casually. "Slippery buggers, aren't they? The Sappers have him now."

"I'd like him sent back to Simla for questioning," Andrew said.

Beynon shrugged. "If you like, old boy, but it's a waste of time. He's only a sneak thief."

"All the same," Andrew said. "I'll question him tomorrow, and then I want him sent to Simla."

The camp settled back down, and Andrew returned to his bed, knowing he would not sleep.

The thief was not after my service revolver. He wanted the Russian pistol back. It's as well I have it under my pillow instead of in the holster.

The following morning, the column moved on before seven, with the wounded and sick sent back under escort. Most men had either forgotten the incident in the night or put it down to the usual small change of the Frontier. Kelly sent forward a company of Kashmir Pioneers as an advance guard, sent the Levies to guard the flanks, and pushed on.

The first few miles were easy, marching along the Nisa Gol *maidan*, a plain of rough grass that provided grazing for the animals and rapid progress for the men. After the cold of the passes, the river valley was hot, with the sun bouncing off the distant hills. As they reached the village of Buni, the grassland gave way to a less pleasant rocky surface.

"You know this place, Baird," Kelly said, and sent him with Humayun to buy supplies.

Andrew asked the usual questions about strangers, and the *malik* of Buni was as outwardly helpful as the rest.

"He saw one stranger," Humayun said. "A tall man who asked about the British."

Andrew felt a surge of interest. "What did he ask?"

Humayun questioned the *malik* further. "He asked where the British garrisons were and how strong they were," he said.

Andrew noted the information and handed over a few rupees.

"He also said there was another stranger," Humayun said. "A bad man who spoke of a rising against the British. The *malik* said he chased him away with stones because he is loyal to the sahibs."

Of course, he is, particularly when a thousand rifles have camped across the river from his village.

"What was this man like?" Andrew asked.

"He was also foreign," Humayun said. "The *malik* said he was not from around here."

Andrew handed over another few rupees and left with his mind busy.

Are the Russians encouraging the tribes to rise against us? I'll have to pass that information on to Simla.

CHAPTER 16

KABUL, APRIL 1895

Asad waited in the shadow of a building, ignoring the dust and the dog that sniffed at his leg. He watched the group of warriors, as he had done for the past three hours, waiting for his opportunity. The men were talking, boasting of their deeds and the *feringhees* they would kill.

Asad listened to their conversation, desperate to be a warrior as they were, desperate to attain martyrdom by killing an infidel and achieving Paradise. The men embraced and walked away with the distinctive high-stepping glide of the hillmen. Asad followed, slipping from shadow to shadow with his bare feet making no sound, and nobody noticed his small, slight body in the crowded streets. A begging *chokra* was not worth anybody's attention.

When the warriors stopped at a market stall, Asad turned away. He knew the bazaar well, for he often stole his food here. Ignoring a group of haggling women, Asad slid under one of the stalls and crawled closer to the warriors. Two laughed as they argued with the trader over the price of a piece of naan bread.

Asad waited until the nearest man was intent on arguing,

grabbed his rifle and ran. He had not gone a dozen steps when the warrior took hold of his hair and dragged him back.

"I wondered what you were after, little thief!"

Asad looked up in alarm, knowing the price of failure.

"I should cut your hand off!" The warrior retrieved his rifle, slung it over his shoulder and drew the long knife from his belt. "What do you mean by trying to steal my rifle?"

"I want to fight the infidels!" Asad shouted. He knew the warrior's threat was genuine. A *chokra's* life was worth little in Kabul.

"Are you not rather young yet?" The warrior seemed more amused than angry.

"I want to chase them from our land and be a martyr and go to Paradise."

The warrior laughed and cuffed Asad across the head. "You'd better live first before you die," he said. "Try this world before hurrying to the next. Have you eaten today?"

Asad saw the *naan* bread in the warrior's hand and was suddenly hungry. "No," he said.

"I thought not," the warrior said. "Hunger gives a boy strange fancies. You'd better grow up before you fight the *feringhees*." He paid the stallkeeper half what he demanded and tossed the naan to Asad. "Here! Eat that, and be more careful who you steal from in future." He leaned closer to the boy. "You might lose your hand next time, and then how could you fight, little one?"

Asad bit into the *naan* and chewed heroically. "Are you going on *jihad*?"

The warrior nodded. "Yes, we are all going on *jihad* when the time is right."

"Can I come with you?"

The warrior laughed again. "It is dangerous, little one."

"I will learn to fight," Asad pleaded desperately.

"What will your father say?" the warrior asked.

"I don't have one," Asad said.

"Let the *chokra* come," an older warrior said casually. "His heart is in the right place, and he can help cook and clean."

"I want to fight," Asad said. "I want to kill the infidels."

"And so you shall," the older warrior told him. "Once you have learned to cook and clean, we will teach you how to fight." He rubbed his hand over Asad's hair. "But no more trying to steal from us, eh? Only from blood enemies and infidels."

Asad looked up with a grin. He knew his destiny, and now he had found a family. Allah was smiling at him.

※

"Mail!" The messenger shouted from fifty yards away. "Mail from India!"

Kelly's column had made progress that day, crossing rough ground that Andrew barely remembered and halting at a deserted fort named Drasan. The fort contained sufficient grain to feed men and horses, and when everybody was camped outside and fires lit, the atmosphere was cheerful.

"Mail!" The baggage arrived in the evening with a packet of letters, both official and personal. The messenger passed over the official mail first, handing one to Andrew from Jack and seven personal letters from Mariana. Andrew scanned Jack's message first and recognised it as an acknowledgement that his telegrams had arrived and an order to look after the Russian pistol. With that out of the way, Andrew lifted Mariana's letters. He read the most recent first, ensuring himself she was fit and well, and then found a quiet corner and began at the beginning.

Mariana wrote long letters full of gossip and trivialities but imbued them with insightful observations about Simla's people and surroundings. Andrew lost himself in her words, smiling at her expressions and wishing she was beside him as she spoke of the social life and hierarchy of the hill town.

"Simla is a hotbed of rumours and assignations," Mariana said. "I can't wait to show you around. Everybody bows and scrapes to Jack, yet some women are rather cool with me because I am not a conventional woman. I find that rather amusing."

Andrew nodded. *They won't find me so amusing if they're cool with you in my company, Mariana. I'll make them hop!*

"The town is filled with scandal, who is walking out with whom and which married woman has secret meetings with which handsome officer. It would be entertaining if I were not missing you so much. Come back safely, Andrew, and be careful up there. Everybody is talking about the expeditions to relieve Chitral when they are not whispering about the shortness of Mrs Captain Smith's skirt and how Mrs Plumpbottom saw Amy MacNewcomer talking with that handsome Lieutenant Griffin of the Royal Staybehinds!"

"Captain Baird! Sir!"

Andrew realised that Borradaile had been trying to get his attention for some time. He tore himself away from Mariana's letters. "Yes?"

"You're chuckling away to yourself, Captain Baird. It's your stint on duty, sir."

Andrew glanced at his watch. He had been reading Mariana's letters for an hour; rain was spreading from the hills, and the column was about to leave. "Thank you," he said, glancing around to ensure Symington was safe.

Andrew took his place in the advance guard as the column marched along a valley. Andrew had wondered how people could live in these barren hills, but they marched past fields of growing grain and orchards of blooming apricot and peach trees.

These patches of fertility are like oases in the desert. It is no wonder the tribes fight so fiercely to defend their homelands.

"We're making good time," Kelly said. "We'll be at Chitral before Lowe's column."

Andrew agreed. "We haven't seen any armed Chitralis for some time," he said. "I could take a small party ahead, sir."

Kelly shook his head. "Ross tried that. We'll stick together."

"Yes, sir."

The column marched on, with Kelly choosing a higher route than that Andrew had travelled, avoiding the villages and dangerous defiles. On the 16th of April, the Levies captured two men who admitted they had fought at the Nisa Gol, and Kelly added them to the porters.

"All hands to the plough," Borradaile said cheerfully, allocating the heavier loads to the more unwilling recruits. The column moved on in fits and starts, frequently stopping to repair the road but without any resistance from the Chitralis.

"What's that?" Symington returned from talking to the coolies. He pointed to the river. "Something's snagged against a rock."

When Andrew investigated, he found the body of a Sikh, partly decomposed but still in uniform and minus the head. "That will be one of Ross's men," he said. "A few refused to join us and remained in the cave. It doesn't seem to have done them any good."

"Poor fellow," Symington commented. He viewed the body. "These Chitrali people seem so charming when one speaks to them, yet life isn't worth much up here."

Andrew saw more decapitated Sikh bodies that day, either bouncing with the current or washed up on the riverbank. He felt the mood of the column alter, with a new anger among the Kashmiris. The column pushed on as Andrew wondered how Symington would survive among the Chitralis.

"How much further?" Symington asked.

Andrew consulted his map. "A few days," he said.

Even without hostile Chitralis, the column struggled to make progress. When the porters proved reluctant, Borradaile encouraged the Pioneers to help them with boots and rifle butts. When the porters stripped naked to ford a river, they left half their burdens on one side until the Pioneers caught them and forced them to continue. The road was poor at best, and the Sappers were busy building bridges and repairing damaged sections to allow the column to continue.

Andrew fretted, knowing they were only a few miles away from their objective without being able to contact the fort in Chitral. The crack of a rifle after incident-free days came as a shock, and the whistle of the bullet startled him.

"What the devil?"

Andrew scoured the hillside opposite, seeing nothing except rocks. The rifle cracked again, with the bullet ricocheting from a boulder ten yards from Andrew.

He's firing at me, whoever he is, Andrew told himself. *Why me? Borradaile and Moberley are in the open, far more tempting targets, and there are hundreds of Pioneers marching along the road.*

The rifle sounded again, and this time, Andrew saw smoke wisping from behind a rock. The bullet ploughed into the ground ten yards away, raising a small spurt of dust.

That's three shots, and none of them came close. Andrew wished he had kept his Martini. He stood up and approached the closest Pioneer.

"I'd like to borrow your rifle," Andrew said in Urdu and Pashto. The man glanced at his havildar, who nodded.

"Thank you." Checking the Snider was loaded, Andrew looked at the hillside opposite. He saw no movement where the shooter had been, and a wind had dissolved the smoke. "Give me some more ammunition, please." Sighting at four hundred yards, he aimed to the left of the rock and fired. He fancied he saw fragments splinter from the rock and quickly reloaded.

A man burst from behind the rock, running erratically up the hillside. Andrew traversed the Snider, got the man in his sights and swore as his target dropped into cover further up the slope.

I could chase him or send over a couple of Levies to hunt him down, but the chances of capturing him are slim.

Andrew waited until his quarry moved again, aimed and fired a single shot. He saw the man spin around, rise and flee, limping badly.

I must have winged him. Andrew reloaded, then sighed.

The Pioneers had marched past, with the rearguard level with Andrew. He watched the shooter limp away and lowered his rifle.

What the devil was that all about? Why shoot at me in particular?

The march continued, with rumours of the enemy making a stand proving false and the Sappers working daily miracles repairing roads and bridges. Kelly ordered the Levies to scout while the Pioneers acted as guards.

"Something's happening ahead!" The news carried from the advance guard. Andrew hurried ahead to see Humayun walking beside a stranger, evidently well-pleased with himself.

"What's happening?" Andrew asked.

"This man has letters from Chitral," Humayun said.

The packet of letters was addressed to "The officer commanding troops advancing from Gilgit."

Andrew was present when Colonel Kelly opened the first letter from Surgeon-Major Robertson. Kelly scanned it and then read it more slowly.

"Gentlemen," Kelly raised his voice. "Sher Afzul has retreated from outside Chitral. Our advance has been successful, and we have relieved the siege."

The officers cheered, with the Levies and Pioneers joining in, although Andrew doubted that many of them knew what was happening.

"The second letter is a casualty list," Kelly said. "The garrison has a hundred and four killed and wounded out of three hundred and seventy men."

The figures sobered the officers.

"Send a messenger," Kelly said. "Tell the garrison that we'll arrive tomorrow."

Stewart looked disappointed, as he had hoped for another battle to use his guns, and most of the officers thought the Chitralis could have put up more resistance. Colonel Kelly was not so sanguinary.

"We have achieved our objective, gentlemen," Kelly said quietly. "We lost quite enough men on the journey here. I am glad to have a peaceful conclusion to our expedition." He allowed himself a small smile. "And we have arrived before General Low's much larger force."

"Low's advance aided us," Borradaile said quietly. "He drew away Umra Khan's men, who could have caused us considerable difficulties."

Andrew pulled Symington aside. "We'll be in Chitral soon," he said. "Are you ready for whatever you have to do?"

Symington grinned through his beard. "I'm looking forward to it," he said. "It's the largest part I've ever played."

"This isn't a play!" Andrew snapped.

"Oh, but it is, Captain Baird," Symington insisted. "This is the greatest play in the world, the contest of empires, with India crucial to the outcome." His face was as serious and intelligent as Andrew had ever seen.

"What can I do to help?" Andrew asked.

Symington grinned again in a lightning return to the young subaltern Andrew had first met. "You kept me alive, sir. I'll slip away without a word. Please convey my respects to General Windrush and tell him you have planted the seed."

"I will," Andrew promised.

Kelly ordered the bugles to blast their arrival at Chitral and marched towards the battered little fort. Robertson, Townsend and his little garrison had held out for forty-seven days and greeted Kelly with firm handshakes but little show of emotion. The garrison filed out to meet the column. Half starved, with many wounded, they stared at Kelly's men.[1]

"Well done," Andrew saw the marks of gunshots and fire on the walls, the unburied bodies of the fallen tribesmen outside

---

1. Rather than face Low's column, Umra Khan fled to Afghanistan, where the Amir threw him in prison. Sher Afzul ended up in an Indian jail, and young Shuja-ul-Mulk became Mehtar of Chitral. He ruled for forty peaceful years, backed by a permanent British-Indian garrison.

and the hidden tears from some of the garrison. He smelled the stink from inside the fort, where the latrines were overflowing and the hospital full of the sick and wounded.

Please, God, I never have to endure a siege. It was bad enough in the Transvaal with a civilised enemy. I can't imagine being besieged up here when surrender would mean a slow, agonising death.

"Captain Baird?" The man looked as ragged as any beggar except for the Khyber Knife at his belt and his clear, intelligent eyes.

"That's right," Andrew said, automatically reaching for his pistol.

"You'll be looking for me," the man said. His slightly Irish accent reassured Andrew that he was no enemy.

Andrew sat at the man's side. "What's your name?"

"General Windrush will want the information I have," the man said. "My name is Stevenson."

"Well, Stevenson," Andrew said. "We'll catch some sleep tonight and head to Simla."

Am I only a courier in this blasted country? Now, I must trek back over those hellish passes. Thank God I'm heading the right way, at least. I hope Mariana remembers who I am.

CHAPTER 17

SIMLA, JULY 1895

"How did you find Kelly's Chitral expedition?" Jack asked.

Shaved, shorn and dressed in stiff scarlet, Andrew felt uncomfortable and out of place in Jack's official office, with the maps of the Frontier adorning the wall and the punkah in the ceiling keeping the air mobile.

"A bit frustrating that I had no official position," Andrew replied. "There were many times that I wanted to take over and give orders."

Jack nodded. "I thought it might be like that since you resigned. I've had you reinstated with your previous rank of Captain and temporary attachment to the Royal Malverns. The Transvaal Dragoons are no more, alas."

"No more?"

"They disbanded a few years ago," Jack replied.

"They were a fine regiment," Andrew said with momentary sadness.

Jack nodded. "They served a purpose in difficult times." He

examined the Russian pistol Andrew had found. "The War Office is a bit sticky about your back pay, though."

"I don't expect any," Andrew said. "The actual relief of Chitral was a bit of an anti-climax."

"What did you expect?" Jack asked. "Brass bands and a parade?"

"Not quite," Andrew said. "Perhaps a last stand by the Chitralis."

Jack laughed. "War isn't like the cheap novels," he said. "Kelly had already defeated the Chitralis in two encounters, Umra Khan had left to face Low, and Robertson defended the fort stubbornly. The Chitralis recognised reality." He stood, paced to the window and stared out. "What's more important is that you delivered Symington safely and brought back Stevenson."

Andrew nodded. "I hope Symington is all right."

"He knows what he's doing," Jack replied. "Did you see this symbol on the pistol?"

Andrew nodded. "Yes. I don't know what it means."

"That's the *Okhrana* symbol," Jack said. "A member of the *Okhrana* must have owned this weapon."

"What's the *Okhrana*?" Andrew asked.

"The Tsar's secret police," Jack said. "They're an unpleasant bunch." He examined the revolver. "This is a Nagant M1895, made this year in Belgium, especially for the Russian market. It's brand new, so somebody will be cursing that he lost it—unless some Pashtun slit his throat to gain the pistol."

"That could be what happened," Andrew agreed.

"You said somebody tried to steal this weapon the same day you bought it?" Jack asked.

"That's correct," Andrew replied. "He came into my tent."

"And you caught him," Jack said.

"I did," Andrew confirmed.

Jack poured them both a whisky. "Who tried to steal it?"

"It's all in my report," Andrew said.

"Remind me," Jack said, smiling.

"A Pashtun named Khattak," Andrew said.

Jack swirled his whisky in the glass. "I've known Pashtuns who could steal a rifle from a sleeping man while the weapon was chained to his wrist. They could remove a man's bed while he was sleeping on it without waking him up."

"Khattak was not as good as that," Andrew said. "I heard him coming."

"That's unusual," Jack said. "Very unusual, and that worries me. You interrogated him afterwards?"

"Yes," Andrew said.

Jack sipped at his whisky. "What did he say?"

"He said somebody paid him to steal the pistol," Andrew said.

"Who?" Jack was relentless in his questioning.

"Khattak didn't know the name. He described him as a tall foreigner."

Jack nodded. "A Russian, I'll be bound. Is this Khattak fellow still in custody?"

"Yes," Andrew said. "I had him sent to Simla so your experts could speak to him."

"Good," Jack said. He eyed Andrew up and down. "It's good to have you back safe and sound, boy. Your wife has been asking for you, so no doubt you'll want to go to her."

"I do," Andrew said.

"Off you go then," Jack said, watching fondly as Andrew marched away. *He's an experienced soldier now, but I haven't finished with him yet. I have other tasks for you, Andrew, my boy.*

❄

MARIANA LOOKED ANDREW UP AND DOWN, SMILING. "You look younger," she said approvingly. "And very fit. You've lost some weight, but it suits you. I thought you would look worn out and haggard like you did when you returned from Mandalay." She touched his arm. "You look delicious."

"Thank you," Andrew bobbed in a mock bow. "You look pretty good yourself."

They stood side by side on the veranda of their bungalow in Simla, with a panoramic view of the Himalayas to the north and the town spread out before them.

"Did you miss me?" Mariana asked.

"Very much," Andrew took her hand.

"I missed you too," Mariana said. She shuffled closer so her hip rubbed against him. "I'm glad you're back."

Andrew interpreted her smile and led her inside the bungalow.

※

"I am Baback, and the old greybeard is Zaram," the warrior grinned at Asad. "You must not mind Zaram's bad temper. It is a thing that comes with age."

Asad nodded solemnly. "I will not mind his temper," he said.

Baback shook his head. "You're a very serious little *chokra*, aren't you? Never mind, we'll soon make you an Afridi warrior."

"Are you Afridis?" Asad asked.

"We are, and so are you, now," Baback said.

Asad looked grave. "It is good to belong."

※

"You were ardent last night," Mariana stretched on the bed and smiled at Andrew.

"So were you," Andrew replied. "It reminded me of our early days."

"You'll have to go up country more often," Mariana walked her fingers across the bed and onto his naked stomach. "Hello; look what's happening again."

Andrew heard the thunder outside and saw the flash of lightning. Electricity crackled in the air. He looked at his wife, seeing the pure love within her. "That's entirely your fault. It never happens with anybody else."

"I should hope not, indeed," Mariana said, nibbling at her lower lip. "It would be a pity to waste it."

"I wouldn't dream of such a waste," Andrew said.

The storm lingered for an hour and passed, leaving Simla bright, washed and refreshed.

"Are you on duty today?" Mariana asked.

"Not unless your esteemed father-in-law decides so," Andrew replied.

"He won't," Mariana said solemnly. "I've had a word with him."

"The poor old man," Andrew said.

"You're mine all day," Mariana told him. "Prepare to get introduced to Simla."

"I can't think of anything better," Andrew listened to the birds singing in the garden that wrapped around the bungalow.

Mariana took Andrew by the hand, smiling. "Simla is a wonderful place, Andrew. You'll love it. It's full of intrigue, hidden passions, hidden meetings between men and women, coy glances from behind fans, dances, balls and gardens for quiet assignations under shady trees."

Andrew raised his eyebrows. "You've found out a lot."

"I've been here for weeks," Mariana said, and added, "alone." She smiled widely.

"You were never alone," Andrew said. "My mother would make sure of that."

"I mean alone without my husband," Mariana corrected herself. "Come on, Andrew. Get dressed, and let's get outside."

Mariana introduced Andrew to some of the public gardens and allowed him to buy her tea and cakes in one of the comfortable tea shops. She smiled as a pair of young women eyed up the passing officers and discussed their attributes. Andrew tried not to listen, but he realised Mariana was intent on hearing every word. He sighed indulgently and leaned back in his cane chair.

"I forgot you liked gossip so much," Andrew told her.

"I didn't get much chance back home," Mariana said. "These so-respectable young ladies are hunting in couples. That means they stay together until they choose some unfortunate young man as their victim and pluck him like a ripe apple from the tree. The poor fellow won't stand a chance; fresh from the jungle or some remote station hundreds of miles from nowhere, he'll have been starved of female company for months. These female wolves will have him dissected and paralysed, turn him inside out, know his prospects and bank balance, and have him at the marriage altar before he can cry help to his mama."

Andrew smiled. "India has worse dangers than angry tribesmen, then."

"Oh, Andrew. Having Pathans take potshots at you is the least of your worries out here." She smiled at him with mischief bright in her eyes. "When that kind of girl wants some less-than-innocent fun, they'll drag a married man into their boudoir." She patted his arm. "Don't despair, husband dear; I'll protect you from their evil clutches."

"Thank you," Andrew eyed the two women without any carnal interest. Even in his pre-married days, he would not have given them a second glance. One was tall, willowy and fair, the other shorter, with a floppy hat half-hiding her dark hair.

Mariana continued to listen, shaking her head. "Did you hear what that girl said about that Highland lieutenant?"

"I did not," Andrew said, holding in his laughter when Mariana leaned closer and whispered in his ear.

"She looks so innocent, too," Mariana said, pretending to be shocked. "Her mama should make her wash out her mouth with strong carbolic soap."

"Would you do that to our children if we had any?" Andrew asked.

"Certainly not!" Mariana said. "My children will know better than to talk about such things."

Andrew was glad he had missed the conversation.

"If we ever have any children," Mariana added.

"It could still happen," Andrew said.

Mariana sighed. "I am not getting any younger," she reminded him. "A woman should start a family in her early twenties, not her thirties."

"We are both fit, healthy and relatively young," Andrew tried to lighten the mood. "Come on, Mariana. Show me around Simla."

Mariana smiled, put down her cup and took hold of Andrew's sleeve. "If you are as enthusiastic as you were last night," she told him, "we could have a whole brood of children."

Mariana had spoken more loudly than she realised, and the two young women looked around with wide eyes and open mouths. Mariana laughed. "You two have a lot to learn about men," she told them, sweeping out of the shop with Andrew on her arm.

With Mariana as his guide, Andrew could see Simla in a different light: a summer retreat for jaded administrators, a hot spot of intrigue and gossip, a pleasure resort for bored wives, and a meeting place for hopeful lovers.

"Everybody has a story," Mariana said as they walked along the twisting Mall, Simla's main street, with fine views all around. "And we can meet all human life here." She held onto Andrew's arm as she acted like a Cook's guide. "Look at these horrible office blocks, full of underpaid clerks toiling over ledgers, nibbling their pens as they scratch out the day-to-day life of millions of people. The faceless administrators in soulless offices within the most vibrant and colourful country on earth."

Andrew smiled. "You are very scathing," he said.

"And rightly so," Mariana replied. "India deserves better than square boxes made of girders, with exterior staircases and ugly verandas."

"I suspect you like Simla," Andrew said.

"I do. I like the contrasts and the vibrancy after our life in

Berwickshire. Now you're here, Andrew, I can attend balls and levees all the time."

Mariana guided Andrew along the Mall, with its long, undulating street that widened into picturesque squares, passing the ornate gates that opened into the splendid gardens of the elite. Although Mariana chose to walk, some people used the ancient *jhampans* for transport.

Andrew shook his head when four men carried a *jhampan* past him.

"It's like a combination of a four-poster bed and a sedan chair," Mariana said, laughing. "Most people use the four-man rickshaw."

"So I see," Andrew agreed. Rickshaws filled the Mall, with their gasping crews propelling the tall-wheeled wickerwork vehicles up and down the steep slopes. One seemed to have trouble as it laboured up the hill, with the pale-faced, bespectacled passenger staring intently around him. A middle-aged couple trotted past, with the man perspiring and the woman, ten years younger, eyeing up every man she passed. When she saw Andrew, she pushed her white Terai hat to the back of her head, smiled and looked away when Mariana glowered at her.

"*Bajke bajao khabar dar*! Look out!" a rickshaw driver shouted as he careened past the woman, running down a slope at full speed to build up momentum for the next incline.

"I'll show you the shops," Mariana said. "The shopping here is better than Berwick but not as good as Edinburgh." She smiled. "Did you know people call Simla the Abode of the Little Tin Gods?"

"I did not know that," Andrew replied solemnly.

"The viceroy is the biggest of the little Tin Gods," Mariana lingered outside a dress shop, hoping to open Andrew's wallet. He allowed her to gaze without falling for her fluttering eyelids and sugared comments. They walked on, past the wine and spirit merchants that boasted of their quality, peered into the window of Hamilton's the jewellers and ignored the establishment of

Phelps and Company at Albion House, the Civil, Military and Political Tailors.

"This town is surprisingly long," Andrew said.

"It is," Mariana lowered her voice. "That woman crossing the Mall is Mrs Hamilton-Phelps. She is quite socially unacceptable, Andrew, and nobody talks to her except me and jungle *wallahs* from the outposts who don't know any better. She was divorced, you see, so respectable ladies avoid her. And that woman there also has a past; that means she knew a man to whom she was not married. Oh, Andrew, we are in fast company here."

"I didn't realise you were such a snob."

"One has to be, or one would be ostracised." Mariana edged closer. "We must at least pay lip service to the niceties," she said. "What we do behind closed doors is our affair."

"Indeed," Andrew replied, remembering his wife's antics the previous night.

"This is Peliti's Restaurant," Mariana stopped beside the bridge at the eastern extremity of the Mall. "If you want to know any local scandal, view the latest arrivals from the fishing fleet, or get an invite to a viceregal ball, Peliti's is the place to eat. Everybody who is anybody eats here."

Andrew smiled. "Are you hinting again, Mariana? It must be three-quarters of an hour since you scandalised those two young ladies."

"What a good idea," Mariana agreed. "Let's go inside."

The interior was cool and seemingly relaxed, although every head turned to view Andrew and Mariana as they entered. The hopeful expressions altered when they realised the newcomers were married, without a hint of scandal, although a few of the young women allowed their interest to linger on Andrew. Noticing their gaze, Mariana tightened her grip on his arm and moved her left hand, so her wedding and engagement rings gleamed in the light.

"What was that all about?" Andrew asked.

"I told you women would be hunting you. Simla is that sort

of place," Mariana told him as a waiter bustled towards them. "With young women fresh out from home, young men and not-so-young men in romantic uniforms and married women whose husbands are away for months at a time, philandering is expected."

"Oh?" Andrew said innocently. "Am I expected to join in?" He nodded to the two young women from their previous tea shop. "With one of these ladies, perhaps?"

Mariana leaned closer and hissed a threat that would have shocked a marine.

"Ah, not for me, then," Andrew said, smiling.

They sat under the slow-moving fan, sipping from Royal Doulton cups while Mariana gave her observations on each person in the room.

"That's the fellow we saw in the rickshaw," Mariana said. "I wonder what he does? He's no soldier with that complexion. He looks like he barely ventures outdoors."

Andrew looked and smiled. "He's probably some minor *babu*, a clerk, full of self-importance and opinions."

Mariana lifted her teacup and examined the pattern. "Quite probably," she said. "Yet he doesn't look right. There is something wrong about him."

"You understand these people, don't you?"

Mariana smiled. "I do," she said. "Some are serious and hard-working, and others treat life as a game. Since your mama brought me here, I have attended eight balls or parties, fended off three hopeless bachelors, played lawn tennis, croquet and archery with a reflexed bow, learned to play billiards – your mama taught me—and watched the fun and games." She nodded to the pale-faced man. "That fellow does not fit in. He has no right to be so pale when other men are either nut brown or peeling red."

Andrew watched as the two girls also glanced at the lone man. They leaned together, whispering and giggling.

"Our predatory friends have him in their sights," Mariana said. "Watch, Andrew, this could be fun."

The younger of the two women left her seat and casually walked past the lone man, dropped her handkerchief and looked at it lying on the floor. The man ignored her, even when she stooped to retrieve the handkerchief, brushing her hip against his shoulder.

"How rude," Mariana whispered. "He didn't even try to help."

"I don't think he even noticed her," Andrew said.

"He was certainly self-absorbed," Mariana replied, studying the lone man. She smiled. "Have I shown you the hat shop yet?"

"Not yet," Andrew said, "but I am already looking forward to seeing a hat shop."

"That's good," Mariana replied. "After you've bought me a new hat, we'll have a nice pot of tea and discuss where else in India we are going to visit."

CHAPTER 18

SIMLA SUMMER AND AUTUMN 1895

"Have you ever held a rifle?" Baback asked.

Asad shook his head.

"You are old enough now," Baback said. "Hold mine."

Asad held the weapon, surprised at the weight.

"This is a Snider," Baback said. "It is a good weapon. The infidels have more modern rifles, and when I get one, I will give this rifle to you."

Asad held the rifle to his shoulder and aimed.

"I'll teach you how to load and fire," Baback said. "Someday, you may fight the *feringhees*." Baback was a patient man and took his time teaching Asad how to hold the Snider.

"Don't you have a son?" Asad asked.

"I had three," Baback said. "Two died of fever, and the third in a blood feud with the Aba Khel."

Asad understood. He had seen disease all his life and knew the Pashtun's honour, when one remark could start a blood feud that might last generations.

"I'll teach you how to fire a rifle," Baback said. "And you can kill the infidels."

※

Andrew accompanied Jack to the lock-up where the army held Khattak.

"We've come to talk to the prisoner Khattak," Jack said to the Sikh warder.

The Sikh slammed to attention and gave a smart salute. "You're too late, Sahib," he said.

"What do you mean?" Jack demanded.

"The prisoner Khattak is dead. Somebody killed him last night," the Sikh said. "It was a good murder," he approved. "A long thin blade thrust behind the man's ear and hardly a trace of blood."

"Was he in solitary confinement?" Jack asked.

"No, Sahib. He was with the others. He shared a dormitory with twenty-two men, and a fight began between Waziris and Afridis."

"Did you find the murderer?" Jack asked.

The warder shook his head. "Not yet, Sahib. We will hang him when we find him."

"Don't hang him until I've interrogated him," Jack said.

The warder nodded. "Yes, Sahib."

"Let me see the body," Jack demanded.

Khattak lay in the morgue, slender and forlorn in death.

"Is that the man who tried to steal the Russian pistol?" Jack asked.

"Yes, that's him," Andrew confirmed.

"Somebody killed him to stop him from talking," Jack said as they returned to his quarters. "Somebody is tying up the loose ends." He strode through the streets with self-important civilians in frock coats and top hats making way before him and officers stopping to salute. "You said somebody tried to shoot you as well."

"Yes, on the approaches to Chitral," Andrew replied. Despite Jack's age and limp, he was walking quickly.

"Are you sure he was firing at you specifically and not merely at any British officer?"

"There were two other officers close by," Andrew said. "All three shots came at me."

Jack grunted. "How far away was the sniper?"

"A fraction under four hundred yards," Andrew said.

"Poor shooting," Jack grunted. "You were lucky. The Pashtuns are normally better shots than that. I've known an Afridi to lie in one spot for seventy-two hours without moving just to fire a single shot at a British soldier."

"I was very fortunate," Andrew said.

Jack nodded. "Perhaps," he said quietly. He walked to the window. "You'd better get back to Mariana. She'll be looking for you."

When Andrew left, Jack paced the room with his hands folded in the small of his back.

How can the Pashtuns, some of the best marksmen in the world, miss a stationary target at such short range? That's not only unlikely, it's damn near impossible. There are too many improbables for my liking.

Jack paced back and forth as he attempted to make sense of the situation. When Mary tapped on the door and entered, he glanced at the clock.

"What time is it?" he asked. "The clock's stopped. The servant's forgotten to wind the damned thing."

"He can't wind it because you're in the room, marching to Moscow or somewhere," Mary told him sternly. "It's half past three in the morning, everybody else in the house is long abed, and you're keeping me awake."

"Good God!" Jack said. "What happened to the time?"

"It's passing. Come on!" Taking his sleeve, Mary guided him to their bedroom.

"This is the Simla Club," Jack told Andrew. "You are fortunate I have some clout, or you would not be allowed in," he smiled. "A mere captain in a colonial unit does not have the same status as a captain of the Guides, the Gurkhas, or even a British line regiment."

"I thought I was in the Malverns," Andrew said.

"You're temporarily attached to the Royal Malverns," Jack reminded. "The extinct Transvaal Dragoons are still your parent regiment until you join somebody permanently."

"I see," Andrew knew his father was suggesting he rejoin the army. "I didn't know the Malverns were in India."

"They'll arrive in a few months," Jack said, smiling. "I do have some say who joins them as I am their colonel."

Andrew nodded. "I am in the family regiment, then." Generations of Windrush males had joined the Malverns, with the regiment being known originally as Windrush's Regiment of Foot.

"Where you belong, Andrew," Jack told him.

Andrew changed the subject. "I thought you would move to Calcutta in the cold season, Father."

Jack nodded grimly. "My duty is to keep an eye on the Russians," he reminded. "As long as Victor Demidov is in Simla, I'll remain here, and he shows no sign of moving." He limped up the steps to the club's front door and acknowledged the uniformed doorman's salute. "In you come, Andrew!"

Jack showed Andrew the billiard room, where a well-dressed civilian was playing a staff major. The civilian looked up when Jack and Andrew entered the room, smiled, and continued with his game.

"That civilian is Ambassador Demidov's manservant, Major," Jack said. "How did he gain entry to the Simla Club?"

"He's my guest," the major said.

Jack nodded to the door. "Come with me, Major. Chornyi,

you remain here. Captain Baird will ensure you don't leave." He jerked his head to Andrew. "Stay with that man!"

Andrew stepped to Chornyi, who held his snooker cue, smiling.

"Why did you invite that Russian to the Simla Club, Major?" Jack asked.

"It's not against the law, sir," the major replied.

"It is now," Jack said. "No more Russians in the Simla Club. Leave this fellow to me."

"Sir?"

"Goodbye, Major," Jack said. He returned to the billiard room.

Chornyi had not moved, with Andrew watching him closely.

"You'll be working for the *Okhrana*," Jack said.

Chornyi smiled. "General Windrush," he said. "You found me out."

"It wasn't hard," Jack said. "The *Okhrana* are normally a secretive bunch, yet you are positively visible."

Chornyi's smile broadened, although his eyes remained expressionless. "So are you, General Windrush."

"I have neither the need nor the desire to hide in my own country," Jack said.

"Are you not British, sir?" Chornyi asked. "You are not in Britain now."

"I was born in India," Jack met the smile. "As was my wife, my mother and my father."

Chornyi nodded. "As the Duke of Wellington might have said, General, if you were born in a stable, would you be a horse?"

"I am as Indian as I am anything else," Jack said, "and India will never be a Russian possession."

"Never is a long time, General," Chornyi told him.

"Leave this club," Jack ordered, "and tell your master that your presence is not welcome in Simla."

Chornyi laid the cue on the table. "I'll tell him, General Windrush."

Jack and Andrew escorted Chornyi from the Simla Club and ordered the doorman, a flint-faced ex-Sergeant Major, to ensure he never returned.

"Now, Andrew," Jack said, "I don't know about you, but I need a drink."

※

ANDREW AND MARIANA TRAVELLED AROUND INDIA FOR THE next few weeks, visiting any place Mariana decided might be interesting.

They visited Lucknow and the Himalayan foothills; Andrew took Mariana on an elephant ride, and they viewed a plethora of Hindu temples and the Ganges River. They spent a week journeying to the Taj Mahal in Agra, which Mariana thought was the most romantic place she had ever seen.

"It's rather sad, though," Mariana said.

"Is it?" Andrew held Mariana's hand as they stood beside the Yamuna River, with the morning light highlighting the white marble.

"Yes," Mariana snuggled closer. "The Mughal emperor Shah Jahan built it as a tomb for his wife Mumtaz Mahal after she died in childbirth. He must have loved her."

"I am sure he did," Andrew said. He hugged her. "All this travelling must be good for you. Because you're looking even better than ever."

"There's a reason for that," Mariana told him solemnly. "I'm with child."

"What?" Andrew stared at Mariana. "Say that again?"

"We're having a baby," Mariana repeated, patting her belly.

"Oh, dear God! After so long!"

"It was the night of the thunderstorm," Mariana told him smugly. "I thought I felt something happen then."

Andrew smiled at Mariana's amazing gift of hindsight. "Something happened, all right."

"Yes. I had considered calling the baby Elaine after my sister, but I've decided we'll call her Simla," Mariana told him comfortably.

"It might be a boy," Andrew said, "and what if I don't like the name Simla?"

"She'll be a girl; we'll call her Simla, and you do like the name. Your eyes smiled when I said it."

Andrew shook his head. "He'll have a terrible time at school with a name like Simla," he teased. He stared at her. "We'll have to book a passage home!"

"No," Mariana said firmly. "You were conceived in India, as was your father," Mariana reminded him. "India's in your blood. Anyway, your mother will ensure we get the best of doctors here, probably better than in Berwick, and Simla is a perfectly healthy station." She smiled, patting Andrew's arm. "Relax, Andrew. I am a Frontierswoman, remember? My mother gave birth in our front room at Inglenook, with my father acting as a midwife. Simla is the height of civilisation compared to the Zulu Frontier."

Andrew shook his head. "I want the best for my wife," he said.

"I'll have the best here. Hundreds of thousands of babies are born in India every year. You were born here, and you turned out relatively human."

"Relatively," Andrew agreed.

"Well, what do you think?" Mariana squeezed his arm. "We're going to have a baby called Simla."

"We'll talk about the name later," Andrew struggled to assimilate the news.

"Yes, and you'll agree with me." Mariana turned on her smile. "Then that's settled."

"So it appears," Andrew said, taking her in his arms. "We're going to have a baby!"

Mary's smile encompassed them all when Mariana told them the news, and Jack nodded, winked at Andrew and produced cigars for them all.

"Except you, Mariana. You must be careful of your health."

"I'll look after her," Mary promised, lighting the most enormous cigar Andrew had ever seen her smoke. "Us mothers must stick together."

For the next few weeks, babies dominated the conversation in the Baird and Windrush household. Andrew realised men were relegated to second place behind more important topics such as washing nappies and morning sickness. Fortunately, Mariana was a fit and healthy Frontierswoman and sailed through the early weeks of her pregnancy, laughing at Andrew's attempts to care for her.

"I'm not made of glass, Andrew. You don't have to do everything for me!"

"You have to take care of yourself," Andrew warned.

"I am fine. Go and talk to your father," Mariana pushed him gently away. "Talk about polo or tiger hunting or something."

"Mariana's right," Mary agreed. "Go and see Jack."

※

JACK LOOKED WORRIED WHEN ANDREW ENTERED HIS OFFICE. He forced a smile. "Have you had enough of baby talk for a while, Andrew? The best thing is to leave it to the women. They understand such matters far better than we do." He ushered Andrew to the chair opposite his desk.

"Sit down, my boy. Chornyi is still wandering around Simla, and as he's officially Demidov's manservant, I can't remove him."

"Why is he here?" Andrew asked. "Why are the Russians remaining in Simla?"

"To spy on us," Jack said. "Demidov is an official representative of Mother Russia. The merchants are here for honest trade, but Chornyi and maybe others are watching us as we watch them." He smiled. "Well, we'll find out in the fullness of time. Let's find you something to do to take your mind off Mariana. You can help me evaluate reports."

Andrew sighed. "Have you nothing more active, Father?"

"Maybe later," Jack said. "I'll tell you what's worrying me, Andrew."

"What's that, Father?" Andrew asked.

"The *Okhrana* are normally a most efficient organisation, not prone to making mistakes, yet they left a cigarette end and a pistol as proof of their existence in Chitral."

"They tried to recover the pistol," Andrew reminded.

"Did they?" Jack asked. "Or did they want us to think they did? The man they sent, Khattak, was a bungler. Any half-competent Pashtun could enter a British tent and lift a revolver, yet your man was noisy."

"I certainly heard him," Andrew said.

"Why would the *Okhrana* send a bungler when they could hire a hundred better men?" Jack asked. He began to pace the room. "Another thing, Andrew. You said that a man fired three shots at you and missed each time."

"That's correct," Andrew said. "The Chitralis were poor shots."

"I think they meant to miss," Jack replied. "Like the thief who was so conveniently and expertly murdered was meant to fail."

"Why?" Andrew asked.

"When I work that out, Andrew, I'll be a happier man."

CHAPTER 19

SIMLA, SPRING 1896

"Have you heard the latest Jubilee poem?" Mariana asked.

"I've had other things on my mind," Andrew admitted. "Like your pregnancy."

Mariana patted her swollen belly. "Little Simla is coming along nicely, except for making me sick and kicking every so often."

"You're doing well," Andrew agreed.

"Yes, indeed. The Queen's Jubilee is an interesting distraction from vomiting every morning," Mariana said. "Listen to Targo Mindien's *Diamond Jubilee Rhyme*."

Andrew nodded. "I'm listening."

Mariana lifted her clear voice.

"Arise! Fair Venus, my dream in Beauty; refulgence!
  Forth
From Father Time's liquid silver sea,
In all thy dazzling splendour, with thy magic
  wand from
Love, it is the Empress-Queen Victoria's Diamond
  Jubilee."

"I will always remember that poem," Andrew said solemnly. "When's the Queen's Jubilee?"

"Next year," Mariana reminded him. "You know that! Sixty years on the throne."

"I had forgotten," Andrew admitted.

The months passed quicker than Andrew imagined. Mariana grew larger each week, coping with the travails of pregnancy with a stoicism that he could only admire, and a smile that made him love her even more. Mary was always ready with advice and support, while the female servants checked on Mariana with anxious eyes and willing hands, so Andrew felt superfluous in this essentially feminine world.

"You see why I could not travel home?" Mariana asked as she carefully sat down. "I'd have sunk the boat." She pushed him away irritably. "Don't fuss over me, Andrew. Go and do something useful."

As Mariana's time neared, Jack tried to keep Andrew's mind occupied, but Mary was more in control. When Mariana's waters broke, Andrew summoned the midwife, who summarily sent him outside the bedroom.

"You will only distract Mother," the midwife was a cheerful Eurasian with decades of experience in dealing with anxious husbands. "Leave us, please."

"Keep out of the way," Mary ordered in a tone Andrew recognised from his childhood. He stepped onto the veranda to pace back and forth, his hands twisting behind his back, looking up at every tiny sound from within the bungalow.

When he heard a baby crying, Andrew started and ran inside. "Is everything all right?"

"Right as rain," the midwife replied. "Mother and baby are fit and healthy."

Mariana lay on the bed, smiling, with her daughter in her arms. "Say hello to Simla," she greeted Andrew.

"Hello, Simla," Andrew said.

For the next few weeks, Andrew forgot about Russians, Chitralis, *mullahs* and Pashtuns as he adapted to his new life as a father. He greeted every experience with wonder, learned that little Simla was now the centre of Mariana's life, and slotted in whenever she had spare time and space.

❄

JACK LOOKED OUT OF THE WINDOW, ENJOYING THE COOLNESS of the hills. India was a land of contrasts. Down on the plains, the dry season ended in abrupt drama in June. A furnace-hot wind would torment the British in their cantonments and bungalows, and then the clouds would pile up, rank after rank. People would grow short-tempered, snapping at one another over unconsidered trifles.

The rains came as a relief, a terrible deluge that hammered the arid earth and brought millions of seedlings to life, blanketing the months-long brown with vibrant green. The blossom followed, and the frogs and toads appeared in their millions.

In the cantonments and barracks, the soldiers, especially those not used to India, welcomed the rains with delight. Often, they would leave the barracks and dance naked under the torrent, exuberant to escape the torturous heat.

"You're smiling, Jack," Mary said. "What's in your mind?"

"I was thinking how lucky we are to be in Simla rather than in the Plains," Jack said. "We could be in Calcutta, where the humidity is torture, and we suffer from dhobi-itch and prickly heat."

"And the insects," Mary said. She shivered. "The hot season brings a rash of suicides, and the rains bring snakes, mosquitoes, cockroaches and the stink bug."

"The jute moth, too," Jack said. "Lovely little things until you touch it and get a horrible rash." He pulled her closer. "We're much better up here in Simla."

Mary laughed. "Mariana certainly thinks so! I've never seen anybody take to motherhood with such delight. I swear she positively likes changing soiled nappies."

Jack nodded. "Andrew chose well, and having them both with us is good."

Mary smiled and pressed against him. "Don't get too cosy," she said. "The great tin god is back in Simla and wants to see you."

"His Excellency, himself?" Jack did not release his hold of Mary's waist.

"Himself, himself," Mary said. "Off you go now, Captain Jack, like a good little general."

❋

ASAD HELD THE RIFLE AS BABACK GAVE HIM QUIET instructions. "Pull it into your shoulder, *chokra*, that's the way. Don't be scared."

"I'm not scared," Asad replied.

"Now, keep your target in sight," Baback said. "Don't jerk the trigger. Squeeze it gently."

Asad obeyed. He visualised an infidel as the target, a man with al-Shaytan's face and a human body. He squeezed the trigger, felt the recoil as the Snider fired and did not see where his bullet landed.

"A hand's breadth to the right," Baback told him. "Now reload as I showed you and try again."

❋

JIGSAW ON THE KHYBER

Jack sighed as he poured out two stiff drinks. The Viceroy had given him orders, and he had to carry them out, however distasteful. He eyed Andrew over the rim of his whisky tumbler, saying nothing.

"What's troubling you, Father?" Andrew asked, unconscious of the baby sick that had stained the shoulder of his jacket.

"You are," Jack said. He swirled the whisky in his tumbler. "You used to be something of a specialist in rescuing people."

"Was I, Father?"

"You were," Jack said. "There was that Burmese fellow."

"Bo Thura," Andrew said.

"And before him, the politician's nephew in the Transvaal and Mariana in Zululand."

"I had never connected the three," Andrew admitted.

"I did," Jack said quietly. "I have another person for you to rescue, Andrew, if you can tear yourself away from Mariana and little Simla."

"Who is that, sir?"

"We have an agent coming in from Afghanistan," Jack said. "He'll come via the Khyber, and I want you to meet him."

"Me?" Andrew asked.

"You," Jack confirmed. "You know what's happening up there, and I trust you." He waited a moment. "You know the agent. You took him to Chitral."

Andrew nodded. "Harry Symington." He thought of little Simla's gurgling laugh and Mariana's tired, happy face and sighed. He was a Windrush, and duty must always come first. "Where do you want me to go?"

"I'm giving you command of a fort in the Khyber Pass, with a mixed garrison of Khyber Rifles and Sikhs."

Andrew nodded. "That's a good combination," he said. "As long as they get on together. The Khyber Rifles have held the Khyber since Colonel Warburton created them, and the Sikhs are as stolid soldiers as you'll find anywhere."

"You've been doing your homework," Jack approved. "Do you think you can handle commanding a fort?"

"Yes," Andrew replied with a faint smile. "It will be good not to have a senior officer giving me orders."

"I remember the feeling," Jack said.

"Where about in the Khyber will I be based?" Andrew asked.

"Razali Fort," Jack said.

"I'll have to find that on the map," Andrew said.

"It's halfway along the pass," Jack told him. "I don't want you too close to Afghanistan, but I want Symington to know he's safe as soon as he's in British-controlled territory."

"Unless the tribes rise, as the *mullahs* hope."

Jack nodded. "Your fort is well within signalling distance of Fort Roberts, which has a battalion-strong garrison, Khyber Rifles and Sikhs. If there is trouble, they'll send a relief column the same day."

"That's comforting," Andrew said. "How large is my garrison?"

"Only seventy men," Jack said.

Andrew nodded. "When am I leaving?"

"Not for a few weeks," Jack said. "Your lady wife would hate me if I sent you away so soon after she'd given birth."

Andrew grinned. "I'm not so sure about that. Little Simla takes up all her attention at present."

Jack laughed. "That's normal, Andrew. Let her enjoy her baby. They grow up fast, and when they do, you'll still be around for Mariana."

CHAPTER 20

SIMLA MARCH 1897

Mary lowered her weekly list of jobs to do in the bungalow. "Are you involved in the Jubilee celebrations, Jack?"

"Not at all," Jack replied. "I've never given them a thought."

"Victoria, Queen-Empress, sixty years on the throne, related to half the royal houses of Europe," Mary shook her head. "You must watch the parade, Jack."

"I probably will," Jack said. "Agreed, they are less splendid in Simla than elsewhere because of the troubles in India. We have unrest along the Frontier, a horrible earthquake in Calcutta, famine in Orissa, plague and political disturbances in Bombay, and civil unrest in Bengal."

"That's correct," Mary said.

When Jack began to pace, Mary knew he was thinking. She sat back, waiting for her husband to work through his thoughts.

"We have unrest along the Frontier," Jack said fifteen minutes later. "I immediately thought the Russians were behind it."

"We all did," Mary said.

"I have been thinking about the situation," Jack said. "I no longer believe the Russians are stirring up trouble among the tribes, although we know the Afghans are. I think the Russians want us to believe they are up there to divert our attention while they operate somewhere else."

"There is trouble up there," Mary reminded him. "Don't forget the cigarette end and the Russian pistol Andrew found."

"I haven't forgotten," Jack said. "I think they were deliberately left for us to find. The *Okhrana* want us to concentrate on the Frontier while they operate somewhere else."

"Where else would the Russians be working?" Mary asked the expected question.

"What have you just reminded me about? The Queen's Jubilee, with all the pomp and celebrations." He poured himself a whisky and swallowed the contents in one go. "And all the big wigs in India will be gathered, including the Viceroy. What a target for the *Okhrana*."

"Why?" Mary played devil's advocate.

"If we're tied up on the Frontier and have civil unrest elsewhere, Mary, who knows what trouble the *Okhrana* can cause to embarrass the British in India."

"What will you do?"

"Police the Jubilee celebrations," Jack said grimly. "If the little tin gods allow."

❄

The weather was turning when Andrew and a small escort of Khyber Rifles rode through the Khyber Pass. A smirr of snow obscured the high peaks as they approached Fort Razali, with the sound of their passage echoing from the surrounding rocks. The fort was smaller than Andrew had expected, little more than a picket or signalling post fifteen miles into the Khyber Pass. Fort Razali stood on a rib of bare rock, overlooking a deep cut in the pass, with the much larger Fort Roberts three miles to the east.

Razali was a routinely square stone-built fortress with a single watchtower, loopholes for the defenders, and little in the way of comfort. The ground on the south sloped steeply, with the other sides gentler, with little to deter any attacker except the defenders' rifles.

Andrew viewed the surroundings with disfavour, for large rocks and deep crevasses afforded cover for anybody who wished to snipe at the defenders.

"Who chose this site for a fort?" Andrew asked.

"I'm blessed if I know, sir," Hugh Innes, the young subaltern of the Khyber Rifles, replied. "I've only been here three days." He grinned. "It's my first posting, sir."

"I'll see if we can find some Sappers to remove these rocks," Andrew growled.

"We're not high on the list of priorities, sir," Innes said. "Colonel Neville at Fort Roberts attracts all the attention."

"Colonel Neville?" Andrew repeated the name. "Is he a red-faced man with pepper-and-salt whiskers?"

"That's the fellow, sir," Innes said. "Do you know the colonel?"

"We've met," Andrew said. He did not mention the incident on the train when he first arrived in India.

"I'm sure he's a good man," Innes said.

"I'm sure he is," Andrew agreed, although privately he had his doubts. "Well, if we can't get the Sappers, I'm sure our men could help."

The Khyber Rifles were recruited from the local Afridi and Waziri tribes, men to whom manual labour was demeaning. The Sikhs proved reluctant to work unless the Rifles pulled their weight.

"How well do you know the area, Innes?" Andrew watched the garrison's slow attempts to remove the surrounding rocks.

"Not well, sir," Innes replied. He was a fresh-faced youth with bright grey eyes. "I've never been on the Frontier before."

"Well, you'll know it a damned sight better before we're

finished here. I want daily patrols outside the perimeter, with one extended patrol every week."

"Yes, sir," Innes seemed pleased at the prospect.

Andrew pointed to the map pinned on the wall of his tiny quarters. "I want you to create a map of the area, with every name marked and every possible ambush spot indicated."

"Yes, sir," Innes replied.

"And keep a watch for strangers coming to the fort," Andrew said. "Pass the word that I am here."

Innes eyed him strangely. "If you say so, sir."

When he was not on patrol or supervising the squads labouring to clear the surroundings, Andrew drilled the garrison. He found the Sikhs as efficient as he expected, while the Rifles were erratic, with some excellent and others reluctant.

"Keep an eye on your men," Andrew ordered Innes.

"Yes, sir."

Andrew took two of the worst offenders on a long patrol along the Khyber towards Afghanistan and was not surprised when one deserted.

"We won't miss him," Andrew told Innes.

As the days merged into weeks, and there was still no news from Symington, Colonel Neville rejected Andrew's repeated requests for Sappers.

"The Khyber is quiet," Neville said. "We pay a subsidy to the Afridis, and they don't cause any trouble. We shall not antagonise them by increasing our defences."

Andrew kept his temper, closed his mouth and kept his men alert. He could sense an underlying tension in the air.

※

"Gentlemen," Jack kept his voice low. "We know the Russians are active in Simla and along the Frontier."

"That's hardly a secret, General Windrush."

Jack nodded. "I also suspect they intend to disrupt the Queen's Golden Jubilee celebrations."

The small circle of senior officers and civil officials nodded. Behind them, the lanterns burned low, casting sufficient light for the men to view each other and little more. Jack had closed the interior shutters on the windows and posted guards on the house.

"Who is in the house?" the police superintendent, a tall man named Buchanan asked. He combed a finger across his neat ginger whiskers.

"Only us," Jack said, "and my wife."

"Any servants?"

"I've given them all the evening off," Jack said, "and the guards have strict orders not to allow anybody in."

"Who are the guards?"

"Royal Malverns," Jack said and smiled. "My regiment and not men who would ever betray us to the Russians or the Pashtun."

Buchanan nodded. "Good."

"We believe the Russians intend to disrupt the Jubilee procession," Jack said. "Our job is two-fold. To prevent that from happening and to arrest the disrupters."

"Why not shoot him?"

"If we arrest him," Jack said. "We can question him and find out who sent him and embarrass the Russians as they intend to embarrass us."

Buchanan nodded. He lit a cigar, with the aromatic smoke coiling around the panelled room.

Jack unrolled a map of Simla on the table, using books to weigh down the corners. "You all know Simla, some of you better than me." He used a pointer to trace the route the procession would take. "I want soldiers stationed the full length of the Mall, with fixed bayonets, and a second line facing outwards, towards the crowd."

The men nodded.

"I want others based in the gardens along the route and more on the taller buildings, watching what is happening."

"Isn't that a bit much?" Buchanan asked. "My men can handle things."

"No," Jack said. "We don't know what the *Okhrana* plan and what the consequences may be."

The officials and officers murmured for a few moments.

"I also want police officers in plain clothes among the crowd and a few NCOs and officers in mufti as well," Jack said. "We'll take no chances, gentlemen!"

"What are we looking for?"

Jack stood at the head of the table. "I don't know," he admitted. "The Russians may want to cause a disruption or even to assassinate the Viceroy. We are looking for anybody who may pose a threat to his life. Our agents are keeping their ears to the ground, listening for whispers. We are looking for anything or anybody suspicious. I wish you all the best of luck, gentlemen."

❄

JACK TOURED THE MALL IN THE DARK HOURS BEFORE DAWN, checking on his precautions. He had posted men in every large garden and on the roofs of buildings, with plain-clothed police, both British and Indian, already in position as part of the anticipated crowd.

The planned celebrations included a handful of parades, the expected church services, and a procession of the elite. Jack considered the procession the most likely target for any attack. He had instructed his men to expect the unexpected, yet not to harass the civilians.

The people gathered slowly: British, Indian, and a scattering of Europeans. Wearing respectable but not new civilian clothes, Jack walked along the Mall, looking into shop windows, nodding to the plain-clothes police and the army officers in mufti. He waited behind one group of Pashtun tribesmen, wondering if they intended mischief. He saw two of the Guides standing casually across the street and walked away. If the Guides were there, his presence was not required.

By an hour after dawn, crowds filled the Mall, British, Indian, European, and Central Asian, all gathered to see the Queen-Empress's Jubilee celebrations. Jack continued his patrolling, checking on his plain-clothes men, ensuring the military and police were in position, and talking to his single, well-positioned agent.

The parade began at nine, with a small band in the van followed by a troop of lancers, splendid in their dress uniforms. The Viceroy was next, dressed in his finery and riding in an open coach.

Jack ignored the parade, concentrating on watching the audience. Unsure what or who he was looking for, he studied every face in the crowd.

Immediately behind Elgin, Victor Demidov sat in another coach, waving to the crowd as though the whole procession had been created for his benefit rather than that of Queen Victoria.

A line of Royal Malverns stood at the next bend, each man the regulation five paces apart. Jack automatically inspected them as he moved through the crowd, keeping level with the procession, looking around for anything unusual.

The band played as they marched, with the Gordons' bagpipers trying to bring some pageantry to what Jack thought was a dismal display.

When the parade approached Peliti's Restaurant, Jack saw a brief flash at the window. He looked across the road and saw a civilian standing apart from the crowd with a light suit and a white pith helmet. As Jack looked, the man pulled a pistol from inside his jacket and aimed it at Elgin's carriage.

"Halloa!" Jack shouted. "That man there!" He glanced at the parade, saw a gap between the band and the lancers, and dashed across the road.

"Hey, you!" A khaki-uniformed police inspector yelled, moving to intercept Jack.

"Stop that man!" Jack pointed to the solitary civilian. "He's got a gun!"

"Who the devil are you to tell me what to do?" The inspector grabbed Jack's shoulder.

Jack threw the inspector's hand off. "I am General Jack Windrush, Inspector. Go after that man!"

"Which man, sir?"

Jack swore. The civilian had vanished. Jack scanned the crowd, searching for his quarry.

"A European man, Inspector," Jack said quickly. "He wore a white pith helmet and a light grey suit and pointed a gun at the Viceroy!"

"I saw him, sir!" a man in civilian clothes pushed through the crowd. "Sergeant Brown, sir, Royal Malverns. He ran that way," he pointed to a narrow lane leading downward.

"You're with us, Brown," Jack said. "You too, Inspector."

Jack led them down the steep lane, glancing into every alley and the side of every house. He pulled his revolver from his pocket.

"There, sir!" Sergeant Brown shouted. "On the roof!"

Jack saw movement above him as the civilian jumped from the roof and doubled back towards the procession.

Jack swore again, turned, and ran up the slope, trying to keep pace with Brown and the inspector, momentarily forgetting he was over sixty years old and not as fit as he had been.

The civilian was fast, jinking from side to side as he reached the Mall.

I'll never catch him, Jack thought.

Brown shouted something and dived forward, grabbing the civilian in a superb rugby tackle that brought him to the ground with a crash.

"Got you!"

"Nice tackle, Sergeant," Jack said, limping to join them.

"Thank you, sir." Brown stood up. "Let's be having you, son!" He dragged the civilian to his feet.

"What's your name?" the inspector asked. "Who are you?"

"Search him, Brown," Jack ordered.

"Sir!" The civilian slipped a knife from his sleeve and slashed at Jack, who blocked with his left arm, gasping as the blade sliced through his sleeve and across his forearm. Brown threw a punch that caught the civilian on the side of the head, temporarily staggering him, and the inspector drew a Webley British Bulldog revolver and fired three rapid shots, hitting the civilian in the chest.

"No!" Jack shouted as the civilian crumpled to the ground. "We wanted him alive."

CHAPTER 21

FORT RAZALI, KHYBER PASS, SUMMER 1897

The news filtered into Fort Razali, carried by passing tribesmen and caravans of camels. "The tribes are up!"

"Double the sentries," Andrew ordered. He had seen the red-bearded mullah pass, riding on a donkey with his loose turban flapping in the breeze and his eyes basilisk-hard as he surveyed the fort.

Andrew noticed that the local Afridis walked with even more of a swagger. They looked the fort's garrison in the eye and spat their contempt on the ground. Each man carried a rifle, and some smiled sardonically as the Sikhs gestured for them to move on.

"There's trouble on the way," Andrew said. He looked towards the northwest, where the road plunged from Kabul and the Afghan heartland, hoping Symington arrived before the Frontier was aflame.

Innes nodded. "I can smell it, sir," he said.

"I want barbed wire around the fort," Andrew said. "With gaps left for killing fields. I want strings of wire laden with tin cans, bottles, and anything else that makes a noise."

"Sir?" Innes looked confused.

"To deter anybody from sneaking up on us during the night," Andrew said. "Get the men to place sharpened stakes in the most obvious hiding places and strew broken glass over the bare patches." He remembered the tricks from the Zulu War nearly twenty years before. "I wish we had a Gatling gun."

Innes smiled. "Whatever happens, we have got The Gatling gun, and they have not."

"Exactly so," Andrew said. "Except we haven't, and nor have they."

Colonel Neville proved reluctant to supply barbed wire, but the Khyber Rifles were adept thieves and smuggled two rolls from Fort Roberts. Andrew had the men string it around the walls at night, with broken glass and any other obstacle he could dream up. He added poles as range markers, white painted on the side visible to the defenders but plain on the outside so any attacker would not know their purpose.

With every day, the atmosphere tightened as men brought news of events elsewhere on the Frontier. In the Tochi, tribesmen shot at a group of British officers as they held a peaceful meeting with the local *malik*s. Breaching the Pashtun rule of hospitality to travellers was abhorrent, but the attack was only the opening scene in a new play whose stage spread across the entire Frontier.

The British officers from the fort of Chakdarra in the Swat Valley were playing polo at Khar, two miles away, when the local tribesmen warned them to return before they attacked the fort. The officers returned, and the Pashtun duly attacked.

"We might be next," Andrew said. "The Khyber is the main route from India to Afghanistan. Whoever controls the Khyber has the advantage."

Innes shook his head. "The boys would let us know," he said. "Ever since Warburton created the Khyber Rifles, they've been faithful to their salt. They won't let us down."

"I hope so," Andrew said, more experienced and less trusting than Innes.

Andrew had gathered information from every passing caravan or lone traveller. He knew there were holy men preaching hate along the Frontier. The three main perpetrators, the Akhund of Swat, the *Mullah* Powindah, and the Hadda *Mullah*, all ranted for a *jihad* against the British, with other minor preachers joining them.

I've seen that red-bearded mullah in Chitral, and now he's here as well, Andrew told himself. *I'll have to keep the garrison alert. I hope Symington arrives with good news soon.*

"I've heard of this sort of thing," Innes said, smoothing a hand over his twenty-two-year-old face with the steady eyes of a man twice his age. "Some half-crazed *mullah* preaches war, the young hotheads and old fools drink it in, and before you can say snap, they are sniping at British columns and attacking some poor innocent Hindu or Sikh merchant who's never done anybody any harm."

"And the Khyber Rifles have remained loyal?" Andrew asked.

"Always," Innes said.

They heard the drums that night, reminding Andrew of the gongs along the Irrawaddy. He walked along the walls, staring into the starlit dark. A ruffle of wind whined around the battlements, sounding like a suffering man. Andrew thought of Mariana and young Simla, wondered if she had taken her first steps or uttered her first words yet, and returned his concentration to the Khyber.

"Don't expect much sleep for the next few days," Andrew said.

"No, sir," Innes said.

"Can you see anything?" Andrew asked the rifleman on the southern wall.

"No, sahib," the man replied.

The sentinels on the other walls reported the same. The

drumming continued, but the darkness hid the drummers. Andrew spoke to the Sikh havildar, who grinned, showing white teeth through his beard.

"They will come, sahib," he said in a deep voice. "And when they do, we will destroy them."

Andrew nodded. "I am sure you will, Havildar."

When the sun rose the following morning, Andrew was behind the battlements with the sentries. The sun slanted behind the ragged hills, first highlighting a host of green banners inscribed with phrases from the Quran and then reflecting from the swords, shields, and rifle barrels of the thousands of men who surrounded the little fort.

"Now, there's a sight I'll always remember," Innes said.

Andrew nodded. "It's like something from the Middle Ages. Take away the rifles, and these men could be fighting in the Crusades or when Muhammad's armies first swept out of Arabia to attack the rest of the world."

"Yes, sir," Innes agreed. "I'm no Richard the Lionheart, but I'm damned if I'll let them intimidate me."

"I never thought they would, Innes," Andrew said quietly.

The drumming continued as the great mass of warriors surrounded the fort.

This siege is my fourth. Once in the Transvaal War, twice in Burma, and now in the Khyber. I have a knack for being in the wrong place.

"Call out the garrison," Andrew ordered quietly.

The bugler blew his brassy tones, and the garrison ran to the walls, Khyber Rifles on two walls and Sikhs manning the rest.

"And hoist the flag," Andrew ordered.

He watched as the Union Flag crawled up the pole to flutter in the fitful breeze, now showing the crosses of St George, St Andrew, and St Patrick. When the breeze died, the flag lay still, close to the pole, as if waiting.

"What are they doing?" Innes asked as the Pashtun warriors remained immobile under their tribal banners.

"They're trying to unnerve us," Andrew replied. He pointed to the red-bearded *mullah* at the back of the warriors, waving his hands in the air and roaring, exhorting the men to battle.

"He'll be promising them seventy-two virgins and martyrdom if they kill an infidel," Innes said.

"Let's ensure the women remain unsullied and the warriors frustrated," Andrew replied.

Innes grinned. "I'll second that," he said. He examined the tribesmen massed outside. "These lads are mainly Afridis, with a few Orakzais, sir."

"Get all the men ready to fight," Andrew said, "but don't show them yet. Keep the normal sentries on the wall, and muster the rest in the courtyard."

"Yes, sir," Innes ran to obey.

"Innes!" Andrew stopped him.

"Sir?"

"Don't run. You're a British officer. Never look hurried in front of the men."

Innes swallowed. "Yes, sir." He slowed down.

Andrew divided the garrison into two unequal portions; one-quarter was on the wall, and the others waited in the courtyard, hidden from the enemy's view. He ensured each of his men had a hundred rounds of ammunition, their bayonets were loose in their scabbards, and their water bottles were full.

"Signal Fort Roberts," Andrew ordered. "Inform Colonel Neville that approximately three thousand tribesmen have surrounded us." He watched the signaller flash the message from the heliograph, fed the men, and settled back.

I've done all I can do. Now we wait for the Afridis.

Andrew surveyed his surroundings. The fort stood on its barren ridge, with an occasional patch of scrub to alleviate the monotony of shattered rock. The mountains around were nearly equally bare, with an occasional belt of sadly sombre pine trees that added to the savage desolation of the scene.

Mariana would put something Arthurian into this picture, but now I see it as older. I could be a Roman legionary manning a fort in the wastes of the Sahara, or perhaps on their Northwest Frontier, facing the untamed Picts of Caledonia.

The *mullah* was shouting, pointing at the fort with a long finger, his nail as untrimmed and dirty as his beard. Spittle flew from his mouth as he harangued the infidels, his voice rising to a scream.

"That silly old fellow will do himself a mischief," Innes observed. "In the old days, people used to pay to see the lunatics in the asylum, and we're getting a free show at our front door."

Andrew glanced over the garrison. "The Khyber Rifles aren't laughing."

Innes nodded. "The old buffer's quoting from the Quran, I suppose, but the Rifles will be all right. They're as loyal as the Brigade of Guards."

Andrew watched the Rifles talk to one another as the *mullah's* words floated into the fort. "We'd better address them, Innes. Remind them they've eaten our salt."

Before Innes moved, one of the Riflemen shouted something and ran to the main gate. Two others followed, and then the Rifles abandoned their posts, pushing past the Sikhs. They tore open the gate and ran outside, some joining the tribesmen and others fleeing into the countryside.

"Let them go!" Andrew shouted as the Sikhs moved to halt the mass desertion. "Let them leave!"

"Sir?" Innes looked confused.

"If we forced them back inside," Andrew explained, "we could not trust them again. If they're outside, they're an open enemy we can kill. If we kept them inside, we'd be forever watching our backs, and we'd have to post Sikhs to guard them."

The Sikhs shouted insults at the deserters, with three men firing until Andrew roared at them to save their ammunition.

When the last of the Rifles had left, Andrew ordered the

Sikhs to close the gate and place a heavy beam of wood across as extra security.

"Now the Afridi will attack," Andrew predicted.

"We're very undermanned," Innes said. "Can we trust the Sikhs not to join the enemy?"

Andrew nodded and ordered the Sikhs to man the walls. They obeyed willingly, clattering up the stairs with Martinis in their hands and yellow turbans gleaming under the sun.

"Havildar Abani Singh," Andrew said, glad he had learned some Punjabi in Simla. "We've just seen the Khyber Rifles desert. My young subaltern here doesn't know much about Sikhs and wonders if you will remain."

The havildar looked at Innes with compassion. "We are Sikhs," he said, as if those three words were sufficient explanation.

Perhaps they are, Andrew thought. *But Innes might need more.*

"Thank you, Havildar," Andrew said solemnly. "Can you add anything to that?"

"Do I need to?" the havildar asked.

"The subaltern is young and inexperienced," Andrew said. "He knows little of the history between the Sikhs and the followers of Islam."

"Tell Innes Sahib we have not forgotten the Muslims buried the two sons of Govind alive beneath the walls of Sirhind. We have not forgotten the Muslims burning the Golden Temple of Amritsar to the ground. Nor have we forgotten the Muslims slaughtering cattle and throwing them into the sacred tank at Amritsar or the Moghul emperors' persecution of our faith."

Andrew nodded. "I will tell Innes Sahib," he promised, glad the Sikhs' religion would strengthen them in the coming contest.

The *mullah* was still preaching, his harsh voice echoing from Fort Razali's walls. Andrew glanced at his Sikh soldiers, neat in their khaki uniforms and yellow turbans, and at the ragged thousands outside in their dark robes, with long hair hanging in ragged locks to their shoulders and their rifles, *jezails*, and swords ready to kill. The *mullah* raised his arms in exhortation, and the tribesmen responded with a roar.

"Bugler!" Andrew shouted. "Sound the stand to!"

The bugler stood at attention, put the bugle to his lips, and blew, with the liquid notes rising over the small fort. Andrew felt a prickle of pride as he looked at the Sikh garrison, waiting for the inevitable assault.

If I am to die now, I could not die in better company, and I leave a daughter to carry my bloodline. Father will look after Mariana, and all will be well in the world. Except I won't see Mariana again or witness my girl grow into womanhood.

When the bugler lowered his instrument, the drums outside beat again, a wild, hard sound that reverberated from the walls of the fort.

The *mullah* raised his arms in a final encouragement to violence, and some of the Pashtun fired. Most of the shots flew high, but some slammed into the parapet, chipping fragments of stone. The Sikhs stood, steady as any Guardsmen. Not one bullet found a human target.

"Present!" Andrew shouted in Punjabi.

The tribesmen surged forward in a purposeful advance.

"Fire!"

※

"DAMN THE MAN," JACK SAID. "NOTHING AT ALL?"

"He had nothing to identify him at all," the army surgeon confirmed. "You checked his clothes and possessions, and I inspected his body. The would-be assassin could have been anybody. His clothes had no label but looked like they came from Calcutta, his weapon was a British Adams revolver, and there was no tattoo or any other identifying mark on his body."

Jack cursed and nursed his bandaged arm. "Damn and blast the man. He could at least have carried a letter from the Tsar or something to help us."

"How very inconsiderate of him," the surgeon agreed.

Jack grunted and limped away. He had a meeting with the viceroy next, and Victor Demidov had invited him for a formal dinner. Jack had no doubt the conversation would centre around the lone assassin.

I know the man was a blasted Russian and an agent of the Okhrana, but I cannot prove a thing. Demidov will play the innocent, and I'll look a fool. I much prefer honest soldiering to this cloak-and-dagger, underhanded political nonsense.

❄

THE SIKHS ALONG THE SOUTHERN AND WESTERN WALLS FIRED a volley, with those on the northern and eastern waiting hopefully for a target. A dozen tribesmen fell, and many of the rest returned ineffective fire, but the remainder continued to advance, with men holding the green flags above the mob.

"Odd numbers from the north wall reinforce the men on the south," Andrew shouted. "Odd numbers on the east wall reinforce the west!" He hoped he had not weakened the north and east walls too much as the *mullah* stalked around the rear of the tribesmen, lifting his arms.

"They're going to charge," Andrew said. "Cease fire!"

The Sikhs obeyed, looking wonderingly at Andrew. "Set your sights for five hundred yards!" Andrew shouted. "I want a volley on my word," he said, "and then independent firing."

The havildar repeated Andrew's words.

"Remember to adjust your sights as the enemy closes!" Andrew shouted. "Ready!" He saw the tribesmen preparing to rush forward, encouraging each other with shouts and religious exhortations.

"*Allah Akbar!*"

The words came clearly across the broken ground to the fort.

"*Allah Akbar!* God is great!"

The warriors surged forward, some waving their swords or

Khyber knives, others firing rifles. A score of men carried the green banners inscribed with phrases from the Quran.

"Fire!" Andrew shouted when the tribesmen reached the five-hundred-yard range markers. The Sikhs fired immediately, knocking down twenty of the attackers. The rest continued, screaming their hatred.

CHAPTER 22

FORT RAZALI, KHYBER PASS, SUMMER 1897

"Independent firing!" Andrew ordered. He watched the horde charge across the broken ground, the long-haired men with slate-coloured clothes carrying swords and rifles facing the disciplined, bearded Sikhs, blood enemies for generations.

The Sikhs fired, loaded, and fired again, showing no fear as the tribesmen closed in their thousands.

"*So Nihaal, Sat Sri Akaal,*" the havildar roared. "The Almighty is the eternal truth!"

Andrew drew his revolver, waited until the enemy was within range, and fired alongside his men. For one moment, he glimpsed somebody standing beside the mullah, a spare, tall man in a neat turban, and then he was busy repelling the Afridi *lashkar*.

The Sikhs fired, loaded, and fired again, moving quickly without rushing, aiming each shot like the professionals they were. Their shooting cut swathes through the advancing tribesmen, with the heavy Martini-Henry bullets knocking men down, smashing open skulls, tearing off arms, and blasting holes in frail human chests.

Andrew saw the attackers leaping over the barbed wire, temporarily slowing them down and allowing the Sikhs an easier target. He fired at any man who came within thirty yards, walking along the parapet to encourage the men. Shots whistled overhead or slammed against the stone, and Andrew saw one Sikh stagger back with blood spouting from a wound in his upper chest.

"Go to the east wall!" Andrew ordered Innes. "This attack may only be a diversion!"

Innes looked at Andrew in consternation. "Sir! I want to fight!"

"Obey my orders!" Andrew snarled.

"Yes, sir!" Innes moved to the east wall, obviously unhappy.

The initial surge of the Afridis slowed, with their casualties mounting and mounds of dead and wounded piling thirty yards before the fort's walls.

The tom-toms continued, throbbing behind the terrible sounds of battle.

When the Afridis' attack weakened, some Sikhs mounted the walls to fire at the retreating enemy.

"Cease fire!" Andrew ordered. "Save your ammunition!"

The Sikhs obeyed reluctantly, aware that the enemy would come again.

"Havildar Abani Singh!" Andrew said, his voice sounding unnaturally loud in the sudden hush. "Take a party outside and bring in as many rifles and as much ammunition as you can carry. Every round helps."

"Yes, sahib!" Abani Singh saluted and led five men outside.

The wounded men outside were moaning, with some attempting to crawl to their friends on shattered limbs. Andrew did not interfere, fully aware that the Pashtun would torture and mutilate any Sikh or British wounded they found. He remembered the fate of the Sikhs captured in the early Chitral expedition.

"Innes!" Andrew said. "Cover the havildar's patrol!"

"Yes, sir!" Innes replied and lined the wall with his men, firing at any Afridi who came too close.

Havildar Abani Singh's patrol returned with twenty rifles, mostly Sniders and Martinis, but also a few *jezails*. They also carried bandoliers of ammunition, a welcome addition to the fort.

"British rifles," Innes said. "Probably looted from our men."

"Maybe," Andrew examined the Martinis. "We allow the Amir of Afghanistan to make Martinis."

"Do we, sir?" Innes asked.

"We do," Andrew said. "God alone knows why. By the look of these weapons, they are Kabul-made. The Amir probably sells them to the Pashtuns or gives them free. Anything to cause us trouble."

"What are you looking for, sir?" Innes asked as Andrew continued to examine the rifles.

"Anything that might suggest Russian influence," Andrew said. "We had reports of Russians in Chitral, and I wondered if they were behind this nonsense as well."

"Can you find anything, sir?"

"Nothing," Andrew admitted. "I thought I might find some Russian-made weapons." He ordered Abani Singh to place the weapons and ammunition in the armoury.

"Get some sleep, Innes," he ordered. "The Afridi might attack at night. They'll hit the east and north walls next."

Except for occasional sniping, the day quietened down. Andrew sent the two wounded men to the makeshift hospital, checked the defences, and ensured the men were fed, watered, and had sufficient ammunition.

Andrew toured the defences, sent a working party out to add more wire to the north wall, and signalled Fort Roberts with his heliograph, informing Colonel Neville of his situation.

"Any reply, sir?" Innes asked.

"Not yet," Andrew said. "Keep an eye open. We don't know

what their situation is. The tribes might have attacked them as well."

"I could take a patrol out and see, sir," Innes offered.

Andrew shook his head. "Too risky, Innes. You wouldn't get five hundred yards with the enemy watching everything we do."

The Afridis were quiet after their repulse but recovered and began to fire at the fort. Sometimes, they only fired a few shots, aiming at any sentries they saw above the parapet, but had periods when scores of rifles fired at the fort.

"They must have plenty of ammunition to waste," Innes said.

"I told you to get some sleep," Andrew reminded him. "You and I will have to take turns in charge of the fort."

"How long do you think the siege will last?" Innes asked.

"The siege of Chitral lasted weeks," Andrew said soberly. "I hope this one is shorter, but we'd best be prepared."

"Yes, sir," Innes replied.

The Afridis occupied the broken ground around the fort and continued to fire, restricting movement inside the fort without causing any significant casualties. Two men suffered minor cuts from flying fragments of stone, scoffed at the wounds, and continued with their duties.

"They're creeping up on the north side, sahib," Havildar Abani Singh warned.

"Allah Akbar!"

The shout came from hundreds of throats as men raised their green banners and launched a sudden charge on the north wall.

"Here they come!" Innes yelled. "Give them a volley, lads!"

The Sikhs had expected the charge and rose, firing a quick volley followed by independent firing that felled dozens of the attackers.

"Send them back!" Innes was in his element, firing one of the captured Martinis and shouting every time he scored a hit. The Sikhs grinned at him, appreciating his enthusiasm.

"Odd numbers from the south wall," Andrew ordered, "reinforce the north wall."

Tempted to join them, Andrew remained where he was, peering over the wall in case the Afridis launched an attack from a different angle.

"Sahib!" Havildar Abani Singh shouted and pointed.

Andrew could see nothing untoward until he realised that one of the rocks had moved. When he studied it, he saw other rocks moving.

"They're crawling to the fort!" Andrew shouted. "Send them back!" He fired a captured Martini, grunted at the kick, and reloaded.

This rifle may look like one of ours, but it handles differently. It's not so well-balanced, and the recoil is greater.

He fired again, and a hundred Afridis threw off the cloaks under which they had been crawling and charged at the wall.

"Allah Akbar!"

"Bole So Nihal, Sat Shri Akal!" the Sikhs replied.

As they started closer to the wall and there were fewer defenders, some of the Afridis reached the wall, with two clambering up to the battlements. The Sikhs met them with bayonets and thrust their dead bodies back down.

"Bole So Nihal, Sat Shri Akal!"

"Fire!" Andrew led by example, hearing the roar of battle on both sides of the fort. He fired the Martini, borrowed a handful of cartridges from a snarling naik, reloaded, and fired again. The rifle barrel was already hot, proof it was an inferior make.

"Send them back!" Andrew roared.

With the element of surprise gone, the Afridis withdrew from the south wall, just as Innes's Sikhs drove them from the north. Silence descended again, punctuated by the moans of wounded men.

"Take the casualties to the hospital," Andrew said, reloading his Martini. Since the Rifles deserted, the Sikhs were thin on the ground and had lost two dead and four wounded in repelling the Afridi attacks.

"It will be dark soon," Innes said.

Andrew nodded. He did not need a subaltern to tell him the obvious.

"Double sentries tonight," Andrew said. "You and I will spell each other. Four hours on and four hours off."

"I don't need sleep, sir," Innes said.

"Everybody needs sleep," Andrew snarled. "If you don't sleep, you'll make mistakes that could cost men's lives. I'll take the first watch." *If I don't, you'll try to stay awake all night and be useless tomorrow, as I would have at your age.*

"Yes, sir," Innes agreed reluctantly.

The night passed peacefully, except for some desultory sniping that did no damage and which the Sikhs ignored. Andrew roused the men an hour before dawn, with the sound of the bugle echoing across the Khyber.

"What will happen today?" Innes asked.

"Whatever happens, we'll cope," Andrew said. He sent another heliographic signal towards Fort Roberts without any response and prepared for the day.

"I want a working party creating lamps and fireballs," Andrew ordered. "I spent half the night expecting an attack when we could see nothing. Tonight, we'll have the capability to see what's happening."

"Yes, sir. Anything else, sir?" Innes asked.

"Yes; two patrols around the fort: one to collect more weapons and replace any damaged range markers for our men, and a longer patrol to scout the enemy. I'll take the longer patrol, and Havildar Abani Singh will command the shorter one."

"I could take the longer patrol, sir," Innes said.

"I know you could, Innes, but I prefer to see for myself."

"Yes, sir," Innes sounded crestfallen.

Andrew scoured the surroundings through his binoculars before selecting a six-man patrol. "Be prepared to give me covering fire, Innes," he said. "We may have to come back in a hurry."

"Yes, sir," Innes replied, happy to be helpful. "Shall I have a section ready to support you?"

"That's a good idea," Andrew encouraged his keen subaltern.

The Sikhs opened the gate, careful of any lurking Afridis, and Andrew led his patrol out. They advanced cautiously, with the last man turning every few steps to check behind him and the others looking alternately to the right and left.

The Afridis did not interfere, although Andrew guessed they were watching him from a dozen vantage points. He led the patrol five hundred yards from the fort to a rocky knoll, which afforded a good vantage point, and readied his binoculars. He was fortunate that he didn't have to teach the Sikhs much about soldiering. They formed a defensive ring around the summit as Andrew climbed up, feeling like every Afridi marksman in the Khyber was aiming at his back.

If they want to shoot me, I'm giving them every opportunity. I hope Innes will hold the fort until Colonel Neville relieves us.

Lifting his binoculars, Andrew scanned the surrounding area. He saw the Afridis' banners on the heights and the occasional flash of sunlight on metal, but there was no sign of any warriors. The dead lay where they had fallen, looking like bundles of discarded rags rather than the brave men they had been only a few hours previously.

Andrew shifted his focus, scanning the road through the Khyber, hoping to see a relieving column from Fort Roberts. The road was empty, without a single camel caravan or itinerant merchant.

It's hard to believe this is the main highway between Kabul and India. Where are all the merchants?

Andrew lifted his binoculars, looking further afield. He could see Fort Roberts' tower, where Colonel Neville must be mustering a relieving force. He could see the flag, colourless at this distance, and a wisp of either smoke from the bread ovens or drifting mist.

Fort Roberts looks quiet. I wonder if Colonel Neville got my message.

The drums started again, throbbing from the hills, and Andrew decided to return to the fort.

"The Afridis have woken up, men!"

The patrol returned quickly, watching for ambushes or hidden snipers. Twice, somebody fired at them, with the bullets passing close to Andrew. Unable to see the marksmen, the Sikhs did not return fire.

"Come on, sir!" Innes had his section two hundred yards from the fort, waiting.

A score of Afridis exploded from behind the broken rocks, running forward to catch Andrew's patrol in the open.

"Face them!" Andrew shouted. "Form a circle!" His men obeyed, presenting their Martinis at the Afridis.

"Fire!" Innes ordered, and half a dozen Sikhs rose from the fort's walls and loosed a volley in support.

When the Afridis hesitated, Innes's patrol fired and followed through with a savage bayonet charge. Shaken by the ferocity of the counterattack, the surviving Afridis fled, with the Sikhs chasing after them.

"Get these men back!" Andrew roared. "Bugler! Sound the recall!"

The Sikhs filed back reluctantly, growling over their shoulders.

"Inside the fort!" Andrew ordered as the frustrated Pashtuns began firing again. The Sikhs on the battlements returned fire as Andrew ushered his patrol and Innes's section inside the fort.

"That was lively!" Innes said, smiling.

"Get your men up to the battlements," Andrew ordered. "The Afridis will attack in a few moments."

"Here they come now!" Havildar Abani Singh shouted.

Andrew split his men, with two-thirds facing this fresh attack and the rest manning the remaining walls. With so few defenders, Andrew knew the gaps between his men were too large, but the Rifles' desertion left him no choice.

The Afridis attacked as before, although Andrew thought they lacked the verve of their initial assault. The Sikhs' shooting was as deadly, leaving scores of bodies as the Afridis' attack ebbed away.

Innes joined the Sikhs in cheering.

"Every third man!" Andrew shouted. "Reinforce the other walls." He patrolled the battlements, looking for any further movement from the Afridis.

The tom-toms began again, throbbing all around the fort. Andrew sent another heliograph message to Neville in Fort Roberts, again without response.

It seems that Colonel Neville is ignoring us.

"Sir!" Innes spoke quietly. He pointed ahead, where the red-bearded *mullah* and the tall man appeared in the centre of a knot of men, with green flags fluttering above. "Something is happening."

The Afridis halted eight hundred yards from the fort and thrust the flags into the ground. The tall man stepped slowly forward.

The Sikhs levelled their rifles.

"Hold your fire," Andrew ordered. "Let him come close. He might want to talk to us."

The tall man seemed unaware of the twenty Sikh Martinis pointed at him as he walked forward.

"That's close enough!" Andrew shouted when the tall man was thirty yards away. "What do you want?" He spoke in English, repeating the words in Pashto.

"I want you to surrender the fort," the man replied in Pashto. "Including all your men and the arms and ammunition. If you do so, I guarantee the lives of your men. If not, we will take the fort and kill everybody inside."

Andrew glanced at his men. Although few of the Sikhs spoke

Pashto, he knew the gist of the conversation would soon be common knowledge.

"Why should we trust you?" Andrew asked.

"I'll show you what happened to the last British officer who refused to surrender," the man said. "He thought he could stand against us."

"Who are you?" Andrew asked.

The tall man did not reply.

"What's happening, sir?" Innes asked.

Andrew related what the tall man had offered.

"The Sikhs will never surrender to Pashtuns," Innes said confidently.

"We had some Sikhs who surrendered to the Chitralis," Andrew told him. "I saw their headless bodies floating in the river a couple of weeks later."

"They were lucky," Innes said quietly. "The Pashtun normally kill their prisoners very slowly."

Andrew nodded. "So I believe."

They watched as a group of Afridis dragged forward a man wearing a British army uniform.

"Colonel Neville!" Andrew said.

That was why Neville didn't answer our heliograph. The Pashtun have captured Fort Roberts.

CHAPTER 23

FORT RAZALI, KHYBER PASS, SUMMER 1897

"What are they going to do?" Innes asked.

"Something unpleasant, I'd guess," Andrew replied.

As the fort's garrison watched, the Pashtun stripped Colonel Neville of his uniform and spreadeagled him on the ground. The tall man watched while a dozen warriors and some women gathered around.

"Sahib!" Havildar Abani Singh approached Innes and spoke too rapidly for Andrew to understand.

"Havildar Abani Singh says the Afridis are going to flay Colonel Neville alive," Innes said. "He asks permission to take a section out to rescue him."

Andrew scanned the surroundings through his binoculars. He saw a slight movement behind some of the rocks, a single sandal showing beside a thorn tree and a momentary flash of sunlight on metal. "Permission denied, Innes. That's exactly what the Afridis want us to do. They'll let us get close, then cut us off from the fort."

The havildar spoke again. "We can't let the enemy torture the sahib."

Andrew lifted his binoculars. Neville was already wounded, with dried blood on his left thigh and across his stomach. He lay on his back with his mouth firmly closed until one of the Afridis wrenched it open. The Afridi thrust a pointed stick inside the colonel's mouth, ensuring he could not shut it.

"What the devil?" Andrew asked, looking at the havildar.

"It is another form of killing," Abani Singh explained. "Women will urinate in the colonel sahib's mouth until he drowns. I think the Afridis are playing with us."

"I'm damned if I'll be a plaything," Andrew said. "Give me a rifle. A Martini, and one of ours, not a Kabul-made copy!"

"You can't shoot them all, sir," Innes said.

"Bring every man to the battlements except three," Andrew said. "Have them keep down beneath the parapet with loaded rifles and ensure the enemy doesn't see them."

Innes nodded. "Yes, sir."

"Have them set the range on their rifles at eight hundred yards," Andrew said, thinking as he spoke. "When I fire, the very second I fire, I want every man to jump up and fire at that group."

"Yes, sir," Innes said.

"Each of the remaining three will watch one wall of the fort. Are there any questions?"

"No, sir," Innes said.

Andrew waited until the Sikhs were in position before carefully aiming his Martini. He took a deep breath.

If I were Colonel Neville, would I want to be slowly tortured to death or killed quickly? I'd rather somebody shot me. But I don't want to shoot a British officer.

One woman was squatting over Neville as the tall man and the *mullah* stepped closer. Another man, an ordinary tribesman by his clothes, slid the blade of his knife under the skin of the colonel's left foot. Andrew took a deep breath, allowed for windage, placed the colonel's head squarely in his foresight and slowly squeezed the trigger. He rode the rifle's kick, but before he had time to observe the effect of his shot, the Sikhs had stood up. Their volley was as uniform as any musketry instructor could demand, and Andrew saw half the Afridis fall or leap backwards as the bullets sliced into them.

Andrew knew he would never be quite the same again. He had deliberately killed a British officer. He lowered his rifle, wondering what the Sikhs thought of him and how he could tell Mariana and his father.

What else could I do? What the devil else could I do?

The Sikhs were still loading and firing, with the Afridis returning fire, so bullets screamed around them. Andrew saw a bullet strike the parapet at his side, breaking off a section of stone and leaving a distinctive blue smear. *Another inch and that shot would have hit me. Innes would have command of the men, but he doesn't have the experience to defeat the Afridis.*

"Cease fire," Andrew ordered. "Get back under cover."

The Afridis' shots were buzzing past like a torrent of angry wasps when a clumsy man upset their nest. A Sikh stiffened and fell, his mouth open in surprise. Andrew stared at the group around Colonel Neville. Most were down, lying prone on the ground, with the *mullah* still standing despite the bullets whizzing around him.

Andrew worked the Martini's underlever to eject the spent cartridge and reloaded, aware a score of Afridis would be aiming at him. At that moment, he did not care if he lived or died. *I killed a British officer.* Andrew thumbed a cartridge into the breech of his rifle, felt something pass half an inch from his head and aimed.

He held the rifle steady, with the *mullah* square in the foresight, and squeezed the trigger. He looked up, expecting to see the *mullah* crumple and fall. The man remained where he was, and for a second, Andrew thought he saw the *mullah's* eyes staring into his.

That's impossible, Andrew told himself. *We are eight hundred yards apart.* He worked the underlever to eject the spent cartridge and methodically reloaded the rifle.

"Sir!" Innes ran to his side. "Get under cover! You too, Havildar!"

Andrew realised that Havildar Abani Singh was trying to shield him with his body while Afridi bullets were hissing and buzzing all around.

"Get down, Abani Singh!" Andrew ordered sternly.

"Sahib!" Singh pushed in front of Andrew. "It is not safe."

Andrew lifted his rifle again to see the *mullah* striding slowly away. The tall man was not among the Afridi casualties.

"Sir!" Innes said, tugging at Andrew's sleeve.

Andrew ducked beneath the parapet, dragging Abani Singh with him. He felt that every man was watching him.

"They'll try another rush," Andrew said. His words seemed to come from miles away, as if he was looking down on himself, the soldier who had murdered a British officer. "Get the men fed, Innes. Havildar, ensure every man has seventy rounds of ammunition."

"Yes, sir."

"When you've done that, hack loopholes in the walls. The enemy will fire high, so we must have another level to shoot at them."

I am giving sensible orders as if nothing has happened, yet the whole world has changed. I am a murderer. I killed a British officer but missed the mullah, although I had a clear shot.

How the devil did I miss? It doesn't matter. Get the men ready to defend the fort. You're a Windrush, Andrew Baird. You do your duty, whatever happens.

❋

ELGIN STARED AT JACK FROM BEHIND A PILE OF LEDGERS.

"Have you made any further progress with your enquiries, General?"

"We have hit a brick wall, your Excellency," Jack admitted. "The assassin is as anonymous as if he never existed. The Russian ambassador denied all knowledge and asked what possible benefit shooting you would bring Russia."

"I wondered that myself," Elgin said. "Could this fellow have been working alone? A man with a grudge against me or against the Indian government?"

"That is possible, your Excellency," Jack said. "Until we have the identity of the man, we cannot progress any further."

"I see. Well, keep pushing, Windrush."

"I will, your Excellency," Jack said.

"I did not ask you here to discuss a dead assassin," Elgin told him. "We have other trouble," he said.

"What's happening, your Excellency?" Jack asked.

"The Waziris are happening, this time," Elgin said. "You'll remember they murdered a Hindu clerk in June last year."

"Yes, your Excellency," Jack said. "The incident was in the *Times of India*."

"We imposed a collective fine of 2,000 rupees on the Waziri villages, which they didn't pay," Elgin said. "In June this year, we sent the local political agent, with a Sikh escort, to the village of Maizar in North Waziristan to collect the fine."

Jack nodded, waiting for the inevitable.

"The people of Maizar were hospitable. They fed Colonel Bunny and the other officers, then ambushed them with gunfire. Colonel Bunny and two officers were killed instantly. Subadar Sunder Singh got the men safely to their camp, and there the situation rested."

Jack nodded again. "We should not let these incidents go unpunished," he said. "The Waziris are the most numerous Pashtun tribe, and they'll see a lack of action on our part as weakness."

"In hindsight, Windrush, you are correct," Elgin said. "We

had reports of tribal gatherings in Swat, beyond the Malakand ridge, strengthened our garrisons and did nothing else. We heard rumours of *mullahs* stirring up trouble and nodded sagely. Have you heard of a *mullah* named Sadullah?"

Jack nodded. "My people are more concerned with possible Russian interference," he said, "but some have mentioned Sadullah. We know him as the Mad Mullah, a ranting troublemaker with a great black beard."

Elgin shuffled his files. "Sadullah has been preaching his poison through the bazaars, claiming he can work miracles and promising to sweep the infidels away at the next new moon."

"That reminds me of the rhetoric before the Mutiny," Jack said.

"That was before my time," Elgin said shortly. "Abdur Rahman, the Amir of Afghanistan, has become more deeply involved, telling the Afghan and Frontier *mullahs* to preach a *jihad*, a holy war."

"A holy war where they stand at the back spouting hate and send young boys and crazed men to their deaths," Jack said.

"That's correct," Elgin said. "You'll note I said more deeply involved."

"Yes, your Excellency," Jack agreed. "I know Abdur Rahman has been stirring up trouble for some years. I am taking steps to combat him."

"Abdur Rahman has been trouble ever since Mortimer Durand fixed the boundary between India and Afghanistan," Elgin said. "It intensified last week," Elgin patted his files in place. "In Chakdara in Swat, in Malakand and along the Khyber."

Jack took a deep breath. "Along the Khyber, too?" *Andrew is out there.*

"I am afraid so, Windrush," Elgin said.

Jack forced himself to sit still. Decades in the army had schooled him in controlling his emotions. "How bad is the situation in the Khyber?"

Why the hell wasn't I informed first? How does the viceroy have military information that I lacked?

"It's unclear," Elgin said. "We know the Afridis have risen and are besieging some of the forts there. We hope the Khyber Rifles hold out."

"Are we organising a relief column?" Jack asked.

"No," Elgin said. "We don't have sufficient manpower." He looked at Jack. "The garrisons will have to hold out as best they can."

"My son is there," Jack said softly.

Elgin looked away. "I am aware of that, Windrush," he replied. "I am afraid I can't organise a relief column because of personal considerations. Captain Baird will have to take his chances like any other soldier."

❄

THE AFRIDIS FIRED FROM THREE SIDES AT ONCE, HAMMERING at Fort Razali's defenders, with bullets screaming overhead and slamming against the parapet. Andrew watched the Sikhs hack at the walls with whatever tools they could find—pickaxes, old, captured rifles, and bayonets—creating loopholes to fire through.

"Don't make the holes too large," Andrew said. "These Afridis are good marksmen!"

The Sikhs understood. Generations of their forefathers had fought against Pashtun warriors.

"The Afridis are trying something," Havildar Abani Singh shouted from the parapet. "There's lots of smoke, sir!"

Andrew ran up the stone steps to the battlements. He glanced aloft, where the Union Flag drooped in the sun, the multicoloured crosses hidden in the folds of cloth.

I won't let you down, he promised.

"Smoke, sir," Innes said.

"I see it, Innes," Andrew said dryly. Blue-grey smoke billowed from a score of fires all around the fort.

"I don't know what they're up to, sir," Innes sounded worried.

"They're making a smoke screen," Andrew said. "Who taught them that trick?" *It might have been the Russians.* "Tell the men to be watchful. The Afridis will come out of the smoke."

Andrew had a third of the garrison on duty all the time, with the others resting and changing duty shifts every eight hours. Each man slept with his rifle at his side, ready for instant action.

Thick and acrid smoke drifted across the hill slopes as Andrew peered through his binoculars.

"Stand to," he ordered when he saw movement in the smoke.

Within minutes of the bugle sounding, the Sikhs were on the walls and standing beside the ragged loopholes, staring outside. Men coughed and rubbed their eyes as smoke billowed into the fort.

"Clever devils, the Afridis," Innes said, smoothing a hand along the barrel of his Martini.

"They've been active a long time," Andrew said. "These lads' ancestors probably fought against Alexander the Great. They'll know all the tricks." He concentrated on defending the fort, knowing he could not afford to let his mind drift to the shooting of Colonel Neville.

"Here they come!" Innes shouted as a mass of Afridis erupted from the drifting smoke. They were only three hundred yards from the fort, hundreds of screaming tribesmen waving swords and firing rifles, with the green flags lifted high, some trailing ribbons of smoke.

"Volley fire!" Andrew shouted. "Aim! Fire!"

He saw the Sikhs' volley knock down half the leading Afridis.

"Independent firing!"

The Sikhs responded, firing and loading with professional calm.

"Sahib!" Havildar Abani Singh ran to Andrew. "Over there!" He pointed to the southern wall, where a large group of Afridis moved forward, some carrying *charpoys* laden with stones and earth.

"What the devil?" Andrew asked. "Havildar, take a section and stop them!"

Abani Singh saluted and gave rapid orders that saw a section run to the north wall. Andrew followed.

"Take over here, Innes!"

There was an area of dead ground beneath the corner of the north and west faces of the fort. Andrew ordered the havildar's section to fire at the men as they approached the angle, cursing when the Afridis huddled behind the *charpoy*.

"Our bullets can't penetrate the soil!" Abani Singh shouted.

Andrew nodded, thinking quickly. The Afridis were clever; the smoke was a screen to hide the mass attack, which itself was only a diversion to cover the assault on the northwest corner.

"Keep firing," Andrew made a rapid decision. "Don't let any reinforcements come through."

Abani Singh gave rapid orders to his men, who stood at the battlements, firing at any Afridis who crossed the open ground.

Andrew ran inside the fort. He guessed the Afridis would be trying to breach the wall. The stones were solid, but the extremes of climate, ranging from near tropical heat to sub-zero cold, would render the mortar friable, easy for determined men to hack through. Calling for four men from the already thin defenders on the south wall, Andrew brought them inside the room on the northwest corner where the Afridis were attacking the stonework.

"Build a barricade!" Andrew ordered. "I want a barrier across the room," he tried to explain in his limited Punjabi. "When the Afridis break through, shoot them flat."

The Sikhs had been unhappy when Andrew removed them from the wall, but they nodded now that they understood their part. They fixed bayonets, placed their Martinis against the wall, and shifted furniture across the room. Andrew used a bayonet to unscrew the door to add to the barrier, then left them, sure the room was in safe hands.

Innes was holding the south wall well, firing steadily at the screaming mob outside, while the havildar's men were limiting the supply of reinforcements.

This is the crisis, Andrew told himself. *Every battle has a crisis. If we survive this, we will hold out for another day. If they break in, they'll kill us all.*

Andrew heard a cheer from outside the northwest corner, and the cry "*Allah Akbar!*" rose high.

The Sikhs responded with their war cry, and for a moment, the two sides were competing with slogans rather than bullets.

That cheer will mean the Afridis are making progress in breaching the wall. I hope my handful of sepoys can hold them.

Andrew decided that the four men inside the room needed him most, reminded himself not to look hurried in front of the men, and walked into the room, holding a Martini.

The Sikhs were waiting expectantly behind their barricade, rifles pointed towards the wall. The sound of picks on the stonework was loud, echoing inside the room, and Andrew saw a trickle of mortar from two of the stones. He saw the point of a pick come through the mortar and heard the yells from outside.

Lifting a hand to his men, Andrew sauntered forward, put the muzzle of his rifle against the hole, and fired. The rifle's report was deafening, and he loaded quickly and fired again, hoping he was doing some damage to the attackers.

He stepped sideways, expecting the Afridis to fire into the room, but instead, they raised another chorus of "*Allah Akbar*" and again attacked the wall with their picks.

Andrew loaded and fired a third time before withdrawing behind the barricade. The Sikhs were waiting, fingers on triggers, eager to fire.

A stone grated and creaked, and somebody pushed it inside the room with a small avalanche of mortar and dust.

"Fire when you have a target," Andrew said quietly.

CHAPTER 24

FORT RAZALI, NORTHWEST FRONTIER,
SUMMER 1897

The Sikhs and Andrew fired together. Five bullets crashed into the men outside, and then Andrew ordered independent firing, with a constant stream of bullets keeping back the Afridis.

The attackers returned fire, with bullets smashing into the barricade, splintering the wood and punching through the door panels. Gunsmoke quickly filled the room, adding to the gloom, with the muzzle flares revealing sudden vignettes of fighting men. Andrew saw brief flashes of warriors attempting to enter, with shouting faces and the gleam of *pulwars* and Khyber knives, the glitter of eyes and spurting blood from the terrible wounds from Martini bullets.

"Keep them back, lads!" Andrew roared. He heard yells from outside and a tremendous crash that sounded like the fort was collapsing, followed by screams, yells and roars. The enemy fire abruptly ended.

"What on earth?" Andrew asked. "Cease fire!"

The Sikhs stopped firing and peered forward. Gunsmoke

billowed across the room, stinging eyes and nostrils. Andrew climbed over the barrier and cautiously approached the gap in the wall. He stared outside to see a mass of masonry on the ground outside the wall, with dead and wounded Afridis lying around, some crushed or pinned beneath the stone. The others had recoiled, and the Sikhs on the parapet were firing at them. Havildar Abani Singh had pushed the damaged section of the wall on top of the assault party.

Well done, Havildar.

Andrew signalled his men forward and began to fire through the hole at the now disheartened Afridis, who withdrew slowly, then broke and ran, losing men to the Sikhs' fire.

"*Shabash!*" Andrew said. He pointed to two sepoys. "You two remain here; the rest join your colleagues on the wall in case the Afridis try again."

They won't come again today. The breach was their main assault, and the havildar destroyed it. I'll recommend Abani Singh for a promotion and a medal.

※

THE HAVILDAR GREETED ANDREW WITH A SALUTE. "What happened, Havildar?"

"The enemy were pressing hard, sahib," Havildar said. "I thought it best to push down the battlements on top of them. We can shift stones as well as the Pashtuns can."

Andrew surveyed the results, with a two-yard section of the battlements missing and the shattered stones lying on top of the remains of the storming party.

"You did well, Havildar," Andrew said. "Now, let's clean this mess up."

They spent the remainder of that day trying to rebuild the damaged wall while the havildar led a patrol to collect the enemy's rifles and ammunition. The Afridis remained at a distance, occupying themselves with desultory sniping.

Andrew posted sentries, ensured the fort was as secure as possible and called Innes and Abani Singh to his quarters.

"Relax, Havildar," Andrew said as Abani Singh stood at attention. "Your opinion is welcome."

The havildar looked astonished.

"Sit down, gentlemen," Andrew invited. "We are in a small fort with a depleted garrison, and an unknown number of Afridis are besieging us. The final decision is mine, but I want your opinions. Do we settle down to the siege or fight our way out to the nearest British base? We know the Afridi have captured Fort Roberts."

"There may not be a British base nearer than Peshawar," Innes said. "If our Khyber Rifles ran, maybe the whole regiment deserted. That would mean the Pashtuns control the entire Khyber."

Andrew nodded. "What do you think, Havildar?"

"We will do whatever the sahib decides," Abani Singh said.

Andrew smiled. "Spoken like a soldier of the *Khalsa*," he said.

"Do you think somebody will send a relief column, sir?" Innes asked.

"Without knowing the situation," Andrew said. "I can't answer that question. We can stay to defend the fort as long as possible, or we leave and fight our way out."

I am here to meet Symington. What is more important, his information or the lives of the men under my command?

"We have food, ammunition and stone walls here, sir," Innes said. "I think we should stay."

Andrew nodded. "I agree, Innes. We'll stay and fight it out."

The havildar saluted, preparing to leave.

"Do we have any more barbed wire, Innes?" Andrew asked.

"No, sir," Innes replied.

"Spare ammunition?"

"Plenty, sir," Innes said with a smile. "The armoury holds ammunition for the Sikhs and the Khyber Rifles; enough for twice our present garrison, plus what we have taken from the Afridi dead. What do you have in mind, sir?"

Andrew smiled. "Some ideas I picked up in the Transvaal, Innes. Let's have an aggressive defence rather than a passive one."

"What do you mean, sir?"

"Dummies," Andrew said. "We'll leave some dummies for the Afridis. Are there any spare uniforms in the fort, either Sikh or Rifles?"

"I don't know, sir," Innes replied.

"Try to find me some," Andrew ordered. "If you can't, then strip some of the Afridi dead."

"Yes, sir," Innes and Abani Singh looked confused.

"Subterfuge can be a useful ally," Andrew explained. "We can't match the enemy in numbers, so we must defeat them with trickery and deception." He grinned, showing confidence he did not feel. "Find me some uniforms, Innes, and you, Abani Singh, collect the ammunition we've taken from the Afridis. Particularly the home-made variety."

Abani Singh brought bandoliers of ammunition from the armoury and looked quizzically at Andrew.

"Extract the explosives," Andrew ordered. "But watch for sparks."

"Yes, sahib."

When Innes found half a dozen Rifles' uniforms, Andrew nodded in satisfaction and stuffed them with straw and anything combustible. He filled small bags with the explosives from the Afridis' bullets and placed them in the chests of the uniforms.

"Now, Abani Singh," Andrew said. "We will take a couple of patrols outside the walls."

"Yes, sahib," the havildar looked confused.

"We'll take these gentlemen with us," Andrew said, "and leave them on guard."

"They don't have any heads," Innes said.

"That is a problem," Andrew admitted. "A headless soldier won't fool anybody."

"Melons," Innes said.

"Melons?" Andrew saw Innes's idea.

"My lads loved them, sir," Innes said. "The Sikhs also like them."

"Can you find me six melons? One for each headless man?"

"Yes, sir," Innes said.

Attaching the heads to the stuffed dummies was a problem until Abani Singh suggested using the ramrods from the captured *jezails*. With one end thrust into the pumpkin and the other wedged inside the tunic, the head looked approximately correct, especially when the havildar added a turban to help disguise the colour. He looked up, smiling.

"We have six more recruits, sahib."

"That's about it," Andrew said. "Let's get these men in place."

Andrew remembered the Sikhs in Burma enjoying a similar deception. He took Abani Singh and six sepoys on three patrols around the fort, each time depositing the dummies. The Sikhs grinned as they left the dummies on guard, complete with broken rifles pointing towards the Afridi positions.

"Three sets of two dummies," Andrew ordered. "Don't make them too obvious, or the Afridis will either snipe them from a distance and blow them up or ignore them."

Abani Singh nodded. "Yes, sahib."

"I can't wait to see the Afridis' faces when they meet our new soldiers," Innes said.

Today's young officers are as promising as ever. Did I share their enthusiasm when I faced the Galekas along the Cape Frontier?

Andrew checked the dummies' positions behind convenient rocks, returned to the fort, and appointed the best marksmen to shoot at them when the time was right.

With range markers surrounding the fort and sufficient food and ammunition to last weeks, Andrew thought they could hold out. *I hope the powers-that-be will send a relief column soon.* Pulling his pipe from his pocket, Andrew wondered what it would be like to be a father.

I am fortunate that Mariana is a good mother. Simla. That's a good name. I only hope I am around to see her grow up.

"Sahib!" Abani Singh hissed quietly. "The Afridis are coming again."

❇

MARIANA SIGHED. SHE LIKED SIMLA WITH ITS GOSSIP, NEVERending social occasions, and invigorating climate. She liked to watch the young couples romancing with coy glances and supposedly secretive assignations as though they were the first to discover the opposite sex. Mariana also enjoyed watching girls straight from rural Britain staring wide-eyed at everything and the handsome young officers and up-country British civilians awkward in female company.

Yet she missed Andrew. Mary could not be a more pleasant companion, and Jack did everything in his power to make her stay comfortable and enjoyable. However, she missed her husband more than she had expected. Little Simla proved diverting company, yet tiring, despite the amiable *ayah* that Mary found to help and who knew everything there was to know about babies.

When the *ayah* took over mothering duties, Mary encouraged Mariana to leave the house, and she became a regular at Peliti's Restaurant. She sat at a central table, watching the world go by, and often nodded to the white-faced, bespectacled man who always looked lonely as he occupied the same seat at a corner table. When what appeared to be an entire shipload of twittering young British women arrived one day, occupying Mariana's regular table, the only available seat was at the bespectacled man's table.

"Good morning," Mariana sat opposite him. "This place is busy today, isn't it?"

The man started, unused to women talking to him. "Yes," he replied, looking as startled as a rabbit in a poacher's lantern light.

"Do you mind if I join you?" Mariana favoured the man with her second-best smile.

"No," the man hurriedly closed the notebook in which he had been writing.

"Thank you," Mariana beckoned to a waiter. "You've picked the best seat here. You have a splendid view over the Mall."

"Yes," the man was in his late twenties, with serious brown eyes and an educated accent.

"You are often in here," Mariana was determined to continue the conversation despite the man's evident reluctance to talk.

"Most days," the man said.

"Ah! Two words," Mariana smiled at him again. "I am Mariana Baird. My husband is Captain Andrew Baird, attached to the Royal Malverns, at present serving on the Frontier."

The man hesitated. "I am Michael Sinclair."

"How do you do?" Mariana held out her hand, and Sinclair stood up politely, shook her hand with a surprisingly firm grip and sat back down.

The waiter arrived, took Mariana's order of a pot of tea and cakes and withdrew.

"What do you do, Mr Sinclair?" Mariana asked Sinclair, wrapping her smile around him.

"I am a writer," Sinclair replied.

"Like Rudyard Kipling?" Mariana asked, genuinely delighted. "I've always wanted to meet a real writer."

Sinclair looked more relaxed. "I am not as good a writer as Kipling."

"Few people are," Mariana said. "What are you writing?"

"A story about Simla," Sinclair said. "I am studying the people walking past, working out their characters and guessing their life stories."

"A bit like Kipling's *Plain Tales from the Hills*," Mariana said.

Sinclair smiled, reached to the bag at his feet, and produced a slim book. "Which I have here," he said. "Kipling is my inspiration. I want to delve deeper into their characters and find out what brought them to India."

"How fascinating!" Mariana allowed Sinclair to pour her a cup of tea. She leaned across the table. "You may start with me. Please tell me more."

CHAPTER 25

FORT RAZALI, KHYBER PASS, SUMMER 1897

Andrew had heard the drums without realising it. Like the Burmese gongs along the Irrawaddy, the sound was inside his head. The tom-toms were insidious, throbbing into his brain to become part of him, a never-ending sound that wrapped around his thoughts.

The Afridis emerged from the hills. They moved slowly, with the green banners held above their heads and the tom-toms hammering in the background.

"How many are there?" Innes asked as the tribesmen continued to arrive, lashkar after lashkar under their tribal banners. "They must have called up every man they have."

"It looks that way," Andrew agreed.

"Afridis and Waziris," Innes said. "And I think these lads are Mohmands. They must want this fort very badly."

"Why?" Andrew asked. "Fort Razali's not significant; we're only a signalling post for Fort Roberts." *Have the Russians ordered them to capture Symington? If so, they are out of luck because he's not here yet.*

"I doubt we'll ever know," Innes said.

The tribesmen halted nine hundred yards from the fort, standing in a great semi-circle encompassing three sides. The drums stopped, leaving a threatening silence.

"That's new," Andrew said, lifting his binoculars.

The red-bearded *mullah* stepped forward and began to preach, too far away for the garrison to discern his words, although the wind carried his voice to the fort.

"I wish somebody would shoot that man," Innes said.

The *mullah* walked in front of the tribesmen, raising his hands in the air as he harangued them.

"Shall I try a shot, sir?" Innes asked.

"How good is your shooting?"

"Fair to middling," Innes replied.

"Then don't try," Andrew said. "If you shoot and miss, you'll encourage the Afridis. The *mullah* claims he can turn our bullets into water, and I've already missed him. I don't want anything to reinforce his importance. They already believe his nonsense."

"I wish we had a seven-pounder," Innes said.

"If wishes were horses," Andrew said, smiling, "we'd all win at Royal Ascot."

"Here they come," Innes said.

The tribesmen spread out and advanced slowly, shouting "*Allah Akbar!*" in deep-throated unison.

"Hold your fire!" Andrew shouted. "Set your sights at eight hundred yards." He watched Innes and Abani Singh check the sepoys' rifles, both seemingly unhurried.

The *mullah* strode before the tribesmen as though challenging the defenders to fire at him. Andrew set his range at eight hundred yards, settled the barrel of his Martini on the battlements, and waited.

Come on; I missed you once, you bastard. I won't miss a second time.

"Will we fire, sir?" Innes asked.

"Not yet," Andrew held the *mullah* steady in his sights. "Wait until they come to eight hundred yards."

"Yes, sir," Innes said.

Andrew felt the Sikhs' anticipation rising. They waited, fingers curled around triggers, eager to fire. He eyed the white-painted range markers his men had put out, calculating distance and numbers.

"Sahib!" Abani Singh gestured to the extreme left flank of the Pashtun advance. "What is that?"

Andrew looked and frowned.

"The *mullah* has called up the trees," an impressionable young sepoy said. "A forest is coming towards us."

Andrew paraphrased Shakespeare's *Macbeth*, whispering the words: "I will not be afraid of death and bane,

Till Birnam Forest come to Dunsinane."

"What's that, sir?" Innes asked. "Was that an order?"

Abani Singh glanced at the flank and returned his attention to the *mullah* in the centre of the Afridi ranks.

"It wasn't an order, Innes. The Afridis have cut branches and bushes," Andrew said. "They're using them as cover."

"Our bullets will go right through them," Innes said.

"Indeed they will," Andrew agreed.

When the *mullah* reached the eight-hundred-yard marker, he stopped, lifted his arms and began to preach.

"Fire!" Andrew said, aimed directly at the *mullah's* head, and squeezed the trigger.

As Andrew fired, the warrior closest to the *mullah* shifted sideways, and Andrew's bullet caught him square in the chest. Andrew swore, worked the underlever to eject the spent cartridge, inserted another and looked up. In the few seconds he had reloaded, the Afridis had advanced ten yards, and the *mullah* was gone.

That man bears a charmed life.

The Sikhs had fired their first volley and were reloading, ready for the next order.

"Volley fire until they reach six hundred yards," Andrew ordered, "then independent firing. Number Three section, concentrate on the men on their extreme left flank, the men hiding behind the branches." He hoped the sepoys understood his words.

Some Afridis were firing now, with shots crashing against the battlements. A naik fell, shouting as a bullet smashed into his shoulder. Another sepoy crumpled without a sound, dead before he landed.

"The Afridis are making better practice," Innes said.

"They have marksmen targeting us while we fire at the mass," Andrew said. "They are a very formidable opposition."

The Afridis were running now, shouting and firing wildly at the fort. The Sikhs responded with disciplined volleys that cut down a dozen men with every discharge.

"Six hundred yards!" Innes shouted. "Independent firing!"

The firing increased in volume, no longer volleys but a constant crackle from the Martinis. One man shouted as his rifle jammed, and Andrew stepped to help him clear away the cartridge. The Martinis had a notoriously powerful kick and were also prone to jamming. Andrew used his knife to free the brass cartridge, levered it out of the breech and returned the weapon to its owner.

"Keep firing, soldier!" he ordered. Already, gun smoke wreathed the battlements. Another defender was down, holding his shoulder from which blood seeped. The rest were firing, some shouting, others in grimly silent concentration.

"They're closing, sir," Abani Singh pointed to the enemy's left flank, where the men carrying branches were making progress. "We can't see the Afridis for the trees, so most of our shots are missing."

Andrew nodded. He could not commit any more men to the flank with the main Afridi attack on two walls. "Keep them firing, Havildar."

"Yes, sahib."

The Afridis' sniping was increasing as their marksmen crept closer to fire at the Sikhs. Another sepoy fell, shot through the forehead, and the Afridis gave a concerted roar and charged.

"Fix bayonets!" Andrew ordered. He glanced around the fort, ensuring the sentinels at the other walls remained on station and alert.

The Afridis surged forward behind their green flags, losing men to Sikh fire. On their left flank, those attackers carrying branches came within two hundred yards and stopped, throwing brushwood and thorn bushes before them.

"Marksmen!" Andrew shouted. "Fire at your targets!"

He saw a knot of Afridis around the first of the dummies' positions, looking confused and stabbing with their swords.

"Birjot Singh is dead, sir," Abani Singh reported.

Andrew nodded. Birjot Singh had been one of the marksmen. "Take his place, Havildar. Shoot the dummy through the heart."

"Yes, sahib!"

The first Sikh marksman fired. His shot missed, smashing into the rocks, and Abani Singh railed at him. The marksman reloaded, aimed and fired again. The bullet hit its mark, blowing up the packed explosive with a satisfying crump. Andrew saw the surrounding Afridis thrown aside as the pebbles he had placed around the charge acted like shrapnel.

"How did you like that then?" Innes asked. "How did you like that?"

The Afridi assault faltered but continued. The marksman fired again, hitting his target with the first bullet. The resulting blast threw a green flag into the air, with the ragged remains of the carrier blown apart. The explosion reduced other men to shreds, killed three outright and wounded another twelve.

I wish we had artillery, Andrew thought. *Every Afridi assault costs us men, and eventually, we'll be too few and too weak to repel them.*

"They're wondering where the explosions come from," Innes said. "They must think we have artillery."

Andrew nodded. "Havildar! Can you get a clear shot in?"

"No, sahib," Abani Singh said. "There are too many men in between."

"Fire when you can," Andrew ordered.

While the dummies distracted Andrew's attention, the Afridis intensified their left flank attack. They burrowed into cover and crawled forward, pushing the brushwood and branches before them.

"What's their plan?" Innes asked.

"I don't know," Andrew replied. "You know these people better than I do."

"I've never been inside a besieged fort before," Innes said.

The tom-toms continued to throb, now surrounding the fort. Andrew searched for the *mullah,* hoping for another shot. He could not see him.

The fire slackened as the attackers sought shelter, and the Sikhs had fewer targets.

"The explosions have confused them," Innes said.

"Temporarily, at least," Andrew said.

The Afridis' marksmen increased their fire, forcing the defenders to keep under cover. Simultaneously, the flank attack developed, with the Afridis moving forward one rock at a time, pushing the brushwood and branches before them.

When the Sikhs rose from the battlements to fire at the flank attack, the snipers opened concentrated fire to pin them under cover.

"One section!" Andrew ordered. "Get to the loopholes below and keep the flank attackers busy."

The Sikhs scrambled from the battlements, and shortly afterwards, Andrew heard them firing. The Afridis continued to ease forward, ignoring their casualties.

"They're getting very close," Innes said.

The Afridis had been quietly reinforcing the men on the flank until one man raised a green flag, and they yelled, "*Allah Akbar!*" and charged for the weakened corner of the fort. The Sikhs at the loopholes fired and reloaded as fast as possible, but the majority of the Afridis reached the walls. A ribbon of casualties lay on the ground, the corpses of brave men looking like bundles of dirty rags.

"I have it!" Abani Singh shouted and fired. He hit the fourth dummy, with the explosion throwing three Afridis into the air and scattering pebbles in a five-yard circle.

"*Shabash*, Abani Singh!" Andrew shouted.

Despite their losses, the Afridis poured against the fort. Thrusting their rifles through the loopholes, some fired at the defenders while others swarmed up the walls. Some hammered at the already weakened corner or prised the stones free, then pushed brushwood and branches inside the fort.

"Three Section!" Andrew roared. "Push these men back! Take over here, Innes!"

Andrew ran to the beleaguered corner with Three Section at his heels. The Afridis attacked in waves, firing through the loopholes, thrusting in brushwood and attempting to clamber up the walls. The Sikhs met them with musketry and bayonets, repelling the few who reached the battlements and firing down at the seething mass below.

Andrew did not see who started the fire as the brushwood inside the fort smouldered and burst into flames. Smoke gushed into the fort's interior, and the searing heat of the fire drove the defenders from the loopholes.

"They're trying to burn us out!" Innes shouted.

"Fire into the smoke," Andrew said.

The flames reached the fort's woodwork, scorching and then setting it afire. Andrew ordered his men to fire through the flames, not knowing how much damage they inflicted. Sepoys coughed, fired, rubbed streaming eyes, reloaded and fired again. Some of the fort's stones creaked and tumbled as the supporting woodwork caught fire.

"Keep firing!" Andrew ordered. "The Afridis have trapped themselves behind the flames." He drew his revolver and fired it into the fire, reloaded and fired another six quick shots.

I'd better be careful with my ammunition. Revolver bullets are scarce in the Khyber.

One Afridi burst through the flames with his clothes ablaze, screaming, "*Allah Akbar!*" Two Sikhs shot him, then plunged their bayonets into his body and returned to firing into the smoke and flames.

"They're coming out!" Innes shouted from the parapet.

Andrew heard the increased firing from the Sikhs, accompanied by shouts of triumph.

"*Jo Bhole So Nihal Sat Sri Akal!*"

"What's happening, Innes?" Andrew yelled.

"They're retreating!" Innes replied hoarsely. "The whole damned lot of them!"

"Send down one-third of your men," Andrew ordered. "We'll have to put out this fire before it spreads."

While the sniping duel continued, Andrew led half the garrison in fighting the fire.

Thank God we have a well, he thought as he organised a bucket chain. "Douse the flames before they spread. Soak the woodwork!"

"Sir!" Innes said. "One of the Afridis isn't dead yet."

"What?" Andrew looked up, dazed by effort and strain.

Innes looked equally tired. "One of the Afridis, sir. One we shot when they attacked the fort."

Andrew tried to make sense of Innes's words. Both men were past exhaustion, and they had difficulty communicating. "What about him, Lieutenant?"

"He's risen from the dead, sir, and he wants to see you." Innes hesitated. "He's asking for you by name, sir. In English."

CHAPTER 26

FORT RAZALI, KHYBER PASS, SUMMER 1897

A watchful Sikh prodded his bayonet into the prisoner's back and propelled him towards Andrew.

"Yes?" Andrew said.

"This Afridi asked to see you, sahib!" The Sikh slammed to attention. "Shall I kill him?"

"No, thank you." Andrew was unsure if the sepoy was serious, so he switched to Pashto. "Who are you, and what do you want from me?"

"Don't you recognise me, sir?" the Afridi said in English, removed his ragged turban and grinned.

Andrew started. "Good God! Symington! It's you!"

"That's right, Captain Baird," Symington smiled.

Andrew nodded to the sepoy. "Thank you, Chamanjeet Singh. This man is one of us. Please inform Lieutenant Innes I wish to see him."

"Sahib!" Chamanjeet Singh saluted and withdrew.

"Sit down, man," Andrew said to Symington. "How the devil did you get through the Afridis?"

"By becoming one of them," Symington replied. "It was the only way I could get close to the fort. Your Sikhs are shooting anything that comes within half a mile."

"Were you in the Afridis' last charge?" Andrew asked. "I am afraid I can't offer you much hospitality. The maid's burnt the toast." He nodded to a string of sepoys throwing buckets of water on the flames.

"You can't get the staff nowadays," Symington said, shaking his head. "Do you have something I can change into? Or somewhere I can wash? I am rather used to the itch, but I'd prefer to lose it."

Andrew nodded. "You'll have to put up with it a bit longer. We're rather busy at present."

"Give me a bucket then, and I'll lend a hand, as long as one of your boys doesn't put a bayonet through me. I had to play dead once already today, and I don't fancy trying it for real."

Lieutenant Innes rapped on the door and stepped inside. "You sent for me, sir?"

"I did. This scruffy gentleman is Second Lieutenant Symington. He'll be joining us for the foreseeable future."

"Welcome aboard, Symington," Innes grinned and held out a hand. "I hope you can keep the good ship Razali afloat."

"I'll do my best," Symington promised solemnly.

"Back to work!" Andrew ordered. "Get yourself a uniform and a bucket, Symington!"

The garrison took three hours to control the fire, and a third of the fort was damaged, fire-blackened, and uninhabitable.

Andrew and Innes surveyed the damage.

"How the devil can we defend this place now?" Innes asked.

"I don't know," Andrew replied, "but we'll have to try."

"We're not engineers. We don't know what damage the fire has done to the internal structure of the fort," Innes said. "Our men might stand on the wall only for it to collapse beneath them."

"We'll prop it up as best we can," Andrew said. "Get the lads working."

"Now?" Innes asked. "They've just repelled an attack and put out a fire."

"I know. Get the sepoys working. Check the supporting pillars and beams, use stones from less important areas of the fort, and build a barricade." Andrew gave rapid orders that saw tired men force themselves to continue working. "You too, Symington! Get to work!"

Smoke-blackened, exhausted, with one man in three wounded, the remaining Sikhs worked until the light faded, then lit fires and worked on. They cleared away the burnt and charred timbers, tested the walls and piled stones into the holes the Afridis had made. They rescued any enemy weapons and threw the enemy dead outside the walls. Andrew did not ask what happened to the Afridi wounded. He did not see any.

Cold moonlight glittered on the fort when Innes eventually stood in front of Andrew. "That's the best we can do, sir."

"Good man," Andrew replied. He looked around, nodding. "It will do for tonight. Get the men something to eat and a couple of hours' sleep." He swayed on his feet as exhaustion threatened to overcome him.

"You too, sir," Innes said. "I'll hold the fort here."

"Literally," Andrew said and staggered to his bed.

I hope whatever intelligence Symington gathered was worthwhile. I'll ask him tomorrow.

❄

Symington had retained his beard but looked quite presentable once he had washed and donned the uniform of the Khyber Rifles.

"Can you tell me what you have found?" Andrew asked. They sat in the smoke-blackened remains of Andrew's room, with the door open to allow relatively fresh air to enter.

"I can tell you a little," Symington said cautiously. "Most of my intelligence is for General Windrush."

Andrew filled the bowl of his pipe with tobacco and offered Symington a cheroot. The agent took it gratefully, lit up from the candle on the desk and inhaled.

"God, that's good. It's been a long time since I enjoyed one of these." He exhaled a ribbon of smoke.

"What can you tell me?" Andrew asked.

"You'll know by now that the tribes are up," Symington said. "You'll guess that somebody's stirring them into a *jihad*, a Holy War."

"We had a hairy *mullah* encouraging the men to throw themselves at our rifles," Andrew said.

"There are at least three *mullahs* preaching their hatred along the Frontier," Symington agreed. "That happens occasionally, but this affair appears more concerted."

"Do you think the Russians are behind it?" Andrew asked. "Remember the Russian cigarette end and pistol we found."

"They may be involved," Symington replied cautiously and smiled. He looked much older than the young actor who had campaigned to Chitral. "I am only one agent of many, Captain Baird. Do you know how intelligence gathering works?"

"I have done a little," Andrew admitted. "Tell me how you see it."

"Agents are all pieces of a jigsaw puzzle. We supply a little bit of information here and there, with no one piece making sense. Only when somebody puts the pieces together does the full picture emerge." Symington drew on his cheroot again. "God, I'd kill for bacon, eggs and devilled kidneys with a decent pot of tea."

"No bacon up here, old man," Andrew reminded.

"I know. It's the simple things one misses." Symington grinned, showing teeth stained by betel juice in a weather-tanned face. "As I was saying, we gather pieces without knowing if they are important or even if they are part of the same puzzle. Some fellow sitting at a large desk in a comfortable office will put the pieces together. He'll never get them all, but he'll have to guess what they mean, ascertain if they are a threat to us and work out a counter."

Andrew lifted his head as he heard something crash into the fabric of the fort. He guessed it was only an isolated shot and puffed at his pipe. "I presume General Windrush is the man at the large desk?"

"That's the fellow," Symington said. "Have you met him?"

"Once or twice," Andrew admitted. "What have you discovered that may affect this fort?"

Symington hesitated. "Fort Razali is not important in itself," he said. "The *mullahs*, and whoever is behind them, want to clear the entire Khyber."

"The Khyber is the main route from Afghanistan to India," Andrew said. "The route the Russians will come."

Symington nodded. "Unless we are fitting in pieces from more than one jigsaw and producing a completely different picture."

※

"Can you hear something?" Innes asked.

Andrew shook his head. "Only the wind." He looked over the fort, with the remnants of the garrison holding their positions, rifles ready. He had lost count of the attacks they had repulsed, knowing only that the ribbons of Afridi dead outside the walls spoke of the gallantry of the Sikh defenders. Smoke from the still-smouldering timber drifted over the walls and smudged the morning sky above.

"Are they coming again?" Andrew asked. He pushed a cartridge into the breech of his Martini.

"It's not that sort of noise," Innes replied.

"I can still hear the drums," Andrew said.

"Yes, sir," Innes replied. "There's something else."

"I hear it," Symington agreed.

Andrew could hear the drums throbbing around the fort and the intermittent gurgle from the nearby river. When Andrew concentrated, he could hear Chamanjeet Singh's low muttering as he intoned a prayer and Havildar Abani Singh as he railed at a man who had fired his cleaning rod during the last attack. Andrew looked upward, where a brace of vultures wheeled, hoping the squabbling humans would provide food in the shape of wounded or dead men.

"Maybe there is," Andrew said. "It's familiar, but I don't know what it is."

It was like a whisper in the wind, something ethereal, a sound like no other. Andrew listened and began to smile. "I know what that sound is," he said and recited part of a poem.

"Oh, they listened, looked and waited till their
    hope became despair;
And the sobs of low bewailing filled the pauses of
    their prayer.
Then upspake a Scottish maiden, with her ear
    unto the ground:
'Dinna ye hear it?—dinna ye hear it? The pipes of
    Havelock sound.'"

Innes stared at Andrew. "That's poetry, sir."

"It's from *The Pipes at Lucknow* by John Whittier," Andrew said. He grinned. "That's what we can hear, Highland bagpipes."

"Dear God in heaven!" Innes said. "Who?"

"Not Campbell anyway," Andrew said. "Or Havelock."

"Maybe the Afridis have learned how to play the pipes," Symington murmured.

"They're Highland pipes," Andrew said and raised his voice. "Bugler! Sound the Stand To! Get yourselves smarted up, men! We'll look like soldiers when the relief column marches in!"

Havildar Abani Singh ran around the men, shouting at them

to smarten up, rearranging a turban here, dusting down a ripped and smoke-blackened uniform there, and generally acting like every NCO in every army in the world.

Now that Andrew had identified the sound, he could hear the pipes clearly, even recognising the tunes. He climbed to the highest point of the fort and focused on the west, willing the column to come close.

He heard the crash of artillery and saw the orange-yellow flower of the explosions in the area where the Afridis had gathered under their green flags.

"That's a nine-pounder mountain gun," Innes said with satisfaction. He smiled as more explosions followed and then the distinctive crash of British volleys.

Andrew looked around the fort with its surviving Sikh defenders and thought of the men who lay in the makeshift hospital and morgue. "We'll take the dead home for burial," he said. "God knows what the Afridis would do to the corpses if we left them here."

Symington passed the news on to Havildar Abani Singh, who told his men.

"Here they come!" Innes shouted.

Andrew lifted his binoculars as men marched along the valley floor. He saw the pipers leading and grinned at the sight of a tall, kilted Highlander side by side with a diminutive, green-uniformed Gurkha, both playing the bagpipes.

Innes pointed to the hills on the opposite side of the pass. "There's fighting going on there, sir," he said.

Andrew lifted his binoculars and saw the puffs of smoke from gunfire and heard the crackle of musketry.

"Our side are clearing the Afridis away," Andrew said. "I don't know which regiments are involved."

Within half an hour, the leading elements of the column arrived at the fort.

"Open the gates," Andrew ordered.

The pipers put down their bagpipes and stood on either side of the gate as a party of mounted officers approached.

"Good afternoon, gentlemen," a tall, stern-faced colonel said. "I am Colonel Alan Webb of the Royal Malverns. Get your men ready to leave. We are evacuating the fort and returning to Peshawar."

CHAPTER 27

FORT RAZALI, KHYBER PASS, SUMMER 1897

"When are we leaving, sir?" Andrew asked.

"Immediately, Captain Baird," Colonel Webb said. "Haven't you heard the news?"

"We haven't heard anything for days, sir," Andrew replied. "We've been pretty busy with the Afridis."

Colonel Webb grunted. "I imagine so. The whole Frontier is on fire," he said. "Most Afridi clans, the Waziri, and no doubt the Orakzai and Yusufzai as well. Somebody's been stirring them up; the *mullahs* have been preaching a *jihad*, and the tribes are attacking our posts all along the border."

Damn and blast! The Russians have succeeded.

"Our Khyber Rifles deserted, sir," Andrew said. "And the Afridis captured Fort Roberts. Colonel Neville is dead." *I won't give the details of Neville's death yet.*

Colonel Webb nodded. "Most of the forts along the Khyber have fallen," Webb said tersely. "Yours is one of the few to hold out."

That's how the Afridis could gather so many men. They have nobody else to fight except us.

"Don't linger," Webb ordered. "We don't have sufficient men to hold back the entire Afridi and Waziri fighting force. We are only here to salvage what we can and relieve you. The general insisted we come this far."

"Which general?" Andrew asked.

"Windrush," Webb said. "He was certain you'd hold out despite what the viceroy believed."

"I'm glad he did," Andrew said.

"Sergeant Brown will take a section to help clear the fort," Webb said. "What's left of it!"

Sergeant Brown was a middle-height, middle-sized man with a row of medal ribbons and a square, tough face. "Tell me what you want, sir." He nodded to his men. "These lads are all right, sir, except Private Hobart."

A freckle-faced man at the rear grinned. "You love me, really, Sergeant!"

"Nobody loves you, Hobart. You're a lazy blackguard, a waste of the Queen's shilling and the worst shot in the army."

"Yes, Sergeant," Hobart agreed, "but you still love me."

"Get to work, you lazy bastard!" Sergeant Brown blasted him.

Innes had organised the garrison, who stood at attention in the courtyard, with the dead and wounded on charpoys and every man as smart as possible.

"Take them out, Lieutenant," Andrew said formally.

With two companies of Gordon Highlanders, two of the Royal Malverns and two of Gurkhas under Colonel Webb's command, together with a battery of four mountain guns, the column had pushed halfway through the Khyber Pass.

Webb mounted the fort's tower and scanned the surrounding heights with his binoculars. "I see the clans have gathered. We're not sufficiently strong to hold them back for long, Baird."

"No, sir. How about the forts that way, sir? Towards Afghanistan? Can we try and relieve them?"

Webb shook his head. "All under Afridi control," he said.

"The Khyber Rifles either fled or the Afridis overwhelmed them. You're the furthest-out fort to fly the flag."

"Could you give me twenty minutes, sir?" Andrew asked. "I'd like to give the Afridis a going-away present."

Webb hesitated, again scanning the surrounding hills. "Be quick, Baird. Once the Afridis work out how few we are, they'll be howling on our heels like a pack of wolves."

"I'll be as quick as possible, sir," Andrew promised. "Innes, march the men outside! Symington! You're with me!"

Andrew led Symington to the armoury as the column consolidated their position and fired a few artillery rounds to discourage the Afridi from interfering. Andrew led Symington to the armoury. He was thankful he had stored the captured ammunition on the opposite side of the fort to the fire. "I want this place rigged to blow up," Andrew said. "We've taken out all the captured rifles, but Colonel Webb doesn't want the ammunition in case it's unreliable."

Symington nodded in immediate understanding. "We could rig a fuse," he said. "Like the old matchlock *jezails*. How long do you want it to burn for?"

Andrew did a quick calculation. "Give the rearguard time to get clear," he said, "but not too long. I want the Afridis inside the fort, yet without time to find the fuse."

"About an hour after we've left?" Symington suggested. "I can't guarantee an exact time."

Andrew nodded. "That should do the trick. No more than an hour. The Afridis are clever blackguards."

"Colonel Webb is asking what's happening, sir!" Sergeant Brown ran into the fort. "He's looking a little impatient, sir."

"My compliments to the colonel," Andrew said. "We'll be ready in ten minutes. If Colonel Webb begins the withdrawal, we'll join the rearguard."

"Yes, sir!" Sergeant Brown saluted and hurried away. Andrew heard the hard rap of the mountain guns bidding the Afridis a fond farewell, followed by the wail of the pipes as the column prepared to withdraw. He watched Symington prepare the trap, light the fuse from his cheroot, and pile old charpoys to hide the trail.

"That should do the trick," Symington said.

"Come on then, Symington," Andrew ordered. He took a last look around the fort and neatly closed the door behind him as he left.

"My mother always taught me to leave the house tidy," he explained.

The Gordons, Malverns and Gurkhas commanded the heights on either side of the Khyber as the column made its slow retiral. Colonel Webb was a methodical commander who ordered his strong rearguard to keep in touch with the main body while two mountain guns hammered the tribesmen whenever they showed themselves.

"Leave nobody behind," Webb ordered. "We won't give the Paythans even the smallest of trophies."

When they passed Fort Roberts, Andrew saw the green flag flying above the parapet. "Could we fire a couple of rounds at the fort, sir? I hate to see that flag where ours should be."

"Nobody's occupying that fort," Webb replied. "Every warrior in the area was around your little command. You drew them to you like iron to a magnet."

"What happened to Fort Roberts' garrison, sir?" Andrew asked.

"We don't know yet," Webb replied. "I hoped you could tell us."

Andrew heard the explosion as his booby trap blew up. He stopped to look back, seeing a column of dirty brown smoke and dust rise hundreds of feet into the sky and a wide scatter of masonry and rubble.

"Let's hope a hundred Afridis were inside the fort," Innes said.

"And that crazed *mullah* preaching a *jihad*," Andrew added.

The mullah who claims to turn bullets to water and who I have twice had in my sights and failed to kill.

The column marched on, passing once-British-held forts that now displayed green flags or where smoke coiled from charred ruins.

"It's like the Mutiny again," Andrew said.

Colonel Webb shook his head. "No, Baird. It's not. It's religiously inspired nonsense, stirred up by fanatics and maybe somebody else."

"Somebody else?" Andrew repeated.

"I've heard reports about foreigners along the Frontier," Colonel Webb said.

Russians. Symington will give his information to Father, and he'll piece the jigsaw together.

Andrew heard musketry behind him and saw the rearguard was in action, firing at unseen assailants.

"Keep the column moving," Colonel Webb ordered. "Gunners! Give the rearguard a hand. Fire where you see any concentration of the enemy."

"Most of these men are new to India and have never been in action before," Webb explained. "This idea of men only serving for six years might keep the army's numbers up, but it deprives us of a hard core of experienced men."

"Yes, sir," Andrew agreed. Most of the Malverns and Gordons appeared very young, little more than boys, to pit against tribesmen who had fought blood feuds and invaders since childhood.

The column eased out of the Khyber, fighting a constant rearguard action against some of the best irregular warriors in the world. Webb oversaw everything, ensuring his most experienced officers and NCOs supervised the younger soldiers and nursed the griffins.[1]

---

1. Griffins: soldiers new to India.

As they neared the mouth of the Khyber, some of the younger men relaxed, believing the danger was past.

"We're nearly back," Symington said. "I am looking forward to a hot bath and a good breakfast." He laughed. "It will be good to be back in civilisation, sir!"

Andrew looked up as musketry broke out on the left flank.

"Here they come!" Sergeant Brown gave the order as a horde of tribesmen rushed the Malverns guarding the left flank. They overcame the rearmost section and surged to the column.

"Shoot those men!" Webb ordered, striding forward.

"With me, Three Section!" Sergeant Brown shouted. "Fix bayonets, lads!"

Private Hobart fired, missed, drew his bayonet and fitted it at the second attempt.

Andrew drew his revolver and fired at the onrushing Afridis. He shot the first, missed the second, saw Brown thrust his bayonet into a screaming *pulmar*-wielding *ghazi*, and then the surviving Afridis turned and fled, leaving five of their number on the ground.

"That was hot while it lasted," Andrew said, reloading his revolver. He turned to speak to Symington. "Symington?"

There was no reply and no sign of the agent.

"Symington!" Andrew yelled. He began to follow the retreating Afridis until Webb grabbed his shoulder.

"Stay here, Baird. I'm not going to the trouble of rescuing you only to have you get yourself killed."

"Yes, sir." Andrew watched the Afridis melt into the landscape.

When the column cleared the Khyber, Andrew stood with the rearguard and looked back. He saw a single green banner held above a group of tribesmen. When he focused his binoculars, he saw the red-bearded *mullah* in the centre of the group, with the tall man at his side.

I lost Symington. I killed a British officer, and the Afridis killed the man I was supposed to bring back.

❄

Elgin stood with his back to the window, frowning at Jack. "I specifically said we could not send a relief column along the Khyber, Windrush."

"You did, your Excellency," Jack agreed.

"Yet Colonel Webb led over eight hundred soldiers to relieve Fort Razali," Elgin said. "You allowed your personal feelings to interfere with a professional decision."

"I balanced my personal feelings with military necessity," Jack countered.

"I had in mind to advise the War Office to consider you for the post of Commander-in-Chief in India," Elgin said, "and that would mean you could rise to the very top of your profession."

"Thank you, your Excellency," Jack replied.

"I can no longer bring myself to give that advice," Elgin said.

"As you wish, your Excellency," Jack kept his voice level.

"You sent a column into the Khyber to save one man's life."

"There were forty-six men in Fort Razali," Jack said, "including a very valuable intelligence agent who unfortunately died in the withdrawal. We also restored some prestige after losing other Khyber forts."

Elgin leaned forward. "Would you have sent a column if your son had not been there?"

Jack did not have to consider his reply. "There is a tradition on the Frontier never to leave a man behind."

Elgin grunted and turned away. "You have damaged your career, Windrush."

"Perhaps so, your Excellency, but Colonel Webb's column saved valuable lives."

❄

"I lost Symington," Andrew said. "We were on the cusp

of success, and the Afridis overcame the flank guard and killed him."

Jack nodded. "Better dead than a captive."

"It was a disastrous mission," Andrew said. "I lost Symington, killed a British colonel and missed an agitator with an easy shot."

"Not all expeditions are successful," Jack reminded him. "Tell me about this *mullah*."

"He's a big man with a red beard," Andrew said. "I saw him in Chitral and again outside Fort Razali."

"Do you know his name?" Jack asked.

"No, but how did I miss?" Andrew asked. "I am a good shot, Father. I had the range correct and had the *mullah* square in my sights, yet I missed him twice. How?"

Jack shook his head. "These things happen," he said. "I've known a shell explode beside a section, killing every man except one, who was untouched. I've seen men fight with wounds that should have killed them, and others die when a shot passes close. There's no logic in war."

Andrew shook his head. "Some of the sepoys say the *mullah* has the power to turn bullets into water. My miss might increase that belief."

"Maybe," Jack conceded. "Or perhaps he didn't even know you shot at him." He shrugged. "How many Afridis shot at you when you were in the fort?"

Andrew shrugged. "I don't know. A few."

"A few," Jack repeated. "Let's say a dozen. A dozen of the best shots in Asia fired at you, and they all missed. That's equally illogical. Let it be, Andrew. You led your men, defended your fort through a difficult situation and survived. That is enough."

"And I killed a British officer," Andrew reminded.

"Colonel Neville would be grateful you saved him," Jack said. "As would I in his situation. War forces you to make impossible choices, and you saved that man from intense suffering."

Andrew looked away, reliving the memory.

Jack swirled his whisky around the glass. "Let's go over this,

Andrew. You have given me a lot of information about a man stirring up trouble in the Northwest Frontier."

Andrew nodded. "Men stirring up trouble, Father, not just one man. There are at least three *mullahs* up there and that tall fellow."

"Do you think the tall man was Russian?" Jack asked.

"Maybe," Andrew replied cautiously. "I don't have all the pieces of the jigsaw."

"Was that a hint?" Jack asked, smiling.

"Just a little nudge," Andrew replied.

"I like your jigsaw analogy," Jack said. "I don't have all the pieces yet, either."

"It's Symington's analogy, not mine," Andrew said. "And I lost him."

"Symington knew the risks better than anybody did," Jack said. "Nobody can blame you."

"I feel responsible," Andrew said.

"We always feel responsible for the deaths of men under our command, but Colonel Webb was in command of the column, not you," Jack reminded. "Don't mention Symington again. I only have sufficient jigsaw pieces to create a rough outline, with many crucial areas left blank. Some of the agents have brought no news, and a few have disappeared."

"Killed?" Andrew asked.

"Perhaps," Jack replied. "Maybe the Russians found them, or maybe they were just murdered by *badmashes*. Life is cheap beyond the Khyber."

Andrew nodded.

"Good, now go to your wife. Don't depress her with bad news, and that's a father's advice, not a general's order." He lowered his voice. "You may not have long with her, Andrew. The Frontier's ablaze."

※

JIGSAW ON THE KHYBER

Mariana juggled little Simla on her knee, smiling across at Andrew. "The newspapers all say you are a hero," she said.

"I'm no hero," Andrew told her.

Mariana laughed, tossing her hair back from her eyes. "Every single newspaper spoke of your heroism in defending Fort Razali."

"I only did my duty."

"Oh, you and your duty!" Mariana laughed.

Andrew held out his hands for little Simla. "It's good to be back," he said. "I haven't had baby sick on my shoulder for months."

"She's passed that stage now," Mariana told him. "She said her first word when you were away."

"What did she say?" Andrew asked.

"It sounded like Mhagha," Mariana replied, "but I am sure she was saying Mama."

"I am sure she was," Andrew said diplomatically.

"Come on, Andrew," Mariana patted his arm. "I'll take you to Peliti's Restaurant. My new friend Michael Sinclair wants to meet you."

"Who?"

"You remember him," Mariana said. "I told you about him in my letters. The writer fellow."

"Ah," Andrew nodded. "I've been looking forward to meeting him."

CHAPTER 28

SIMLA AUTUMN 1897

Andrew tapped on Jack's door, waited for permission to enter, and stepped inside.

Jack looked up from his desk, hastily removed the round-lensed spectacles perched on his nose and placed them in the top drawer. "I've changed my mind," he said abruptly.

"About what?" Andrew pretended not to have seen the spectacles. General officers required their vanity.

"I've changed my mind about the *Okhrana* stirring up trouble among the tribes and planning to assassinate the viceroy," Jack said. "Sit down."

Andrew sat and waited as Jack opened the whisky decanter and half-filled two glasses.

"I thought there was something wrong," Jack said. "In my previous dealings with the *Okhrana*, they were always very professional. Things were neat, clean and tidy. The men you met in Chitral seemed amateurish, leaving clues where you were bound to find them. The cigarette end, for instance; was he smoking a cigarette in Chitral? If so, he may as well proclaim he was a foreigner, for how many Chitralis smoke cigarettes?"

Andrew nodded. "I see," he said.

"The *Okhrana* would not make such a fundamental mistake," Jack said. "The pistol as well. Leaving it in a sangar for us to discover, with the *Okhrana* symbol plainly on the butt, was either rank amateur or coldly deliberate."

"Why?" Andrew asked.

Jack finished his whisky. "I can only think of one reason," he said. "Somebody wanted us to blame the *Okhrana*. They wanted to make us think the *Okhrana* was responsible for the troubles up the Grim[1] and the attempted murder of Lord Elgin."

Andrew sipped at his whisky. "Why? Who would do that?"

"I am not sure, although I have my suspicions," Jack said. "I am still fitting the pieces of your jigsaw together. As well as the too-obvious clues, there was the man who shot at you and missed three times, although he was only three hundred yards away with a clear field of fire."

"Maybe he was nervous," Andrew said.

"Maybe," Jack said. "I think he meant to miss."

"Why?" Andrew asked.

"I will come to that in a minute," Jack replied. "The next piece in the jigsaw was the bungled attempt to steal the Russian revolver from you. The *Okhrana* would never select an amateur to do a professional's job. Somebody sent that man to fail."

"Why?"

"To make you think you had gathered important information," Jack replied. "And when the supposed thief, Khattak, ended up in prison, somebody murdered him to prevent us from finding out more." Jack poured himself another drink. "They made a mistake there."

"Did they?" Andrew asked.

"Yes. It was a professional murder, as the Sikh warder told us. An ordinary prison murder would be messy and brutal. Whoever

---

1. Up the Grim: along the Northwest Frontier

murdered Khattak killed him swiftly and without effort." Jack shrugged. "Let's fit the jigsaw pieces together."

Andrew nodded, intrigued.

Jack tapped a finger on his desk. "You found the Russian cigarette end and the Russian revolver and heard all about the foreigner operating in one of our most vulnerable areas. Now, what conclusion did we draw?"

"That the *Okhrana* was stirring up trouble on the Frontier," Andrew said.

"We both believed the *Okhrana* was involved," Jack agreed. "We thought somebody tried to retrieve the pistol and tried to shoot you. Both attempts failed, but somebody intended to make you believe your information was valuable."

"Yes," Andrew said. "That's what I believed."

"I think there is a Russian involvement," Jack said. "Not the *Okhrana*, but a completely different organisation."

Andrew shrugged. "I am lost," he admitted.

"Have you heard of *Narodnaya Volya*?"

"No," Andrew said and considered for a moment. "I think I read about them in the newspapers. The name is vaguely familiar. Did they not assassinate the last Tsar?"

"They murdered Tsar Alexander II in 1881," Jack confirmed. "You were in Africa at the time, fighting the Boers. The *Okhrana* were supposed to have suppressed the organisation in the late 1880s, but there have been a few splinter movements since then."

"I know nothing about this sort of thing," Andrew admitted. "I have little interest in British politics, let alone Russian."

"Politics is a murky, ugly business," Jack said. "You'd best stick to honest soldiering and avoid politics. Cloak and dagger skulduggery is sordid and leaves one tainted."

"I came to India to show Mariana the sights," Andrew said. "Not to involve myself in Russian politics."

"It's too late to stop now," Jack said. "Once we start these things, we have to see them through to the end."

"What do you think is going to happen?"

"I believe the *Narodnaya Volya* intended to cause ructions at the Jubilee celebrations to create a rift between us and the Russian Empire. They want to bring down the Tsar, and what better way than to have him accused of murdering Lord Elgin in Simla and start a war."

"A war between us and Russia will cause thousands, maybe tens of thousands of casualties," Andrew said.

"Hundreds of thousands," Jack said soberly. "The Crimean War cost over five hundred thousand lives, and that was nearly fifty years ago, before magazine rifles and the Maxim machine gun." He was silent for a moment as the memories returned. "The good Lord save us from that sort of horror." Jack shook his head. "So far, you've only been in small wars, Andrew. Oh, they're brutal enough for anybody at the sharp end and terrible for those involved, but for casualties, they can't compare with Crimea or the Mutiny." He looked up, unsmiling. "I hope you never have to live through anything like that."

"So do I," Andrew agreed.

"Let's find out what's happening," Jack said, "catch these people and end this thing before it spreads."

"How can we catch them if we don't know who they are?" Andrew had never seen Jack so determined.

"I'd do anything to stop another major war, another Mutiny or Crimea," Jack said quietly. "These *Narodnaya Volya* people might well be fighting against the Tsar's oppression. That does not give them the right to stir up the Pashtun tribes and cause needless deaths in India."

"I agree." Andrew waited, knowing that his father had more to say. "They're certainly stirred up."

"The Mohmands, Orakzais and Afridis have attacked our posts and garrisons," Jack said quietly. "It's the Afridis I am most concerned about. They've been peaceful in the Khyber area for the last sixteen years, and suddenly, they attack forts manned by the Khyber Rifles, a unit we recruit from the Afridis. Now the

Pashtuns have demanded we withdraw all British forces from Swat and the Samana range."

"We've rejected these proposals, I hope," Andrew said.

"Yes," Jack replied. "And we are about to strike back on two levels. We're counterattacking militarily and with intelligence."

Andrew nodded. "Where am I going?"

Jack looked serious. "I don't like sending anybody into danger, Andrew, least of all you."

"I am a soldier," Andrew reminded him. "I must do my duty."

Jack sighed. "I know," he said. "I know that word only too well."

"Where will my duty take me?" Andrew asked.

Jack poured himself another drink, offered the decanter to Andrew and nodded when he refused. "It will take you into a place where angels fear to tread, a place that even the British army has never penetrated."

"That sounds interesting," Andrew began to fill his pipe. He pushed away the thought of Mariana and little Simla.

Jack pushed across a map of the Northwest Frontier and the border regions of Afghanistan. "Since you've lived on the Scottish-English Border, have you ever visited Liddesdale?"

The question was so unexpected it caught Andrew off guard. "Liddesdale? Southwest of Hawick?"

"That's the place," Jack said. "When Walter Scott's Border Reivers were rampaging around causing mayhem, Liddesdale was the worst valley in the Borders and maybe the most dangerous valley in Europe."

"If you say so," Andrew said. "Am I going back to Scotland?"

"No. You're going to the Frontier's equivalent of Liddesdale. We're going to see what's beyond the *Purdah nashin*, [2] what's concealed behind the curtain." Jack's grin took years off his age. "We're sending an expedition to the Tirah, the homeland of the

---

2. Purdah nashin: concealed behind the curtain.

Afridis, and we're going to teach them not to attack British forts on the Khyber."

Andrew took a deep breath. He had heard men talk about the Tirah around the campfires and in the darkest recesses of the forts. "The Tirah. I believe that no foreigners have ever been there."

"Only as prisoners," Jack said. "A ring of mountains surrounds it. Even when we send punitive expeditions against the Afridis, we don't venture beyond the Samana Range, the mountains that protect the Tirah Maidan."

Andrew nodded. "The Afridis are among the wildest of the wild tribes," he said. "It will be a tough campaign to invade their homeland."

"It will," Jack agreed. "I was with Wolseley when he penetrated the African forests to burn the Ashanti capital of Kumasi, and I fought at Suakin and up the Nile towards Khartoum. The Tirah is the same. We're sending a British army into a hitherto inaccessible country."

"We're gradually reducing the wild places, one by one," Andrew said.

"Think back to Liddesdale," Jack said. "It was once the wildest valley in Europe, but now it's one of the quietest. I like to think that the Frontier and Afghanistan will be the same in fifty years. A beautiful, peaceful place where people can sleep without fear of badmashes and raiders stealing their livestock, killing them and stealing their women."

"Do you think it will happen?" Andrew asked.

Jack smiled. "That's our mission out here, I think. Trying to bring peace to the world. Maybe that's what the Empire is for." He sighed. "Do you remember General Arthur Elliot? You met him a few times."

"I remember him," Andrew said.

"He once said the British Empire was here to fight some future evil, and when it defeats that evil, its reason for existence would have passed, and it would end."

"What will replace it?" Andrew asked.

"Maybe we will achieve peace in the world and bring these semi-savage people to a civilised state," Jack said. "Maybe our schools, hospitals, anti-slavery patrols and anti-pirate patrols will do some good. But in the meantime, we have another fight on our hands."

"Why have the tribes risen, sir? What lever did the *mullahs* or the Russians use?"

"I don't know what the *mullahs* said. I know the Durand Line upset them, and the *mullahs* exploited their upset." Jack shook his head. "They'll cause trouble and send the gullible or the young to their deaths while he'll be safely out of the firing line."

"Yes, sir," Andrew said.

"When you're in the Tirah, keep your eyes and ears open, Andrew."

"For the Russians?" Andrew asked.

"For anything untoward," Jack said. "Especially news of that tall troublesome fellow. And for God's sake, keep your head down."

"I'll do my best," Andrew promised.

Jack turned to a pile of papers on his desk. "Here are your official documents telling you where to go and when to attend. Say goodbye to your wife and daughter first."

"I will, sir," Andrew said.

※

ANDREW READ HIS ORDERS WHILE TRAVELLING TO KOHAT TO join General Sir William Lockhart's Tirah Field Force.

"You will take command of the Mounted Infantry in Tirah and search for any outside interference while also aiding General Lockhart in reducing the Afridis.

At last! Command of my own mobile force. No more crawling along, obeying other men's orders, or staying static within the walls of a fort. I will be free to roam with an independent command."

CHAPTER 29

NORTHWEST FRONTIER, AUTUMN 1897

"You are Captain Baird." Heavily built, with a fine moustache and hard eyes, Lockhart possessed a Scottish accent as evident as the chest full of medals indicating service from the Mutiny, Bhutan, Abyssinia, and the Black Mountain Expedition.

"Yes, sir," Andrew admitted.

"I remember you from Burma," Lockhart said. "You were in the forefront of the Irrawaddy Flotilla all the way to Mandalay."

"I was there, sir," Andrew admitted. "I never served directly under you."

Lockhart scrutinised Andrew's medals. "You also served in Africa," he said. "And you were on Kelly's Chitral expedition, I believe."

"Yes, sir," Andrew said.

"As a mounted officer, Baird, you are allowed one mule for baggage," Lockhart said. "You may have heard that I am keen on scouting and outposts, which comes in handy in wild country."

"Yes, sir," Andrew agreed.

"You'll have done your share in South Africa," Lockhart continued.

"I did, sir."

Lockhart nodded. "You have command of our unit of Mounted Infantry, Captain. I will use your MI to scout and support the infantry. I know General Windrush has also given you other orders, which are subordinate to my requirements while you are under my command."

"I understand, sir," Andrew said. "However, I must still pursue my other duties."

"You are free to do so, Captain, after you complete your duties with me." Lockhart leaned forward. "I have some good fighting regiments in this force, Baird, but people with fine scouting experience are hard to find. I knew your record and requested you in my force."

"Thank you, sir," Andrew said.

"Some of the MI are raw and will need careful handling," Lockhart said. He prodded a finger at Andrew's medal ribbons. "These may help, but your personality will be as important as your rank with such men. Do you understand?"

"I do, sir," Andrew said. "The MI are not easily impressed."

"Exactly so," Lockhart said. "Can you handle them?"

"Yes, sir," Andrew nodded.

"I hope so," Lockhart eyed Andrew for a few moments. "You had a good name in Burma, Baird, and I know your father." He nodded. "Dismissed. Now make yourself known to your MI and tell them what you expect of them."

Lockhart had two divisions to invade the Tirah, with British battalions among the mainly Indian and Gurkha force. With over 34,000 men, including supporting brigades and reserves, Lockhart faced around 50,000 Afridi and Orakzai tribesmen on their own ground. A further twenty thousand camp followers and a mobile field hospital accompanied Lockhart's fighting men.

Andrew toured the camp, remembering Chelmsford's

column advancing into Zululand and the invasion that ended with the victory of Ulundi. The small numbers involved in the Boer War paled by comparison, while Andrew's experiences in the Burma War had mainly been along the River Irrawaddy. He was impressed by the quality of support Lockhart had for the infantry. Two squadrons of cavalry, a Gatling gun detachment, four batteries of screw guns, and companies of Pioneers completed the force.

Andrew smiled at the wail of the pipes, remembering the Gordon Highlanders and Gurkhas relieving Fort Razali. He saw the orderly lines of the Royal Malverns, wondered if he should introduce himself, but decided his MI took priority over everything else.

Lockhart had given Andrew the paperwork for the Mounted Infantry, which he scrutinised before he took them over. Each man had completed the two-month course at the Mounted Infantry School at Poona, and Andrew studied their certificates, Army Form B.2078, supplied *gratis* by a benevolent War Office.

Andrew checked the qualifications against each man's name. The certificates had four columns on the front: Riding, Stable Duties, Mounted Infantry Duties and Remarks, with explanations at the back of the form. The qualifications for Riding rose from Bad to Very Good, with most of his men being in the lower half, Indifferent or Fair. The instructors had also marked them as Indifferent for Stable Duties, and Quick, the lowest level, for Mounted Infantry Duties, with a few exceptions. The remarks column included such comments as "not willing to work" or "tries hard without success." Only one man, Sergeant Brown of the Malverns, had better qualifications, with "Section Leader" and "Intelligent" after his name. Private Hobart, from the same unit, was consistently poor, having the lowest qualifications in every column.

I have a lot of work to do here, Andrew told himself.

The Mounted Infantry had camped slightly outside the main camp and looked up without interest as this unknown officer arrived. Andrew watched them for a while, then changed his horse. He had brought Tweed and Teviot, preferring to work with horses he knew rather than find an expensive, if more powerful, charger.

"Come on, Teviot," Andrew spoke to his horse. "Let's show these lads what we can do."

He remembered his father's teachings when he first learned to ride many years ago. "If you're going to jump, throw your heart over first, and the horse will follow."

Andrew rode Teviot around the irregulars' camp, getting their attention, and then increased his speed. When he knew most were watching, he jumped over fallen logs or any other obstacle, swung from the saddle to land beneath the horse, dismounted and mounted on the move and came to a sudden standstill in a cloud of dust.

Andrew did not like showing off but knew he must make an instant impression.

"My name is Captain Andrew Baird," he told them. "I am in command of this unit of Mounted Infantry."

The men looked at him, some suspicious, a few smiling, others impassive.

"We are riding into the Tirah to face the Afridis in their homeland. Are there any questions?"

The men looked at him, a mixture of all the British regiments in Lockhart's command plus a few others that Andrew did not recognise. He allowed them a few moments to observe him before he spoke again.

"How many of you are proficient on horseback?"

Some of the men raised a hand; others slowly shook their heads.

"How many volunteered for the MI?"

As Andrew expected, the better horsemen raised their hands. He guessed the others were the unwanted, the bad characters and the useless. He nodded.

"Well, men, before I am finished with you, everybody will be at least proficient. We're headed into some wild country, and the better horsemen and soldiers you are, the more efficient a unit we will be, and the better chance of all of us coming out alive."

He moved slightly, allowing the sun to highlight his medal ribbons. He saw some of the older men narrowing their eyes, working out his campaigns.

"We'll begin with basic horsemanship and marksmanship," Andrew said, "and see how good you all are."

There were twenty-five Mounted Infantry, with one sergeant and a corporal. Andrew led them on a small route march to assess their skills. He sighed as one man did not know how to mount his horse; two fell off within the first half mile, and he despaired when most failed to keep up. He led them to a plain where kites circled above, and people watched curiously from a small village.

"You're not very good yet," Andrew told his MI. "Let's start with getting to know your horses." He spent the remainder of that day practising mounting and dismounting until even Private Hobart could get on his horse without swearing and gasping. In the evening, Andrew showed them how to groom and feed the horses, ensured each man had an individual mount and told them they were a unit.

"Man and horse together," Andrew said. "You are like man and wife, except without the arguing." He waited for the rueful laughter from the married men and continued, "Or the other thing." That brought more laughter and a few comments he chose to ignore.

Andrew was unsure how much time he had to train his MI, so he crammed as much as possible into every day. After his experiences in Chitral, he was glad Lockhart had armed the MI with rifles rather than short-range carbines, even though the latter were handier on horseback.

"We have the Lee-Metford rifle," Andrew addressed his men, displaying a Lee-Metford for all to see. "Some of you will be familiar with this weapon; others will not. It is slightly longer than the old Martini-Henry, which has served us well, and fires a rimmed .303 bullet rather than the .45, so it has slightly less stopping power."

He saw the interest in some of the older men, while Hobart smiled at some private joke in his head.

"However," Andrew said. "These disadvantages are more than offset by three things." He paused for effect. "Firstly, the Lee-Metford does not jam as often as the Martini. Those of you who have been in action understand the feeling when a dozen Zulus or *ghazis* are charging towards you, screaming their heads off and waving spears or swords, and your Martini refuses to fire. There is less chance of that happening with this little girl."

The veterans nodded, and some even mustered a smile.

"Second is the kick. The Martini's recoil bruised shoulders after only a dozen shots. I've known men change their shoulders from right to left purely to ease the bruising, with consequent deterioration in their marksmanship. The Lee-Metford kicks less and is easier to fire."

Some of the men looked restless. Andrew came to his final point.

"Lastly, and most important, the Lee-Metford is a bolt-action rifle with a box magazine invented by the Scottish-born American James Lee, with a rifling design by the Englishman William Metford." Andrew showed his men how to load the magazine and work the bolt.

"The magazine holds ten cartridges; a decent soldier can fire twenty-five rounds a minute. Those of us who have been in action know how important an increased rate of fire can be." He acknowledged the nods of the veterans. "It also means we can use up our ammunition faster, so be careful not to overuse the bolt action."

With the theory complete, Andrew took his men on firing drill, ensuring they knew how to use the bolt action, aim, and fire at a static target. Most were proficient shots, so Andrew advanced quickly to firing at moving targets, distance shooting, and firing up and downhill. He did not expect Hobart to hit anything, and his expectations were proved correct.

"Your range is up to 2,900 yards," Andrew told them, "more than twice the old Martini and more than anything the Afridis have." He made them practise long-distance shooting, and two men proved to be outstanding shots. One was a veteran named Pearson, and the other was a young troublemaker named Moffat, whom the Gordons had been glad to push onto the MI.

"What were you before you joined the army, Moffat?" Andrew asked.

The youth looked away. "Nothing much, sir," he mumbled.

Andrew looked at his tanned face and hands. "You're no city boy, that's for sure. If you were, the sun would burn you to a crisp. You worked outdoors."

Moffat smiled as if at some secret joke. "I was outdoors a lot, sir," he agreed.

Andrew understood. "Did a magistrate send you into the army?" he asked.

Moffat grinned and nodded. "Yes, sir. He gave me the choice of the Gordons or the jail. I chose the Gordons."

"And you've been the bane of your NCOs and officers ever since," Andrew hardened his voice. "You were a poacher, weren't you?"

"Yes, sir," Moffat was a lean, lithe man of eighteen with a long, mobile face and darting eyes.

"Well, Moffat, as of today, you are a scout and marksman with the Mounted Infantry. I will put you in for your marksman badge, which means extra pay." Andrew leaned closer. "And if you give me any trouble, even one little whiff of trouble..." He tried to dream up a threat to frighten this man. "Do you know your Bible, Moffat?"

"No, sir," Moffat said.

"Find one," Andrew said. "And read about Uriah the Hittite."

With Moffat looking confused, Andrew returned to training

his men. He had limited time to teach them the intricacies of scouting and mounted operations, so he drove them hard.

"We are Mounted Infantry," Andrew reminded. "Not cavalry. We do not charge into battle waving bayonetted rifles like lances." He held up the new, shorter leaf bayonet. "I prefer the older eighteen-inch bayonets anyway. We ride when we scout, ride to battle and fight on foot."

Teaching a mainly city-bred unit how to scout in the wilds was one of the hardest things Andrew had ever done. He showed them how to keep under cover and avoid showing themselves on the skyline. He taught them how to look for objects that moved against the wind. He ordered them to remain still even when insects were crawling across their faces and snakes coiling past their legs. And finally, Andrew showed them how to communicate with hand signals rather than speech.

"That's the basics," Andrew said. "We're going against experts in their homeland. They will know every square inch while we feel our way. You'll need to be at your best all the time."

The Mounted Infantry nodded.

"One more thing," Andrew said. "Don't get captured, and don't allow the Afridis to capture any of us."

"Will you shoot us if you do, sir?" Moffat asked, with his eyes challenging.

Andrew felt the sudden tension. He knew that the story of him killing Colonel Neville had spread.

"I will say this," Andrew replied. "If the Afridis are about to skin me alive, I hope you shoot me."

The veterans nodded, and even Moffat and Hobart looked thoughtful.

"That's all. Feed and groom your horses, men, and get some rest. We're off first thing tomorrow."

CHAPTER 30

NORTHWEST FRONTIER AUTUMN 1897

"Sir!" Lieutenant Innes threw a smart salute. "General Lockhart ordered me to report to you."

Andrew restrained his smile. "What the devil for?"

Innes remained at attention. "General Lockhart has sent me to join the Mounted Infantry, sir."

"God help us," Andrew said. "Why did he pick you?"

"Probably because I volunteered, sir," Innes replied.

"I thought so," Andrew nodded. "Welcome, Hugh."

"Thank you, sir," Innes allowed himself a smile.

"Come and meet the men."

Innes and the MI viewed each other, with Innes showing his enthusiasm and the troopers appearing dispassionate, although Andrew knew they would discuss their new officer at great length later.

"I hope your riding skills are better than most of the MI," Andrew said as they walked to the horse lines to inspect their mounts.

"Passable, sir," Innes said. "I know how to ride."

Andrew grunted. "That's a good start," he said. "Have you any news for me?"

"Yes, sir," Innes said. "The *mullahs* have made a new claim to cause trouble."

"Have they?" Andrew said. "What are they saying this time?"

"Many centuries ago, before even Lord Roberts was born, a holy and honourable man named Sheikh Mali Doba blessed a red-and-green flag and stuffed it in an earthenware pot, which he promptly buried somewhere in the Tirah."

"Ah!" Andrew said, nodding solemnly. "That's the sort of thing Sheikh Mali would do."

Innes laughed. "Stop mocking my story, sir, or I won't tell you the rest."

Andrew held up his hands. "I won't say another word, Lieutenant," he promised.

"The good sheikh said that in a time of terrible trouble, away in the future, the Afridis could dig up the flag, which would show them if their tribe would survive." Innes paused, waiting for Andrew's comment.

Andrew nodded, saying nothing.

Innes continued. "Well, sir, with the *mullahs* and whatnots stirring up trouble all along the Frontier, the Afridis dug up the pot containing the flag a few weeks ago. As the contents were sacred, Said Akbar, one of their greatest religious leaders, held a large ceremony with all the Afridi tribes present. They gathered with their tribal standards, making a great circle around the pot with all the tribal standards waving and the holy men doing whatever holy men do."

Andrew nodded, hiding his impatience as he inspected each horse.

"Said Akbar sacrificed nine cows, sir," Innes said, "and splattered their blood over the pot."

Andrew listened, remembering the fanaticism with which the Afridis attacked Fort Razali. He put a horse aside for the farrier to reshoe.

Innes smoothed his hand over a horse's withers and nodded his approval. "When Said Akbar spattered the blood, the pot shattered, and everybody saw the flag. Somebody, I don't know who, hoisted the sacred flag, and all the tribal standards bowed down to it, which was an obvious sign the Afridis would defeat us." Innes glanced at Andrew. "That's the story going through the Peshawar bazaars, sir."

Andrew sighed. "It's a bit scary that at the end of the nineteenth century, people still believe this superstitious rubbish," he said. "The *mullah* who faced us promised he could turn bullets into water, and hundreds of brave men ran into our musketry. They died for nothing."

"Yes, sir," Innes agreed.

Andrew led two horses to the farrier. "Come to my tent, and I'll show you where we're going."

Innes waited until Andrew produced a map of the Tirah and spread it on the ground, weighing down the corners with rocks.

Innes shook his head. "Information is a bit scanty, isn't it? There's not much there."

"Nobody's been there to make maps," Andrew said. "The Afridis don't need them and probably would not understand them anyway."

Innes grinned. "This looks like fun," he said.

"That's one way of viewing it," Andrew said. "General Lockhart wants the Mounted Infantry to help fill in the gaps. We'll be explorers as much as soldiers in this campaign in one of the most hostile areas of the world." He mustered a smile. "We're in the advance guard, Innes; first in, last out. Welcome to the MI."

Innes nodded. "Thank you, sir."

At the beginning of October, Andrew mustered his MI, placing them in a semicircle with Sergeant Brown at one end and Innes at the other. The men sat on their horses, rifles in bucket holsters, and their faces composed, waiting for Andrew to speak.

"We're going into the Tirah with the advance guard, men, so

watch out for ambushes and anything that doesn't look right. If you are in doubt, ask Sergeant Brown, Lieutenant Innes, or me."

The men nodded.

"Anything you see might mean the difference between life and death, and I'd rather we inspect something that turns out to be a false alarm than ignore a half-hidden Afridi with a rifle and a grudge."

Some of the men smiled.

"Our first destination is Shinwara," Andrew said. "All right, boys, column of twos and follow me."

Andrew looked over Lockhart's column. He heard the Gordons' pipes, and those of the King's Own Scottish Borderers and saw the sturdy Gurkhas in their green uniforms, kukris bouncing at their hips. Andrew looked for the Sikhs and wondered if he knew any of the men who marched steadily to Shinwara.

I wouldn't like to fight a campaign without the Sikhs at my side.

The Royal Malverns, Dorsets, and Devons plodded along manfully, griffins new to India and the Frontier, yet each man was determined to do his best. The troops kicked up dust that rose all around them, covering uniforms and pith helmets, boots and faces, seeping into eyes, nostrils, ears and mouths. Dust hid the lower half of the Indian cavalry, so their long lances seemed to protrude from a khaki haze, each with a drooping, dusty pennon.

Andrew heard the rattle-clank of the mountain guns and saw the gunners riding alongside. Strings of imperious camels padded along with the marching infantry, each laden with ammunition, fodder, or supplies for the advancing army.

There is glory in this scene. The Afridis have declared war on us, and they won't like the response.

Andrew led the Mounted Infantry in the van of the column, the leading man of the Queen-Empress's response to the Afridis' attack on her peace. He was experienced in scouting in Southern Africa, but India had different rules and tactics. Every night,

Andrew spoke to the Indian officers, picking up hints and friendly advice, and every day, his men gained experience, becoming more competent as they pushed into the tangled, ragged hills that fringed Tirah.

"Watch for movement on the hills," Andrew advised his men. "Anything that shifts against the wind. Look for rising dust or the flash of sunlight on metal."

The MI learned, the best of them listening, picking up lore from Andrew and the Indian regiments, with the others catching up as best they could.

The Afridi watched them come. Andrew saw men on the hills, waiting at extreme rifle range or out of range. The Afridis allowed themselves to be seen, and Andrew knew they were there, counting Lockhart's men, assessing the danger and gathering their forces.

After three days, Andrew thought his MI troopers were sufficiently experienced to move independently and he led them on the flank of the army.

"Extended order, boys," Andrew ordered. "Keep within five yards of one another, and don't stray. If we bunch up, we offer the Afridis a perfect target, and if we ride alone, we're vulnerable to capture."

The MI rode on, with Andrew nearly tasted the hostility in the air. The villages were typically Pashtun, with high walls, heavy locked gates, and a watchtower glowering over the surrounding countryside.

When they approached the first village, Andrew called his men together. "Ensure your rifles are loaded, boys, and be ready to retaliate." The tribesmen on the watchtowers watched them through brooding, impassive eyes, tall, lean Pashtuns with untidy turbans and rifles held in experienced hands.

I wonder what these lads are thinking when we invade their supposed inviolate homeland.

As the villagers did not respond to the MI, Andrew rode past, cautious but without firing. He lifted a hand to acknowledge the watchmen, who stared at him without moving. The solid wooden gate was closed, with a drift of smoke from cooking fires coming from within the village. Andrew sensed a dozen eyes watching him and forced himself to ride slower. His men, normally talkative, were strangely subdued.

That's no bad thing. The lads are learning.

"What do we do, sir?" Innes asked. Andrew noted the flap of his holster was unbuttoned, ready for a quick draw.

"We scout, Lieutenant," Andrew replied. "We report on the size of the village and the number of armed men we see, and we only fight if they attack us or General Lockhart orders us in."

"Yes, sir," Innes replied.

The MI filed past a hundred yards distant with Andrew ordering them to treat the fields and crops with respect.

"Ride around the fields, lads, not through the grain." *The harvest must be late this year.*

Other villages proved equally unresponsive, and then Lockhart's army reached the first major obstacle, a savage pass that marked the doorway of the Tirah.

A unit of the Guides were first to reach the heights, with Andrew's Mounted Infantry only an hour behind. They were ahead of the advance guard, with Lockhart's main body with the supplies and the bulk of the men half a day's march behind.

"What's this place called?" Innes asked.

Andrew studied the map each morning so he had an idea of the terrain. Nevertheless, much of his patrolling consisted of correcting the cartographers' discrepancies and adding features and villages to the rough blanks.

"This is the Dargai Heights," Andrew said. He paused to scan the Heights with his binoculars, for the name sent a chill through him.

Something has either happened or will happen here. I can sense it. My Windrush blood is tingling.

After generation after generation of military service, the Windrush men had developed a feeling for trouble. Until recently, Andrew thought the skill had passed him by, but something about this Northwest Frontier awakened the old genes.

"Do we go up, sir?" Innes asked hopefully.

"We report back to the brigadier," Andrew replied. "And wait for orders."

Andrew reported to Brigadier Kempster, who ordered the MI to scout towards the left flank and keep back any enemy.

"Hold that ridge, Baird," Brigadier Kempster indicated a partially wooded ridge that extended from the heights, "and signal if you see anything hostile."

"Yes, sir," Andrew led his men out. The ridge was long and rugged, with topes of scrubby trees and a wide view to the west.

"Dismount, hobble the horses and let them graze," Andrew ordered. Every fourth man was a horseholder, ordered to look after the horses when they dismounted. Andrew had chosen the least effective men as horseholders. "The rest, watch all around, keep under cover and be ready for snipers."

Andrew positioned his men in small, mutually supporting groups, found a prominent spot to supervise, and set up his heliograph.

"Now we watch and wait," he said. "Innes, take the left flank. Sergeant Brown, take the right. Send a runner to me immediately if you see anything."

Andrew lifted his binoculars and scanned the land in front, watching for movement. He heard voices behind him, swivelled and saw the 3rd Gurkhas advancing against a small village. When the inhabitants resisted, firing from the walls and tower, the Gurkhas opened into extended order and charged, with one company giving covering fire.

"*Jai Mahakali, Ayo Gorkhali!*" the Gurkhas shouted, "Victory to Goddess Mahakali, the Gurkhas are coming!"

Andrew watched, impressed, as the Gurkhas swarmed over the wall and into the village. He heard the rattle of musketry but forced himself to return to his duty of guarding the flank.

He heard shouting and firing behind him, a single terrifying cry of "*Ayo Gorkhali!*" and, moments later, silence. When Andrew glanced over his shoulder, he saw Gurkhas standing on top of the tower and knew the village was in Lockhart's hands.

Overlooking the village and dominating the route into Tirah, the Dargai Heights towered over the column. The Heights commanded the left flank of the road into the Chagra Valley, Lockhart's first objective.

We'll have to capture the Heights next, Andrew told himself. *That won't be easy. If the Afridis are as tactically alert as I think they are, they'll have a strong garrison up there.*

Andrew watched as the Gurkhas and the King's Own Scottish Borderers prepared for the assault. Andrew knew the KOSB had won laurels for their part in Low's advance during the Chitral Expedition and were experienced in Frontier warfare, while the Gurkhas had the reputation of being amongst the best soldiers in the world.

Andrew watched as the Borderers and the Gurkhas swarmed up the Heights. He heard the distant popping of musketry and saw puffs of smoke as the Afridis fired on the attackers. A handful of the Gurkhas and Borderers fell; the remainder swarmed up, pushing the defenders aside.

Within half an hour, the Gurkhas and Borderers captured the Dargai Heights and signalled for ammunition and supplies to consolidate the position.

"What's happening, sir?" Innes asked.

"I am not sure," Andrew replied. "We'll sit tight and wait for orders."

Six hours after the Borderers and Gurkhas captured the Heights, they withdrew, as the advance guard lacked the ammunition, food and water to supply them.

"Logistics," Andrew told Innes. "Logistics are as vital in war as intelligence of the enemy's position and morale for the fighting men."

As the advance guard waited for supplies and ammunition from the main body, the Afridis and their Orakzai allies gradually reoccupied the Heights, with a profusion of tribal standards erupting from the top.

"Now we have to do the whole thing all over again," Andrew said. "And this time, the Afridis will be ready and waiting for us."

Innes nodded. "Will we be involved, sir?" he asked as Sergeant Brown stamped his boots on the ground and eyed the Heights through narrow, cynical eyes.

"That depends on the Brigadier," Andrew replied.

The Mounted Infantry remained on their ridge for two days, camping overnight and watching the flank. Andrew had flashed heliographic reports every two hours, mainly negative, but with an occasional warning of groups of warriors advancing to strengthen the Pashtun position on the Dargai Heights.

"How many Afridis are on the Heights now, sir?" Innes asked.

Andrew scanned the Heights with his binoculars. "I'd say at least five thousand. Maybe more," he replied. "I count eighteen standards."

Innes focused his binoculars. "I'd say nineteen standards, sir, and a whole host of men. It will be a hard fight to take it now."

"Let's hope the guns can make a difference," Andrew said. "I'd hate to fight without the artillery. The guns make all the difference in the world."

The MI watched Lockhart's main body trundle up, with the guns in the van and the infantry slogging behind through a curtain of dust. The supply wagons and all the paraphernalia an Indian army needed followed behind, with a strong escort.

"Sir!" Sergeant Brown pointed to his front. "I saw movement in that tope, sir."

Andrew lifted his binoculars and nodded. A powerful body of Afridis had occupied the tope, five hundred yards from the ridge. "Keep watching them, Sergeant. If they come any closer, let me know." He turned to Jamieson, the signaller. "Send a message to the Brigadier: company of Afridis five hundred yards from ridge."

Jamieson nodded. "Yes, sir." He bent to the heliograph and began flashing the message across.

As Andrew watched the tope, Lockhart had deployed his eighteen nine-pounder mountain guns and opened fire. The sound of artillery was reassuring, and Lockhart's men watched the explosions flaring on the crest of the Dargai Heights.

Andrew watched through his binoculars. "The artillery is firing shrapnel," he said. He saw the shells bursting above the Afridis' sangars, with the green banners waving in defiance and warriors appearing on the skyline, waving weapons. "They'll be screaming Allah Akbar, like as not," Andrew said, returning his attention to the tope.

Three Pashtun warriors stalked towards the ridge, with others lingering at the fringes of the trees.

"Sir!" Moffat nodded to the oncoming men. "Shall I shoot them?"

"Not yet," Andrew replied. "Let them fire first. Keep them covered."

The MI settled down, aiming their rifles. Andrew wanted to see how his men acted in a fight yet did not want to begin a skirmish. He watched the Afridis striding purposefully towards the ridge, knowing three men were no threat to his MI.

Behind Andrew, the British artillery continued to hammer the Dargai Heights, with the explosions raising a cloud of mixed dust and smoke.

"They're getting closer, sir," Brown warned.

"What the devil are these three doing?" Andrew asked. He raised his voice and shouted. "Halloa! Who are you?" repeating the words in Urdu and Pashtu.

The three men stopped as if surprised to be addressed. One raised a hand in greeting. "Why are you in Tirah?" he asked.

"To teach you not to attack British possessions," Andrew replied.

"We will kill you all," the Afridi said.

"We will not let that happen," Andrew told him.

"We are not afraid of death," the Afridi said. "When unbelievers die, they go to hell. When the true believers die as martyrs, we go to Paradise where *houris* await us."

"Do the *houris* have any choice in being there?" Andrew asked.

"They are blessed with the presence of a martyr," the man replied. Andrew estimated his age as at least sixty, with a henna-dyed beard and a wrinkled, scarred face. He wondered that any woman, let alone a beautiful, doe-eyed *houri*, would welcome the presence of such a man.

"Do they choose such an honour?" Andrew asked.

The Afridi looked confused. "Why would they choose anything else?" he countered.

"Sir! On the right!" Sergeant Brown shouted. While Andrew and the elderly Afridi had been talking, more tribesmen had left the copse to creep closer to the ridge.

"Order your men to withdraw," Andrew said. "Or my men will shoot."

"More martyrs for Paradise," the elderly man said, lifted his hand and shouted, "*Allah Akbar!*"

The tribesmen echoed the elderly man's shout and charged forward, yelling.

Andrew sighed. "All right, Sergeant! Send them back. Innes: stand firm and don't get involved."

The Afridis are testing us to count our numbers.

Brown's section opened fire. For most of them, it was the first time they had fired their Lee-Metford rifles against an enemy, and the first volley was ragged. Brown shouted angrily, and the next volley was more controlled, with bullets kicking up dust and fragments of rock from the ground.

Andrew saw two Afridis crumple, and the others seemed to merge with the ground as they returned fire. Brown was issuing crisp orders, with his section now firing independently. The magazine rifles gave them a rate of fire the Afridis could not match, and they gradually pushed the enemy back.

Andrew did not interfere, measuring the sergeant's performance. He nodded as the surviving Afridis withdrew, carrying their dead and wounded. The elderly man with the henna-dyed beard lay still, his wish of martyrdom granted.

I hope you get your houris, old fellow, Andrew thought.

"Cease fire!" Sergeant Brown ordered, and peace descended on the ridge. Andrew ordered the signaller to heliograph the events to Brigadier Kempster.

As the MI emerged victorious from its skirmish, the bombardment of the Dargai Heights continued. Andrew saw the plume of dust and smoke where the shells had landed, but the green standards still stood defiantly, and now Andrew heard musketry as well. Focussing his binoculars on the Heights, he counted twenty-nine flags thrusting from the ridge.

"A message from General Lockhart, sir," Jamieson said. "The enemy includes the Ali Khel, Mamuzai and Alisherzai Orakzais, Malikdin Khel, Kambar Khel, Kamrai, Zakha Khel, Sipah and Kuki Khel Afridis."

"Thank you, Jamieson," Andrew said. *Half the clans of the Afridis must be represented on the Heights.*

"Sir, the general says there are up to twelve thousand Paythans, mainly Afridis."

"Thank you, Jamieson," Andrew repeated.

"Somebody's coming, sir!" Moffat pointed to the main force.

Andrew saw a plume of dust as a lone rider galloped from the army. *Why does Kempster not use the helio?*

"Captain Baird!" the galloper rode up to the crest of the ridge and dismounted with a flourish.

"That's me," Andrew admitted.

"Brigadier Kempster sends his compliments, sir, and the Sikhs are relieving you on the ridge. Could you move your men to the main body as soon as is convenient?"

Coming from a brigadier, that means immediately.

Andrew saw a denser column of dust approaching from the main body and guessed that was his relief.

"Thank you, Lieutenant. We will leave as soon as the Sikhs arrive."

The handover was swift and efficient, with the relieving Sikhs familiar with Frontier conditions. Andrew led his MI back to the main body, satisfied with their stay on the ridge and the outcome of their first skirmish. The men had behaved well, Sergeant Brown had proved himself a steady man, and the new rifles were efficient.

CHAPTER 31

TIRAH, NORTHWEST FRONTIER, AUTUMN 1897

"Baird," Brigadier Kempster greeted Andrew with a curt nod. "You'll see we are about to force the Heights."

"I see, sir," Andrew said.

"We have elements of the Second Division advancing against the tribesmen while the artillery keeps them occupied." Kempster tugged at his whiskers. "The Gordons may also help."

The Maxim machine gun and the Gordon Highlanders occupied the Mama Khan ridge, over a thousand yards behind the Dargai Heights, with the Maxim's fire passing over the heads of the assaulting troops. On the northern side of the Chagru Kotal, a mile away, Numbers One, Five and Eight Mountain Batteries hammered the Pashtun positions. Number Nine Mountain Battery fired from Samana Sukh, nearly two miles away, with the shells screaming above the Indian and British infantry to explode amongst the enemy sangars.

At 11:45, Andrew saw the leading battalions, the 3rd Gurkha Scouts under Lieutenant Tillard and Major Judge with the 1/2nd Gurkhas, advancing across an area of open ground that the Pashtuns swept with rifle fire.

As Andrew watched, the guns fired a salvo that exploded on and above the tribesmen's sangars, momentarily forcing them to take cover. In the few seconds of safety, a dozen Gurkha Scouts scrambled across the open ground and threw themselves into the shelter of loose rocks below a cliff. Even in those few moments, the ground was littered with the green uniforms of Gurkha dead and wounded.

"How the devil will they get out of that?" Brigadier Kempster asked and gave orders to reinforce the Gurkhas.

Andrew checked his watch. He was always surprised by how quickly time passed in action. At a quarter past two, the Dorsets advanced to support the pinned-down Gurkhas. Although new to the Frontier, the Dorsets moved confidently, sturdy men in khaki, with sun helmets at the same angle and Lee-Metfords over their shoulders. Andrew watched a platoon ready themselves; Captain Arnold gave an order and led them in a charge across the open space. The tribesmen were waiting, hundreds of expert marksmen with a clear field of fire. They opened fire as soon as the Dorsets appeared and hit nearly every man, with Arnold lying prone on the ground among his men.

Andrew swore and swore again as another group of Dorsets tried, with the tribesmen shooting every man except the young lieutenant who led them. The Dorsets tried a third time, and then men from the Derbys attempted the open space, always with the same results.

"The Gurkhas are trapped, and the supporting troops can't cross the open space," Andrew said. "Can the guns not quieten these Afridis?"

"It seems they can't," Brigadier Kempster replied.

An outburst of firing from the Samana Sukh attracted Andrew's attention as a company of Afridis arrived from the Khanki Valley in a half-hearted assault. The 36th Sikhs responded with enthusiastic volleys.

"Come on, lads!" Andrew shouted, happy to do something positive. "Give the Sikhs a hand!"

The MI joined in, firing careful volleys that helped repel the assault.

A few moments after the abortive attacks, Lieutenant Colonel Piercy of the Dorsets heliographed General Yeatman-Biggs, saying he could make no progress without reinforcements. Jamieson read the heliograph flashes and relayed the message to Andrew.

"Our advance has stalled at the first hurdle," Andrew said.

Andrew saw the Gordon Highlanders and 3rd Sikhs advancing towards Dargai, but the Dorsets and Devons again attempted to cross the open space. A wing of the 21st Madras Pioneers marched to replace the Gordons on the Mama Khan.

General Lockhart was watching events. He lowered his binoculars and summoned Lieutenant Colonel Mathias of the Gordon Highlanders.

"That ridge must be cleared at all costs," Lockhart said.

Mathias looked over the open ground, littered with bodies clad in Rifleman Green and Khaki, with the Afridi riflemen waiting for events. "The Gordon Highlanders will take it," he said.

Andrew felt a surge of something; he did not know what, when he heard the colonel's words.

Pride, perhaps? Why? I am not a Gordon but remember them at Majuba in the Boer War.

Lockhart ordered the artillery to lay a three-minute barrage on the Afridis' sangars, with the Gordons going in immediately after the shelling lifted.

When Mathias addressed his men, telling them what they had to do, the Gordons cheered, lifting their sun helmets in the air and waving their rifles.

Andrew felt that surge of emotion again. *Whoever wins this battle, it won't be the Afridis. God help them if the Gordons get amongst them with the bayonet.*

Andrew watched as Colonel Mathias led his men from the front. The Gordon Highlanders, with their green tartan kilts beneath khaki tunics, readied for the charge across the bare area of rock.

The pipers began to play, Piper Milne and Piper George, "Jock" Findlater marching before the men, as was their wont. The Afridis started to fire, and the Gordon Highlanders charged forward over the shelterless neck of rock. Andrew saw Piper Milne fall, shot through the lungs, and then Findlater stagger and crumple, shot through both ankles. The pipe music ended, and Andrew could only hear the rattle of musketry and the scream and whine of ricochets.

That's a bad start, Andrew thought, and then he saw Findlater crawl to a boulder, lift his pipes, and begin to play again. Andrew could not distinguish the tune through the hammer of battle but knew it inspired the Gordons, who pushed on, with men falling like khaki-clad dolls before the Afridi fire. Andrew heard a thin cheer, saw the flash of sunlight on bayonets, and the Gordons cleared the Heights.

Mathias and Colour Sergeant Mackie both survived the advance over the bullet-tortured ground.

"Stiff climb, eh, Mackie?" Mathias said. "Not quite as young as I was."

Mackie patted him on the back. "You're going very strong for an old man," he said.

The Gordons had thirty-two men killed crossing the open ground and continued the advance, charging up the rock-strewn slope towards the Afridi sangars. The Gurkhas followed in the Gordons' wake, with the Sikhs, Dorsets and Devons not far behind.

"On you go, my bonny lads," Lockhart breathed, and Andrew saw the worry in his eyes as his men thrust upwards, with the Highlanders clambering up a narrow goat track to reach the enemy. Piper Findlater, weak from pain and loss of blood, continued to play his pipes, so the strains of *Cock of the North* followed the Gordons.

The advance continued, with the kilted men dodging Afridi

bullets as they moved from rock to rock, carrying their bayonets toward the enemy. Perhaps sensibly, the Afridis fled before the Gordons and Gurkhas reached them, for the Highlanders from Scotland and Nepal had casualties to avenge.

"The Gordons have taken the Dargai Heights, sir," a red-faced staff officer reported to Lockhart.

"So, I see," Lockhart murmured. "So, I see."[1]

Andrew knew he had witnessed something historic. He removed his hat as a token of respect.

"That'll show the Afridis," the staff officer said, nodding approval.

When the Gordons returned from the Heights with their casualties, they also carried the wounded Gurkhas and Dorsets. Every regiment present cheered them, and many men emerged from the camps to offer their water bottles to the returning Highlanders.

Andrew nodded, appreciating what the simple gesture meant. Water was a precious commodity, strictly rationed, and lending it would mean hardship to the giver and relief to the receiver.

That will help ease the sting of Majuba, Andrew thought as the Highlanders marched with their heads held high.

The day was fading when Lockhart's men secured the Heights, and the general ordered them to dig in for the night.

"They'll be cold up there," Andrew remembered crossing the Shandur Pass. He knew the staff officers did not send up tents, or extra supplies, food, or water, so the men on top of the Heights braved sub-zero cold and a wind that cut like a scimitar. The British and Indian soldiers held on, and the Afridis did not attempt to retake the Heights.

---

1. The battle of the Dargai Heights resulted in a handful of Victoria Crosses: Piper Findlater, Private Edward Lawson of the Gordons, Private Samuel Vickery of the Dorsets and Captain Henry Pennell of the Sherwood Foresters. Colonel Mathias survived a minor wound, and Lieutenant Dingwall was hit four times, none of the wounds serious.

"We're fighting two wars here," Andrew told Innes. "The official war with the Afridis, and another against stupidity and neglect from our higher command. If the KOSB and Gurkhas had been properly supplied a few days ago, the Gordons would not have needed to attack. These deaths were the staff's fault."

Innes looked unhappy. "Maybe you should not say such things, sir."

"Maybe not," Andrew said, "even though it's true."

"If the staff officers hear you, sir, it might damage your career."

Andrew shrugged. "I didn't come to India to return to soldiering," he said. He felt Innes's eyes on him, closed his mouth and walked away. *Innes was correct. I said too much there. I don't like wasting lives in retaking positions because of the stupidity of those in charge.*

Andrew's lack of faith in some officers was proved correct when the officers detailed to care for the expedition's transport failed to feed and water the mules or remove their loads at night.

"What was that?" Andrew listened to the news with disbelief. "How many mules died?"

"Hundreds, sir," Innes stepped back from Andrew's obvious anger. "We can't move forward until we find transport animals."

Andrew swore in frustration. "Damn and blast! How the devil are we going to do that? Conjure them out of the sand? Ask the Afridis to borrow their horses?"

"I don't know, sir," Innes said. He hesitated. "Brigadier Kempster wants us to help search for camels."

"Camels? Do the Afridis grow them here?" Andrew tried to control his response. He had heard that senior officers used the Mounted Infantry for every unwanted job. Now he had the proof. "Of course we could," Andrew said quietly. "Tell the men we're riding in half an hour. Each man to carry food and water for two days and a hundred and twenty rounds of ammunition. I want half a dozen spare horses with fodder for the horses and tents for the men."

"Yes, sir," Innes replied. "Are we camping overnight, sir?"

"Yes," Andrew said. "We are camping overnight."

Leading his Mounted Infantry around the local area, Andrew continued his quest for the tall Russian. As he bartered for camels with *maliks* and merchants, Andrew also asked about any foreigners. After the British success on the Dargai Heights, the local people were slightly more tractable, and Andrew managed to round up half a dozen camels, although he suspected he paid over the odds for them.

"Strangers?" the *malik* of one village laughed. "Your General Lockhart has brought thousands of strangers into the area. How can I pick out one face from so many?"

"He may have been Russian," Andrew said. "A tall man without a beard."

The *malik* put a handful of betel nuts in his mouth and spat juice onto the ground. "Oh, the Russian. Yes, he was here."

"What did he say?" Andrew tried to disguise his surge of interest.

"The usual," the *malik* said. "If you Pashtuns all rise, the British will leave. The Russians are on the Pashtun's side and will send thousands of brave Cossacks to aid you. He told us the Turks had defeated the British and captured the Suez Canal, and if we fought against the British, Tsar Nicholas II would support us."

"Did you believe him?" Andrew asked.

The *malik* ejected more betel nut juice. "No more than I believe the British when they make stupid promises or the *mullahs* when they claim to turn bullets into water."

"You don't believe the *mullahs*?"

The *malik* laughed. "When you're as old as I am and have seen as many sword cuts and bullet wounds, you learn nobody can turn lead into water." He hesitated and gave a red-toothed grin. "Except Allah, and he does not come to our land often."

"Not often," Andrew agreed. "Although *Iblis* does."

"*Iblis* brings war, famine, pestilence, drought and floods," the *malik* said. "He marches alongside the British to Tirah."

"He also marched with the Afridi when they attacked the forts in the Khyber and murdered British soldiers," Andrew replied softly.

"*Iblis* whispers war wherever he goes," the *malik* said. "When cultures clash, Iblis shouts, and fools listen."

"Then we are all fools," Andrew said sadly.

"That is the way of the world," the *malik* said. "Perhaps that is Allah's will."

"The ways of God are mysterious," Andrew extended his hand. "God be with you."

"And with you," the *malik* replied. "Look for your Russian in the Place of Many Bones. *Iblis* sat on his shoulder, laughing."

"The Place of Many Bones?" Andrew repeated the name. "Where is that?"

The *malik* smiled. "I have told you all I can, Captain. May Allah bless your endeavours if it is his will."

"Thank you, Father," Andrew said.

Andrew checked his map for The Place of Many Bones without success. He asked the officers and men of the Sikhs and Gurkhas.

"Nobody knows what lies behind the *purdah*," the Sikhs replied.

Andrew wrote the name above his map, added a large question mark and continued to search for camels.

It took a week for the column to find three thousand camels, and only then could Lockhart push his army onto the next obstacle, the Sampagha Pass.

"Another pass," Andrew said. "This land is all hills and passes."

"And Pashtuns," Innes replied. "They seem to grow from the barren soil."

Cold rain greeted Lockhart's men on the 25th of October as they camped beside the Khanki River.

"We have a choice here," Innes said. "Parch with thirst, freeze in the winter, or get washed away by floods in autumn."

Andrew laughed. "Life would be boring otherwise," he said.

Lockhart sent Major Wade and a strong party to forage ahead, with the Mounted Infantry scouting for a mixed force of a half-battalion of the Devons, another from the Derbys, the 2nd/1st Gurkhas and No 1 Mountain Battery.

"With me, lads!" Andrew shouted. "A hundred and twenty rounds each, and food and water."

They advanced over three miles beside the Khanki River, gathering what forage they could, with the MI acting as a screen in front of the marching infantry.

Andrew saw the Afridis first, flitting between rocks five hundred yards ahead.

"Sergeant," he said, "tell the major we have company. A few hundred tribesmen on the left flank."

"Yes, sir," Sergeant Brown trotted back to the column. He returned ten minutes later as Andrew scanned the Afridis through his binoculars. "The major wants to speak to you, sir."

Major Wade listened to Andrew's information and nodded. "I don't want these Afridis to believe they chased us back," he said. "We'll continue for another half mile."

"As you wish, sir," Andrew said. Putting his men into extended order, he moved on, watching as the Afridis melted into the surroundings.

"Be careful here, Innes," Andrew said. "We don't want the enemy to cut us off from the main body."

"I'll watch them, sir," Innes promised.

After another hundred yards, Andrew saw more warriors ahead, some standing in open defiance and others crouched behind rocks.

"They're waiting for us, sir," Andrew reported to Wade.

"Yes, that's far enough," Major Wade agreed. He scanned the rocks through his binoculars, nodding. "Time to return to base. Act as rearguard, Baird."

Andrew had expected the order. "Yes, sir."

When the column halted and marched back, the Afridis, emboldened, pressed closer.

"Don't fire yet," Andrew ordered. *The enemy has the advantage here, so the longer we can hold off a battle, the better.*

The Afridis emerged from cover, running three hundred yards behind the column, shouting to each other yet still not firing.

"Wait!" Andrew said.

The column was not hurrying, returning in order along the riverbank as growing numbers of tribesmen mustered in the rear.

"Don't stay in one place," Andrew warned his men. "A static target is easier than a mobile man."

The MI obeyed, constantly moving, riding around the rear of the column, watching the tribesmen edge ever closer.

When one young Afridi lifted his Martini, Andrew marked the man down, daring him to fire.

You're the hot-headed youth that starts the battle, my young friend.

Andrew ducked as the Afridi fired. He heard the bullet whizz over his head and returned fire, hitting the youth in the right shoulder. He rode on, hoping that example would be sufficient.

Other tribesmen fired, with the MI returning fire, only targeting the riflemen. The column moved steadily on, with Major Wade ensuring they did not encourage the Afridis by appearing to hurry.

"Keep them at a distance," Andrew ordered.

Apart from the occasional sniping, the Afridis did not attack the column until it arrived at Lockhart's camp an hour before sunset.

"Usher them in," Andrew said as his Mounted Infantry patrolled the camp entrance. The infantry marched past without having fired a single shot, thankful to be back.

The Afridis remained outside the camp perimeter until the sun dipped and then approached within a couple of hundred yards; some fired and withdrew, taunting without being a significant danger.

"Double the sentries," Lockhart ordered. "Fire if you see a target."

"Permission to engage them, sir?" Andrew asked.

"Off you go, Baird," Lockhart agreed.

"Come on, lads!" Andrew formed his MI into a V formation and rode out of the camp, firing at the enemy. When the Afridis withdrew into the dark, Andrew retired to the camp. The Afridis returned, and Andrew rode out again, with both sides firing without inflicting casualties.

The bloodless engagement continued for fifteen minutes until Lockhart organised the camp into a proper state of defence and ordered the bugler to sound the recall. As the Afridis followed the MI, a hundred yards behind, the Malverns fired controlled volleys that sent them reeling back.

"Cease firing," Lockhart ordered. "I want double pickets outside and inside the camp. How many casualties do we have?"

"One soldier killed, sir," a staff officer reported. "Two officers and thirty-six men wounded, and some transport animals hit."

Lockhart grunted. "Send men up to the heights tomorrow morning. I want sangars built and heavily manned. We'll have no more raids on our camp."

"Yes, sir," the staff officer replied.

"The Afridis won't let us into Tirah without a fight," Innes said. "They'll wait for us on the Sampagha Pass, and that's some height to climb."

After Chitral, the pass's height did not concern Andrew, but the Afridis did.

"If they hold the Sampagha Pass in strength," Andrew said. "It will be the devil of a job to force."

That night, Andrew wrote a long letter to Mariana. He knew the following day would be challenging but did not mention the danger. As an afterthought, he wrote a short note to Simla telling her to be good, shook his head at his foolishness, and folded Simla's note inside Mariana's letter.

When he lay down on his *charpoy*, Andrew thought about his wife and daughter and wondered what misadventure had brought him back into the army.

I should be farming at Corbiestane, not exchanging bullets with tribesmen at the back of beyond.

CHAPTER 32

TIRAH, NORTHWEST FRONTIER, OCTOBER 1897

"Baird!" Lockhart said. "Take your MI with the Gurkha Scouts and see what's happening up the Sampagha Pass."

"Yes, sir."

The MI troopers were now used to the terrain and followed Andrew without question.

"Sergeant Brown, take two men on the flank and watch for ambushes. Innes, you have the rearguard. Ensure the Afridis don't try to cut us off from the main body."

Innes looked crestfallen. "Should I not be with the advance guard, sir?"

"You should obey orders, Lieutenant Innes," Andrew told him.

"Yes, sir," Innes moved to the rear, leaving Andrew to lead from the front. The MI moved confidently past the village of Nazeno, where the inhabitants stared at them with interest and no hostility. Andrew led them past a hillock at the base of the pass and halted at the settlement of Kandi-Mishti.

A man sped from the village, zig-zagging up the pass without looking back.

"He's gone to warn his friends that we're coming," Andrew said.

"I reckon so, sir," Brown replied.

Andrew had become familiar with the passes of the Frontier, the sheer drop to a boisterous river below, the sudden spurs that cut off the view ahead, and the tangled rocks and vegetation that could hide a single sniper or a thousand *ghazis*. He pushed forward slowly with his Lee-Metford across his saddle, his eyes constantly roaming. The wind hissed over the rocks, carrying occasional spurts of cold rain, and mist drifted, cold, clammy, and dangerous.

"This is some place," Moffat commented. "It reminds me of the Lecht in the Cairngorms. All we need is Corgarff Castle and a horde of Highland caterans bounding from the heather."

"Thank you, Moffat," Andrew replied. "The Afridis are bad enough without dealing with the Camerons or MacGregors as well."

They pushed on, slowly and carefully, until a hidden Afridi fired a single shot. Andrew heard the whine of a passing bullet and saw a faint puff of smoke from a group of rocks.

"Over there, sir!" Moffat shouted. "Bloody MacGregors!"

"Push on!" Andrew ordered. "Return fire if you have a target." He moved quicker now, not willing to halt before a single rifleman but with his body tingling in anticipation of a soft lead bullet plunging into him.

When the marksman fired a second time, the MI were ready, and five Lee-Metfords replied.

"Well done, lads," Andrew said. He had not fired, knowing his men were ready to retaliate. Andrew rode on, waiting for the inevitable next attack. He rounded a spur and halted, ordering the men to keep open order behind him.

"Sir," Brown stopped at his side. "The Afridis are here."

Andrew nodded. The Afridis had erected sangars on either

side of the road, with green flags flying above three of them. Andrew saw the morning light reflecting from sword blades and rifle barrels.

"They're very confident, sir," Sergeant Brown said. "Or they wouldn't allow us to see them. They're inviting us on, challenging us to penetrate their purdah."

"*Allah Akbar!*" Somebody shouted ahead, with a hundred voices taking up the cry. "*Allah Akbar!*"

"That doesn't sound too promising, sir," Brown said as the challenge echoed from the surrounding hills.

"We'd better report to General Lockhart," Andrew replied. "We'll tell him the Afridis hold the pass in force and are waiting for us."

Lockhart listened to Andrew's report. "The Gurkha scouts reported the same thing," he said. "Your report gives me confirmation. Thank you, Captain. We're marching out for Ghandaki tomorrow. I want your men in the advance guard."

"Yes, sir," Andrew said.

On the 28th of October 1897, Lockhart marched from the camp with over seventeen thousand fighting men and a long trail of camp followers, camels, mules, and other baggage animals. After a slow march of two miles, they camped in the early afternoon.

"Keep the sentries alert," Lockhart ordered. "Place pickets on the hills, build sangars. I want mounted patrols around the perimeter. Baird, accompany Brigadier General Hart."

"Yes, sir."

The MI were only one component of Hart's reconnaissance force, riding in support of the Guides as they returned to the Sampagha Pass. The MI advanced cautiously, with Andrew a length in front, inspecting every rock, tree, and patch of scrub on the route. He saw the gun smoke from the heights above.

"Dismount, men!"

Half a dozen bullets buzzed around the MI as they

dismounted and searched the slope for the enemy. Moffat lay prone behind a rock, lifted his Lee-Metford, fired, and grunted.

"That's one less, anyway."

"Can you see them, Moffat?" Andrew asked.

"Aye, sir," Moffat replied. He fired again and worked the rifle bolt. "Twelve of them, sir. There used to be thirteen."

Andrew lifted his binoculars. "Tell me where you see the closest Afridi, Moffat."

"See that white-splashed rock, sir? Look to the right."

Andrew looked and saw a fingernail's width of grey. "I see him," he said grimly.

The Afridi moved a fraction, Moffat fired, and the man jerked up with the force of the striking bullet.

"Got him!" Moffat said.

The Afridis responded with a fusillade that crashed around the Mounted Infantry, chipping the rocks and clipping branches from the scrubby trees.

"How many are there, Moffat?" Andrew asked from the shelter of a boulder.

"More are arriving all the time, sir," Moffat replied. "I'd say fifty or sixty."

Andrew lifted his binoculars and scrutinised the path. He saw sangars on the high ground at the side, with a flutter of movement within.

Andrew raised his voice. "That's far enough, lads! Withdraw by sections! Sergeant Brown, take your section away first!"

The MI withdrew down the pass, with each section covering the others and one man lightly wounded. When they reached the foot, Andrew ordered them to mount, and they returned to the camp.

"I think the Afridis will make a stand on the Sampagha Pass," Andrew reported to Brigadier Hart. "They've increased their numbers since we were here yesterday and seem determined to stop us."

"We'll advance a little further and see what they do," Hart decided. "Take the rearguard, Baird."

Hart pushed his force up the path, halted as the Afridis met him with accurate rifle fire, examined the sangars through his binoculars and withdrew to the base of the pass. The Afridis followed, exchanging shots with Andrew's rearguard.

"I can't see anybody!" Hobart complained. "I'm firing at rocks!"

"That's all right, Hobart," Sergeant Brown said. "You'll probably miss them anyway."

When Hart reported to Lockhart, the general pondered for a moment. "The more we delay, the stronger the opposition. We must force the Sampagha Pass," he said, brushing his whiskers. "We're going in tomorrow."

"Early start tomorrow, boys," Andrew informed the MI. "We're heading up before dawn." He checked the horses, ensured the pickets were alert and lay down. He did not like to sleep when men were on duty but knew a commander, even of such a small unit as the MI, needed rest to remain alert.

The camp roused at four the following morning, the 29th of October 1897. After the usual bustle of breakfast, checking ammunition and horses, and last-minute orders, the 1st Division marched from the camp, with the artillery rolling behind them. Andrew led the MI at the front as the Devons occupied Nazeno and the nearby hill spurs without resistance.

"That's a good start," Innes said.

Andrew nodded. He watched the Derbys climb the small hill at the entrance of the pass, with a battery of artillery toiling up behind them. On the left flank, the 2nd/1st Gurkhas took over the Kandi-Mishti villages.

"The Afridis have taught Lockhart caution," Innes approved. "That raid a few days ago benefitted us more than them."

Andrew nodded, checked his men and pushed them up the pass for the third time. As the sun rose, he saw Afridi standards fluttering above their sangars and heavily concentrated to the west, where the Gurkhas were advancing.

"What's happening there?" Innes asked.

"The Afridis must think we're attacking to the west of the pass," Andrew replied. "They're concentrating on the Gurkhas."

Innes nodded, checked his revolver and replaced it in its holster. "The more men they have there, the less they have to oppose us here."

Andrew pushed the MI in front until Hart ordered them to halt.

"Dismount, lads! Form a defensive screen in case the Afridis attack."

"What now?" Innes asked.

"Now we wait for developments or orders," Andrew replied. "And keep an eye on the enemy." He pointed to an isolated hillock half a mile ahead. "I can see Afridi sangars on that hill. Tell Jamieson to helio Lockhart with the information."

"Yes, sir," Innes replied, and five minutes later, the heliograph was winking back down the pass.

Shortly before half past seven, the artillery opened fire, concentrating on the sangars on the single hill.

"Message from Brigadier Hart, sir!" Jamieson reported. "You are to advance up the pass until you meet stiff opposition, then wait for support."

"On we go, lads!" Andrew said. "Mount and ride!"

The MI moved on slowly, checking every rock and wind-twisted tree. The artillery bombardment of the single hill continued for five minutes, and then Lockhart sent in the infantry. The MI watched as the khaki-clad men captured the hill with minimal resistance. After half an hour, British artillerymen dragged their guns up the slopes and fired on the Afridi positions higher up the pass in front of Andrew's men.

"Orders, sir," A red-faced runner panted up the path to Andrew. "The MI are to guard the flank and let the Queen's pass through."

Andrew's men cheered as the Queen's Royal West Surrey Regiment marched past, with mutual insults, both jocular and barbed.

"Stand aside, boys, and let the real soldiers pass!"

"Here come the Queen's! The fighting must be over!"

The artillery barrage ended as the infantry closed with the crest, and the Queen's were on their own against the Afridis in their stone sangars.

Andrew heard a spatter of musketry and a loud, prolonged cheer.

"That's the Queen's taking the bayonet to them," he said.

Innes nodded. "The Queen's is a fighting regiment. They'll do the business."

Ten minutes later, a pink-faced subaltern hurried down the track. He saw Andrew, stopped, and gave a hurried salute.

"Are you Captain Baird, sir?"

"I am," Andrew admitted.

"Major Smith's compliments, sir, and the Queen's have cleared the summit of Paythans for you."

"Thank you, Lieutenant," Andrew replied solemnly.

"If you'll excuse me, sir, I have to report to the brigadier." The subaltern saluted again, knocking his pith helmet askew, and hurried down the path, full of self-importance and impetuosity.

They're too young to go to war. Britain sends its brightest and best, uses them hard, and discards them when they've fulfilled their usefulness.

"Right, boys," Andrew shouted. "You've had your little rest, and now it's back to work. No more idling behind rocks for a fly smoke. Open order; Lieutenant Innes, take the rearguard."

Andrew led them back up the pass, acknowledging the Queen's by removing his pith helmet with a flourish and rode on, wary of an ambush. He expected the musketry and ordered his men to dismount when he heard the heavy thump of a Martini. The bullet crashed into a rock beside Hobart, who stared at the resulting chip.

"Somebody's firing at me!"

"Get off your bloody horse, Hobart!" Sergeant Brown roared, "Or I'll fire at you!"

The MI dismounted, handed the reins to the horseholders, and found cover as they searched for their attackers.

"Over there, sir," Moffat pointed to a group of sangars to the northwest.

"I see them," Andrew focussed his binoculars. The sangars were well sited, mutually supporting, with high, loopholed walls. He raised his voice. "Give them a few rounds, boys! Three rounds each!"

The MI responded immediately, and Andrew felt their morale lift. There was nothing worse for soldiers than being fired at without being able to retaliate. Firing back was always helpful, even if they could not see the result of their shooting.

"I got one!" Hobart yelled. "I saw his head jerk back."

"You must have eyes that can see through stone," Pearson replied. "I cannae see a single one of them."

Andrew ducked as an Afridi bullet chipped the rock at his side. "There are more to the northeast," he said. "They've got us in a crossfire."

"Jamieson!" Andrew shouted.

"Sir!"

"Set up the helio and inform Brigadier Hart that we are beyond the summit and the enemy occupy sangars to our northeast and northwest. Tell them the Afridis are in considerable strength and have the main path in a crossfire."

"Yes, sir," Jamieson hesitated. "I'll have to get back down the path a little to signal, sir."

"Then do so," Andrew said.

The Afridis increased their fire, with bullets whining and spitting around the MI's position. Andrew swore when one of his men grunted and fell back, holding his leg.

"Withdraw fifty yards," Andrew pointed to a spur. "We'll take up position at that point. Move by sections; Number One section retire first, Two section fire northeast, and Three section northwest. On my word. Go!"

Andrew had practised this manoeuvre in training and now saw the benefit as his men moved out of danger, one section at a time. "Keep the enemy occupied," he ordered, wishing he had brought more ammunition.

Magazine rifles are grand for speed of firing, but unless I keep the men under control, we'll use up our ammunition in short order.

Jamieson ran up to Andrew. "Sir! A message from Brigadier Hart, sir. We've got to hold out here until the artillery fires on the sangars."

"Thank you, signaller. Tell the brigadier we are holding on but would appreciate some more .303 ammunition."

A few minutes later, the rapid blink of the heliograph told Andrew his message was on its way.

The MI were firing steadily, with Afridi bullets hammering back, chipping the rocks, burrowing into the ground, or ricocheting around the men's ears. One man yelled and rolled away, clutching his leg.

"Look after that man!" Andrew roared. "Check your ammunition! How many rounds do you have left?"

The answers came back, anything from thirty to fifty. The best shots had the most ammunition, as they only fired when they had a definite target.

"Ration your firing!" Andrew understood why many officers limited the men to volley fire. That way, the officers could regulate the ammunition use rather than allow the too enthusiastic to blast away all their cartridges in a short time. "Sergeant!"

"Sir!" Brown replied.

"Send two men to the horses and bring back our spare ammo boxes."

Andrew cursed himself for not thinking of the spare ammunition earlier. *I'll indent for bandoliers the next chance I get. The men hate them, but it's an extra eighty rounds each.*

"Sir!" Brown pointed above them, where a group of Afridis had left their sangars to move above the MI's position.

"One Section! Control these men!" Andrew ordered.

Innes reorganised his section, pointing out the best places to shelter and still be able to fire at the Afridis. Andrew checked the wounded man and found he was heavily bandaged and happily ensconced behind a rock, with a stubby pipe in his mouth as he fired at the northeastern sangar.

"They're getting close, sir," Innes said.

The Afridis were at the edge of the spur, firing irregularly but accurately, with their shots pinging and whining around the MI.

"They'll cut us off soon," Innes said.

"Ammo, sir!" A gasping trooper arrived from the horses. "We only brought one box." Sweat ran down his face, and his uniform was torn.

"One box is all you could carry," Andrew agreed. "Distribute it to the men, then fetch another."

"Yes, sir," the private said.

"Calderwood!" Andrew selected a man known for his speed. "Go to the horseholders and tell them to withdraw towards the crest. We can't afford to lose the horses if the Afridi get too close."

"Yes, sir," Calderwood moved away, jinking from rock to rock with an agility Andrew could only envy.

The Afridi were threatening to outflank the MI, moving stealthily across the spur and down towards the track. Andrew wanted to move against them himself, but he knew his position was with the bulk of his men.

"Sergeant! Grab some more ammo, take three men and blunt the Afridi flanking attack. Don't get killed."

"Yes, sir," Brown said. "MacLeod, Hawkins, Ambleworth; you're with me!"

Andrew watched Brown move away. "Come on, lads! We're better than the Paythans!" He ducked as a bullet chipped the boulder at his side.

"They're getting very close," Innes said. "Permission to lead a bayonet charge, sir?"

"No!" Andrew denied. "The Afridi would shoot you the moment you emerged from cover. Keep firing."

Andrew lifted his rifle, aimed at a puff of smoke and fired, feeling satisfaction at the kick. He worked the bolt and fired again.

Show yourself, you bastards. Show yourselves so we can kill you.

Andrew heard a roar from the flank and saw Brown rearing up from behind a rock. There was the flash of sunlight on steel, and Brown plunged down with his bayonet. Somebody screamed, Brown shouted, and the firing began again.

"With me, lads!" Sergeant Brown yelled and moved on.

"Give the sergeant covering fire!" Andrew ordered and fired three rounds rapid.

"There's too many of them, sir!" Hobart shouted.

Andrew saw the Afridis flitting from rock to rock, emboldened when they saw the few men they opposed.

"Keep them back!" Andrew said.

The terrible crack of the screw-guns surprised the MI. They looked up to see the first orange-white flashes of shells exploding around the Afridi sangars.

"The gunners are at them!" Moffat shouted. "*Shabash* the guns!"

Andrew lifted his binoculars. While the MI had held the Afridis' attention, the 5th and 9th Mountain Batteries had pushed to the summit of the pass. Under cover of their fire, Lockhart sent in the infantry to take the sangars. On the left, the 36th Sikhs and the KOSB pressed forward, while the Queen's and the 3rd Sikhs stormed the sangars on the right. Bayonets flashed in the sunlight, and a thin cheer rose from both flanks.

"The Afridi are withdrawing, sir!" Moffat shouted. All along the spur, the tribesmen were retreating, with the MI having only glimpses of their erstwhile attackers.

"Shoot them," Andrew ordered.

"It goes against the grain to shoot men in the back," Innes said.

"Think what they would do to you," Andrew reminded grimly. "The more we kill today, the less there are to kill us tomorrow."

The MI obeyed, firing as the Afridis retreated. Andrew saw the British and Sikhs capture the sangars, routing the defenders and taking over the positions.

"What time is it, Innes? I forgot to wind my watch."

"Half past eleven, sir," Innes replied.

One morning's fighting had cleared the Sampagha Pass. Lockhart had forced open the outer gate to the Tirah, and his forces poured in.

I still have to find that blessed Russian, Andrew told himself. *The military campaign is only part of my duty.*

CHAPTER 33

MASTURA VALLEY, TIRAH, NORTHWEST FRONTIER, OCTOBER 1897

"What were the casualties?" Andrew asked. The MI rested in the Mastura Valley on the far side of the pass. The men cleaned their rifles, lit cigarettes or pipes and discussed the recent action. "How is Private Wooler?"

"I sent him to the hospital," Innes said. "Apart from a few minor scrapes and cuts, he's our only casualty. Lockhart forced the pass with surprisingly few losses, considering we're storming the Afridis' inviolate homeland. The column had one officer and one other rank killed, and one officer and thirty other ranks wounded."

Andrew nodded. He knew the families of the dead would be grieving as much as if there had been a thousand killed. "Now we face the next pass, the Arhanga, and into the Tirah proper."

"Yes, sir," Innes agreed. "General Lockhart requests your presence, sir. Immediately."

"Thank you, Innes," Andrew replied, straightening his crumpled uniform as he left.

Lockhart held a conference with all his officers above the rank of lieutenant to discuss the campaign so far.

"One thing that I've noticed," Lt-Colonel Mathias of the Gordons said. "Some of these Paythans have long-range breech-loading rifles. Thankfully, most have Sniders or Martinis, with a maximum range of 1,500 yards, and some still have the old *jezails*." He stopped as the gathered officers nodded. "I'd say about fifty have Lee-Metfords stolen from us or taken from our dead."

"Thank God it's only fifty and not five hundred or five thousand," Colonel Webb said.

"Fifty is bad enough," Mathias replied. "Our flanking parties will have to be a mile from the main body to clear away the Afridi marksmen."

Lockhart nodded. "Did you all hear that, gentlemen? The flankers will be deployed at a greater distance from the main body. We will search every village for arms and confiscate any rifles, particularly Lee-Metfords."

The officers nodded.

Lockhart settled into his chair. "Now we have cleared the first obstacle, we'll rest the men and march towards the Arhanga Pass. The 3rd Brigade will lead, with the 15th Sikhs as advance guard." He nodded to the colonels. "The 3rd Sikhs and Yorkshire Regiment will supply the flank guards, remembering Colonel Mathias's words about the Afridis possessing Lee-Metfords. The flankers will have to dominate the heights overlooking the valley."

As the officers took notes, Lockhart continued. "The Gurkha scouts will be in the van, and the MI will remain with Hart's First Division."

Lockhart pushed his army forward towards the Arhanga Pass, with Andrew listening to events further north.

"I can't hear any gunfire," Andrew said. "The Afridis can't be resisting."

"Maybe they've already had enough," Innes said.

Andrew smiled. "We can only hope," he said. "I'd be surprised if they didn't try to hold us at the Arhanga Pass."

When the last of the baggage toiled up the Sampagha Pass, Hart's 1st Brigade followed the main body, acting as rearguard and shepherd for any straggling animals.

"Baird," Brigadier Hart said. "Continue with your mapping and scouting. This area is supposed to be under our jurisdiction, so the more we know about it, the better."

Andrew was happier leading his men to map the Mastura Valley. He asked each remaining *malik* and traveller about any stray Russians, without any success. Andrew found few *maliks*, for the Afridis had deserted most villages to drive their flocks over the Arhanga Pass away from the British advance.

Searching for a lone stranger on the Frontier is like a blindfolded man searching for a needle in a haystack.

When all the baggage had negotiated the Sampagha Pass, Lockhart pushed forward with the 3rd Brigade.

"They're not going to make a stand," Innes reported hopefully. "The Gurkha scouts have hardly seen any Afridis."

"Lockhart's doing well," Andrew replied. "Let's hope our luck holds."

On the 31st of October, Lockhart ordered the entire column forward.

"Ready, lads!" Andrew shouted cheerfully. "Mount and ride! We're with General Westmacott's 4th Brigade today."

"We're at the front again," Innes said. "They can't do without the old MI!"

Andrew eyed the 4th Brigade, nodding in satisfaction when he saw the Northamptons, 36th Sikhs, 1st/3rd Gurkhas, and the familiar uniforms of the KOSB, Sappers and Miners.

"They look a handy bunch," Andrew said.

"Yes, sir," Innes agreed.

Lockhart advanced cautiously, sending the KOSB to capture the hill-foot village of Unai. The infantry advanced at the front, and both flanks overcame slight resistance and occupied the settlement. With Unai in British hands, Lockhart sent in the artillery.

"The Afridis hold the summit of the pass," Andrew explained to the MI as the artillery opened up. The range was 1,350 yards, and the gunners made good practice, hammering the enemy positions while the 4th Brigade advanced up the steep pass for a frontal assault. Lockhart sent the 2nd Brigade up the east side of the pass and the 3rd Brigade on the west.

"Here we go again!" Innes said as the MI moved ahead of the 4th Brigade. After a couple of hundred yards, Andrew realised the horses were struggling and ordered the men to dismount.

"Horseholders, look after the horses," Andrew ordered. "The rest, follow me!" He looked ahead, where the orange-white blasts of explosions showed where the artillery was pounding the Afridi positions. By the time the MI reached the summit, the Afridis had withdrawn, and the column marched over the Arhanga Pass with only three casualties, none in the MI.

"Push on!" Lockhart urged. "Get the men over the pass."

The column obeyed, tramping up and across the rough track and into the Tirah Maidan. Lockhart sent strong pickets to occupy the hills on the north side of the pass, waiting for the Afridi response.

"Where are the Pashtuns?" Innes asked. "I think we've scared them all away!"

"I doubt it," Andrew replied. "They won't fight the way we want them to. They'll know we're their masters in open warfare, so they'll fight their own way. I expect a guerrilla war, like the Spanish against Bonaparte or Garibaldi against the Austrians."

"Yes, sir," Innes said. "Here's a runner, sir!"

"Captain Baird!" the messenger panted. "General Westmacott's compliments, sir, and could you take your MI back to find the baggage column? It seems to have got lost."

"Please tell the general I am on my way," Andrew responded, whistling up his men. "The army's lost the baggage, lads. They need our help. Carry a full complement of ammunition and rations for a day."

"Do you expect trouble, sir?" Innes asked.

"Always," Andrew replied.

As the advance guard marched to the next campsite, Andrew led his men back over the Arhanga Pass. As dusk approached, they heard gunfire and hurried forward.

"Extended order, boys," Andrew peered through the swiftly gathering gloom. "Trot!" He had never commanded the MI in a night battle before and hoped his men remembered their training.

The gunfire faded to a few echoes from the surrounding heights. Andrew continued forward. He saw a muzzle flare ahead, then heard the sharp crack of a Martini.

"Come on, boys," Andrew shouted. "Keep in formation and watch the flanks."

The supply column loomed through the dark, with the mules hurrying forward and the meagre escort nervous.

"Who are you?" the subaltern in charge asked. "Quickly! Identify yourself, or I'll fire!"

"Captain Andrew Baird of the MI," Andrew replied. "What's happening here?"

"The Afridis!" the subaltern shouted. "They've attacked us three times, sir, killed two of our drivers and stolen three ammunition mules!"

"All right," Andrew tried to calm the boy down. "We'll take over the escort. You head northward along the road, and we'll take care of the Afridis." Andrew hoped he sounded more confident than he felt. He split his men, with eight riders on each flank, four as rearguard and four as advance guard.

"Innes!"

"Sir!"

"Take the advance guard. Sergeant Brown, take the left flank. Pearson, you're now a corporal; congratulations on your promotion. Take the right flank; I have the rearguard."

Guarding a convoy was one of the most thankless jobs of the MI, with no possibility of glory or recognition but every chance of hard knocks. Andrew ushered the convoy over the pass, with his men firing at every sound and responding to every Afridi attack with concentrated musketry.

The Afridis' attack gradually faded away as the MI escorted the convoy down the pass to Lockhart's camp.

"Will we get any thanks for this night's work?" Innes asked.

Andrew shook his head. "We are the MI," he replied. "Neither cavalry nor infantry. Nobody knows what to do with us until there is trouble."

Innes grinned ruefully. "I understand, sir. We get the jobs that nobody else wants."

"That's about it, Innes," Andrew agreed.

※

MARIANA SIGHED AS THE TWO YOUNG WOMEN ENTERED Peliti's Restaurant. For all the effort they had made, neither seemed any closer to snaring a husband. They selected a table near the window, and one checked her very elegant watch.

"It's nearly time," she said, and both giggled like little schoolgirls. Mariana watched them staring out the window. A carriage whirred past, with a very dignified couple sitting inside, and then a tall young officer strolled along the Mall.

"Isn't he the handsome one?" the blonde woman sighed.

"What did you say his name was?" the other asked.

"Major Eustace Lloyd-Jones," the blonde replied. "He's a staff officer from Norfolkshire."

The other watched Lloyd-Jones walk in the wake of the carriage. "Eleven-fifteen," the blonde said. She glanced at Sinclair, busy with his book. "That one never looks at us."

The second snorted. "He wouldn't notice if a dozen girls passed him."

Mariana felt her anger rise. She rose from her seat and approached Sinclair. "You are still writing, I see, Mr Sinclair."

"I am," Sinclair agreed, clearing a space on the circular table. "I am surprised the restaurant allows me to stay here all day, every day."

Mariana saw the coffee pot beside Sinclair's papers and notebooks. "You must drink a lot of coffee."

"Gallons of the stuff," Sinclair said, smiling.

"May I see what you're writing?" Mariana asked.

"Most of it's in note form," Sinclair replied. "It's very rough. Here." He handed over one of his notebooks.

Mariana read the first page. "You're describing everything and everybody you see from the window!"

"That's correct," Sinclair said. "And before you ask, yes, you're included." He turned a couple of pages and pointed to a paragraph. "There you are."

Mariana read the paragraph, with her initial curiosity changing to pleasure. "Do you really think I am a beautiful and charming lady?"

"None better," Sinclair said, leaning back in his chair.

"You said my presence lights up the room," Mariana reread the paragraph.

"Everybody likes you," Sinclair told her. "I am sure you already know that."

Mariana looked at him, unsure how to reply. When she glanced around, the two women had gone. Mariana smiled, although something nagged at her mind. Something was wrong, but Mariana did not know what.

※

Andrew and Innes rode to the entrance of the Tirah Maidan, the heartland of the Afridi lands. He knee-haltered his pony and scrambled up a small hill, reaching the summit just as the sun rose. They watched the golden rays slowly illuminating the land. Pulling out his pipe, Andrew stuffed tobacco into the bowl and scratched a match.

"The Afghans have a saying," Innes said quietly, "when Allah made the world, he had some rocks left over. He was unsure what to do with them, so he threw them in a corner, and the rubble became Afghanistan."

Andrew nodded. "I didn't know that story," he said.

"This place, the Tirah Maidan, is not like that," Innes continued. "I've never seen anywhere so beautiful. No wonder the Afridis keep it a secret."

Andrew puffed aromatic tobacco smoke into the crisp air. "I agree," he said. "It's a wonder that somewhere so lovely produces such a warrior race."

"Maybe they're a warrior race to protect this secret Garden of Eden," Innes said.

The Tirah Maidan was wide, with sweet water easing from the mountains. Andrew saw individual houses, two-storeys tall, solid and neat, surrounded by groves of apricot and walnut trees. The fields were well cultivated, and the atmosphere was one of comfort and security.

"The Afridis have made a paradise of the Tirah," Innes said.

Andrew agreed. "I thought we would walk into a robbers' den of fortresses and walled towns," he said.

"If the Afridis come from such a paradise," Andrew wondered, "why do they spread such violence to their neighbours?"

"I don't know," Innes replied. "In this season, the colours remind me of England in autumn."

"The English are also a predatory race," Andrew murmured, "attacking their neighbours and keeping their homeland inviolate. Maybe we are closer to the Afridi than we care to imagine."

Innes looked confused. "We are English," he replied. "The most civilised of people."

Andrew thought of the walls of Berwick-upon-Tweed and the multiplicity of battles, raids and skirmishes along the English borders with Scotland and Wales. "So we are," he said, and descended to his horse.

"Captain Baird!" Andrew recognised the runner as he began the ride back.

"Yes, Lieutenant?"

"General Lockhart requests your presence, sir."

"Take over the MI, Innes," Andrew ordered.

"Yes, sir," Innes looked pleased at the responsibility.

Lockhart looked up as Andrew arrived at his travelling desk. "I've had a message about you from General Windrush, Captain."

Andrew wondered if he was expected to reply. "Yes, sir," he said.

"He wants you to go to the mosque at Bagh," Lockhart said dryly.

"Yes, sir," Andrew replied.

"Bagh is the insurgency centre of the Tirah," Lockhart unbent to explain. "And the mosque of Mullah Said Akbar is undoubtedly the centre of Bagh. The *mullah* is one of the leaders in the present troubles and announced the uprising from his mosque."

"Yes, sir," Andrew said for the third time.

"Here," Lockhart passed a sealed envelope to Andrew. "Orders from General Windrush."

"Thank you, sir," Andrew lifted the letter and slipped it, unopened, inside his jacket.

"I am sending a strong party to Bagh tomorrow," Lockhart said. "It leaves at five in the morning. You can join them, Baird. If General Windrush's orders permit, you may take your MI with them. Otherwise, Lieutenant Innes will assume command of the MI."

"Yes, sir. Thank you, sir." The letter felt as if it was burning a hole in Andrew's pocket. He opened it as soon as he left Lockhart's tent, standing in the shelter of a shattered rock as he slit the seal and unfolded the single sheet of paper inside.

"My agents inform me there are two foreigners inside the mosque at Bagh."

Andrew read the note twice before shredding it between his fingers and allowing the wind to scatter the fragments. He had hoped for something more.

Two foreigners. Am I meant to capture them, question them or kill them?

CHAPTER 34

TIRAH, NORTHWEST FRONTIER, NOVEMBER 1897

Bagh was only three miles away, and Andrew joined the KOSB, 1st/3rd Gurkhas, and No 8 Mountain Battery on the march. The column stopped half a mile away, and Andrew scanned the settlement and mosque through his binoculars. He peered through the surrounding trees, searching for any sign of life.

"Don't damage the mosque," Major Wade ordered the column. "We don't interfere with these people's religion."

"How about the trees, sir?" Lieutenant MacQueen of the Gurkhas asked.

"Ring them," Wade replied. "We have to punish them for attacking us."

When they heard the news, the Gurkhas laughed and sliced off the bark in a ring around the trunks, ensuring the trees would die.

"Should we be doing that, sir?" Andrew remonstrated with Wade. "I was taught never to interfere with other people's religion."

Wade shook his head. "We have to teach the Afridis a lesson," he said. "They took our salt and turned against us. Faithless people don't deserve mercy or pity." Wade was an intelligent man in his mid-thirties, no cherub-cheeked one-pipper fresh from Sandhurst. "Have you seen what the Afridis do to our wounded?"

"I have," Andrew nodded. *I shot a man to save him from Afridi torture.*

"Exactly," Wade said.

Andrew saw British and Gurkha soldiers enter the mosque side by side, carrying out the pulpit and other objects. He heard their rough laughter.

"You look troubled, Captain Baird," Wade said softly.

"I am troubled, sir," Andrew replied.

"The Afridis set the rules," Wade told him. "We play by their rules. Do you think they would respect a Christian church, a Hindu temple, or a Sikh Gurdwara?"

Andrew considered for a moment. "Probably not," he replied.

"When the Moghuls conquered much of the Indian subcontinent, they destroyed hundreds, maybe thousands of Hindu temples and built mosques on top," Wade reminded him. "When the Afghans captured Hindu prisoners in the 1840s, they murdered those who did not immediately convert to Islam."

Andrew nodded. "I see," he said.

"They made the rules," Wade repeated. "Not us."

"Do you take any prisoners here, sir?" Andrew asked. "General Windrush thought there might be a foreigner inside the mosque."

Wade shook his head. "The place was deserted when we arrived," he said. "The mullah and his followers fled."

"It's not the *mullah* I am after," Andrew said. He entered the mosque, removed his shoes at the entrance, and examined the interior. The walls were made of solid stone, simply built.

Andrew had hoped for a hidden doorway or a man hiding, but he found nothing and left disappointed.

Andrew spent the next day riding around the area, not sure what he was searching for. Most of the inhabitants had fled when Lockhart invaded the Tirah. The few people who remained were elderly and looked blank when Andrew questioned them about foreigners.

"Do you know of a Place of Many Bones?" Andrew asked, and the reply was a slow shake of their heads.

Andrew sent a sealed despatch to Jack when he returned to the main force. *My time on the Frontier has not been a success. I've lost Symington, failed to find the Russian agent, and killed a British officer. The only bright spot is little Simla.*

Lockhart camped his men in the Maidan, posted strong sentries, and mounted patrols around the countryside. His political officers, men who had spent years working on the Frontier, rode to the scattered tribes to invite the *maliks* to *jirgas* to surrender peacefully.

"Will they surrender, sir?" Andrew asked.

"They'd better if they know what's good for them," Wade said grimly. "They've tweaked the lion's tail once too often. If they fight us in the open, we will smash them."

"They know that, sir," Andrew said. "They'll use guerrilla tactics, stabs in the back, night-time ambushes on soft targets, murdering sentinels and civilians."

Wade nodded. "God help them if they do," he said. "God help them if they do."

The Afridis retaliated by targeting the British lines of communication, a long, slender, vulnerable track from Maidan to Kushalgarh across a hundred miles of rough country. They attacked the convoys, shot the drivers and pack animals, and retreated before the thinly stretched escort could arrive.

Lockhart sent Andrew's MI to help patrol the track, concentrating on the area north of the River Mastura.

The Afridi attacks continued. They were sudden and devastating, either with long-range sniping or an unheralded rush on the weakest section of the column. They killed or wounded a handful of men without halting the convoys but became a persistent nuisance.

Rather than remain on the road, Andrew spread his MI in an extended line, left half of them in two-man observation posts, and waited to see from where the Afridis launched their attacks.

"That way, sir," Sergeant Brown said, pointing to a faint track heading east. "They come from that great lump of a hill in the dusk and dawn."

Andrew consulted his map. "That hill's called Saran Sar, and it's eight thousand feet high," he said. "Let's have a look."

Beyond Saran Sar was another valley where the Bara River flowed and the Zakha Khel Afridis.

"Zakha Khel?" Innes said. "They're supposed to be the most truculent of the Afridi clans, sir. They were prominent during the attacks on Fort Razali."

Andrew loosened his rifle in its bucket holster. "Warn the men, Innes. Tell them this expedition could get ugly."

Andrew led his MI towards Saran Sar. They rode cautiously, following a *nullah*, a dry riverbed.

"This *nullah* will be a torrent in the wet season," Innes said, watching all around.

Andrew nodded. "Thank the Lord that it's dry now." A few fortified villages stood on the hill flanks, abandoned since the British invasion, but each one with a watchtower and defensive wall. Smaller *nullahs* ran into the main track, with the depth altering between ten and a hundred feet.

"What a place for an ambush," Andrew said. He sent flank guards to the lips of the *nullah* and moved on. When they reached the foot of Saran Sar, the ravine shallowed, so the MI emerged into the open, feeling even more vulnerable.

We must be visible to anybody on the mountain, like ants crawling over an ostrich egg.

"Extended order," Andrew ordered, and his men spread out.

There were three small villages visible, all empty of their inhabitants.

"I thought the Afridis would fight for their land," Innes murmured.

"They don't fight as we do," Andrew replied. "We'll leave the horses here." He pointed to a slight depression. "The horse-holders will guard them." He pushed on up the steepening path to the summit of Saran Sar. The path narrowed as it curled around the vertical cliff that soared to the peak and then plunged down to the Bara Valley.

Andrew surveyed the valley through his binoculars. "That's the home of the Zakha Khel," he said.

The cockpit of the Tirah, with the Zakha Khel, the Frontier equivalent of the Armstrongs of Liddesdale, God help us.

"And a clan that encourages the Aka Khel to fight against us," Innes said.

"Sir!" Sergeant Brown pointed downward, where a host of tribesmen were heading toward the path. "They've seen us."

"Right, lads, we've reconnoitred the road, time to get back." Andrew acted as rearguard as the Zakha Khel Afridis climbed towards them.

The MI withdrew rapidly. Andrew put Pearson and Moffat, his best marksmen, at the rear, ready to retaliate if the Zakha Khel chose to fire.

"They seem content just to chase us away," Innes said.

"Maybe so," Andrew replied. "Go to the head of the column and ensure everything is all right. I'll remain with the rearguard." Andrew raised his voice. "Sergeant Brown, guard the flanks."

Andrew ushered his MI downhill as the Zakha Khel opened a desultory fire.

"Target the riflemen!" Andrew ordered. He was a fair shot, but Moffat and Pearson were better, so he allowed them the freedom to choose their vantage points. A few moments later, a double crack sounded as his marksmen fired.

"You three!" Andrew picked men at random. "Cover the marksmen!"

The MI withdrew in stages, moving steadily to show the enemy they were not running and inflicting a few casualties on the Zakha Khel without receiving any.

The final leg in the *nullah* was nerve-wracking as they trotted through the deepest sections, leaving the Afridis behind.

Brigadier Hart listened to Andrew's report without expression. "I'll pass on your intelligence to General Lockhart," he said.

"Thank you, sir," Andrew replied. He wanted to sleep, but first, he had to write a letter to Mariana and little Simla.

At the beginning of November, the Orakzai *maliks* entered Lockhart's camp to discuss peace terms. The Orakzai had borne the brunt of the British assault at Dargai and decided further resistance would only bring disaster. After protracted negotiations with Lockhart and the political officers, they agreed to hand in most of their modern weapons and pay a hefty fine.

"That's one major victory," Lockhart said. "Now we can concentrate on the Afridis. Including your Zakha Khel, Captain."

"Yes, sir."

Lockhart nodded. "We have told the Afridis that if they don't surrender, we'll burn their villages and destroy their crops." He sighed. "It's not a nice way to wage war, but war is never nice."

"I see, sir," Andrew said.

"We're sending a major reconnaissance over the Saran Sar," Lockhart said. "Following your little adventure."

Andrew nodded. "The Zakha Khel will expect us, sir."

"I hope so," Lockhart said. "I hope they stand and fight so we can thrash them." He smiled. "That's why I sent you first, Baird. Burning crops is not the answer; defeating them in battle is the best way to impress a warrior people like the Afridis."

"Perhaps so, sir," Andrew said cautiously.

"I want your MI with the reconnaissance force," Lockhart said. "You know the path."

"Yes, sir."

"Has your other mission shown any success, Baird?"

"Not yet, sir," Andrew replied.

"There's time yet, Baird. Dismissed."

CHAPTER 35

TIRAH, NORTHWEST FRONTIER, NOVEMBER 1897

General Westmacott commanded the reconnaissance over the Saran Sar. Andrew scrutinised the assembled force of the 1st Northamptons, 1st Dorsets, a company of the Madras Sappers and Miners, two Mountain Gun Batteries, and the 15th and 26th Sikh Infantry.

"Westmacott has a powerful little army," Innes said.

Andrew nodded. "The Zakha Khel might find them a bit hot to handle."

An hour after dawn on the 9th of November, Westmacott led his men out of the camp at Maidan. Andrew's MI was part of the advance guard, and as they approached the *nullah*, Sergeant Brown trotted towards him.

"The tribesmen are waiting ahead, sir."

Andrew nodded. "We thought they would be."

Westmacott sent the Northamptons and the Sappers directly up Saran Sar, with the 36th Sikhs on their right flank and the Dorsets on their left.

Andrew grunted when he saw the Northamptons march past, hundreds of very young faces peeling from sunburn. "These lads look pretty raw. I'd prefer more experienced men to fight the Afridis."

Innes smiled. "We've all got to learn, sir, and anyway, they're British soldiers. They'll obey orders and fight until they drop."

"They'll fight as best they can," Andrew gave a qualified agreement. He watched as teams of mules dragged the mountain guns up the hill beside Saran Sar, with the 15th Sikhs acting as escort. "Check the men, Innes. A hundred and twenty rounds per man, with a full day's rations and full water bottles."

"Yes, sir," Innes saluted and left.

The Northamptons marched up the *nullah* and emerged at the top, where the Afridis waited in newly built sangars. The Afridis' torrent of rifle fire sent the Northamptons back into cover.

The Mounted Infantry watched from a distance, with Sergeant Brown shaking his head and grasping his rifle in white-knuckled hands.

"What happens now?" Innes asked.

"Now we wait for orders," Andrew replied. He lifted his binoculars and scanned the slopes. "I can't see the Dorsets at all. They're meant to support the Northamptons."

"I can't see them either, sir," Innes said.

"Captain Baird!" A runner panted up to Andrew. "General Westmacott wants you to take a patrol and find the Dorsets, sir. They haven't been in touch with us."

"Tell General Westmacott I'm on my way," Andrew said. He chose Number Two section and rode halfway up the hill before dismounting to continue on foot. Andrew heard the crackle of musketry from the head of the *nullah*, Lee-Metford and Martini, and then the heavier crash of a mountain gun. The angle of the hill prevented Andrew from seeing where the shell landed, although he guessed it was on the Afridi sangars.

"Sir!" Moffat pointed. "Somebody's coming down the braeside."

Andrew focused his binoculars and saw two privates of the Dorsets were carrying a third down the hill.

"What's happened?" Andrew asked when they met.

The older of the two young soldiers replied. "Peter here, I mean Private Simms, sir, fell and twisted his ankle. We're taking him back down the hill to General Westmacott." He hesitated. "Which way is it, sir?"

"That way," Andrew indicated the bottom of the hill. "Where are the Dorsets?"

"Over there, sir," the private waved behind him to the left.

"They should be that way," Andrew said dryly, pointing up the hill and to the right. He pushed on, with Number One section behind him in extended order.

"I can hear them, sir," Moffat said. "Over that way."

Andrew altered their route in the direction Moffat indicated, and within five minutes, he found the Dorsets floundering across the hill. Andrew pointed them in the right direction. "Over that way, sir."

"Are you sure, Captain?" A confused-looking major asked.

"Yes, sir," Andrew replied, saluting. "If you'll excuse me, sir, I've left my unit in a precarious position."

When Andrew returned his MI to the main force, he discovered the artillery had cleared the Afridis from their sangars, and the Northamptons had renewed their assault.

"Take your men up there, Baird," General Westmacott ordered wearily. "Make sure the Northamptons don't get lost."

"I'll do my best, sir," Andrew promised. He gathered his MI and pushed up the hill.

The artillery covered the advance, blasting any possible Afridi hiding place until they reached an isolated hillock with a gnarled tree. The Afridis waited until the Northamptons arrived at the tree and opened fire again.

"Come on, lads. The Northamptons have struck trouble."

Before the MI arrived, a combination of Northampton musketry and shells from the mountain guns cleared away the

Afridis. The advance continued. When they arrived at the curve at the summit, the Northamptons' colonel sent five companies to the left to climb the peak and the remaining three to march along the track to the viewpoint overlooking the Bara Valley. Andrew arrived with the MI a few minutes after the Northamptons secured the position.

The crest of Saran Sar was different from Andrew's previous visit. On his previous visit, the summit was bare. Now, there were remnants of campfires, a broken knife, a handful of cartridges, and spaces for latrines.

"The Afridis abandoned this position when we advanced," Innes said.

Andrew glanced around, looking for the Dorsets, who had still not appeared on the left flank.

"The Dorsets have got lost again," Innes said. "Maybe we should train the men better before we send them into the Frontier."

"That would be sensible," Andrew said. *No wonder Father was so keen on constant training. I'll remember that; the old man knew what he was talking about.*

Andrew looked left, where a thick forest lapped around the hill flank, affording cover to the Afridis.

"Sir," Innes said. "I can hear voices in the woodland."

"Inform the Northamptons," Andrew said. "Give their colonel my compliments and advise him to watch his right flank. Tell him the Afridis will probably attack while we withdraw."

From their position on the summit, the British could see most of the Bara Valley, and a clutch of senior officers studied the terrain. General Westmacott sent out strong pickets and ordered the surveyors to start work. He toured his defences, looking for the Dorsets through his binoculars.

"Where the hell are they? They've got lost again. Baird!"

"Sir?"

"Take your men to that forest," Westmacott ordered, "and try and find the blasted Dorsets."

The forest was quiet when Andrew's MI approached. He penetrated the outer trees without seeing any enemy or the Dorsets, lingered for an hour to tempt the Afridis to reveal themselves, and withdrew, keeping a strong rearguard in case of attack.

"No sign of the Dorsets, sir," Andrew reported.

"Afridis?"

"We didn't see any, sir, but I know they're there."

At quarter past twelve, with the surveyors' work completed and a rough map of the Bara Valley, Westmacott began the withdrawal back to the camp. The Sikhs were first to leave the summit, halting at the gnarled tree until the rest caught up.

"Sir! General Westmacott!" a signaller ran to the general. "General Lockhart has sent a heliograph message from the camp below. He's coming up the hill to see for himself. He sends his compliments, sir, and asks you to wait."

"As you were!" Westmacott said.

Andrew saw the anger on Westmacott's face as he consulted his watch.

Westmacott had everything timed to the minute; Lockhart's interference will delay his retiral.

General Lockhart and his staff rode to the summit and examined the valley through his binoculars. He looked at the surveyors' maps, nodded approval, made a few suggestions, and returned.

"It's two o'clock now," Andrew said. "We'll be hard-pressed to get back before dark."

"Yes, sir," Innes agreed. "I was thinking the same."

Westmacott resumed the withdrawal, ordering the Northamptons' three companies to join the Sikhs at the wind-twisted tree. They doubled down, panting on the narrow track and waited beside the Sikhs.

"We'll go just before the rearguard," Andrew decided. "If we leave with them, the Northamptons will think we don't trust them."

"We don't, sir," Innes said.

Andrew nodded. "All the more reason not to tell them."

The remaining five Northampton companies followed, scrambling down in the glare of late afternoon.

Andrew brought his MI down next, leaving G Company of the Northamptons as the final British unit. As the MI slid away from the summit, the Afridis in the forest opened fire on G Company.

"The Dorsets should be there," Innes said. "Should we support the Northamptons?"

"Stand ready to assist," Andrew said. He raised his binoculars. "Damn and blast! The Northamptons have casualties. Run to their colonel and ask if we may help."

Innes returned in ten minutes. "The colonel says the Northamptons can look after themselves, sir."

"I thought that would be his reply," Andrew said. "G Company is in trouble. They'll need to bring down their casualties under fire. Stand ready to help, whatever their colonel wants."

The Northamptons' A Company returned up the hill to cover their comrades, firing volleys at the wood.

"The Afridis will slip behind cover whenever the officer orders a volley," Andrew said. "If we heard them talking, they'll hear us."

"What will we do, sir?" Innes asked. "Their colonel doesn't want us to interfere."

"Their colonel is as inexperienced in Frontier warfare as his regiment," Andrew reminded. "We lend a hand. Lives matter more than a colonel's pride."

Andrew led the MI back up the hill, with the sunset blazing in the west and the Bara Valley already in darkness. "Fire at will, lads. Don't wait for orders."

The MI welcomed the order, firing between A Company's volleys, with the two marksmen grunting with satisfaction when they scored a hit.

"That's another Afridi in Paradise," Pearson said.

"I hope they can find enough virgins up there," Moffat replied and began to sing the *Ball of Kirriemuir*.

"Four and twenty virgins,
Cam doon frae Inverness,
And when the ball was over,
There were four and twenty less.
Wha'll dae ye, lassie,
Wha'll dae ye noo?
The mon wha did ye last nicht,
Cannae dae ye noo."

"Stop the noise, Moffat," Andrew ordered. "You'll attract the Afridis. Keep them occupied without the free entertainment!"

"Aye, sir," Moffat said, working his rifle bolt.

"There are hundreds of them, sir," Pearson commented.

"Plenty of targets, then," Andrew replied.

A and G Companies of the Northamptons were struggling and unable to retire while carrying their casualties. No regiment would willingly leave men behind on the Frontier, for the Pashtun would torture them to an agonising death.

The Northamptons refused to panic, but unused to Frontier conditions, they stuck to the drill book of aimed volleys as their training demanded. Andrew watched, frustrated, knowing the men were excellent material.

"Come on, MI!" Andrew shouted. "Help the Northamptons!"

General Westmacott had seen the Northamptons' difficulties and ordered the 36th Sikhs back up the hill. Much more experienced in Frontier warfare, the Sikhs sent skirmishers to keep the Afridis at a distance, enabling the English regiment to carry their casualties behind the Sikh screen.

Andrew kept his men mobile, firing and moving as they returned with the Sikhs.

The Afridis followed at a distance, firing at the Northamptons more than at the Sikhs and MI. By the time they reached the foot of the hill, the Northamptons carried a dozen wounded men, and darkness loomed over them.

"Keep the Afridis back, boys," Andrew encouraged. He saw Hobart firing wildly into the dark. "Aim at the muzzle flares, Hobart!"

"Get these men to hurry up!" Westmacott ordered.

Vulnerable without their infantry escort, the artillery rattled back to camp. With the threat of shrapnel removed, the Afridis moved closer, harassing the flanks and rear of Westmacott's retiring reconnaissance force.

The Northamptons staggered down the main *nullah*, depending on the 15th Sikhs and recently returned Dorsets to cover their flanks.

"Baird!" Westmacott snapped. "Take your men to the front and ensure the road to the camp is clear!"

"Yes, sir!" Andrew pushed his MI forward as the 36th Sikhs shifted further to the left flank and darkness gathered. The Afridis followed, firing and searching for stragglers.

"Keep the road clear, lads!" Andrew ordered.

He saw a muzzle flash ahead, extended his leading section, and rode down on the Afridi marksman, saw a blur of movement in the dark, aimed, and fired. The MI followed, spread out as he had trained them, with each man in touch with his neighbour.

The MI cleared the road of stray Afridis, reached the camp just after seven, and returned five hundred yards to escort the returning infantry. The Sikhs were composed, the Dorsets slightly less so, and the Northamptons arrived in penny packets, some carrying their casualties.

"Roll call!" Westmacott ordered as the last company staggered in, still firing.

Each unit formed up, company by company, under the flickering glare of torches, with the senior NCOs calling the roll and the men answering their names.

Andrew's men were all present, as were both Sikh regiments and the Dorsets, but the Northamptons were less fortunate.

"What's happened?" Andrew asked.

"Part of the rearguard got left behind," an anonymous lieutenant told Andrew. "The regiment was extended in the *nullah*, and we lost touch with the rearguard."

"How many men?" Andrew asked.

"Second Lieutenant McIntyre, Colour Sergeant Luck, and eleven privates are missing, sir," the lieutenant replied.

Andrew looked back to the sinister darkness of the night. *Putting an inexperienced second lieutenant in charge of the rearguard during a contested withdrawal was foolish. If these men are fortunate, they'll already be dead.*

"Sir!" Andrew approached Westmacott. "Permission to take the MI back to search for McIntyre's party."

"Refused," Westmacott replied at once. "McIntyre will have to fend for himself tonight. We'll search tomorrow morning."

"It may be too late then, sir," Andrew said.

"I won't send men to their deaths, Baird. Dismissed."

Andrew returned to his men, angry and frustrated. "Grab some sleep, boys," he said. "We'll search for McIntyre's men tomorrow."

CHAPTER 36

TIRAH, NORTHWEST FRONTIER, NOVEMBER 1897

Andrew's MI led Westmacott's brigade back towards the pass the following morning, but they had not ridden far before they found the remains of McIntyre's men. They lay in the *nullah*, dead, with frost covering their bodies and their rifles and ammunition missing.

"It looks like they fought to the last," Innes said.

Andrew nodded. "I'll never doubt the courage of British soldiers," he said. "Only the stupidity of senior officers who send them out half-trained against some of the most dangerous warriors in the world." He worked out what had happened.

"The Northamptons straggled down the *nullah*," Andrew said, "and McIntyre's party were at the rear. The Afridis cut them off, lined up at the edge of the *nullah* and fired down on them. It was a perfect place for an ambush, with nowhere to hide." He shook his head. "It was an unnecessary waste of life."

"Yes, sir," Innes agreed, "but they died like British soldiers."

"That will be a great consolation to their families!" Andrew fought his impotent bitterness. "We had fifty-five British and nine Sikh casualties on this reconnaissance," he said.

"You sound very angry, sir," Innes said.

"I am angry," Andrew replied. "I am angry at the total waste of good men."

"Sir!" Sergeant Brown rode to Andrew and saluted. "We have a prisoner who asks to talk to you."

Why?

"He asked for you by name, sir, Captain Andrew Baird."

Andrew sighed. "Very well, Sergeant, bring him here."

The man looked like a typical Afridi warrior, with steady eyes, a hook nose and a loose turban. Tall and rangy, he stood beside an escort of two MI, disarmed yet still dangerous.

"What's your name?" Andrew asked in his now-fluent Pashto.

"Shahid Khan," the man replied, holding Andrew's gaze.

"Why do you want to see me, and how do you know my name?"

"I am from the Aka Khel," Shahid Khan said. "We want a truce with the British, but the Zakha Khel want us to keep fighting."

Andrew nodded.

We have a breakthrough. Andrew knew the Afridis were split into eight different clans, each with its own agenda. "It would be better if you spoke to General Lockhart," he said.

"You are looking for a foreigner," Shahid Khan said.

Andrew started. He had questioned scores of people in the Tirah without success. "I am," he agreed cautiously.

"The Zakha Khel are hiding four foreigners."

Andrew hid his surge of enthusiasm. *Four Russians? No wonder the unrest is so widespread.* "Where are these foreigners hidden?"

"Near the Bagh Mosque," Shahid Khan said.

"Why are you telling me this?" Andrew asked. *We've already checked the Bagh Mosque. Is this man leading me into a trap?*

"I am telling you this to show the Aka Khel want a truce with Lockhart's men," Shahid Khan said.

"Can you take me and my men to the foreigners?" Andrew asked.

"No. Once the Zakha Khel see British soldiers, they will gather, destroy you and move the foreigners away. I will take you alone if you dress as a Pashtun warrior."

I've done that before, Andrew reminded himself.

"How can I trust you?" Andrew asked.

"Take my son as a hostage," Shahid Khan replied immediately. "If I betray you, give him to the Sikhs. They will kill him slowly."

Andrew knew the Sikhs and Pashtuns despised each other. "Where is your son?"

"I will fetch him," Shahid Khan offered.

"No," Andrew shook his head. "I'll trust you." He knew he was taking a considerable risk travelling with an unknown Pashtun into tribal territory. However, he also knew the man might not hand over his son, but some stranger and showing trust might help win the Aka Khel's neutrality.

Devil take it! This man could hand me over to the Zakha Khels or just slit my throat as soon as we leave the camp. He could have shot me at any time if he wanted me dead.

Shahid Khan smiled. "And I will trust you to speak well of the Aka Khel."

"I'll have to speak to my superior first," Andrew said.

General Lockhart reluctantly agreed to Andrew leaving the camp, with Innes in charge of the MI.

"Does Lieutenant Innes have the experience?" Lockhart asked.

"He's as good a junior officer as any I've served with," Andrew replied. "And Sergeant Brown is a sound man who will keep him right."

Lockhart sighed. "Junior officers should know their place. If General Windrush was not in your corner, Baird, I'd have you on convoy escort duty until this campaign ends." He scowled at Andrew. "On you go then." He waited until Andrew was at the flap of his tent. "And Baird!"

"Yes, sir?" Andrew turned around.

"The very best of luck."

"Thank you, sir," Andrew replied.

❄

THEY SLIPPED OUT OF THE CAMP IN THE EVENING TO MINIMISE the possibility of the Afridis seeing them and headed for the pass.

"You said the foreigners were in the Bagh Mosque," Andrew said.

"They are," Shahid Khan replied. "The Bagh Mosque in the Bara Valley."

"Are there two Bagh Mosques?"

"Yes. Keep up with me." They rode quietly up the pass and were in the Bara Valley by first light.

"I am surprised the Afridis didn't see us," Andrew said.

"They saw us," Shahid Khan said calmly. "We passed three sentries, but they didn't know who we were." He grinned. "They know the British are too stupid to disguise themselves."

Andrew smiled. "A lot of British lack guile," he agreed. "Or imagination."

The atmosphere in the Bara Valley differed from the Tirah Maidan. Andrew found it tense, with warriors on guard at the watchtowers and the village gates closed. Groups of warriors passed Andrew and Shahid Khan, greeting them with questions and suspicious looks. Andrew kept quiet, trusting his companion to reply.

"Who are these foreigners?" Andrew asked.

"British prisoners," Shahid Khan said. "Taken in the Khyber."

"I didn't know the Afridis had any British prisoners," Andrew said. *I am still no closer to finding these damned Russians!*

Shahid Khan nodded. "The Zakha Khel have four."

"Are there any other foreigners here? Any Russians?" *I've never heard of the Afridis taking prisoners before.*

"No," Shahid Khan replied.

Every mile took Andrew deeper into hostile country and further from Lockhart's camp.

Shahid Khan could have betrayed me any time since we left the camp. Have faith.

They passed a ruined fort with two crumbling watchtowers and a tumbledown wall before reaching a level plain scattered with shattered boulders.

"We call this place the Place of Many Bones," Shahid Khan said quietly.

"What?" Andrew remembered the old *malik*'s words. "The Place of Many Bones? Why is it called that?" Even for the Frontier, the name was ominous.

"Two armies fought a battle here thousands of years ago," Shahid Khan said. "One of Sekundar's[1] generals fought a local chieftain. Thousands of men died, and the bones remained on the plain for centuries. Something about the ground or the air keeps them from turning to dust. Look." He dismounted and scraped his shoe through the dust, stooped and lifted the skeleton of a human hand.

"That's interesting," Andrew said, looking at the arid plain. "Where are your four foreigners? Take me to this mosque." He felt for the revolver hidden inside his robes.

The mosque stood at the side of the Place of Many Bones, a plain building slowly crumbling into ruin beside a grove of walnut trees.

They halted outside the building, with a chill wind raising the dust and the distant hills sharply etched against a clear blue sky. Andrew dismounted.

"Are there no guards?"

"They are inside," Shahid Khan said.

Andrew took the Martini from beside his saddle and stepped towards the mosque.

---

1. Sekundar: Alexander the Great, who passed through Afghanistan and what is now Pakistan on his journey to India.

Shahid Khan accompanied him as he pushed open the door, rifle held ready.

The interior was gloomy, with the only source of light a long window at the far end of the building. Three men saw Andrew enter, and one called a challenge.

"We're here to take the prisoners away," Shahid Khan told him.

"On whose orders?"

"Mullah Sadullah," Shahid Khan replied smoothly.

The three men were elderly, with white beards, but they still looked fit and capable. Andrew kept his Martini pointed at the spokesman, ready to fire.

"We heard nothing," the spokesman said. "Who are you?"

"I am Shahid Khan of the Aka Khel."

"Who is he?" the second man looked closely at Andrew. "I know him! He is one of the *feringhees* who defended Razali Fort in the Khyber!"

Andrew cursed. He had not expected anybody to recognise him for his past exploits. When the second man reached for the knife at his belt, Andrew shot him in the chest, then swung the butt of his rifle at the spokesman. The spokesman tried to duck, but the butt smashed against the side of his head, knocking him to the floor.

The third man was faster, running at Andrew with a pulwar. Shahid Khan drew his Khyber Knife and thrust underhand, catching the third man in the stomach and ripping upwards.

In the meantime, the spokesman had recovered and lunged at Andrew, who crashed the butt of his Martini on his head again, smashing it until the man lay still.

"Somebody will have heard the shot," Shahid Khan sounded worried.

Andrew reloaded quickly, thumbing a cartridge into the Martini's breech. "We'll have to move fast," he said.

Three doors opened from the main prayer room; the closest was directly beneath the *mihrab*, the niche on the wall indicating the direction of Mecca. Andrew opened this door first, peered inside, saw the room full of religious books, and moved to the second.

A large key protruded from the lock. Andrew turned it and stepped inside.

Three men were tied to the wall, emaciated, bruised and filthy. A fourth sat on a padded chair, calmly smoking a long black cigarette. He smiled as Andrew entered. "You must be Captain Baird," he said in perfect, if slightly accented, English.

Andrew pointed his Martini at the speaker. "I am," he said. "Who the devil are you?"

The man bowed without standing and blew smoke into the air. "I am Alexis Sokolov," he said. "I am the man for whom you have been searching."

"Wait there," Andrew said. "Shahid Khan, ensure this fellow does not get away."

Shahid Khan pointed his Snider at the Russian while Andrew moved to the prisoners.

"I am Captain Andrew Baird," he said as he sawed through their bonds. "Who are you?"

"Oh, thank God! I am Second-Lieutenant Trueman, sir, and these men are Privates Robinson and Hartley." All three were huge-eyed and bruised.

"Can you stand?" Andrew asked.

"I don't know, sir," Trueman was dazed. "What's happening? Where are we? Have you come to rescue us?"

"I'll answer your questions later," Andrew said. "See if there's any food in this place and grab the weapons from the dead men in the hall outside. I must speak to this man."

Sokolov looked amused as he puffed at his cigarette.

"Was this fellow your jailer?" Andrew asked as an afterthought.

"He worked with the Paythans, sir," Trueman said. "I don't know what he said, but they listened to him."

Shahid Khan pressed his Snider against the Russian's chest.

"He was one of the men who told the tribes to rise against the British," he said.

"I thought so," Andrew watched Trueman and Robinson limp outside. "How many others were there, Sokolov?"

Sokolov drew on his cigarette. "I don't know, Captain Baird. It doesn't matter now. There may have been ten or a hundred." When he languidly stood, Andrew knew he was the tall man who he had seen with the red-bearded *mullah*.

Sokolov's attitude angered Andrew. "You have caused hundreds of deaths and injuries, Sokolov."

"That's just the start of it," Sokolov said. "I played a very minor part." He eyed Andrew levelly through a plume of smoke. "More minor than you assume."

Andrew heard Trueman moving next door. "What do you mean?"

"I am only one man, Captain," Sokolov spread his hands. "Do you think I could travel from Chitral to the Malakand, to Tirah and the Khyber at the same time?"

Andrew felt his anger grow. Private Hartley was watching, his eyes mobile beneath a shaggy fringe of hair.

"He's playing games, Captain Baird," Hartley said. "Only one Russian helped raise the tribes. The Afghans did the rest."

"How do you know?" Andrew asked, bewildered by the events in the mosque.

"I know the difference between an Afghan and a Russian, sir," Hartley said. "The Amir of Afghanistan has been stirring up trouble ever since Mortimer Durand fixed the border between Afghanistan and British India. He called for a Holy War, not the Tsar."

"Keep quiet, Private!" Andrew concentrated on the Russian. "Why did the Russians become involved? Do you intend to invade India?"

Sokolov shrugged. "I don't know what the Tsar intends," he said. "Nor do I care."

"Aren't you from the *Okhrana*, the Tsar's secret service?" Andrew tried to make sense of the situation.

Sokolov laughed openly. "No, my naïve British friend. You could not be more wrong! I am from the *Narodnaya Volya*."

"Why?" Andrew was unable to hide his surprise. "We ended your plot to assassinate Lord Elgin."

"You British have no imagination," Sokolov said. "Lord Elgin was not the target, and the man you caught was a martyr, as am I. We are part of a movement to overthrow the Tsar and bring a most just society where the people have control."

"Who was the target?" Andrew asked as Trueman and Robinson entered the room.

The Russian's smile vanished. He glared at Andrew. "I'll tell you nothing, Captain Baird."

Andrew pulled the revolver from inside his poshteen. "You've helped cause a war, Sokolov. I can shoot you here and now and the world would be a cleaner place."

"You wouldn't shoot me! You're a British officer," Sokolov did not look quite so confident as his words suggested.

"Try me," Andrew said. He held his revolver to the Russian's head with first pressure on the trigger. Sokolov faced him, with his eyes suddenly wide with fear. Andrew frowned. *Those eyes! I've seen those eyes before.* "Who are you?" He glared into the Russian's face, trying to remember.

"Oh, dear God!"

CHAPTER 37

TIRAH, NORTHWEST FRONTIER, NOVEMBER 1897

Andrew hesitated as the memory returned. He was back on the Shandur Pass, with the altitude crushing his chest and the snow glare blinding him. Two men rescued him, carrying him over the summit through deep snow. One had the same bright blue eyes.

"You carried me on the Shandur Pass two years ago," Andrew said slowly. "You saved my life."

Sokolov nodded. "You would have died if we had left you," he said.

"Why save me?" Andrew asked. "I am your enemy."

"You are not our enemy. Our enemy is the Tsar and the aristocracy. Anyway, we needed you," Sokolov replied. His confidence returned as he realised Andrew would not kill him. "We needed you to spread misinformation about the Tsar's men creating unrest."

Andrew replaced his revolver in its holster. "Thank you for saving my life," he said. "What happened to the other man?"

"Your army shot him in the Khyber," Sokolov replied.

Andrew nodded. "You'd better get out now. If I see you in British territory again, I will surely kill you."

"I knew that British officers were gentlemen," Sokolov said, smiling. "Yet still naïve."

"Maybe," Andrew said. "What do you plan?"

Sokolov laughed. "We are going to assassinate Victor Demidov in two days, Captain Baird, and there is nothing you can do to stop us. Not even you can travel to Simla in time."

Andrew felt a cold shiver from the base of his spine to his neck. If the *Narodnaya Volya* assassinated the Russian ambassador in Simla, the Russians would blame the British, who already suspected the *Okhrana* of causing the Pashtun violence along the Frontier.

The jingle ran through Andrew's head.

We don't want to fight, but by jingo, if we do,
We've got the men, we've got the ships, we've got the money too.

"That might lead to war," Andrew said.

Sokolov nodded. "We hope so," he said. "A war would show the corruption in the Tsar's regime and the terrible conditions in which the people live. A war between Great Britain and the Russian Empire would surely rid us of the Tsar. The proletariat would triumph."

Andrew took a deep breath. "Half a million people died in the Crimean War, and we have more modern weapons now, more powerful artillery, Gatling guns, ironclad ships. There would be hundreds of thousands of deaths."

"Their sacrifice would be worthwhile," Sokolov said.

"The dead might not agree," Andrew said dryly.

"What's happening, sir?" Trueman asked. "What do you want us to do?"

"We're getting back to the British camp," Andrew said. "As quickly as possible."

"What about him?" Trueman nodded to Sokolov.

"We let him go," Andrew said. "He saved my life once."

"His words cost many Aka Khel lives," Shahid Khan said. He drew his knife and thrust it into the Russian's chest.

"No!" Andrew was too late to save Sokolov, who was already dead before his body hit the ground.

Shahid Khan wiped the soles of both feet on the Russian's body.

"You men strip the Pashtuns' bodies," Andrew said. "Take their clothes."

"Sir?" Trueman looked startled.

"We'll have to act as Afridis to get away from here," Andrew said. "Move!"

Dazed by their captivity, Trueman was slow to comprehend, so Andrew explained further. "If the Afridis see British soldiers wandering around, they'll kill us without compulsion. Wearing Pashtun clothes will give us a better chance to get away."

The men obeyed, stripping the dead guards and hauling their outer clothes over the rags that remained of their uniforms.

"Are you men fit to walk?" Andrew asked.

"We'll try," they replied. Hartley looked more like a Pashtun than a Pashtun.

Andrew frowned, shook his head and pushed a memory away. "Come on, then." He led them from the mosque and onto the barren plain. They blinked and shaded their eyes from the sudden harsh light after the gloom of their confinement.

"How long have you been prisoners?" Andrew asked.

"I don't know," Trueman said. "What's the date?"

"November 1897," Andrew told him.

"They captured us in August," Trueman said. "Where are we going?"

"Back to the main force in the Bara Valley," Andrew said. "We're in the Tirah, if you were wondering, and I must get a message to Simla."

"Simla is hundreds of miles from the Tirah!" Trueman was already wilting in the sun, while Robinson was staggering, hardly able to walk.

Andrew swore.

These men are not sufficiently fit to make the journey.

"Shahid Khan! How far is the nearest Aka Khel village?"

"Three hours on foot," Shahid Khan understood immediately.

Andrew worked out the times in his head. He had to pass his information to the British, yet he could not abandon these men.

What's best to do now? Remain with these men until they are safe? Or try to pass on my message? Andrew agonised for a moment, aware of the men's gaunt appearance and what they had already endured.

I am a Windrush. I do my duty, as generations of Windrushes have done before me.

"How long on horseback?"

"An hour," Shahid Khan replied. "Maybe less."

"Ride to the nearest Aka Khel village and bring back horses. Take these men to safety, Shahid Khan. When the British come, as they will, tell them what has happened and give them my name and assurance you are friendly." Andrew hesitated a little. "No, tell them you are acting for General Jack Windrush. Have you got that?"

"General Jack Windrush," Shahid Khan repeated.

"Let's get these men somewhere sheltered for the present," Andrew said.

"What will you do?" Shahid Khan asked.

"Contact the British," Andrew replied. He looked around the barren plain with the distant mountains tall and grim, already smeared with snow. "Where is safe for these men?"

"This way," Shahid Khan said. He altered direction, heading deeper into the valley.

Andrew told Trueman what was happening.

"Trust Shahid Khan," Andrew said. "He'll look after you until the British come."

Trueman looked up, gaunt-faced beneath his four-month

beard. Andrew could only imagine what the prisoners had endured. "Yes, sir," Trueman said.

The privates tried to come to attention as the faint hope died from their eyes. "We thought you were part of a larger expedition come to rescue us, sir," Robinson said.

"I am," Andrew said. "It will take a little longer than I hoped, that's all. The Aka Khel are more friendly to the British than the other clans."

God, I hope I am doing the right thing and not transferring these men from the frying pan to the fire.

"Sir!" Private Hartley saluted. "Permission to accompany you."

"Refused," Andrew replied.

Hartley's sudden grin surprised Andrew. "Come on now, old boy, surely you won't leave an old companion behind."

"What?" Andrew peered closer. Behind the beard, bruises and dirt, he recognised the face. "Harry Symington!"

"None other, sir," Symington replied.

"We thought the Afridis killed you in the Khyber," Andrew said.

"They nearly did, sir," Symington pushed back his tangled hair to reveal a raw wound across his scalp. "I was the lucky one! I'm not sure why they took us prisoner. I thought it would be better to be in uniform than in mufti, so I took these togs from an unfortunate corpse and took his paybook for the name."

"You're with me, Symington."

"Yes, sir."

Shahid Khan led them off the plain to a jumble of weather-shattered rocks where a small pool of water and shade welcomed them.

"Thank you, Shahid Khan," Andrew said.

Andrew hardened his heart, hating himself. "I am going to leave you here," he told Trueman. "I must contact Simla and try to prevent a major war. Trust in Shahid Khan. He's a good man and will follow their rules of hospitality."

The soldiers nodded, eyeing the water.

"Good luck, lads, and may God be with you." Andrew was tempted to salute them, decided that such a dramatic gesture would not be suitable, and rode away. He wondered if he would ever see them again.

Andrew and Symington pressed forward, riding hard for the pass out of the valley. With his travel-battered Pashtun clothes and ragged beard, Andrew looked like any Afridi tribesman while Symington rode, spoke, and even spat betel juice like a Zakha Khel.

"*Allah Akbar!*" Andrew heard the familiar shout as a group of horsemen rode towards him.

What the devil do I do now? Join them! The last thing they will expect is a lone British soldier riding through their territory.

"Follow my lead, Symington, and hope your disguise is effective."

Symington grinned. "Yes, sir!"

"*Allah Akbar!*" Andrew shouted and rode behind the tribesmen, with the leading rider raising a large green flag in the air.

Other Afridis joined them, singly or in small groups, as they trotted towards the pass. One man grinned at him, shouting something Andrew could not understand above the hammer of hooves. Andrew smiled back, lifted a hand in acknowledgement and ducked his head to concentrate on riding. Teviot was tiring, lagging behind the main group. Andrew strove to keep up, using the *lashkar* as cover to reach the pass without being questioned. Symington rode between Andrew and the warriors, occasionally spitting onto the ground.

They reached the hill in the evening, with darkness a welcome cloak as Andrew and Symington remained behind the Afridis, yet sufficiently close to be regarded as one of them.

When the warriors dismounted, Andrew and Symington rode on, ignoring the shouts of his companions. After a few moments, Andrew slid off Teviot and signalled for Symington to follow suit.

"We walk from here," Andrew said.

Symington nodded, drooping from exhaustion.

Andrew led them, long striding and hoping not to be challenged. He heard men talking on the right of the track, greeted them in Pashto and walked on.

Andrew sang a song by the famous Pashto poet Kushkhal Khan Khatak, the only Pashtun song he knew, hoping the words would disguise his accent.

"It is for the Afghan honour that the sword I have beside me
I, Kushkhal Khatak, am the only proud Afghan of the day!"

While a few men joined in, and some laughed, an authoritarian voice warned him. "Be quiet, *ghazi*. You will attract the attention of the *feringhees*."

Andrew lifted a hand in acknowledgement, closed his mouth, and walked on. He hoped he had given the impression he was a *ghazi*, uncaring of the British, as he walked on through the gathering darkness.

Two sangars guarded the summit, with men crowded around cooking fires, laughing high-pitched as they prepared their evening meal. Andrew lingered for a minute to dispel any suspicion and count their numbers. Somebody shouted something, either a challenge or a greeting; Andrew was not sure which. He replied with a wave of his hand, sang the same couplet of his song, and led his weary horse over the summit with Symington a few steps behind.

"The infidels will shoot you!" an elderly man warned.

Andrew continued, with his heart hammering and his throat dry. Leaving the valley had been easier than he expected, but now he had to avoid the pickets, reach the British camp and pass on his message.

"Close up, Symington," Andrew said. "Try to walk like a soldier rather than a Pashtun. We must be approaching our forward pickets."

Even though he expected it, the challenge took Andrew by surprise.

"Halt! Who goes there? Advance and identify yourself!"

CHAPTER 38

TIRAH, NORTHWEST FRONTIER, NOVEMBER 1897

"I am Captain Andrew Baird and my companion is Lieutenant Harry Symington," Andrew replied. "And say, sir, when you are addressing an officer!"

"Officer, my arse!" the crude reply assured Andrew the challenger was a British soldier. "You're a bloody Paythan. Stand there, or I'll blow your bloody head off."

"Is your officer present?" Andrew asked. He knew a nervous British sentry was every bit as likely to shoot him as an Afridi warrior. "Or an NCO?"

"Hey, Sergeant!" the voice from the dark called. "There's a raggy-arsed Paythan here who wants to talk to you."

"I don't want to talk to him!" the sergeant replied.

"I assure you, Sergeant, you'd better talk to me," Andrew called. "And snap to it!"

Andrew heard the crunch of boots on the ground, a torch flared, and a startled sergeant gaped at him. "Who did you say you are, sir?"

When Andrew repeated his name and rank, the sergeant

came to attention, saluted, apologised and invited him into the British sangar. "You too, sir," the sergeant said to Symington.

"Do you have a heliograph?" Andrew asked.

"Not here, sir. Company headquarters has, back at the solitary tree knoll."

"Send a runner to inform them I'm on my way," Andrew said. "No, hang it all; I'll go with the runner."

"Yes, sir."

❊

"Sir!" Lieutenant Cotton, the aide-de-camp, stood at attention within Jack's office door. "A message for you from the Tirah, sir. It's marked Urgent and Top Priority!"

"Who's it from?" Jack snatched the telegram, saw it was from Andrew, scanned it and reread it slowly.

"Cotton!"

"I'm here, sir," the aide-de-camp had not moved from his position inside the door.

"When did this message arrive?" Jack reached for his belt and revolver.

Cotton checked his watch. "Three minutes ago, sir."

"Damn!" Jack said. "It's alerting us to a proposed assassination today. Which regiment is on duty in Simla today?"

Cotton looked doubtful, following Jack as he hurried from his office. "I don't know, sir."

"You don't know? It's your job to know!" Jack stalked outside. "Never mind. Rouse them, whoever they are. I want every man on duty. Send their colonel to me, and I want whoever commands the police as well."

"Civil or military, sir?" Cotton asked.

"Contact both. And send a message to every officer under general rank to be on alert." Jack strode to the stables. "Is my horse ready?"

"No, sir," Cotton hurried after Jack. "Where can I reach you, sir? Where will I tell these people to find you?"

Jack stopped. "I'll be with the viceroy," he said. "Tell them to meet me at Peterhoff in half an hour."

"Yes, sir."

Lord Elgin looked up when Jack barged into his office. "Look here, Windrush. You can't crash in like that. There's a proper procedure, you know."

"Yes, your Excellency. I've no time for that. Russian dissidents are going to assassinate Demidov."

"When?" Elgin asked, standing up.

"Today, sir."

"Is it a credible source?"

"Yes, Your Excellency. Unimpeachable. I've asked the head of police and colonel of the garrison to meet here," Jack checked his watch, "in ten minutes."

"Good. Do we know who the assassin is?"

"No, sir. Only that he's Russian and a member of the *Narodnaya Volya*," Jack said.

"What's that?" Elgin asked.

"It's a Russian revolutionary socialist group, your Excellency, dedicated to overthrowing the Czar," Andrew said.

Elgin took a deep breath. "As if we hadn't got enough trouble here," he said. "What are we going to do about it?"

"We're going to catch the assassin, Your Excellency, and ensure Demidov is still alive tonight."

Superintendent Buchanan was the first to arrive at Peterhoff, followed by Colonel Wainwright, the garrison commander. Andrew gave them brief details.

"What do you suggest, Windrush?" Elgin asked.

"Summon Demidov here, Your Excellency; tell him to come secretly and don't allow anybody else in. We can't interfere with the internal workings of the Russian Embassy, but I suggest we seal it off, let nobody in or out and let their secret service find the assassin."

"The *Okhrana* have a reputation for ruthlessness," Buchanan said.

"That's not our affair," Jack said. "Our duty is to look after India."

"Isolating an embassy may cause a bit of a stink," Buchanan said.

"Having an ambassador murdered in Simla will cause a much bigger stink," Jack told him. "Where are your men?"

"My men are patrolling the streets," Buchanan said.

"As are mine," Colonel Wainwright added. "But we don't know who or what we are looking for."

"How large is the garrison, Colonel?" Jack asked.

"Not large, sir," Wainwright admitted. "Most of the fighting men are on the Frontier. I have the sick, the lame and the recovering with a small detail for Embassy protection."

Jack grunted. "I want them all on the streets, Wainwright. I don't care if they have to march on crutches or with a medical orderly at their side carrying a bedpan."

Wainwright snorted. "That's a bit strong, sir."

"Strong or not," Jack said. "That's an order!"

"I'll send one of my staff with a note to the Russian embassy," Elgin decided. "The ambassador will be safe here. I can inform him of the current situation on the Frontier."

"No," Jack said. "I'll go. He knows me."

"That's highly irregular," Elgin protested.

"So is killing off ambassadors," Jack reminded. He glanced at the longcase clock in the corner of the room. "I'll leave as soon as we finish this meeting. I want all your men patrolling the streets, Colonel Wainwright, and every British and Indian officer in Simla on high alert. Lay aside all other duties." Jack stopped. "Your Excellency," he said quietly. "I have an idea."

"An idea?" Elgin asked. "What the devil do you mean?"

Jack began to smile. "Listen, gentlemen," he said and elaborated.

JIGSAW ON THE KHYBER

❄

Andrew sat on Tweed, watching Brigadier General Francis James Kempster lead his column over the Tseri Kandao Pass and into the Waran Valley: Aka Khel territory. The men marched well: a mixed force of Gordon Highlanders, Dorsets, 1st/2nd Gurkhas, 15th and 36th Sikhs, Sappers and two Mountain Gun batteries. Andrew's MI acted as a flank guard.

"Are you fit to travel with us, Captain Baird?" Kempster asked for the third time that day.

"Yes, sir. I left two British soldiers with the Aka Khel, and I'd like to get them home."

Kempster nodded. "We'll see what we can do, Baird, but our primary objective is to bring the Aka Khel to heel."

"It was Shahid Khan from the Aka Khel that helped me, sir," Andrew said. "I don't think they'll cause trouble."

Kempster tapped the sword that hung beside his saddle. "I hope not," he said. "But if they do, we'll be ready for them."

With the 36th Sikhs guarding the Tseri Kandao Pass, Kempster pushed into the valley. Warriors stood on the slopes, watching the British file down without attempting to interfere.

"Keep the men in extended order, Innes," Andrew ordered. "Don't fire unless they do." He scanned the slopes with his binoculars. The warriors remained in the open.

"If they were hostile," Andrew said, "they'd be hiding and would have fired as we crossed the pass."

Innes nodded. "Yes, sir, but I'll ensure the men remain alert."

He's learning.

Andrew rode away as Kempster spoke to his senior officers.

"The Aka Khel are not hostile, sir," Andrew said. "They're only observing us."

"As long as that's all they're doing," Kempster said. "They held a *jirga* yesterday and accepted our peace terms, but the Pashtun are renowned for breaking their word."

"I trust these men, sir," Andrew said. "I'll vouch for them."

Kempster looked amused. "All of them, Baird?"

"If they accepted our terms at a *jirga*, sir, I'll believe them." Andrew knew he was putting men's lives and his reputation on the line.

That evening, as the Gordon Highlanders guarded the camp and the MI patrolled three hundred yards further out, Sergeant Brown reported movement to Andrew.

"I saw quite a few tribesmen passing, sir."

"Did they threaten the camp, Sergeant?" Andrew asked.

"No, sir," Brown replied. "They went straight to the nearest village."

"Did they remain in the village?" Andrew asked.

"No, sir," Brown said. "They left after an hour or so."

Andrew pondered for a moment. "That suggests they did not belong there, Sergeant."

"Perhaps so, sir," Brown conceded.

The following morning, Andrew asked Kempster for permission to visit the village.

"Why?"

"I want to know what their nocturnal visitors wanted," Andrew said.

Kempster nodded. "How many men do you wish, Captain?"

"Only one, sir," Andrew said. "Somebody to hold my horse. I want to appear as if I trust the villagers."

"Very well. Take care, Baird," Kempster said.

Andrew took Moffat as his horseholder and rode slowly, raising a hand to show he came in peace. The village looked no different from any other along the Frontier, with solid stone walls and a tall watchtower from where two guards watched Andrew approach.

Andrew reined up outside the gate.

"I am Captain Andrew Baird," he said. "I wish to speak to the *malik*."

The grey-bearded *malik* greeted Andrew with a smile and an

invitation for a meal. Andrew accepted, aware of the Pashtun law of hospitality.

"You are of the Aka Khel," Andrew said.

"We are," the *malik* said.

"You had visitors last night," Andrew said.

The *malik* agreed.

"Were they Aka Khel or Zakha Khel?" Andrew asked directly.

The *malik* did not hide his smile. "They were Zakha Khel," he said.

Andrew nodded. He thought it better not to ask further. "I believe the Aka Khel are friendly to the British."

The *malik* agreed.

"Let's hope that arrangement continues," Andrew said.

"Let us hope so," the *malik* said.

The men from the village watched Andrew from their homes. He wondered how many had participated in the actions against Lockhart's column and whether any had attacked Fort Razali.

"The Aka Khel have two British guests," Andrew said. "Lieutenant Trueman and Private Robinson. I wish to bring them back to General Kempster's column."

The *malik* looked grave. "I will arrange to send them to you."

"Thank you," Andrew said.

"What do you think, Captain?" Kempster asked when Andrew returned to the column.

"I believe the Aka Khel will keep the peace," Andrew said. "With your permission, sir, I'd like to station a couple of men to watch the village tonight."

"Why?"

"In case of any visitors, sir. I'd like to see who they are."

"Your MI?" Kempster shook his head. "No, Captain. I'll place some Gurkhas there. They can see the devil's shadow crossing a pile of coal on a moonless night, and not even a Paythan will see them."

Andrew smiled at the analogy. "Yes, sir. I've heard they are pretty good sepoys."

Andrew had little experience with the Gurkhas but now witnessed their relationship with the British soldiers. After fighting together on the Dargai Heights, the Gurkhas and Gordon Highlanders formed a close companionship, with the Gordons even putting up the Gurkhas' tents when the latter returned to camp after a long expedition.

Not only the Sikhs are good soldiers, Andrew told himself, *the Gurkhas are also special. We are very fortunate in the quality of our sepoys.*

❄

ASAD LAY QUIET. HE HAD ACCOMPANIED BABACK AND ZARAM as he followed the infidels out of the valley and waited his time with all the patience of the Pashtun. Now, he rolled from his bed and sneaked from his place in the camp. Ignoring Baback, Asad crawled to Zaram, who snored gently in his sleep with his Martini clutched in his gnarled hand with the grey hairs curled over a white scar gained in a long-forgotten skirmish. Asad took a branch from a thorn tree, gently prised Zaram's hand open, removed the Martini, and placed the branch within the hard fingers.

Zaram grunted in his sleep, muttered something and pulled the branch close to him.

Asad waited for a long moment and snaked away. He threw a pebble to his left, slipped past the sentry when he looked in that direction and vanished in the night.

CHAPTER 39

SIMLA, NOVEMBER 1897

Mariana sat in Peliti's Restaurant, sipping her tea. She watched Sinclair working on his book and the two young women twittering as they eyed up every officer who passed. She glanced at the clock on the wall and saw the minute hand move closer to nine.

Only fifteen minutes before I return to little Simla. Having an hour to myself is good, but I already miss my little girl. I wish Andrew were home.

Mariana reread the letter she was composing to Andrew. She heard the women laugh, saw the blonde glance at a passing subaltern, and added another paragraph to her letter. The blonde whispered something to her friend, stood and walked to the door. Her friend followed, holding her umbrella, ready to open against the pelting rain.

Mariana glanced out the window, saw a couple of people watching something rolling along the Mall, and remembered the Russian ambassador was due to pass. *Victor Demidov is a creature of regular habits; his coachman drives him around Simla at the same time every day, whatever the weather.*

Mariana checked her last paragraph, nodded, and looked up to see Demidov's carriage. The ambassador was alone today, heavily bundled in a greatcoat and with the carriage's hood pulled up, while the coachman drove faster than usual. The wheels threw up a fine spray as they passed through puddles.

Mariana drew a sheet of blotting paper from her writing case and pressed it over her letter. She glanced again at the clock. If she hurried, she should catch the mail for Peshawar, and from there, her letter would be forwarded to the Frontier. Mariana looked down at herself and patted her belly, proud that she would have even more good news to tell Andrew when he came home. Mariana wanted her husband to be the first to know, apart from Mary, of course. Mary knew everything.

Demidov's carriage was nearly level with Peliti's when the two women moved. The blonde pushed the subaltern aside and threw something at the carriage while the brunette pulled a pistol from inside her umbrella.

"Ambassador!" Mariana screamed a warning. She realised Sinclair was no longer in his seat, and the coachman had leapt from his perch.

The object the blonde threw bounced from the raised hood, landed on the road and rolled away. Demidov jumped out the opposite side of the carriage as the coachman ran at the brunette.

"Stay there, Mariana!" Sinclair shouted. He no longer looked like a thin and studious writer but a lithe warrior as he ran outside with a pistol in his hand. He fired twice, hitting the blonde woman as the object she threw exploded with a loud crash. The brunette fired at Demidov a second before the ambassador and the coachman fired at her.

Mariana saw the brunette fall, dropping her pistol. Sinclair ran to her, kicked the weapon away, checked her condition and glanced at the blonde.

"Both dead," he said tersely.

"Good shooting, boys," the ambassador said. He threw off his cloak and revealed himself as Jack, with Chornyi acting as coachman at his side.

"Sorry about the excitement, Mariana," Jack said "Sinclair is one of my men; he's been keeping an eye on the Mall for weeks."

"Oh," Mariana replied. "Now I have something more to tell Andrew."

❄

AS THE BRITISH CAMPAIGNED AROUND TIRAH, THEY LEFT their mark on the lands of the Zakha Khel. They flattened the crops, removed the population and burned the villages and grain stores.

"It's called economic warfare," Kempster said to Andrew. "If we deprive the Afridi of the means of living, we will break his will to fight."

"It's hard on the women and children," Andrew said.

"War is always hard on the women," Kempster replied. "But these Afridi women would skin you alive without a qualm."

At night, the flames of burning homes reflected on the clouds above, and acrid smoke perfumed the British camp. A curtain of fire surrounded the British camp as the British and Indian troops spread destruction everywhere. Byres, forts, outhouses and homes burned fiercely all night. The Zakha Khel retaliated with ambushes and attacks on British convoys and camps.

The shooting that night began with a single rifle. The bullet pierced a hole in an officer's tent, splintered the tent pole and exited without causing any other damage. The Gurkhas were on guard and replied with a quick volley.

"Call out the guard!"

The bugles sounded the alarm, and British, Sikh, and Gurkhas tumbled out of their tents in various states of dress and undress, took their assigned places, and waited for orders.

The lone Afridi fired again, with the bullet ripping through a tent.

"Gurkhas! Fire a volley," Kempster ordered, "then three rounds rapid."

The garrison fired, with the sound tearing through the night.

The following silence was nearly painful as the British waited for the Afridi response. Andrew heard a few shouts with the ubiquitous "*Allah Akbar!*" and obscene insults about the infidels, then silence again.

"Maintain your positions," Kempster ordered.

The men remained where they were for another half hour with no movement from the enemy.

"Permission to take a patrol out, sir?" Andrew asked.

"No," Kempster replied. "The Afridis will expect that, and they'll be waiting for you."

After another uneventful fifteen minutes, Kempster sent most of the men back to bed, leaving double sentries on watch.

"Innes, wake me at two in the morning," Andrew ordered.

"Yes, sir," Innes replied.

The following morning, Kempster called his officers to him. "Well, gentlemen," Kempster said. "Our patrols found a handful of brass cartridges three hundred yards from our perimeter and no sign of enemy casualties, no dead bodies or blood trails."

The officers nodded.

"How about Kohkar, sir?" Andrew asked. "The local village?"

"The Gurkhas reported no movement in the village," Kempster replied. "We can safely say the Aka Khel were not involved."

"I don't understand, sir," a young artillery officer said.

"I think the Zakha Khel wanted to end the peace between the Aka Khel and the British," Kempster explained. "They want us to blame the Aka Khel and burn down their villages, so they rejoin the fight against us."

"Sir," Andrew said, "the Aka Khel are still looking after two British soldiers."

"I haven't forgotten," Kempster said.

"Permission to take my MI to collect them, sir?"

"Granted," Kempster said. "Do you want supporting infantry and artillery?"

"No, sir," Andrew said. "That may make the Aka Khel think it's a punitive expedition and encourage them to attack. It would play into the Zakha Khel's hands."

Kempster eyed Andrew for a moment. "Very well, Baird. While you collect the two men, I'll take a force to strike at the Zakha Khel. The dual action will show the Aka Khel we trust them and warn the Zakha Khel that their actions have consequences."

"Yes, sir," Andrew agreed.

Andrew left before dawn the following day, with his MI behind him with flank and rear guards. They rode through the crisp night with fading starlight reflecting from the frosty ground and the sound of their horses' hooves hollow through the silence.

"These people in Khokar are friendly," Andrew reminded, "but the Zakha Khel might have infiltrated them. Don't fire unless I give permission."

"What if they fire first, sir?" Sergeant Brown asked.

"Don't retaliate for a single shot," Andrew replied. "It may be a young hothead trying out his birthday rifle or the village idiot out on the spree."

As Andrew intended, the men laughed and rode with relaxed wariness. They halted at a rocky ridge overlooking the village.

"Sir!" Moffat lay beneath the skyline on a rocky ridge, scanning the valley. The MI lay behind the crest, with pickets watching for the Afridi and the others relaxing, sleeping or playing cards. Andrew had banned them from smoking. "Somebody's coming, sir."

Andrew lifted his binoculars. A group of riders came slowly from the west, heading directly for Kempster's camp. "Let's see who they are, Moffat." He raised his voice. "Ride and go, MI. Extended order and keep fifty yards behind me."

As he came closer to the approaching Pashtuns, Andrew recognised the leading rider.

"They're friendly! That's Shahid Khan and our lads!"

Andrew halted the MI a hundred yards from the Aka Khel and rode forward alone. Shahid Khan greeted him with an upraised hand.

"*Assalamu alaikum* – peace be upon you, Shahid Khan," Andrew said.

"*Wa alaikum salaam* – and unto you, peace, Captain Baird," Shahid Khan replied. "Here are your friends."

Trueman and Robinson were mounted awkwardly on two ponies. They walked their mounts slowly forward.

"You're safe then," Andrew said.

"We are," Trueman replied.

Andrew nodded. "Let's get you back to General Kempster." He was relaxed as he returned to the camp. The campaign was going as well as expected; the Russian agent was dead, Symington and the prisoners were safe, and he would soon be back with Mariana. He glanced over his men, saw they were riding confidently, and nodded. Life was as good as it ever could be during a war.

❇

"We've shown the flag and warned the Zakha Khel," Kempster said that evening. "We're returning to the Maidan Camp today. The main body will march with the transport. The 36th Sikhs will march from the summit of the Tseri Kandao Pass to guard the Maidan side, and the 15th Sikhs will guard the hills on both sides of the pass."

Andrew nodded. The British had learned to take the high ground on either side of hill passes.

"The 1st/2nd Gurkhas will act as rearguard while we cross the pass," Kempster said, "whereupon the 15th Sikhs will act as rearguard until we reach the Maidan when the 36th Sikhs will take over as rearguard."

Andrew nodded. Kempster was giving the hardest and most dangerous jobs to the more experienced Indian regiments.

"Baird," Kempster said, "you're with the rearguard."

"Yes, sir." Andrew understood. By placing a British unit with the rearguard, Kempster had ensured nobody could accuse him of keeping the British safe.

Andrew organised his men to ride on the flanks of the Gurkhas, with Brown on the right and Innes on the left. He took the rearmost position with Pearson, Hobart and a stocky Dorset man named Comben, stopping every two hundred yards to survey the land for any danger.

"Sahib," a Gurkha *naik* said. "The enemy is watching us." He nodded towards a group of rocks.

When Andrew focused his binoculars, what he thought were rocks became crouching tribesmen in grey cloaks. "They might be friendly Aka Khel," he said.

"No, Sahib," the *naik* said. "They are Zakha Khel. Five men with rifles and more are behind the rocks over there."

Andrew did not doubt the *naik*'s word. He glanced ahead, where the main body and the transport trundled towards the pass. Trueman and Robinson were there, moving to safety with British and Sikh regiments guarding them. Now, he had to get back to Mariana and little Simla.

The Zakha Khel fired from long range, with the men in the rocks firing first. The shots sounded like whipcracks, with the bullets passing high.

"Terrible shooting," the *naik* said, laughing.

Andrew returned the smile, knowing the Gurkhas were not usually renowned for their marksmanship.

"Fire only when you think you can hit your target," Andrew ordered his men.

"Yes, sir!" Hobart said, firing wildly.

The MI kept moving, spoiling the Zakha Khel's aim by never riding in a straight line. As the number of attackers increased, the MI returned fire. Andrew could not see if there were any enemy casualties as the rearguard moved steadily towards the pass. He saw a Gurkha fall, wounded, and another crumple, shot through the head.

"With me, MI!" Andrew shouted and led a counterattack at one group of Zakha Khel, who came too close. His men trotted forward, firing from the saddle. Andrew thought he saw one of the enemy fall before the group fled into an area of broken ground where men on foot had the advantage.

"Retire, MI," Andrew shouted, fired a final shot, wheeled and returned to his position with the Gurkhas.

The main body and the transport wagons were approaching the summit of the pass when the Gurkhas reached the foot.

Andrew saw more Gurkha dead and wounded, with the rest firing and withdrawing by sections, chattering to each other as they fought.

The Gurkhas are different to the Sikhs. They don't posture or make dramatic gestures, but they are every bit as good soldiers.

"Up the pass, Gurkhas!" a tall Gurkha officer ordered calmly. "The 15th Sikhs will take over the rearguard now."

Lieutenant-Colonel Abbott of the 15th Sikhs greeted the Gurkhas calmly. "You can relax now, Johnnies. My lads will see off the Zakha Khel."

Abbott had posted two companies at the north of the pass, two at the south and another two on a wooded spur that jutted from the Saran Sar. He stood on the pass with one company, with another in reserve on rising ground, ready to move wherever it was needed.

"Baird, I might need your MI. Remain with the rearguard."

"Yes, sir," Andrew said.

The Afridis swarmed over the mountain, some moving from cover to cover and others advancing boldly, secure in their numbers.

Andrew extended his men along the path, exchanging fire with the warriors they could see as Abbott gradually withdrew his men. The Zakha Khel attacked the spur first, running at them in numbers. The Sikhs delayed their withdrawal, stood fast and responded with accurate fire that cut down a dozen of the enemy.

"Dismount and give these lads a hand!" Andrew ordered his MI. He slid behind a tree and joined in the battle, aiming, firing, working the bolt and firing again. When he emptied the magazine, he reloaded. The attack faded away, leaving Zakha Khel dead and wounded on the ground and some Sikh casualties.

The reserve company joined Abbott as the Afridis pushed at the rearguard, firing from cover. The Sikhs withdrew slowly, carrying their wounded rather than leaving them for the Zakha Khel.

"We're hard-pressed here, Baird!" Abbott said.

"Yes, sir," Andrew ordered Innes to take his section to reinforce the Sikhs' left flank while Sergeant Brown moved to the right. As their casualties mounted, the 15th Sikhs found it hard to pull back and remained where they were, exchanging fire with increasing numbers of tribesmen.

Abbott fired his revolver at the encroaching warriors. "I've sent a man back to inform General Kempster."

Andrew looked up as a deluge of soldiers, 36th Sikhs and Dorsets arrived.

"Morning, sir," Colonel Haughton of the 36th Sikhs said. "We heard you might need a hand."

"I thought it was about time your boys did something rather than sit on their hands and admire the scenery," Abbott replied. He nodded to the Dorsets' officers. "Have you come to learn how real soldiers fight?" A moment later, an Afridi bullet smashed into Abbott, and Colonel Haughton took over command of the rearguard.

With the reinforcements holding back the Zakha Khel, the Sikhs and Dorsets withdrew from the Tseri Kandao Pass, carrying their wounded. When they descended the pass, they passed a solid, two-storey house where a company of the Dorsets remained to cover them. The MI remained with the rearguard, shepherding any stragglers, ensuring nobody was left behind and firing at the pursuing Afridis.

"Is this a victory or a defeat, sir?" Innes asked.

Andrew shook his head. "I count any day we survive on the Frontier as a victory, Innes," he replied.

As darkness fell, Andrew sent Innes and most of the MI away, remaining with Sergeant Brown, half a dozen men and around two hundred of the rearguard.

When the rearguard came under heavy fire, Brown pointed to a cluster of deserted houses on a slight rise above the track.

"That's their base, sir."

Colonel Haughton grinned. "Then that's where we'll dispose of them. These Afridis may be experts in firing from behind cover, but they can't hold a candle to my men in close action." He raised his voice. "Sikhs! Fix bayonets!"

The Sikhs complied, with the sinister snick resounding as the Sikhs fitted their wicked eighteen-inch bayonets to their Martinis.

Haughton drew his sword, spoke to his men in Punjabi, and strode forward with the Sikhs at his heels.

"Damn and blast it all," Andrew said. "I won't have anybody say the MI were backward in coming forward. Come on, lads, up and at 'em!"

The MI joined the Sikhs in their night-time charge to the houses. The Afridis resisted for a few moments and then broke and fled, with the Sikhs firing bullets and insults after them.

Haughton looked at the scatter of Zakha Khel casualties. "We'll stay here the night," he said. "We're better here than wandering off in the dark."

※

ASAD WATCHED THE INFIDELS FROM BEHIND A ROCK. HE HAD waited all day without finding his target, and now the enemy was settling for the night. He saw the sentries stirring, British and Sikhs, and remained still. The flies and insects did not bother him. Taking the Quran from inside his clothes, he began to read, searching for inspiration.

When he had read a few pages, Asad saw the infidels lighting fires in the cluster of ruined houses they occupied. He held the Martini steady, waiting for his chance.

After an hour, Asad saw a group of infidels talking, silhouetted by the fire behind them. Lying prone behind his rock, Asad thought of the pleasures of Paradise and took careful aim. He saw the tall *feringhee* stretch forward with his hand outstretched and squeezed the trigger.

❈

"Your lads did well today, Baird," Haughton said.

"Thank you, sir," Andrew replied.

"If you ever want a transfer to the 36th Sikhs, Baird, give me a shout," Haughton said, holding out his hand.

"That would be an honour, sir," Andrew stretched forward to shake Haughton's hand. He did not hear the sharp crack of Asad's Martini, only the hammer blow of a bullet smashing into his leg. He spun around without knowing what had hit him, and a second bullet cracked into his chest, knocking him sideways onto the ground.

"Baird!"

Andrew heard Haughton's voice and saw his face as a wavering shape looking down at him.

"Mariana?" Andrew said, confused. He tried to struggle up, gasped and coughed up blood. He saw the face bending over him without realising who it was. "Mariana?" Andrew repeated and closed his eyes.

❈

Asad smiled as he saw his target spin around. He half stood to reload his Martini and yelled as an infidel's bullet smashed into his chest.

It can't be a bullet. The mullah said he could turn the infidel's bullets into water. This sensation must be Allah bringing me to Paradise. But why is it so painful?

Asad looked upwards, searching desperately for his promised reward for killing an infidel. He was still hoping when his life bubbled away, and he lay prone, another forgotten casualty of the war.

❄

Private Hobart lowered his rifle. "I got him, sir," he said. "One of they *ghazis*. A big ugly fellow with a beard. I got him straight through the head, sir. Sir?"

CHAPTER 40

SIMLA, JANUARY 1898

Jack was in his office in Simla when a harassed Cotton knocked on the door.
"You look flushed, Cotton," Jack said. "What's the matter?"
"It's your son, sir," Cotton said.
"What about him?" Jack felt the cold chill of dread clutch at his heart. He controlled his emotions as decades in the army had taught him.
Cotton took a deep breath. "He's been shot, sir."
Jack closed his eyes and took a deep breath. *How will I tell Mary?* "Oh, dear God. Is he dead?"
"Not a bit of it!" Andrew shouted from the hall below. "If somebody could help me up these damned stairs, I would prove it!"
Jack pushed past Cotton, unable to stop his grin. "What are you doing with a plaster on your leg?"
"Some hairy great Afridi shot me in the thigh," Andrew said, "then another bullet grazed my ribs. I think it was Private Hobart. He's the worst shot in the army, that man. Worse than

you with a pistol, General Father, sir, and that's saying something."

"I hope it hurt, you cheeky young rascal!" Jack limped down the stairs.

"Hurt? The worst was when I bit my tongue when I fell," Andrew said. "Now, where have you hidden my wife? I need some tender loving care to get better."

❄

ANDREW SAT WITH HIS PLASTERED LEG BALANCED ON A CHAIR and a tumbler of whisky in his hand. Symington sat on his left, with Jack on the opposite side of his desk.

"You both got back safely," Jack said. "Your information helped stop an assassination, Andrew, which could have led to war with Russia."

"I'm glad it reached you in time," Andrew said. "Mariana gave me the details, but how did you know the women were the assassins?"

"Sinclair brought them to my attention. I wasn't sure, but Mariana gave me a clue," Jack said. "She told me the woman called Norfolk, Norfolkshire, and was in Peliti's every time Demidov passed."

Andrew smiled. "Mariana is a clever woman," he said. "She notices things."

Jack nodded to Symington. "All I had to do was put the pieces of the jigsaw together. We already knew that Abdurrahman Khan, the Amir of Afghanistan, was stirring up trouble, but Lieutenant Symington has given us the names of most of the main agitators. We will deal with them."

Andrew sighed. "It wasn't the *Narodnaya Volya* or the *Okhrana*, then?"

"No. The *Narodnaya Volya* contributed a minor part, pretending to be from the *Okhrana* to provoke a war between us and Russia. While you were concentrating on the Russian involvement, Andrew, Symington teased out the Afghan influence." Jack raised his glass to Symington. "We have a five-cornered ring, gentlemen, with us, the Pashtun tribes, the *Narodnaya Volya*, the *Okhrana* and the Amir of Afghanistan all jockeying for position."

Jack nodded. "The Amir sent his agents across Afghanistan and the Northwest Frontier, telling the tribes to prepare for a *jihad*. He also sold thousands of rifles to the Pashtun tribes at the bargain price of half a crown each."

"Where did the Amir of Afghanistan get so many rifles?" Andrew asked.

"From the factory in Kabul where he makes them, under licence from us," Jack said.

"How can he afford that?" Andrew asked. "I thought Afghanistan was a poor country."

"We afford it for him," Jack said soberly. "We give the Amir a large annual subsidy." He smiled. "Our politicians paid for these tribes to attack us, and our ally encouraged them."

Andrew grunted. "I never did shoot that red-bearded *mullah*."

Jack smiled. "There's no reason to regret not killing somebody, Andrew. If you shot him, another would have taken his place."

"That's true," Andrew agreed. "What happens now?"

"Nothing," Jack said. "I write a report and send it to Elgin, who either forwards it to London, ignores it or throws it in the wastepaper bin."

"How about all the men that died, ours and theirs?" Andrew asked.

Jack shook his head. "Small pieces in the jigsaw, Andrew. Politics is the most sordid, ugly business in the world. We don't mention what really happened and who is to blame; we smile nicely, bow and shake hands at the next official bun-fight, and the world moves merrily on."

Andrew nodded. "I didn't realise jigsaws were sealed in blood."

"Only political jigsaws, Andrew," Jack said.

"I'll keep clear of politics in future," Andrew said. He thought of little Simla and Mariana with the child growing within her and closed his eyes.

APPENDIX

It is a very Victorian scene, the beleaguered garrison holding out with the Union Flag flying above and the relieving column battling against immense odds to rescue them. It is also accurate. Cawnpore, Lucknow, Chitral, Mafeking, Ladysmith, Gordon in Khartoum: all famous in their day and mostly forgotten now. Many of the men who engaged in these small but vicious actions also featured in the much larger battles of the First World War. Ian Hamilton, who was seriously wounded at Majuba, commanded the landings at Gallipoli, for instance, while Bobs Roberts, who led the Kabul to Kandahar march to relieve the siege of Kandahar during the Second Afghan War, died in France in 1914 while visiting Indian troops.

The siege and relief of Chitral filled many columns of contemporary newspapers, with the defenders and relievers becoming temporary celebrities. Townshend, who became known as Chitral Charlie for his part in the defence, later defended Kut during the Mesopotamian campaign against the Ottoman Turks. He again held out during a long siege, but this time unsuccessfully.

Besieging and relieving fortresses and cities has been a feature of warfare for centuries. Scotland had notable sieges of

Stirling and Berwick during the Middle Ages, while the sieges of Gibraltar and Yorktown were vital during the American War of Independence, and the siege of Vienna was a turning point in the Ottoman advance into Europe. In the twentieth century, Tobruk, Verdun, and Stalingrad come to mind. Hopefully, there will be no more bloody sieges, for war is undoubtedly the most sordid horror that humanity has devised.

ABOUT THE AUTHOR

Born in Edinburgh, Scotland and educated at the University of Dundee, Malcolm Archibald has written in a variety of genres, from academic history to folklore, historical novels to fantasy. He won the Dundee International Book Prize with *Whales for the Wizard* in 2005 and the Society of Army Historical Research prize for Historical Military Fiction with *Blood Oath* in 2021.

Happily married for over 42 years, Malcolm has three grown children and lives outside Dundee in Scotland.

❄

To learn more about Malcolm Archibald and discover more Next Chapter authors, visit our website at www.nextchapter.pub.

Printed in Great Britain
by Amazon

48044293R00219